THE PRIMATE'S DREAM

BOOKS BY JAMES W. TUTTLETON

A Fine Silver Thread
Vital Signs
Thomas Wentworth Higginson
The Novel of Manners in America
The Works of Washington Irving
    History, Tales, and Sketches (editor)
Henry James's The American (editor)
The Sweetest Impression of Life (editor)
Edith Wharton (editor)
Washington Irving (editor)

JAMES W. TUTTLETON

The Primate's Dream

Literature, Race, and Ethnicity in America

IVAN R. DEE   CHICAGO

THE PRIMATE'S DREAM. Copyright © 1999 by Mrs. James W. Tuttleton. All rights reserved, including the right to reproduce this book or portions thereof in any form. For information, address: Ivan R. Dee, Publisher, 1332 North Halsted Street, Chicago 60622. Manufactured in the United States of America and printed on acid-free paper.

Publication of this book has been aided by a grant from the Abraham and Rebecca Stein Publication Fund of New York University, Department of English.

Library of Congress Cataloging-in-Publication Data:
Tuttleton, James W.
    The primate's dream : literature, race, and ethnicity in America / James W. Tuttleton
      p. cm.
    Includes bibliographical references and index.
    ISBN 1-56663-234-X (alk. paper)
    1. American literature—History and criticism. 2. Afro-Americans in literature. 3. American literature—Afro-American authors—History and criticism. 4. Ethnicity in literature. 5. Race in literature.
I. Title
PS173.N4T88 1999
810.9'896073—dc21   98-50376

THIS BOOK IS FOR

RK

WRITER, EDITOR, CRITIC, FRIEND,
MASTER COMPOSITOR

Since all of your work was really an effort to appease
the past, a need to be admitted among your peers,
let the inheritors question the sibyl and the Sphinx,
and learn that a raceless critic is a primate's dream.
You were distressed by your habitat, you shall not find peace
till you and your origins reconcile; your jaw must droop
and your knuckles scrape the ground of your native place.
Squat on a damp rock round which white lilies stiffen,
pricking their ears; count as the syllables drop
like dew from primeval ferns; note how the earth drinks
language as precious, depending upon the race.
Then, on dank ground, using a twig for a pen,
write Genesis and watch the Word begin.

      Derek Walcott, *Midsummer* (LI)

Contents

Preface	*xi*
The Mind of a Black Abolitionist: Frederick Douglass	*1*
The Mind of a White Abolitionist: Thomas Wentworth Higginson	*25*
An Uncertain Abolitionist: Lincoln in Fact and Fiction	*54*
Lincoln's Generals: Grant and Sherman in Their Memoirs	*74*
Twain's *Huck*: Fresh Tears and Race Flapdoodle	*91*
Pride and Shame: The Winning of the West	*116*
Ethnic Blues and All That Multicultural Jazz	*144*
Loathing Western Civilization: Christianity and Race in America	*156*
Countee Cullen at "The Heights"	*176*
The Negro Writer as Spokesman (1969)	*207*
The Problematic Texts of Richard Wright	*222*
Derek Walcott and the Vision of Homeric Grandeur	*243*
Ralph Ellison: Indivisible Man	*280*
Notes	*299*
Acknowledgments	*329*
Index	*331*

Preface

This is a book about race, black American literature, ethnic minorities, and American multiculturalism. It is a response to President Clinton's call, in the late 1990s, for a dialogue on race and ethnicity in America. Like him, I too believed that it was timely for blacks, whites, Hispanic Americans, Asian Americans, and others in this country to come face to face and to speak to each other in an honest, direct, and faithful way about common interests, issues, and concerns. But how could I, an English teacher, contribute to the national dialogue? Only, perhaps, through an analysis of what I know best. My concerns in this book are thus principally with American literature, the role of ethnic writing in the mainstream of our art, what constitutes its canon, some important white influences on the historical experience of blacks, the themes and techniques of specific minority writers who have engaged my mind, and a just estimate of their quality *as writers*.

In its discussion of minority issues, this book takes as a given the theoretical adequacy of representational art.[1] It presupposes that a novel or play, for instance, can show us more or less as we are. But questions of verisimilitude in literature have obliged me to reconsider how such influences as books, movies, TV, university classes, and print journalism have actually dealt with minority experience in this country. What I have found striking—particularly in the accounts of the settlement of the West and the fate of the Native American—is the extent to which the past is being rewritten today to satisfy a contemporary "progressive" political agenda. In other words, the critic of minority literature has to address not only the adequacy of the way minority experience used to be represented in art but also the historical revisionism at work today in our criticism. This revisionism succeeds remarkably well because most of our contemporaries do not really know much about the history of ethnic relations in America. Oh, people know there was a thing called slavery, that the Civil War was fought, that the American Indian was sequestered on reservations, and so on. But how and why these significant events came about are substantially unexplored. Most Americans simply persist in holding to Henry Ford's view of the past: "History," Ford said, "is bunk."

In *A Different Mirror: A History of Multicultural America*, the ethnic historian Ronald Takaki expresses the belief that our vision of the future will be dictated by the image of the past that is victorious. And he is intent on seeing that his view of our past will win out.[2] To him, the documentary record of our nation's history seems largely to be material for propagandizing an ethnic-centered vision of the future. This is a distorted view of the function of historical understanding. For the past has a reality—a factual, documentary, testamentary, and material actuality—that is substantially available to objective understanding. And this understanding is independent of the utilitarian purposes to which it is being put by contemporary ethnic or multicultural ideologists. In other words, American history is something other than a tool for effecting political correctness today. Whether the view of America that Professor Takaki stumps for is sufficient and whether his viewpoint makes for an instructive understanding of the past I discuss below in the chapter called "Ethnic Blues and All That Multicultural Jazz." But for the moment it is sufficient to note that not only is contemporary minority experience a field of sometimes abrasive contestations; so too is the historical record of the ethnic past, which is undergoing a political revisionism unlike anything we have seen before in this country.

All the essays in this book, in one way or another, deal with the general problem of language and communication. One important communication on race, it is worth remembering, was the Kerner Report of 1968, which declared that America was "moving toward two societies, one black, one white, separate and unequal." That report was a chilling official indictment of our culture. Since then we have regularly been told that, indeed, America has broken up into estranged societies, each defined by race. The view that racism is more than ever a rampant force for destruction in America has most recently been proclaimed by Derrick Bell, Andrew Hacker, and Jonathan Coleman.[3] This argument is, in my view, substantially wrong and has actually served to divide blacks and whites. It is an instance of what the black sociologist Orlando Patterson has called the liberal need to see blacks as permanent victims.[4] Incontrovertible factual evidence of the improvement of racial attitudes has been compiled by the sociologists Paul M. Sniderman, Edward G. Carmines, and others. But the most decisive evidence of this positive change has been brought forward by Abigail and Stephan Thernstrom, who have rightly concluded of the Kerner report that "What is striking, with the benefit of hindsight, is not how prescient the report was, but how far off the mark it has turned out to be."[5]

Still, the alert witness may well ask what communication is now possible between a Leonard Jeffries and a David Duke, between a Louis Farrakhan and a Rabbi Marc Tannenbaum, between a Jesse Jackson and a Jesse Helms. Even when there is a bona fide public effort to hold a forthright dialogue on race, the deck may be stacked against candor and objective understanding. This certainly was the case with the first open meetings on race convened by President Clinton in the fall of 1997. His commission included an honor roll of important Americans appointed to explore ways to reduce racism and foster diversity in every aspect of American life. Chaired by the black historian John Hope Franklin, the committee held its first open sessions in November that year. It was evident, however, that neither the president nor his chairman was really interested in a dialogue on race or in considering a diversity of opinions about common racial concerns. At the first meeting at the University of Maryland, on the subject of how to attain diversity in university admissions, chairman Franklin deliberately excluded opponents of affirmative action as people who had nothing to offer to a national dialogue on race. Ward Connerly, the University of California regent who had led the opposition to affirmative action that culminated in voter approval of Proposition 209, was simply ignored. In view of the manifest opposition of the American people to racial preference quotas, this was simply stunning. But as Congressman Charles T. Cannady of Florida observed, "It's been clear from the outset that the board was designed to support the

President's position" on affirmative action.⁶ A dialogue hardly seems possible if alternative viewpoints on race are suppressed or ignored. Such episodes in the national life make it all the more necessary for each of us as citizens to try to make our own perceptions of race heard and understood. This I propose to do through an analysis of important literary reflections of America's racial experience.

II

Ethnic discontent in the nineteenth century partly took the form of abolitionist protest against slavery or liberal attacks on Jim Crow legislation such as *Plessy v. Ferguson* (1896), the case that established "separate but equal" educational facilities and by extension all racial segregation. This book undertakes to define at least some aspects of the prewar abolitionist mind in the persons of two prominent nineteenth-century racial activists, Frederick Douglass and Thomas Wentworth Higginson. In my account of their work, I have sought to elicit the sources of their strength as writers but also to educe the moral vision that animated them—a moral vision that still may have power to shape our own future.

Some of the essays that follow enlarge upon the consequences of the intransigent propensity to violence in the abolitionist mind —particularly the essays on Grant and Sherman, who led Union troops into battle against the slave-holding Confederacy, and the essay on Abraham Lincoln, who commanded them and finally authorized the 1863 Emancipation Proclamation that freed the slaves. These essays bring home the still evident truth that the destiny of blacks in America has always been dependent, in some measure, on the politics of powerful whites. If I am critical of secular rationalism as an avenue to understanding racial difference, the reason will become plain in the essay "Christianity and Race in America," which rejects the effort in some versions of modern history to blame Christianity for the presence of racism in America. The violence of the Civil War, a military solution antithetical to Christian values, was played out further in the Indian Wars on the Western plains. I take up the discomfort Americans felt then (and still feel now) at how peace was finally achieved, at great cost to Native Americans, in "Pride and Shame: The Winning of the

West." Further, the immigrant history of selected ethnic groups (such as the Irish, Italians, Chinese, and Japanese) is taken up in "Ethnic Blues and All That Multicultural Jazz."

Literature most interests me, however, and the substance of this book deals with black writers, the representation of black experience in America, and the critical interaction between blacks and whites who have commented on American racial experience in our life and letters. Sometimes significant issues are clearly brought out in white writing; and I have not hesitated to educe it. The essay "Twain's *Huck*: Fresh Tears and Race Flapdoodle," for instance, is especially useful in exploring the problem of whether a text that is claimed to be racist in its treatment of blacks can ever be a classic; and it analyzes various conflicting views of one of our most important works of nineteenth-century American fiction.

A quarter-century ago, while I was chairman of the English Department at New York University, my job involved not only teaching and administration but filling the occasional role of building superintendent, caterer, lay psychiatrist, funeral director, and night watchman. One day a burst water pipe in our office building obliged me to get into a storeroom to rescue a half-century of English Department senior honors theses. These had come down to Washington Square College from University College, the other NYU liberal arts college in the Bronx, familiarly called "The Heights." In the process of drying out the waterlogged theses, I took occasion to see whether any of these undergraduate majors had gone on to fame or fortune. Amongst the work of these largely forgotten authors I discovered the unknown thesis of the black poet Countee Cullen, who had graduated from NYU in 1925. "Countee Cullen at 'The Heights'" presents Cullen's thesis on Edna St. Vincent Millay, sets it in the context of his student life and early writing, and relates his career to the development of American poetic modernism.

In preparing the Cullen essay, I had the invaluable help of a senior colleague, Ralph Ellison, who was then Albert Schweitzer Professor of the Humanities at NYU. During my nine years as chairman (and afterward until his death in 1994), Ralph was an essential intellectual resource to me and the department. He was also a great pathway to friendship with others since he knew everyone. It was Ellison who seized my arm one evening at the Century Club and dragged me over to Robert Penn Warren, introducing me, in all my callow youth, as—after a pregnant pause—"my *boss*, Jim Tuttleton." As no one *ever* bossed Ralph Ellison, I can still see Red Warren's amazed inspection of my person and hear his booming horse laugh echoing down the passage of the years. Yet one could tease Ralph equally as well. As we both came from the Southwest and shared a Cherokee ancestry, after a martini or two I used to twit him with the possibility of our having had a common great grandfather, an idea he found hilarious. I also introduced him to various friends of mine over the years, friends like John Lewis, founder of the Modern Jazz Quartet, whose music had meant so much to both of us. The essay presented below, "Ralph Ellison: Indivisible Man," deals with Ellison's major themes and techniques and defines my sense of the continuing utility of his critical perspective for American culture as a whole.

III

I confess at the outset to some concern about how, in the academy at least, comments on race, class, and gender are ruthlessly interrogated for signs of political incorrectness in the speaker. While this surveillance goes on in some other areas of American society today, the academic pursuit of incorrectness is especially virulent and likely to be unleashed at the first sign of the serious criticism of the literature of minority groups. (I mean genuine criticism, not mere puffs that enhance self-esteem.) Unfortunately the charge of "racism" is all too easily bandied about. I have no idea about how to forestall it, especially since we are all guilty of "racism"—at least as philosopher David Stove defines the term in *Cricket versus Republicanism*:

> "Racism" is the belief that some human races are inferior to others in certain respects, and that it is sometimes proper to make such differences the basis of our behaviour towards people. It is this proposition which is nowadays constantly declared to be false, though everyone knows it is true; just as everyone knows that it is true that people differ in age, sex, health, etc., and that it is sometimes proper to make *these* differences the basis of our behaviour towards them.[7]

Throughout history few have complained about "racism," which is a charge of recent invention. According to the *Oxford English Dictionary*, "racism" as a term did not exist before the modern era. It was not until recent times that people were condemned for recognizing that there are differences amongst the races and that these may rightly be invoked to guide us in making decisions. Racism, as Stove defines it, is frankly endemic in human experience; it is a rational tool in making worthwhile discriminations and is not necessarily a destructive attitude toward other people. The reason is that men and events customarily have fore-meanings for people who have had some experience of the world—as Martin Heidegger in *Being and Time* and Hans-Georg Gadamer in *Truth and Method* have shown; and it is reasonable to invoke these fore-meanings in the presence of the new or the unknown. Understanding and interpretation would be impossible if we were not already situated within the so-called "hermeneutic circle" that permits us to understand the unknown by reference to the known.[8] Consequently we ought all to object to frivolous charges of racism simply because there is value in recognizing the existence of such differences as Stove here enumerates.

Still, some of my colleagues feel that to defend such positions as the rational utility of prejudice, even on philosophic grounds, will only inflame the shrill ideologues who dominate racial discussion today. I am told that there are some black activists, white liberals, and academic Marxists who think that they alone have a lock on the subject of race and black literature in America, that only their views are entitled to be heard, and that any observation by anyone who is said to enjoy the privileges of "the cultural hegemony" is *ipso facto* prejudiced and immoral. I hope this will not be the case. Race intolerance, on the other hand, *is* indefensible, a sign of ignorant know-nothings.

But if I have some residual anxiety that *The Primate's Dream* will provoke an ignorant charge of racism, the future tense and the conditional mode are really all wrong. The charge has *already* been made against me. To explain. Some of the essays in this book appeared elsewhere. All of them save one have been extensively rewritten, revised, and updated. The one essay left unchanged—"The Negro Writer as Spokesman"—was commissioned in 1968 by C. W. E. Bigsby. It has often been cited by other critics and, I believe, remains in print.[9] It is, however, distinctly a period piece. For one thing, at the time it appeared blacks insisted on being called Negroes. Nowadays no one would use the word in a title. Moreover, in 1968 there were no language cops around to protest the use of a good old genderless term like *spokesman*. Finally, this essay was an immediate response to an explosion of bitterness that had manifested itself in the violence of the Black Panthers, the deranged cultism of the Symbionese Liberation Army, and the extremist politics and journalism of Eldridge Cleaver, Imamu Amiri Baraka, Bobby Seale, Huey P. Newton, Malcolm X, and a great many others of that long ago time. I saw no way that I could update the piece without substantially altering its relation to the racial conditions of the middle and late 1960s, so I have let it stand as a reflection of my thinking, thirty years ago, about some problems that continue to vex us. Period piece though it may be, I still hold to the central moral judgments and the critical estimates expressed in that argument.

It was not that essay, however, that brought down on me the charge of racism. It was another—"The Problematic Texts of Richard Wright." This piece first appeared as a short book review in the Summer 1992 issue of *The Hudson Review*. In that review I commented on the strengths and weaknesses of Wright's remarkable fiction as reprinted in the Library of America edition.[10] In the course of the essay I discussed Wright's political, aesthetic, and philosophical development. If the essay expressed any irritation, it was critical of the editor Arnold Rampersad, a black professor of American literature at Princeton, who, I thought, had misrepresented Wright's textual intention in *Native Son* and thus had issued a flawed text of his most successful novel. In any case, I was pleased to have the piece appear in *The Hudson Review*, for the co-editors of that magazine (Frederick Morgan and Paula Dietz, both of whom I later got to know) have for years produced a superb literary quarterly internationally known for its distinguished creative writing and excellent literary criticism. This is a journal that had attracted the work of Pound, Eliot, Auden, Lowell, Wilbur, and many other modern masters. My review involved aesthetic and textual criticism, pure and simple. Nothing there about race at all—or so I thought.

The next year *The Hudson Review*, which had for some time been given a small annual grant from the National Endowment for the Arts, was inexplicably denied the award. The editors were naturally curious to know why. Since the allocation of taxpayer money requires freedom of information, the editors asked to see the report of the rating committee. To their surprise, the grant was denied because the panel felt that "writers of color were significantly under-represented in *The Hudson Review*." Moreover, although I had declared the Library of America publication of Richard Wright to be "an event of great cultural importance" which rightly established him alongside Hawthorne, James, Twain, and other American masters, the panel specifically faulted my essay as "isolating and condescending." The panel observed that "this concern was exacerbated when this essay was compared with the fulsome essay on Zola in the same issue." (The Zola essay was not mine.)

Needless to say, I was quite surprised that my remarks on Wright had been read as condescending and racist in character. In a long career of teaching and writing about black authors, I had never before been accused of racism. At first I thought there must be some error or a personal vendetta against me on the part of someone on the committee. I too requested the committee report. As it turned out, I knew no one on the evaluating committee. None of them was of recognizable stature in the world of letters. There was evidently nothing personal in their arraignment. But it was plain and simple: if I said things critical of a black writer or his editor, I was *ipso facto* condescending and a racist.

I gave it up in disgust. And there the matter might have ended had not the story been picked up by the *Wall Street Journal*. There the managing editor of *The New Criterion*, Roger Kimball, rightly identified this episode as an instance of the government's effort to "impose quotas and politically correct thinking," even while making great claims about the desirability of a diversity of viewpoints.

> The message from the NEA's panel is clear: Only institutions waving the banner of political correctness need apply.
>
> The freeze on unorthodox opinion works in two ways. First come the bean-counters and quota-mongers. How many blacks, Hispanics, Asians, women and people of varying "sexual orientation" do you publish? If you fail to meet the established quota, forget about getting a grant.

Then come the PC-police. Even if you have published articles about, say, black authors, were the articles sufficiently—that is, unequivocally and unreservedly—enthusiastic? And if you dared criticize an "author of color," surely you cannot have praised a dead white European male in the same issue! (In fact, the offending article about Zola is descriptive and biographical, not "fulsome," but who pays attention to such niceties nowadays?)[11]

Despite Mr. Kimball's explanation, I was still appalled to think that something I had written had cost *The Hudson Review* a publication grant.

But there really is a law of compensation. Such was the widespread public outrage at the NEA's effort to dictate political correctness that private contributions came pouring in to *The Hudson Review*, more than making up for the loss I had evidently caused them. Still, the episode confirmed me in my conviction that the government ought not to be in the business of subsidizing the arts and humanities. Creative and critical work can only be corrupted when political ideologists dictate who does and does not get a grant of taxpayer money based on extraneous considerations such as political orthodoxy and a correct identity politics.

One final word about the Wright essay. I have revised and expanded it. Why didn't I leave it alone so that the reader could see it as the NEA committee got it in 1992? The reason is this. In that review I criticized Professor Rampersad—the editor of the Wright volumes—for falsifying, as I viewed it, the textual intention of Richard Wright. (For example, Wright's manuscript had included some coarse sex scenes in *Native Son* that, on advice of editors and friends, he decided to delete from the published novel. The Library of America text restored these scenes, thus corrupting the text that Wright had approved for publication. I was not alone in my criticism of Professor Rampersad, as my citations in the essay below will attest.)

Recently, however, I have learned that the editorial decision about this contested textual matter was not in fact made by Arnold Rampersad, though he was probably obliged to acquiesce in it in order to get the collection published. The changes in the Wright texts appear to have been dictated by someone whose name does not appear anywhere in the Library of America volumes. I refer to

Preface

Hanna Bercovitch, a white editor whose 1997 obituary identified her as the Library of America in-house employee who "oversaw the publication of the first 90 volumes in the Library of America, including editions of Richard Wright's *Native Son*. . . ." According to this obituary,

> Ms. Bercovitch often undid what earlier editors had done. For example, when Harper & Brothers published Richard Wright's "Native Son," they made some changes to suit the Book-of-the-Month Club. They deleted the passages that showed that the novel's black protagonist, Bigger Thomas, was sexually attracted to the white woman he ended up smothering. Under Ms. Bercovitch's supervision those passages were restored.

The obituary goes on to praise Ms. Bercovitch for "rescuing" American literary texts, and it cites a frankly dubious commendation by Henry Louis Gates, Jr.: "It is hard to find anyone who has been more central to institutionalizing the canon of American literature. . . ."[12]

Of course it is risible to think that Ms. Bercovitch had any significant influence on the shaping of the American canon. Hawthorne, Irving, Wharton, and Wright were all canonized long before she came along. But she did exercise a malign influence on those texts she is claimed to have "rescued." The changes and deletions in Wright's manuscript were not made by his editors or the Book-of-the-Month Club, as this obituary wrongly has it, but by Wright himself—in response to their detailed criticisms of his imperfect texts. He was by no means a passive victim of white editors, as these remarks falsely imply. These textual issues are so important for American literary study that I felt obliged to expand the argument of *The Hudson Review* essay and to provide additional bibliographical evidence in support of my remarks on the genesis of Wright's fiction.

I am, however, frankly appalled at the idea of a behind-the-scenes manipulation of the received canon of American writing by a shadowy, unnamed in-house editor whose dubious textual decisions were forcibly imposed on an academic consultant whose name had been purchased in order to lend to the Library's text a measure of scholarly credibility.[13] The task of revising the Wright essay, then, gave me opportunity to rescind my criticism of Professor Rampersad and to lay the blame for the Wright fiasco precisely where it belongs: at the feet of Hanna Bercovitch. In any case, it has come to a sad pass in this country when a magazine of superb literary quality is silently denied a grant in aid of publication by a government agency like the NEA on the spurious ground of race. I stand by *The Hudson Review* comment on Richard Wright. I do not believe that it can in any sense be deemed racist or condescending; but if it is to be regarded as such, then literary criticism will have become impossible in our time.

As will be evident from the essays below, this book also assumes the practical necessity of recognizing and acting on racial differences. Blacks are not whites; whites are not Native Americans; and so on. Of course, how and to what we attribute racial differences will have a bearing on how we look at others and behave in our daily interrelations. In the academy it is fashionable nowadays to invoke DNA and other scientific data in order to prove that nothing fundamental distinguishes one group from another. As Anthony Appiah has remarked, "The truth is that there are no races: there is nothing in the world that can do all we ask 'race' to do for us. The evil that is done is done by the concept and by easy—yet impossible—assumptions as to its application." Henry Louis Gates has likewise affirmed this idea in protesting that "'races,' put simply, do not exist, and that to claim that they do, for whatever misguided reason, is to stand on dangerous ground."[14]

Professors Appiah, Gates, and others who take this tack seem to be at war with the philosophical conception of essence itself; and they evidently would like nothing better than to dismantle the whole of Western metaphysics that undergirds it. The effect, they suppose, would be to abolish racial difference. This is a hopeless task—not only as an intellectual project (as Derrida's evaporation has proved)—but in relation to human experience itself. People are simply not going to ignore the evidence of their own experience and its instructive value in grasping what presents itself to us for understanding. And this fact will inevitably make for the kind of observation and behavior to which Gates objects.

IV

Finally, a word about the title, *The Primate's Dream*. Readers may distantly associate it with Professor Gates's *The Signifying Monkey*. But my title (and the epigraph of the book) are really drawn from *Midsummer*, a volume of verse by the black poet Derek Walcott. This is a beautiful lyric sequence of more than fifty poems, composed at various times and in various places, dealing with a variety of themes in a variety of poetic techniques. It was published in 1984 at the height of the poet's powers. It would be impossible to do full justice here to *Midsummer*, even to poem LI, which gives my book its title.[15] But perhaps I can indicate something of its present critical suggestiveness for me.

> Since all of your work was really an effort to appease
> the past, a need to be admitted among your peers,
> let the inheritors question the sibyl and the Sphinx,
> and learn that a raceless critic is a primate's dream.
> You were distressed by your habitat, you shall not find peace
> till you and your origins reconcile; your jaw must droop,
> and your knuckles scrape the ground of your native place.
> Squat on a damp rock round which white lilies stiffen,
> pricking their ears; count as the syllables drop
> like dew from primeval ferns; note how the earth drinks
> language as precious, depending upon the race.
> Then, on dank ground, using a twig for a pen,
> write Genesis and watch the Word begin.
> Elephants will mill at their water hole to trumpet a
> new style. Mongoose, arrested in rut,
> and saucer-eyed mandrills, drinking from the leaves,
> will nod as a dew-lapped lizard discourses on "Lives
> of the Black Poets," gripping a branch like a lectern for better
> delivery. Already, up in that simian Academe,
> a chimp in bifocals, his lower lip ajut,
> tears misting the lenses, is turning your *Oeuvres Complètes*.

In elucidating the title, I note that the poet addresses first of all himself. He meditates on the extent to which the inspiration of his poems has been the desire for fame and the task of reconciling himself to his lineage and his inheritance. This inheritance is the racial, religious, linguistic, and literary line from which he has evolved. In the chapter on Walcott below, I discuss this lineage at length. Given the lush primeval landscape, we may understand the habitat that distresses him to be the Caribbean island chain that was the homeland of his Indian ancestors (Walcott was born in St. Lucia), and, even further back behind that, the African subcontinent from which his black forebears had come. But the "you" of the poem is also the reader, who learns that "a raceless critic is a primate's dream." This pronoun "you" implicates the reader in a comparable task—that of attaining a reconciliation to his own troubling past, whatever it might be.

The primate image arises from Darwin's idea of our having evolved out of furry arboreal quadrupeds who left the trees, descended onto the African plain, and began to ambulate upright, moving in gregarious herds, then forming tribes, nations, and states. The Darwinian theory of evolutionary development defines our origin and lineage as (in the first instance) that of a naked ape. However difficult the task, Walcott has made a reconciliation with this figure an essential part of his poetic purpose. Evolution argues transformation from the simple to the complex, from the lower to the higher, the transfiguration of the ape into the man, an onward-and-upward process (perhaps the man's ascending to the Superman or even to God). Darwin thought that every aspect of our lives as human beings could be traced to an evolutionary adaptation in the process of natural selection. But Walcott, in seeking to reconcile himself to his origin, is troubled that Darwinism finds no τέλος in existence, no aim or purpose to the whole evolutionary process. Given the pointlessness of mere change, *devolution* is just as likely a future possibility as evolution. Walcott does not shrink from imagining a regression from his present state into a simian origin that he embraces as his own. This atavism has nothing to do with his being black but rather with his being a fully evolved human. And it is a regression that the poem, in its address to "you," invites us to experience as well. This visionary atavism—in which the speaker or reader becomes for the moment the slack-jawed, long-armed, knuckle-dragging ape—is put to the service of discovering our origins so as to become reconciled to them and at peace with ourselves. Specifically, for the poet, this backward motion toward the source involves a rediscovery of the world as it originally was, and

Preface

as you and I originally were, and of locating in the rich particularities of that primordial existence the ground of voice, language, expression, form, and even poetic meter (the perceived tempo of the dropping dew).

In undertaking to make clear what is meant by "the primate's dream," let me observe that the point of this imaginative regression is for the poet to reach the originary moment at which his humanity began to emerge from its simian origin; and in this poem it is the point at which the ape starts to become man by picking up that twig and, employing language, beginning to write. The ascent begins, then, in the moment of expressive articulation. The ascent is a slow *Assumption,* or rising, and its miraculous character is also suggested by the religious terms *Genesis* and *the Word*—terms that designate the moment of God's creation and man's relation to the world and to speech. Speech as discourse is self-expression in words. But it has its counterpart (and finds its culmination) in the *Logos,* which is God made manifest through language and incarnate in the flesh. What is implicit in Walcott's image is the age-old longing for an ascent from ape to man to God that, in its processes, even transfigures the order of nature and its diverse creatures (the mongoose and the mandrills and the chimp).

The idea of a simian Academe is frankly hilarious. But Walcott evidently feels that this conceit captures the present abysmal level of poetic understanding—especially the degree of understanding of the lives of the black poets apparent in academic classrooms and organizations like the MLA. Partly this lyric is about an island writer's trying to establish himself as a poet in a long continuum that has included Moses (supposing that he wrote Genesis), Homer, Ovid, Virgil, Shakespeare, Pope, Tennyson, Eliot, and Brodsky. He, though English-speaking, is black; and the assessment of his work, that is, his worthiness to be admitted as a peer of these Masters, is inseparable from the question of his race and from the race of the critic who takes up his complete works.

With respect to "the primate's dream," though he does not yet exist, the raceless critic is naturally the reader for whom the poet longs. The raceless critic is the expositor who can make clear what words mean and the relation of words to the Word; it is he who can transcend every difference in skin color. Not yet fully evolved, he is *still* (meaning *nevertheless* as well as *always*) the dream of the primate-writer. "Primate," of course, refers to more than the order of *Primata* or simians and their relatives. A primate is also an exalted religious figure—a high priest, let us say. Walcott's primate-poet has been, as it were, to the mountain. He has had a divine vision. He has ascended in the spiritual scale, and the line here expresses the capacity of poetry to convey truths of a transcendent character known to the poet who has had a vision. In its dream of a raceless critic, the lyric also expresses the hope of a future in which a poet will be judged by the character of his verse rather than by the color of his skin. Walcott's viewpoint as a poet is of course much more complex than the theme of this one poem. At times he even contradicts its theme, as I try to indicate in the overall assessment below. But, needless to say, the vision of a raceless critic has impressed me as an ideal worthy of readerly emulation. Walcott's dream has become one with my own.

V

We each arrive here by a circuitous route; and mine has featured an ethnic history that includes English, German, and French ancestry (on my father's side), and English, Scots-Irish, and Cherokee Indian (on my mother's). The fact of my Native American ancestry in the Old Southwest reminds me that many Cherokees held black slaves or intermarried with them. Could I have a partial black ancestry? Probably not, but the answer is lost in the mists of an illiterate past. Whatever the answer might be, I claim each of these ethnic or racial strains. I could not bring myself to say that I am simply a white or simply an American Indian (although I have as much "Indian blood" in me as many who claim it on the federal census form) or simply a black (the effort would be conspicuously preposterous). Mostly, though, the effort is repugnant because to identify myself with only one strain of my racial or ethnic inheritance would constitute—in my mind—a denial of all the others.

In *Thirteen Ways of Looking at a Black Man*, Henry Louis Gates, Jr., speaks of the heavy burden of feeling that you "can really represent your race, thus that your actions can betray your race or honor it."[16] But iconic status is hardly possible to one of mixed race—as Gates is, as I am, as (trace one's lineage back far enough) most people (dread thought) might possibly be. My father held the view that true Americans were a "Duke's mixture." His metaphor was drawn from that exceptionally fine tobacco mixture produced by the Dukes of North Carolina, who years ago sold a little cloth bag of superb blended tobaccos for fifteen cents. Dad thought this blend the best. Likewise, the quintessential American was a unique blend of different ethnic and racial strains: in our own case, English, Scots-Irish, French, German, Indian (and perhaps even black). He was sure that the resultant blend of these ethnic types—the American—had every reason to be proud of his heritage (as well as of each component part of the fusion).

For those who, unfortunately, cannot claim the rich ethnic diversity that is distinctively mine, there is something just as satisfying, it seems to me. And that is the *cultural diversity* that each of us can lay claim to as his own rightful heritage. This is the cultural equivalent of the physical intimacy that has always existed between blacks and whites and Indians. I claim as my rightful heritage—and any American can so claim it—the gift handed down to me in the writings of Frederick Douglass, the jazz improvisations of John Lewis, the superhero sport exploits of Michael Jordan, the lyric purity of Jessye Norman's song, the engaging fictional creations of Zora Neale Hurston, Odetta's moving spirituals, the cinematic brilliance of Sidney Poitier, and so on. Add to this the ways in which American Indian culture has enriched our lives through its multi-talented champions like the All-American Jim Thorpe, its splendid tribal leaders like Chief Joseph, the superb fiction of N. Scott Momaday; through its remarkable mythographies of creation and cosmology, its brilliant intricacies of varying artistic design, its probing rumination on political organization and confederacy. I also triumph through passionate identification with those who have willed me other precious assets—from England, Ireland, and Germany. Nathan Glazer in *We Are All Multiculturalists Now* has rightly remarked that no political separatism, much less cultural segregation, is possible here because we are all beneficiaries of each other's creative brilliance which has fused us into a single American cultural identity. This is a point Henry James tried to elaborate in his portrait of Milly Theale in *The Wings of the Dove*: the American heroine is "heiress of all the ages" in that she is the beneficiary of what other cultures have contributed to our making. And that is the lesson that Ralph Ellison's career made particularly plain to us. It is not an especially felicitous phrase, but the black journalist Stanley Crouch has even ventured the term "cultural miscegenation" for the inextricably interrelated cultural interconnections that we now enjoy, an intimate blending of modes and styles of living that create something new and distinctly American, available to us all.[17]

Despite the gloom of the Kerner Report, which was frankly distorted in its racial views by the temporary passions of the anti–Vietnam War movement, the United States is not two societies, one black and another white, divided and hostile. It is one nation. There are of course notable differences amongst the races, and it is rational to recognize them and act on them accordingly. Mistakes as to the character of a given individual will be made from time to time. But the several races and ethnic groups in America are not alien to each other and not at each other's throats. The fact is that American blacks and other immigrant minorities who have settled here know in their heart of hearts that the United States—amongst all other nations in the world—offers the greatest chance for attaining ethnic peace, freedom, education, and personal economic improvement. We sometimes think that only material inducements lure the immigrant poor to our shores. Not so. They know that only when the conditions of peace and freedom are propitious will there be any possibility for something even greater than economic security—that spiritual transcendence that is the goal of human aspiration everywhere.

Even the most vocal and aggressive blacks who chastise whites for the persistence of racism—the Farrakhans, the Jesse Jacksons, and the Al Sharptons—know, as journalist Stanley Crouch has remarked, that "they would prefer to be here in the United States than to be in any place in Africa, which they can buy a one-way ticket to any time they want."[18] Deep down, we are all aware that despite our past racial failures, a remarkable transformation has peacefully altered America since the 1950s. As Orlando Patterson correctly observes, the changes that have occurred in America during the past half-century are unparalleled in the history of minority-majority relations. The separation between the races is significantly closing in high school and college graduation rates, in housing and employment, in full-time income, and so forth. Irrefutable statistical data support Patterson's claim: "relations between the races are getting better, as are the conditions of most African-Americans."[19]

Although what we have in America is the envy of the world, there is much left to do to alleviate poverty, to educate the American people, to level all the playing fields without racial quotas, and to encourage an appreciation of the distinctive gifts each group has given to American culture. But whether we have it in us to realize the dream of the Founders for a more perfect social order—for, among other things, a society in which race ceases to be a value, pro or con—depends in large measure on who speaks up positively for what we have already achieved. Recently we have not heard enough from those who, in spite of historical indignities, still find something to affirm in our interracial experience. Only when our historical progress in attaining racial harmony is fully understood and appreciated will we be able to build upon it so as to attain something even better.

J. W. T.

THE PRIMATE'S DREAM

The Mind of a Black Abolitionist: Frederick Douglass

That we live in a decadent age will seem evident to anyone who has been numbed by the moral horrors that occur daily all over this country and that are reported with a bland reportorial neutrality—or with supercilious amusement—by all the news media. These horrors—involving squalid prostitutes loitering on our city streets, drug dealers in every park and mall, armed children shooting it out in the schools, network pornography, fetal murders, medical research on aborted fetuses, doctor-assisted "suicides," congressional malfeasance and presidential smarminess—all of these have become so routine that they evoke hardly more than a shrug. Pedophile priests: what did you expect? A televangelist with his hand in the till or a hooker in tow: so what else is new? All of this is taken as a form of public amusement, like *The Late Show with David Letterman*, but it is just as stale and contrived. If any emotion stirs nowadays, it is likely to be a false compassion for a spurious victim—for the three-time loser who is said to deserve the weekend furlough and conjugal rights, or for the sports superhero with AIDS who brags that he slept with scores of women, or for the entertainment idol, caught in the pederastic act, who buys his way out of jail.

Passivity in the face of such evils is in fact nowadays admired as evidence of "open-mindedness," "compassion," and "tolerance" for differing "values" and "behaviors." In fact, to believe that evil is a reality or to have strong convictions about how to deal with the forms that evil takes in the national life is usually to be dismissed as an absolutist, a crank, and a bigot. Public moralists are a nuisance, and we usually do not like to listen to them. I am therefore led to wonder whether, if this were the nineteenth century, we would be capable of recognizing *as evil* something so huge and monstrous as the institution of slavery. Probably not.

In any case, such reflections on the ubiquity of evil and the too human readiness to deny it—especially when it is mirrored in the lines of one's face—occur to me as a result of rereading the autobiography of Frederick Douglass. This tragic and truly extraordinary black American had the bad fortune to be born a slave in Tuckahoe Creek, Maryland, in 1818. For most Americans in the early years of the Republic, it was perfectly "natural" that an "inferior race," like the blacks, should be enslaved to the "superior whites." After all, the Founding Fathers, in their constitutional wisdom, had—for all their declarations about born equality—provided the "natural law" of slavery with many American legal and political protections, hadn't they? And these constitutional guarantees to slavery were long supported by many of the other institutions of Northern and Southern society—the churches, the universities, the press, the "intellectual community," and the vast majority of just plain folks like you and me. Slavery an evil? Hardly, most people would have said in 1838. Only insolent blacks and the Northern religious right, those Yankee moral cranks who demonstrated and got arrested, thought so. But in the light of the highest ethical principles, they and a few others had it right.

The author of *Narrative of the Life of Frederick Douglass, An American Slave* (1845) was one of those insolent blacks who had it right. His remarkable account of what it was like to be a slave made inescapably plain to many of his contemporaries that this "peculiar institution" was in fact a socially organized manifestation of evil. While nearly everyone with the capacity of moral reason recognizes this now, few enough did in the 1830s, when he ran away from his owner. But the publication of this autobiography in 1845, in conjunction with many other kinds of abolitionist activism by Douglass and others, eventually moved many Northerners and some Southerners to agree with Lincoln's decision to publish the

Emancipation Proclamation in 1863. The *Narrative* is thus a major document in the racial, social, and political history of the nation.

Its historical importance aside, however, it is also the best of the American slave autobiographies—a work of extraordinary psychological, moral, and *literary* importance. This fact has been obscured of late, in the surge of new energy devoted to unearthing neglected narratives by slave women or novels by forgotten black women writers. Anyone who wants to know what slave life was like for women must read works like *The History of Mary Prince: A West Indian Slave* (1831), *Memoir of Old Elizabeth: A Coloured Woman* (1861), *The Story of Mattie Jackson* (1866), Kate Drumgoold's *A Slave Girl's Story* (1898), and Annie L. Burton's *Memories of Childhood's Slavery Days* (1909), which have all been republished in recent years. But of all such slave stories, by either men or women, the best was Douglass's *Narrative*.[1] As it took him him only up to age twenty-seven, however, the *Narrative* should be read alongside Douglass's subsequent autobiographical writings—the volumes *My Bondage and My Freedom* (1855) and *Life and Times of Frederick Douglass* (1881; revised, 1892).[2]

These autobiographies constitute a remarkable unfolding account of the life of an exceptional black American. The first takes him from slavery in the South to freedom in the North; the second from servile anonymity to worldwide celebrity as the most powerful black abolitionist orator in the world; and the third expands the earlier accounts in taking him through the Civil War and the triumph of black emancipation to great personal celebrity, high government office, and international fame—even as America was relapsing into Jim Crow laws, resegregation, and what Mark Twain was to call "The United States of Lyncherdom." Douglass's was a remarkable life. His narrative of that life is likewise remarkable in its moral vision, social judgment, and psychological power.

II

Born the son of Harriet Bailey, Douglass never knew who had fathered him. Frederick Bailey, as he was named, was rumored to be the son of his mother's master, the white man Aaron Anthony, who worked as the general overseer of the immensely wealthy planter Edward Lloyd, who owned five hundred slaves and thirteen farms in Talbot County, Maryland. Since his mother seems to have been used as a breeder, Frederick had an undetermined number of brothers and sisters, including Eliza, Ariana, Harriet, Kitty, Perry, and Sarah Bailey. Separated from his mother at the end of his first year, Douglass was reared by his grandmother, Betsey Bailey, while his mother was sent back to the fields. Then, at the age of six, he was removed from his grandmother's cabin and taken to live on the Lloyd plantation on the Wye River. There he was befriended by the twenty-year-old white woman Lucretia Anthony Auld, wife of Thomas Auld. She was, quite possibly, whether she knew it or not, his half-sister. In any case, the light-skinned Douglass was made the companion of Daniel Lloyd, the young son of the white master, and both boys had the run of the planter's "Great House." The two were inseparable and came to love each other; and Douglass must have fantasized about his also being the son of the rich white man Edward Lloyd, who owned so many farms and slaves. But no one stepped forward to enlighten Frederick about his father; and when he was seven or eight his mother, who might have told him, died unexpectedly; in all he had seen her only four or five times —usually briefly and at night, when she walked miles to the Lloyd plantation, after a long day of working in the field, to see her children.

Because he was a favorite of Lucretia Auld, Douglass was sent to Baltimore in 1826 to live with her brother-in-law, Hugh Auld, a ship carpenter, and his wife Sophia. Now, at age eight, Douglass was to be the companion of the Aulds' young son Tommy. Life in Baltimore was much safer than on the plantation; there was more food to eat; Douglass had a bed of his own for the first time; and Sophia Auld's kindness was a revelation of white generosity and affection. Life for a slave, however, was never secure. His owner Aaron Anthony died almost immediately, and his daughter Lucretia, who had taught and protected him in his childhood, died the next year. Such turning points in the lives of white families were often catastrophic for the slaves. At such times slave families were often broken up and relatives were sold and dispersed, sometimes to the deep South, into the cotton states, where agricultural life was much more difficult. Aaron had in fact already sold a number of the boy's relatives to deep South planters, and there was an expectation that ominous change awaited him. Douglass was inherited by Thomas Auld, Lucretia's widower. At the moment he did not want the boy, but instead of selling him off, Thomas Auld luckily returned young Douglass to the Hugh Aulds in Baltimore.

Douglass remarks in the *Narrative* that soon after he went to live with the kindly Sophia Auld, she began to teach him the ABCs. This was an extraordinary act of generosity on her part, and it promised to open up alternate worlds for young Douglass. But Hugh Auld put his foot down, refusing to hear of the boy's being educated, and reprimanding his wife that

> "If you give a nigger an inch, he will take an ell. A nigger should know nothing but to obey his master—to do as he is told to do. Learning would *spoil* the best nigger in the world. Now," said he, "if you teach that nigger (speaking of myself) how to read, there would be no keeping him. It would forever unfit him to be a value to his master. As to himself, it could do him no good, but a great deal of harm. It would make him discontented and unhappy."[3]

These words, overheard by the sensitive boy, were a revelation to young Douglass of how whites had always managed to enslave blacks. They kept his people in an ignorance borne of illiteracy. From that moment on, literacy represented for Douglass "the pathway from slavery to freedom."[4] And, during the next seven years while he lived with the Hugh Aulds, the passion to read and write was all-consuming. Douglass "appropriated" little Tommy's copy books and readers and studied them with avidity. He "borrowed" the Webster's speller and got white youngsters on the street to show him how letters were made. He joined a Bible study group at the Bethel AME Church in order to read more widely, and he bought and devoured a used copy of *The Columbian Orator* (1797), a well-known collection of prize speeches. Immersed in this book, Douglass memorized long passages from Richard Brinsley Sheridan, Caleb Bingham, and other great orators. Some of the speeches dealt with slavery and emancipation from oppression.

> The reading of these documents enabled me to utter my thoughts, and to meet the arguments brought forward to sustain slavery; but while they relieved me of one difficulty, they brought on another even more painful than the one of which I was relieved. The more I

read, the more I was led to abhor and detest my enslavers. I could regard them in no other light than a band of successful robbers, who had left their homes, and gone to Africa, and stolen us from our homes, and in a strange land reduced us to slavery. I loathed them as being the meanest as well as the most wicked of men. As I read and contemplated the subject, behold! that very discontentment which Master Hugh had predicted would follow my learning to read had already come, to torment and sting my soul to unutterable anguish. As I writhed under it, I would at times feel that learning to read had been a curse rather than a blessing. It had given me a view of my wretched condition, without the remedy. It opened my eyes to the horrible pit, but to no ladder upon which to get out. In moments of agony, I envied my fellow-slaves for their stupidity.[5]

This burning awareness of his servile condition ate upon his soul, alienated and embittered him, but what could he, a mere child, do about it? From time to time young Douglass had heard sinister things about Northern abolitionists; they piqued his curiosity, and he vowed to learn more about them.

In 1832, at age fourteen, Douglass was summarily returned to his owner, Captain Thomas Auld, who was still living back in rural Talbot County. This was a disastrous development, for Auld was a cruel and cowardly master who, Douglass wrote, did not care about his slaves or feed them enough. Throughout the first two autobiographies Douglass relentlessly condemned Thomas Auld as a mean-spirited master who was the embodiment of the evil of slavery as such and as the incarnation of all irreligion. In fact, Douglass appended to the 1855 *My Bondage and My Freedom* an open "Letter to His Old Master," accusing Auld of wantonly inflicting "the chain, the gag, the bloody whip" and of dragging him "at the pistol's mouth, fifteen miles, from the Bay Side to Easton, to be sold like a beast in the market, for the alleged crime of intending to escape from your possession."[6] Where, he asked Auld, were his "dear sisters"? And he asked about his "dear grandmother, whom you turned out like an old horse to die in the woods—is she still alive?"[7] Auld had supposedly been converted to Christianity at a Methodist camp meeting, but for Douglass any church that justified the perpetuation of slavery was unworthy of the name of religion. This master was, if anything, even more cruel after his conversion than before.

> I have seen him tie up a lame young woman, and whip her with a heavy cowskin upon her naked shoulders, causing the warm red blood to drip; and, in justification of the bloody deed, he would quote this passage of Scripture—"He that knoweth his master's will, and doeth it not, shall be beaten with many stripes."
>
> Master would keep this lacerated young woman tied up in this horrid situation four or five hours at a time. I have known him to tie her up early in the morning, and whip her before breakfast; leave her, go to his store, return at dinner, and whip her again, cutting her in the places already made raw with his cruel lash. The secret of master's cruelty toward "Henny" is found in the fact of her being almost helpless.[8]

All slaves were more or less helpless, but Henny Bailey's hands had been injured in a horrible fire, and her inability to work as fast and efficiently as Auld wanted was an irritant to him. Pornography was taboo in the nineteenth century, but something like soft porn was allowable in the description of the whipping of these female slaves. The point was twofold. In whipping, the masters were shown to be brutal monsters. But we are also to understand the whippings as an elaborate displacement of the sexual abuse of these vulnerable women, a degradation mixed with perverse and sadistic erotic impulses. Since Auld's conversion seem to have made him even more ruthless, Douglass turned against Christianity, became a cold rationalist, and put his seething intelligence to the service of destroying the institution that had enslaved him.

Witnessing such whippings eventually made Douglass insolent and obstreperous; he frequently intervened or spoke out of turn and was often whipped himself for his troubles. Eventually Auld determined to punish Douglass by renting him out as a field hand to Edward Covey, a well-known local "nigger-breaker."[9]

> Mr. Covey succeeded in breaking me. I was broken in body, soul, and spirit. My natural elasticity was crushed, my intellect languished, the disposition to read departed, the cheerful spark that lingered about my eye died; the dark night of slavery closed in upon me; and behold a man transformed into a brute![10]

Douglass ran away, back to Auld's farm, and begged his master to hire him out to another. But Auld refused and ordered Douglass back to Covey's farm.

One of the most crucial passages in the *Narrative* concerns Covey's attempt, three days later, to get revenge by whipping the sixteen-year-old boy. Douglass had been beaten many times before, but for some reason, this time, he did not intend to let himself be whipped again. Covey did not expect a fight and got more than he could handle. The fight was quite prolonged (two hours long, in fact), and Douglass drew blood in defeating the white man. For such an offense any slave might have been killed on the spot or immediately sold downriver to the cotton states. But strangely enough, after being beaten by the boy, Covey left him alone; he growled and threatened and menaced, but he did not try to whip him again, and eventually the slave rental agreement expired at the end of the year. The effect of the fistfight was that Douglass's self-confidence returned, his spirits rose, and he decided to gain his freedom by escaping. This he finally tried with five other slaves in 1836. At that time he was under lease to another nearby farmer, William Freeland, known in Talbot County as a more lenient master than either Auld or Covey. In fact, Douglass remarked that Freeland was "the best master I ever had, *till I became my own master.*"[11] At the Freeland farm Douglass fell in with and became closely attached to the other slaves John and Henry Harris, Handy Caldwell, Charles Roberts, Henry Bailey, and Sandy Jenkins. On Sundays, after a week's work in the fields, Douglass undertook to teach them to read and soon had more than twenty young men eager to attend his forbidden Sabbath school. In due course a few of them began to talk about freedom and conspired to escape. Douglass planned it. All of them vowed to stand by each other. But one slave, Sandy Jenkins, had a dream in which he saw Douglass in the claws of a huge bird. Sandy retained what Douglass later described as an African belief in voodoo and superstition and insisted "Dare is sumpon in it, shose you born; dare is, indeed, honey." On the fateful Saturday of their planned escape, Douglass, working in the fields, had a sudden presentiment that they had been double-crossed. "Sandy," he said, "we are betrayed"; and Jenkins replied, "Man, dat is strange; but I feel just as you do."[12]

Douglass and his fellow conspirators were arrested by the local authorities, and Douglass, as the chief malefactor, was marched to Easton and jailed. As he left the paradoxically named Freeland farm, the shrill screams of Mrs. Freeland echoed in his ears: "You devil! you yellow devil! It was you that put it into the heads of Henry and John to run away."[13] In the Easton jail, he was on the point of being lynched when his owner Thomas Auld suddenly appeared, demanded custody of the slave, and told the jailers in Easton that he was retrieving Douglass in order to sell him to a slaveholder in Alabama. Then, however, quite inexplicably to Douglass, he sent the boy back to the Hugh Aulds in Baltimore—to learn a trade. The person who betrayed them in the escape attempt was always a mystery, but the autobiographies suggest rather strongly that it was their fellow slave Sandy Jenkins.

III

The situation of blacks in Baltimore at the time Douglass returned to live there was a confusing matter. Perhaps only 20 percent of the population—some 25,000 people—were black; but of these perhaps three-fourths of the blacks were free, having been manumitted by their owners or been born to free parents of color. Blacks therefore came and went without much or any white supervision. A number of the blacks who remained slaves were, like Frederick Douglass, apprenticed out to learn a trade. After serving his apprenticeship as a caulker in a shipyard, Douglass in fact was allowed to hire himself out and to board where he chose, although he was obliged, once a week, to surrender most of his wages to Hugh Auld. Once he had mastered his trade and saved enough money, Douglass, in these loosely supervised circumstances, planned his escape. In 1838, at age twenty, he went underground, headed north, evaded the prowling slave-catchers and bounty hunters, and made his way to freedom in New Bedford, Massachusetts.

One might expect that the story of the actual escape would be the centerpiece of the *Narrative,* but in fact Douglass gives it short shrift. We must remember that Douglass was still a fugitive vulnerable to arrest at any time and susceptible to a forced return to his Maryland owner. Hence, in his anti-slavery speeches, he did not disclose his Bailey identity, identify his master by name, or reveal the way stations northward on the journey to freedom.[14] In fact, when he arrived in New Bedford, he was traveling under the name of Stanley. He and his new bride, Anna Murray, thought they would set up house as the Fred Johnsons. But his local contact, a man named Nathan Johnson, told him there were already too many black Johnsons in New Bedford and that another name would be preferable.

What's in a name? The slave has nothing but his body, his labor, and his name. Some slaves had secret African names, but Douglass did not. He had been born Frederick Augustus Washington Bailey but had himself dropped the middle names. Yet in running away, this slave Fred Bailey had had to renounce his name, his patronymic (or rather matronymic), in order to become *par excellence* an actor, an imposter, and a confidence man rolled into one. By pulling up stakes, moving to a new location, and changing his identity, this slave had begun to participate in what has always been a very distinctively American *rite d'identité*. Douglass reports that

> I gave Mr. Johnson the privilege of choosing me a name, but told him he must not take from me the name of "Frederick." I must hold on to that, to preserve a sense of my identity. Mr. Johnson had just been reading the "Lady of the Lake," and at once suggested that my name be "Douglass." From that time until now I have been called "Frederick Douglass;" and as I am more widely known by that name than by either of the others, I shall continue to use it as my own.[15]

But there is perhaps another reason why this newly named Douglass gave the actual escape such scant treatment in the first two narratives. A close reading of Douglass's two antebellum autobiographies suggests that his essential emancipation had in fact already occurred four years earlier, at age sixteen, at that fistfight with Edward Covey, the "nigger-breaker." This will seem surprising to the reader. But Douglass states and then restates a point of view that puts the psychology of the slave in a new light. "This battle with Mr. Covey," Douglass wrote in the *Narrative*,

> was the turning-point in my career as a slave. It rekindled the few expiring embers of freedom, and revived within me a sense of my own manhood. It recalled the departed self-confidence, and inspired

me again with a determination to be free.... It was a glorious resurrection, from the tomb of slavery, to the heaven of freedom. My long-crushed spirit rose, cowardice departed, bold defiance took its place; and I now resolved that, however long I might remain a slave in form, the day had passed forever when I could be a slave in fact. I did not hesitate to let it be known of me, that the white man who expected to succeed in whipping, must also succeed in killing me.[16]

This is a remarkable redefinition of the meaning of freedom. Here freedom is equated with the absolute possession of one's ownmost spirit, with psychological self-confidence, with an autonomous interior selfhood. Freedom is not so much a matter of who controls one's body as who has control of the soul. As such, this definition of liberty is not unlike that of the philosopher-slave Epictetus, to whose Stoicism the imprisoned and enslaved, in many nations, have oft turned for consolation. Nor is this definition of freedom alien to one strand of Christian thought, which sees us all as slaves—to the body, to the appetites, and to perversions of the will, if not to worldly powers. Under this conviction, St. Paul counsels patience and obedience to one's masters, in the expectation of eventual heavenly emancipation.[17]

Douglass appears to have sensed the extremity of this subjective definition of freedom and later backed off from it in the 1881 *Life and Times of Frederick Douglass*. There he writes: "I was a changed being after that fight. I was *nothing* before; *I was a man* now. It ... inspired me with renewed determination to be a *free man*." He wrote that he was resurrected

> from the dark and pestiferous tomb of slavery, to the heaven of comparative freedom. I was no longer a servile coward, trembling under the frown of a brother worm of the dust, but my long-cowed spirit was roused to an attitude of independence. I had reached the point at which I was *not afraid to die*. This spirit made me a freeman in *fact*, though I still remained a slave in *form*. When a slave cannot be flogged, he is more than half free. He has a domain as broad as his own manly heart to defend, and he is really "a power on earth."[18]

One likes the adjective in "comparative freedom," but it is followed by considerations of form and fact and percentages of liberty that do not add up in my own calculations. Still, the point seems preserved, even in Douglass's final and more florid 1881 figure: the essence of freedom is always a condition of the mind and heart.

IV

Between 1838 and 1841 Douglass supported his family by unskilled labor—sawing wood, shoveling coal, and loading ships. (The white New Bedford shipyard workers would not tolerate a black caulker.) Yet he was now reading *The Liberator,* attending speeches by William Lloyd Garrison and Wendell Phillips, and occasionally speaking himself from the pulpit of the local Zion Methodist church. In 1841, at the Massachusetts Anti-Slavery Society convention in Nantucket, Douglass was invited to describe his life as a slave. The performance was electrifying and so enthusiastically received that he was hired by the Society to be its general agent and to tour the country—with Garrison, Phillips, Abby Kelley, Stephen S. Foster, Parker Pillsbury, and other radical abolitionists—advocating the nonviolent emancipation of blacks, their civil equality, and their right to live in America (rather than suffering exile to a distant black colony). In 1845 he published the *Narrative,* and, because he disclosed his Bailey connections, movement leaders deemed it prudent to send him on a lecture tour to Great Britain, where, during the following two years, he was an immense success. While abroad, some of his English friends (notably, Anna and Ellen Richardson and John Bright) negotiated with the Aulds to secure his freedom—thus initiating the first of many great public furors over the conduct of Frederick Douglass. Hugh Auld, who in 1846 had bought Douglass for $100 from his brother, agreed to free Douglass in return for £150. After Douglass secured his freedom in this way there was an immense outcry, many purists arguing that the English anti-slavery radicals had trafficked with—and indeed enriched the coffers of—the hated slave power. But Douglass and his friends justified the negotiation on the ground that Douglass had not been *purchased* by the English. Instead, for a consideration, Hugh Auld had merely agreed to *manumit* him. The paradox in all of this is that some of the abolitionists would have preferred Douglass to remain a fugitive slave: it made for better anti-slavery propaganda.

Back in America in 1847, a free man, Douglass resumed lecturing and touring the country. But he was becoming restive with the tight controls placed on him by Garrison and the Massachusetts Anti-Slavery Society. He wanted to edit his own abolitionist newspaper, but the Society had other ideas. They wanted to use and control him, to employ his talents for their own programs and purposes. But Douglass, who already had a reputation for being uppity, was his own man. And it was with some irritation that the Garrison abolitionists finally acceded to Douglass's moving Anna and his household to Rochester in 1848, where he commenced his own radical newspaper, the *North Star,* a competitor with *The Liberator.* The prospectus for the paper promised that it would "attack slavery in all its forms and aspects; advocate Universal Emancipation; exact the standard of public morality; promote the moral and intellectual improvement of the colored people; and to hasten the day of freedom to our three million enslaved fellow-countrymen."[19]

The Garrisonians did not like the *North Star* and were frankly appalled by developing events in Douglass's personal life. Once again, it seemed, a radical *social* idea—black emancipation—was getting entangled with the idea of *sexual* emancipation—and miscegenation. Douglass had brought to America and installed in his own house the white radical Julia Griffiths, a member of the English anti-slavery movement. She served as his business manager for the *North Star,* but there is no reason to doubt that she was also his mistress, living in the same household with Anna and their five children. None of these relationships is clarified in the autobiographies. Douglass is wonderfully reticent about his courtship of Anna, their marriage, his women friends, and his own sexuality. And we know next to nothing about Anna's response to Frederick's abolition work or to women friends. Anna Douglass was a very shy woman and did not participate in movement activities; and, despite many unsuccessful efforts to teach her to read, she remained illiterate and did not forward, directly, her husband's developing career. But what seems unmistakable is that many women, of both races, found Frederick Douglass sexually attractive.

Douglass was a remarkably tall, muscular, and handsome young man with thick, black, curly hair, a pair of piercing eyes, a straight nose, thin and well-formed lips, a musical voice, and a light mulatto complexion—a combination that melted hearts on two continents. In addition, he was the brightest and most articulate slave ever to have joined the movement, almost too talented and exceptional to be believed. Some were so struck with his abilities that they doubted he had ever been a Southern slave. Others did not believe that Douglass himself had really written the 1845 *Narrative*. Most slave narratives were, in fact, dictated or ghost-written. But we have no evidence that anyone helped Douglass with the writing or editing of the *Narrative*. Still, Douglass's first life is preceded by the usual "Attestation" of its authenticity: two stirring prefaces—one by Garrison, the other by Wendell Phillips—confirming that, yes, Douglass really was a black slave and, yes, he had written the work himself. (In subsequent editions, after his break with the Massachusetts Anti-Slavery Society, these prefaces by the white abolitionists were replaced with introductions by black friends.)

Douglass's mixed blood, light complexion, and sexual charisma were a problem for many abolitionists, black and white. The Englishman Thomas Clarkson worried: "I wish he were full blood black for I fear pro-slavery people will attribute his preeminent abilities to the white blood that is in his veins." And so some of them did. Douglass, whose identity was securely that of a black man, wrote back comically from England that "I am hardly black enough for the british taste, but by keeping my hair as wooly as possible—I make out to pass for at least a half a negro at any rate." Because of his mixed ancestry, the argument about the source of his talent went on and on. In the preface to *My Bondage and My Freedom*, a black friend by the name of James McCune Smith undertook to answer in print whether "Mr. Douglass's power [was] inherited from the Negroid, or from what is called the Caucasian side of his makeup." Smith concluded that "for his energy, perseverance, eloquence, invective, sagacity, and wide sympathy, he is indebted to his negro blood."[20] William S. McFeely, in his excellent biography *Frederick Douglass*, has reported some of the other wonderful but paradoxical responses to this remarkable slave:

> One of Douglass's Dublin admirers had a somewhat different slant on the problem: "Faith, an' if half a Naigar can make a speech like that, what could a whole Naigar do?" At least one American knew

the right answer to this excellent question: years later, Lizzie Lavender, a former slave herself, reflected "that if a man who is only half black can become great like that, what may not be achieved by a person who is all black like me?"[21]

What seems obvious is that Douglass attracted quite a number of radical groupies in England and America; and in Julia Griffiths he had brought one of them home to live with him (and Anna and the children) in Rochester. As Douglass was by this time too well known, too popular, and too successful to be controlled by the white anti-slavery establishment, he thought he could weather the sexual scandal. But, with even *The Liberator* publicly critical of this ménage, the pressure became too much, and in 1855 Julia Griffiths returned to England.[22]

V

In any case, the Garrisonians were coming to seem more and more irrelevant, in Douglass's view, to American political developments. That Douglass had been fully accepted by whites in England helps, as David Brion Davis has observed, "to explain his underlying optimism about the imminent conquest of racial prejudice."[23] But that optimism was becoming increasingly rooted in political rather than moral possibilities. Garrison and *The Liberator* group saw the Constitution as an evil document which enshrined and protected slavery. Any participation in American politics was therefore corrupt and immoral. Some abolitionists wanted the North to secede from the South and its slave-defending federal government; others wanted Massachusetts to secede from the Union; the most radical of the Garrisonians even wanted Essex County to secede from Massachusetts. The point was to maintain one's moral purity and remain free from the squalid compromises required in the political life. A long train of events had convinced Douglass that this hostility to the political process had not achieved any positive results. Moreover, Douglass had become convinced by new arguments to the effect that the Constitution was in fact anti- rather than pro-slavery. It was clear that Douglass now needed to forge some new political alliances. So in 1853 he threw in his lot with Gerrit Smith, merged his *North Star* with Smith's *Liberty Party Paper,* and so produced a new journal that he called *Frederick Douglass's Paper*. He now joined with many others in an open *political* dialogue—and so provoked a bitter break with Garrison and the Massachusetts Anti-Slavery Society.

Douglass's activities thenceforward, until the outbreak of the Civil War, are what might have been expected from an ardent, nationally known abolitionist. He continued to tour the country giving lectures on anti-slavery and urging other liberal causes in the "Sisterhood of Reforms" (Northern desegregation, temperance, anti-vivisectionism, female suffrage, more generous labor laws). Very often Douglass and his fellow speakers were hauled out of railroad cars, ejected from restaurants, heckled and shouted down, set upon by mobs, or beaten by racist thugs. Nevertheless, courageously and persistently he followed this anti-slavery calling. He published the second version of his autobiography, *My Bondage and My Freedom*, in 1855. Jean Fagan Yellin has said that here "the mature Douglass produced an autobiography which ranks with the memoirs of his greatest countrymen, and critics judge it his most finished work." This 1855 text does have a refinement of style produced by Douglass's years of speechwriting and editing. But I am inclined to agree with Yellin that the book lacks the dramatic impact of the *Narrative,* which "stands on its own, a complement to the fuller [1855] autobiography."[24]

When the Republican party came into being, Douglass urged its leaders to turn it into the party of abolition. He knew and supported John Brown in assisting escaped slaves to reach Canada. But when in 1859 Brown told him of the plan to assault the Harpers Ferry arsenal and to arm the slaves for an insurrection, Douglass knew that his friend had gone round the bend and declined to participate in the raid. Still, Brown's confiscated papers mentioned the name of Douglass, and a request for his arrest was issued. This led Douglass to take off on an immediate unplanned voyage to Europe, where he met up with Ottilia Assing; and on the lecture circuit he acclaimed, from afar, the martyrdom of Old Osawatomie.

When it was safe to do so, Douglass returned to America, supported Lincoln for the presidency, and went about the country campaigning for the Republican party. Lincoln's opponent, that *other* Douglas—the Little Giant Stephen Douglas—had shrewdly foreseen, in the Second Debate in 1858, that support for Lincoln could be eroded by invoking the specter of social equality with blacks and the fear of miscegenation. And in Freeport, Illinois, as well as in other places, he appealed to the racism of his audience by warning that Frederick Douglass was the portent of the sexual horrors to come. Calling Lincoln the tool of black abolitionists, Judge Douglas said,

> I have reason to recollect that some people in this country think that Fred. Douglass is a very good man. The last time I came here to make a speech, while talking from the stand to you, people of Freeport, as I am doing to-day, I saw a carriage and a magnificent one it was, drive up and take a position on the outside of the crowd; a beautiful young lady was sitting on the box seat, whilst Fred. Douglass and her mother reclined inside, and the owner of the carriage acted as driver. (Laughter, cheers, cries of right, what have you to say against it, &c.) I saw this in your own town. ("What of it.") All I have to say of it is this, that if you, Black Republicans, think that the negro ought to be on a social equality with your wives and daughters, and ride in a carriage with your wife, whilst you drive the team, you have a perfect right to do so. (Good, good, and cheers, mingled with hooting and cries of white, white.) I am told that one of Fred. Douglass's kinsmen, another rich black negro, is now traveling in this part of the state making speeches for his friend Lincoln as the champion of black men. ("White men, white men," and "what have you got to say against it." That's right, &c.) All I have to say on that subject is that those of you who believe that the negro is your equal and ought to be on an equality with you socially, politically, and legally; have a right to entertain those opinions, and of course will vote for Mr. Lincoln. ("Down with the negro," no, no, &c.)[25]

Despite the evident public conflict aroused by these debates and by provocative abolitionist agitation, Frederick Douglass did not foresee secession and the attack on Fort Sumter. He did, however, welcome it. During the war—while Lincoln played that devious political game over what would be done with the slaves—Douglass held Lincoln's feet to the fire. Emancipation, desegregation, education, and equality of opportunity were Douglass's objectives. He wanted blacks enlisted into the Union army, paid equally with whites, and accorded all the rights of citizenship. Douglass hoped to receive a commission himself and wanted to recruit black volunteers; and indeed Lincoln thought him "one of the most meritorious men in America."[26] But there was much opposition to Douglass in the cabinet and, when the commission did not materialize, he withdrew to his home and resumed his civilian agitation on behalf of black emancipation. As Benjamin Quarles has remarked, "a commission to a Negro was too far in advance of Northern sentiment" at that time.[27]

The nineteenth century was the great age of oratory, and, in an era of extraordinary public spellbinders, Frederick Douglass was a master indeed. He modeled his delivery on that of William Lloyd Garrison, one of the best speakers of the age. But Douglass commanded an even more impressive rolling stentorian style and employed a remarkably fluent vocal range. There are many reports of "the magnetism and melody of his wonderfully elastic voice."[28] He had in fact a repertory of roles, dialects, and voices that could evoke wonderful responses of pity and fear, joy and laughter. His gift for satirical mimickry—of Southern slaveholders, redneck overseers, and pompous pulpit defenders of slavery—was wicked indeed and brought down the house in frequent laughter. Yet, more seriously, Douglass could also mesmerize an audience of two thousand and more for two or three hours at a time. (How different are modern politicians, who cannot master the thirty-second sound bite.) Elizabeth Cady Stanton, who acclaimed the "burning eloquence" of this fugitive slave, said that, when he warmed to the topic of the evils of slavery, he stood on the abolitionist platform "like an African prince, majestic in his wrath." And all around him "sat the great antislavery orators of the day [Garrison, Pillsbury, and Phillips], earnestly watching the effect of his eloquence on that immense audience, that laughed and wept by turns, completely carried away by the wondrous gifts of his pathos and humor."[29]

Some have said that the power of his writing derived from his platform techniques, others from the rhetorical mode of the black pulpit.[30] But these propositions seem unlikely. In his autobiographies Douglass is a *writer* and a very good one indeed. We have little in the published lives of the oral storytelling manner so common in Douglass's time and nothing of the iterations and repetitions so typical of verbal tales. In these autobiographies we do not find the satirical mimickry that continually convulsed

Douglass's audiences with laughter. And, unlike Twain, Artemus Ward, Paul Laurence Dunbar, and others in the vernacular oral tradition, Douglass almost never descended into dialect—the vehicle of comedy—to represent the speech of blacks.[31] I like the first of the three narratives for its deceptive simplicity and the directness of its style and story. The later versions are increasingly filled out, more copious and factually detailed, and are marked by more imaginative invention. The later accounts even raise a question in my mind about Douglass's striking ability to visualize scenes and remember exact conversations that he had only sketchily represented years before. And I am not much taken by the false flowers of rhetoric that were so much admired in the later Victorian period. Still, all three forms of the life are remarkable expressions of human dignity, moral seriousness, psychological strength, and literary power.

After the war Douglass continued to lecture on the lyceum circuit and publicly campaigned for successive Republican candidates—Grant, Hayes, Garfield, Blaine, and Harrison. He wrote widely and well on a wide range of topics—from the need for education and self-help to segregation, race relations, the failures of Reconstruction, and international politics. Though he hoped to be appointed to high office, Douglass was perhaps too abrasive and independent (if not too scandalous) for most Republican administrations. In 1871 Grant gave him a commissioner's post to investigate the idea of annexing the Dominican Republic for blacks. Hayes made him the U.S. marshal for the District of Columbia in 1877, but President Garfield afterward demoted him to the post of recorder of deeds.

After Anna died, the sixty-six-year-old Douglass shocked nearly everyone by marrying, in 1884, Helen Pitts, a white woman from New York twenty years younger than he. Neither his children nor her family approved of this match, and the interracial marriage was widely criticized in the American press. Many blacks thought he had turned his back on his race, while many whites saw it as another step toward the "mongrelization" of the Caucasian race. But Douglass knew in his own parentage that neither law nor custom can control desire or prevent love and affection from crossing racial lines; and without apologizing or explaining he simply acted on the principles by which he had always lived.

Frederick and Helen Douglass comported themselves with the greatest dignity, were very happy together, won over many of their detractors. In 1889, Douglass was appointed minister resident and consul general to Haiti, a post he held until 1891. The appointment in Haiti was richly symbolic, since in many respects Douglass was to his people something of what Toussaint l'Ouverture had meant to Haitians. His final years were quiet, but toward the end he made the friendship of the young black journalist Ida B. Wells, and, spurred by her ardor and burning indignation, he recovered his passion for reform with a prolonged and effective attack on the appalling wave of black lynchings in the South. He died in 1895 and was buried with Anna in Rochester, New York.

VI

In retrospect it is clear that Frederick Douglass was the most important black in nineteenth-century America. His courage, conviction, and fiery eloquence created admiring audiences all over the United States and Britain. He will therefore always have a place in the history of black emancipation and of American eloquence and platform oratory. Douglass's public performances are lost to us, since he lived before the invention of voice or audio recordings. But a distinct personality well worth knowing was created in these three autobiographies, which are the work of a remarkable, versatile, and accomplished *writer*.

As a writer, Douglass has not escaped a painful flogging at the hands of some modern literary theorists. The effect of a great deal of politically correct contemporary writing about Douglass is to diminish the historical importance, moral authority, and rhetorical power of his work. Unfortunately, some of these theorists are of Douglass's own race, and their thinking is decidedly peculiar. One of them, Henry Louis Gates, Jr., has said that the "refusal to use sophisticated analysis on our own literature smacks of a symbolic inferiority complex as blatant as were treatments of skin lightener and hair straightener."[32] This sounds all right until we remember that sophisticated analysis means things like deconstructionism and neo-Marxism. Infected by the deconstructionist virus, Gates now believes that nothing has an essence and everything is a text. So in his postmodern account of things, Douglass is a mere "creature of language"—rather than the master of language, of literacy, and of powerful self-expression. Especially fearful to Gates is the idea of a "knowable and unchanging black and integral self." So perturbed is Gates that Douglass's identity might have had an *essence* or core of black selfhood that he reduces the writer to an inconstant and elusive verbal shapeshifter in whom we can repose no confidence. The effect is that our belief in Douglass is diminished and the objective of racial equality demanded in his autobiographies is accordingly subverted.³³

But the most remarkable devaluation of Douglass's achievement is found in the criticism of Houston A. Baker, Jr. I have been arguing that Douglass's achievement—in learning to read and indeed *to write* those extraordinary autobiographies—represents a triumph of the human spirit for which every reader can justly, if vicariously, be proud. But, according to Baker, a discontented black, Douglass's work is inauthentic *because it is written in English*. Poor fellow, Douglass lacked "a separate, written black language" and so was entrapped in "the linguistic codes, literary conventions, and audience expectations" of literate Christian America. These, of course, "compromised" his integrity as a "prototypical black American self." It is Baker's opinion that, "Had there been a separate, written black language available, Douglass might have fared better." As it was, the existing social and linguistic structures of Douglass' time "seemed to force him to move to a public version of the self—one molded by the values of white America."³⁴

Most of his white antebellum contemporaries, Northern and Southern, would have been surprised to hear that Fred Douglass actually embodied their own sexual, racial, and religious values. They thought of him as a shocking radical with newfangled ideas—although in fact he was merely reminding them of the high ethical standard they said they believed in. In any case, what else than English could Douglass have used in the *Narrative*? Did he have a white audience who could read Guinean? Were there any American blacks in 1845 who could read Zulu? Did the African languages spoken by the imported slaves have a written alphabet or a literature for reading, in America, in 1845? Whatever the condition of written texts in African tribal languages then, how many American slaves in 1845 could remember, much less read, the tongues of their African forefathers? Very few indeed. I would be surprised if Houston Baker—who was once the president of the Modern Language Association of America (an office, in my view, that obliges its holder to have a better appreciation of the English language and its literature)—I would be surprised if Houston Baker himself could speak or write in any black African tongue that might have been used by his forefathers. But why should either he or Douglass be criticized for that?

In fact, many contemporary postmodern literary critics do not think that Douglass was radical enough. Not merely did he, in the words of Thad Ziolkowski, use "hegemonic discourse [i.e., English] as a mode of representation."[35] Even worse, he stood for higher education, self-reliance, self-discipline, and personal responsibility. He stood for the Protestant work ethic, and for the Americanness—rather than the Africanness—of the Afro-American. Douglass's belief in assimilation, integration, and active political participation in the American way of life, as a means of improving the lot of blacks, has made him for many postmoderns another Booker T. Washington. He is therefore almost *persona non grata* to black nationalists, separatist Muslims, and the MLA Marxists whose "non-hegemonic discourse" encourages a latter-day incitement to violence. Far from a wimpy accommodationist to honky oppression, Douglass, for most Americans, is and will always be a genuine American hero.[36]

VII

One of the most affecting passages in the autobiography appeared in the *Life and Times of Frederick Douglass,* where he described his return in 1876 to Talbot County, Maryland, to meet with the eighty-year-old Thomas Auld, his former master. After his escape Douglass had relentlessly and publicly attacked Captain Auld, by name, as the sadistic personification of slavery itself. By the outbreak of the Civil War, Auld was almost as well known in antebellum America as Douglass himself. But now, in 1876, the dying Captain Auld had requested an interview. Although Douglass had harbored a lifetime of bitterness against his master, the visit produced a remarkable "turn."

We addressed each other simultaneously, he calling me "Marshal

Douglass," and I, as I had always called him, "Captain Auld." Hearing myself called by him "Marshal Douglass," I instantly broke up the formal nature of the meeting by saying, "not *Marshal*, but Frederick to you as formerly."

We shook hands cordially, and in the act of doing so, he, having been long stricken with palsy, shed tears as men thus afflicted will do when excited by any deep emotion. The sight of him, the changes which time had wrought in him, his tremulous hands constantly in motion, and all the circumstances of his condition affected me deeply, and for a time choked my voice and made me speechless. We both, however, got the better of our feelings, and conversed freely about the past.[37]

In the scene as constructed, both speak simultaneously: neither is accorded preeminence, priority, or superiority. Further, the dignity of both men is preserved in Douglass's having them address each other by their titles—"Marshal" and "Captain." Yet "Marshal" is repeated three times in the paragraph—a reminder that Douglass is no longer chattel. His rank and public office remind us that it is the majesty of the law, incarnate in all its officers, that preserves the equality of the races. Even so, cordiality and affection predominate in the exchange. The affection goes to a depth that makes for trembling, tears, and speechlessness, perhaps as befitting the reunion of brothers-in-law long separated. One notes too that this depth of human affection is, in that distinctively masculine American way, denied, as if the affective states generated by this encounter were really the effect of Auld's old age and palsy and Douglass's witness of it.

For all of Douglass's lifelong bitterness, despite every whip lash he had suffered, this was a scene of mutual forgiveness and final reconciliation. Auld told Douglass new facts about the Bailey slaves that he had not known before, and Douglass discovered Auld to be blameless of some of the accusations of cruelty that Douglass had earlier brought against him. In fact, far from turning out Douglass's grandmother like an old horse, Auld, who had really never owned her, had in fact taken her in, in old age, and had provided for her to the end of her life. Douglass discovered, in short, that he could no longer hate his former master, who was more of a Christian than he had supposed.[38]

Slavery *was* a monstrous evil, but into the interstices of any such barbaric system there will always slip that incalculable element—human feeling. Call it the human equation. Call it by its name, affection. Affection led Lucretia Auld to see that the young Douglass was assigned to the service of Master Lloyd and his son; it was affection that led Sophia Auld to want to lift the appealing young Douglass toward literacy; and it was affection, perhaps, in some warped and distorted form, that moved Captain Auld to rescue Douglass from that Easton jail in 1836—when he was on the point of being lynched for trying to escape—and return him to the Hugh Aulds in Baltimore. It takes nothing away from Douglass, a genuine American self-made man, to note that in some corner of his mind he always knew that at crucial moments the Aulds, perhaps unconsciously, had opened doorways and created unexpected opportunities for his advancement. While the intent of Douglass's writing is always relentless anti-slavery propaganda, and while Captain Auld as the incarnation of evil was a rhetorical necessity in the anti-slavery campaign, all three narratives move us, psychologically, toward this delayed acknowledgment of Auld's essential humanity and toward Douglass's final reconciliation with him. "He was to me no longer a slaveholder either in fact or in spirit," Douglass wrote, "and I regarded him as I did myself, a victim of the circumstances of birth, education, law, and custom."[39] Douglass was of course denounced by some blacks in the 1870s for making his peace with a onetime slaveholder. And even now some radical critics are sullen at the overtones of Christian forgiveness that illuminate this passage. But, in transcending the desire for revenge and perpetual punishment, Frederick Douglass preserved his soul intact; and in realizing and recounting this peaceful reconciliation of racial differences, Frederick Douglass gave the American people their best hope for racial harmony.

The Mind of a White Abolitionist: Thomas Wentworth Higginson

The history of race relations in America has sometimes been obscured by the evanescence of reputations that once seemed formidable and unforgettable. Such is the case with Thomas Wentworth Higginson (1823–1911). He is perhaps most often remembered nowadays as the critic who told Emily Dickinson that her poems needed revision and that young authors ought to delay publication until their works were ready. In the minds of a great many modern critics (as well as feminist fanatics), Higginson has been transmogrified into the monster who repressed her genius and kept her from publishing her verse. This is of course nonsense, as Dickinson took orders from nobody. If he were in fact the villain that some modern critics describe, Dickinson—no fool—would not have continued to correspond with him for two decades. She always regarded him with affection and playfully addressed him as "Dear Preceptor," though they both knew that she was her own woman. To Higginson she sent more than a hundred poems; to him we owe a debt for co-editing her verse in two volumes after her death.

If the literary life was important to Higginson, so was Emersonian transcendentalism. I do not think I am wrong in calling Higginson Emerson's most faithful, even slavish, disciple. But Emerson was principally reflective; Higginson was always in search of ways to translate his convictions into action. And the two most important principles that animated him had to do with the emancipation of blacks and that of women. He was one of the great abolitionists and one of the great male feminists of his time. This essay is principally about his notions of race.

Throughout the 1840s and 1850s, while the abolition movement was a-building, this transcendentalist *littérateur* was absorbing the political enthusiasm of anti-slavery reformers such as William Lloyd Garrison, Wendell Phillips, Lucy Stone, Mrs. Child, the Grimké sisters, Theodore Parker, and Samuel Gridley Howe. Emerson had remarked in his journal in July 1846 that "the Abolitionists should resist, because they are literalists; they know exactly what they object to, and there is a government possible which will content them."[1] Higginson knew what would content him. If abolitionists such as Frederick Douglass held to the necessity of participating in the electoral process, in order to change the law, he, like Thoreau, advocated disunion and secession from a national government unwilling to abolish slavery. As Higginson reflected on the matter, he wrote to a close friend that "the great reason why the real apostles of truth don't make any more impression is this—the moment any person among us begins to broach any 'new views' and intimate that all things aren't exactly right, the conservatives lose no time in holding up their fingers and branding him as an unsafe person—fanatic, visionary, insane, and all the rest of it. . . ." This, he felt, had rightly been the case with all reforms, since "it is the enthusiastic (i.e. half-cracked people) who begin all reforms." Mrs. Child, he observed, "has long been proscribed as an entirely unsafe person and as for Mr. Emerson and Mr. Alcott, it doesn't do for a sober person even to think of them."[2]

So vocal was he, in his opposition to slavery, that conservatives called him "swart-minded Higginson" and accused him of substituting his private opinions for the law. But Higginson, like other Yankee transcendentalists, held to a Higher Law, the law of human freedom, which would be served—even perhaps, unfortunately, through the instrument of violence. Had not even Jefferson said that the tree of liberty might need to be refreshed from time to time with the blood of patriots?[3]

Higginson was a quintessential political activist. When the Fugitive Slave Law was passed in 1850, he stood for Congress as a Free Soil party candidate. Thoreau's "Civil Disobedience" (1849) had counseled that "those who call themselves Abolitionists should at once effectually withdraw their support, both in person and property, from the government of Massachusetts,"⁴ and Thoreau had gone to jail to dramatize his own withdrawal. Higginson admired the nonviolent resistance of Thoreau and the pacifism of Whittier and of the Garrisonian abolitionists. But he went further, telling his neighbors that since the Fugitive Slave Law "must . . . yield to a higher law," right-thinking Massachusetts men would refuse to catch or return escaped slaves.

His sermons were so insistently about the righteousness of abolitionism that the Newburyport Unitarians felt obliged to let him go for not addressing their other congregational needs. The Newburyport *Union* even accused him of openly advocating "the nullification of the laws of the land, when they do not correspond with his individual opinions." But in his "Address to the Voters," referring to the fugitive-slave provision of the Compromise Act of 1850, he said "DISOBEY IT . . . and show our good citizenship by taking the legal consequences!" He abhorred bloodshed, he told his would-be constituents. But in "terrible times" it became "necessary to speak of bloodshed." When push came to shove, he warned, "it is hard to say where a man must stop in defending his inalienable rights."⁵

Several test cases of the Fugitive Slave Law inflamed Higginson's antagonism to this "immoral legislation" in the 1850s and shoved him in the direction of that violence he so abhorred. One case involved an escaped slave named Sims, who was arrested in Boston and returned to Georgia, to be publicly whipped. Higginson was dismayed with the "great want of preparation on our part for this revolutionary work," and he tried to persuade Marshal Tukey of Newburyport of the immorality of pursuing escaped slaves. And to his classmate Charles Devons, then a United States marshal, he wrote:

> For myself there is something in the thought of assisting to return to slavery a man guilty of no crime but a colored skin [at which] every thought of my nature rebels in . . . horror. I think not now of the escaped slave, though he has all my sympathies, but of the free men and women who are destined to suffer for this act. And I almost feel as if the nation of which we have boasted were sunk in

the dust forever, now that justice and humanity are gone; and as if the 19th century were the darkest of all the ages.[6]

In the meantime his powerful oratory and his moral energy became known to the leaders of the Free Church at Worcester. He had supposed himself "to have given up preaching forever," but the Worcester congregation—"with no church membership or communion service, not calling themselves Christian, but resembling . . . [modern] ethical societies"—offered Higginson "a new sphere of reformatory action."[7]

During his Worcester pastorate (1852–1858), Higginson resumed the ministry of nondenominational Christianity based on man's "intuition" of "the great Law of Nature," God's love manifest in the humanity of Jesus. In practical affairs he supported the ten-hour bill, land reform, penal legislation, temperance, anti-slavery, and women's rights—all popular causes in Worcester, a workingman's town. In 1853 he helped organize the World Temperance Convention in New York City. Since he loved to be in the thick of convention politics, where the wires are pulled, he moved the appointment of Susan B. Anthony to the Committee on Arrangements. Thereupon the convention disintegrated into an uproar of hissing and catcalls, for Miss Anthony was widely despised as a feminist radical. During the uproar Higginson resigned from the committee, warning that no World Temperance Convention could possibly be effective that excluded representatives of half the human race. He led the walkout that resulted in the formation of a "Whole World's Temperance Convention," featuring the support of some of the great radicals of his day—Elizabeth Cady Stanton, Susan B. Anthony, Lucy Stone, Lucretia Mott, Abby Foster Phillips, Garrison, Parker, and Horace Greeley. Higginson was the unanimous choice as its chairman.[8] But the Sims case and others like it rankled. All he asked of fate, he recorded in his diary, was "one occasion worth bursting the door for—an opportunity to get beyond this boy's play."[9]

II

That opportunity came to Higginson, then thirty, on Wednesday, May 24, 1854, when he received word from Samuel May that Anthony Burns, an escaped slave, had been seized in Boston and that a public protest was scheduled at Faneuil Hall on Friday night. Higginson immediately went to Boston and closeted himself with the Vigilance Committee. Composed of Higginson, Theodore Parker, Wendell Phillips, Samuel Gridley Howe, Austin Bearse, Martin Stowell, and William Kemp, the committee debated a forcible rescue of the slave Burns. Most opposed any violence, but they agreed to formulate a plan on Friday at the Faneuil Hall demonstration.

Meanwhile Stowell privately urged Higginson to action, citing their ineffectuality in the Sims affair. On Friday night, while the crowds were filling up the hall, Higginson, agreeing that they must take *some* action, purchased a dozen hand axes from a nearby hardware store, hid them in the office of Henry Bowditch, across from the Court House, and went over to Faneuil Hall. Higginson and Stowell then presented to the committee their plan for an assault on the Court House, while the meeting was in session, on the ground that the police and deputies would be expecting trouble after the demonstration broke up. Howe and Kemp agreed to the plan. Parker also consented, although in the noise and confusion he misunderstood the plans. Phillips's consent could not be secured, as he was lost somewhere in the crowd. Austin Bearse opposed the idea. While Parker harangued the Boston crowd ("Fellow citizens of Virginia"—"No, no!"), Higginson and Stowell slipped out of the hall, returned to the office of Henry Bowditch, and Higginson distributed the hand axes. Stowell and a few others were armed with pistols as well. Meanwhile Phillips had begun to speak at the hall. At a prearranged time, Higginson's "plant" interrupted the meeting to announce that Negroes were already storming the Court House and attempting a rescue. At this Faneuil Hall dissolved into an uproar and the sympathetic crowd surged for the exits and headed for the Court House.

Higginson's men, hearing the tumult of the approaching crowd, led the assault on the Court House with stones, axes, and a fourteen-foot battering ram. Higginson had been a detached planner and director of these events. But in the excitement of the moment he threw down his umbrella, seized hold of the battering ram himself, and helped to smash in the door. Almost immediately he found himself pushed inside the darkened Court House, where the guards were laying about with clubs and cutlasses. He and a black collaborator were momentarily trapped inside, and in the melee Higginson was gashed in the face by a cutlass. When the mob fell back, Higginson roared out to those behind him, "You cowards, will you desert us now?" In the darkness and confusion, someone answered with a pistol shot, killing a Court House guard. The mob was paralyzed by the gunfire. A number of those outside, including Stowell, were arrested by a swarm of police, and in the confusion Higginson somehow contrived to recover his umbrella and escape into the crowd. Taking refuge in W. F. Channing's house, Higginson wrote his wife Mary that "there has been an attempt at rescue and failed. I am not hurt except a scratch on the face which will prevent me from doing anything more about it, lest I be recognized."[10]

Little more could be done in any event, since the U.S. marshal brought in federal troops to guard Anthony Burns. Back in Worcester the next day, Higginson—his wound bandaged—was greeted as a hero by a throng of cheering supporters. He told Mary that he had heard "rumors of my arrest, but hardly expect it. If true, I hope no U.S. Officer will be sent up, for I cannot answer for his life in the streets of Worcester." Meanwhile—although he felt this to be "the greatest step in Anti-Slavery which Massachusetts has ever taken"—he urged the Vigilance Committee to provide "assistance to the family of the man shot, supposing it to be so arranged as to show no contrition on our part, for a thing in which we had no responsibility, but simply to show that we have no war with women and children."[11] Burns, however, was lost to the Slave Power. Not even the fifty thousand people who lined the Boston streets, booing and hissing, could obstruct the two thousand armed guards who conducted the prisoner to the boat which returned him to the South.

Richard Henry Dana confided his surprise at Higginson's conduct to his journal: "I knew his ardor and courage," he wrote, "but I hardly expected a married man, a clergyman, and a man of education to lead the mob." Few could have been more surprised than Higginson himself. He was living in a dream state, like that during the Sims affair, when he had confessed: "It is strange to find one's self outside of established institutions; to be obliged to lower one's voice and conceal one's purposes," and "to see law and order, police and military, on the wrong side, and find good citizenship a duty." In the pulpit on Sunday after the Court House attack, Higginson defined the duty of good citizenship in "Massachusetts in Mourning." Preaching on the text of Jeremiah 15:12—"Shall iron break the northern iron and steel?"—he declared that the time for words was past, that resistance to tyranny was obedience to God, and that, for himself, "I can only make life worth living for, by becoming a revolutionist."[12]

Although Higginson warmed to the prospect of his trial on the charge of riot and prepared a defense based on the immorality of the Fugitive Slave Law, he was never tried. The first grand jury in Boston found no cause to indict, and though the second brought charges, the indictment was quashed on a technicality. Many years later he observed that it seemed "almost incredible that any condition of things should have turned honest American men into conscientious law-breakers."[13] But the shameful compromise of 1850, with its Fugitive Slave Law, created the conditions for a guerrilla warfare, fought by men of democratic principle, of Christian conscience, based on faith in a law they held higher than that of the United States in 1854.

A further field for underground warfare against the evils of slavery opened up in Kansas during the 1850s. In the contest over whether that territory would be slave or free, many of the Free Soil settlers in Kansas were being victimized by the advocates of slavery from Missouri, the "border ruffians." Higginson supported the recruitment of men, arms, and ammunition for Free Soil Northerners wishing to emigrate to Kansas, and even went west to report on the welfare of the New England men who had settled there. His "Letters from Kansas" depict the open insurrection constantly threatening, as marauding bands of Southerners plundered the wagon trains and settlements of the Northerners. He rode shotgun with a wagon train bound across the prairie for Topeka, telling his mother: "Imagine me also patrolling as one of the guards for an hour every night, in high boots amid the dewy grass, rifle in hand and revolver in belt." Here was manly action aplenty. But fortunately no marauders laid siege to the wagon train, although "once, in the day time, the whole company charged upon a band of extremely nude Indians, taking them for Missourians." While in Lawrence, Higginson preached on the text of Nehemiah 4:14: "Be not ye afraid of them: remember the Lord, which is great and terrible, and fight for your brethren, your sons and daughters, your wives and your houses." The power of his sermons spread his reputation through the settlements, and his life was continually threatened.[14] In Kansas, Higginson found the living revolution in behalf of the freedom for blacks he so ardently desired.

John Brown, the instrument of that revolution, approached Higginson in the winter of 1858 and requested money for his "secret service." Brown was about to realize what he called "the *perfecting* of BY FAR the most *important* undertaking of my whole life."[15] He was necessarily secretive about his "undertaking," but Higginson understood him to intend the rescue of fugitive slaves in Virginia and the transport of them to safety in Canada.

The Brown plan seemed unobjectionable, and between early 1858 and October 1859 the "Secret Six"—Higginson, Parker, Howe, G. L. Stearns, Frank Sanborn, and Gerrit Smith—conspired to raise money for Old Osawatomie to effect this plan. Their dream exploded in gunfire and smoke on October 18, 1859, when Brown led a small band of followers in a futile assault on the federal arsenal at Harpers Ferry, Virginia. This news was stupefying to Higginson and the other five. Frank Sanborn immediately fled to Canada, and was soon followed by Stearns and Howe. Smith entered an insane asylum. Parker was then dying of a terminal illness in Italy. Only Higginson remained in the country, in the expectation of arrest for his part in supporting what had turned out to be an insane scheme. Yet he expressed sorrow that Brown's Northern supporters had not been at Harpers Ferry. During the trial he rode down to North Elba, New York, to persuade Brown's wife of the desirability of an armed attempt to rescue her husband. But Brown would not hear of an escape attempt and so, after his trial, was executed on December 2. Nor were Higginson's efforts to rescue Brown's confederates any more successful. Higginson was never arrested for supporting Brown's "undertaking"; nor, strangely, was he ever called to Washington to testify before the Mason Committee, even though his complicity was known to the United States government. The Congress, he concluded, where "white men are concerned," would "yield before the slightest resistance" and dared not try to arrest him in Worcester.[16]

Well before 1857, Higginson had insisted that the irreconcilable differences between the North and the South required "the expulsion of the Slave States from the confederation in which they have been an element of discord, danger, and disgrace."[17] Consequently, in January of that year he called to order the Massachusetts Disunion Convention to lay the groundwork, whether by peaceful or violent means, for that expulsion. At the time Higginson, Phillips, Garrison, and their allies were denounced by conservatives as wild-eyed fanatics and lunatic demagogues. Even as late as the spring of 1861 these abolitionists were often the target of violent crowds, and Higginson and his friends were often forced to serve as armed bodyguards for Phillips, Emerson, and Parker at public meetings in Boston. But the firing on Fort Sumter in April changed all that, resolving the North into a troubled unanimity and vindicating, finally, the political foresight of the anti-slavery reformers.

In a series of articles in the *Atlantic* on "Nat Turner's Insurrection," "Denmark Vesey," "Haitian Emigration," and "Ordeal by Battle," Higginson prophesied the eventual emancipation of the slaves, whatever the outcome of the war. But he remained indecisive about his own role in the conflict, contenting himself with "a quiet life with literature and nature,"[18] for when the war broke out—after a decade of abolitionist exhortation, riot, and gunrunning—he was drained of physical and spiritual energy. Nor was he any longer a *young* firebrand, being thirty-seven at the commencement of hostilities.

Nevertheless, the reasons for this hesitation at enlisting were complex and constitute no discredit to his character. First, he was, after all, a Christian minister who felt unequipped for military service. Second, his wife Mary was a total invalid, and he felt responsible for her welfare. But even more important, Higginson was deeply suspicious of the aims of the federal government in prosecuting the war. He had no wish to put down the Southern secession if Washington was not committed to the abolition of slavery. (In fact, Lincoln dithered and the Emancipation Proclamation was not issued until 1863.) Disunion, he had always felt, might be the best course for the North, and the prospect of a return to the *status quo ante* was intolerable.

As the weeks passed into months, however, Higginson became more and more restive. An activist, he wanted action. Consequently, in August 1862 he raised a group of Worcester volunteers and was appointed captain of a company of the 51st Massachusetts Regiment. During that fall Higginson mastered the manuals and drilled his men. But shortly after he began to prepare his company, he received an offer from General Rufus Saxton, military governor of the Southern Department, which changed the course of his military career.

In November, Higginson learned that the U.S. Army was considering the creation of a regiment of freed South Carolina slaves. There was considerable doubt among military strategists that these ex-slaves could be trained properly or that they could be counted on under fire. Higginson had few reservations, believing that the liberated blacks would fight for their freedom even more resolutely than their white Northern liberators. Who was more appropriate to lead them than he? In mid-November he went to South Carolina and, under General Saxton, Colonel Higginson took command of the 1st South Carolina Volunteers, the first regiment of ex-slaves in the Union army.

A full discussion of Higginson's active service I shall defer until the later analysis of his splendid autobiographical *Army Life in a Black Regiment*. Nevertheless, it is worth noting here that Higginson had the distinction of organizing, administering, and leading into battle a regiment that conquered Jacksonville, Florida, in March 1863, and liberated hundreds of slaves from the plantations along the Edisto River in the interior of South Carolina. But on one of his upriver patrols, in July 1863, Higginson was wounded by a concussion of shellfire which shattered the pilothouse of the boat. Though the injury was outwardly slight, his constitution, enfeebled perhaps by the fevers of malaria, did not respond to treatment satisfactorily. The army discharged him in April 1864 with a medical disability. He returned home to Massachusetts and a hero's welcome. He and his men, he later wrote in *Army Life in a Black Regiment*, "had touched the pivot of the war. . . . Till the blacks were armed, there was no guarantee of their freedom. It was their demeanor under arms that shamed the nation into recognizing them as men."[19]

On his discharge, Higginson and his wife Mary returned to Newport, Rhode Island, then becoming a watering place for the wealthy. They did not move in the social circles of the summer parvenus,[20] but were intimate with "the whole 'Atlantic' force" of writers who had settled there: Mrs. Julia Ward Howe, author of "The Battle Hymn of the Republic"; Helen Hunt Jackson, later the author of *Mercy Philbrick's Choice* (1876) and *Ramona* (1884); John La Farge, artist and future author of *Considerations on Painting* (1895) and *An Artist's Letters from Japan* (1897); and other members of the Town and Country Club. In Newport, Higginson chaired the school committee, which abolished "separate but equal" black schools in the town; he organized the town library corporation and became one of its directors; he founded a local gymnasium and taught a large class in calisthenics and physical culture; he fostered the work of the Sons of Temperance; and several times he attended and spoke at women's suffrage conventions in Washington and Cleveland.

During the Reconstruction era, Higginson labored in behalf of black enfranchisement, opposed the conciliation of the treasonous political and military leaders of the South, and attacked the softness of President Andrew Johnson and others who wished to bind up the nation's wounds by restoring power "to the former lords of Southern soil" who wished only to reestablish "slavery under the name of 'Apprenticeship.'" Still, he doubted that Reconstruction politics would change men's hearts. He noted sadly that "We can make no sudden changes in the constitution of men either at the North or South. I do not look to see in this generation, a race of Southern white men who shall do justice to the Negro."[21]

In addition, he had become deeply fatigued by the whole antislavery, abolitionist, and Reconstruction movements. In 1865 he was offered a job as agent for the Freedman's Aid Society in New England but declined, observing: "I do not want to give any more years of my life exclusively to those people now, as much as I am attached to them." The work of liberating blacks, he concluded, could not be accomplished in his lifetime; and though he continued to support it, he felt he could no longer lead the freedman's cause. He eventually urged on blacks the patience that had sustained them through slavery; "not special legislation, but centuries of time," he concluded, would be required to erase color prejudice.[22]

During this period in Newport (1864–1878), Higginson, like Thoreau, had many lives to lead, and that of the social reformer alternated with that of the writer, for, as he told Emerson, he wished to be "an artist . . . lured by the joy of expression itself."[23] The burden of supporting an invalid wife required him to write essays, short stories, a novel, biographies, and histories, and to lecture widely to a large and and increasingly admiring public. Among his works are *Malbone: An Oldport Romance* (1869), *English Statesmen* (1875), *Young Folks' History of the United States* (1875), *Common Sense About Women* (1882), *Margaret Fuller Ossoli* (1884), *Henry Wadsworth Longfellow* (1902), and *John Greenleaf Whittier* (1902). "To keep up my interest in slavery," he told his old army surgeon, "I am translating Epictetus who is far superior to your dear Antoninus."[24] Epictetus was superior because the philosophy of that Roman slave argued irresistibly the "inevitable laws of retribution" tending toward the restoration of human liberty.[25]

Meanwhile Higginson began to edit the *Harvard Memorial Biographies* (2 volumes, 1866). Twelve of these brief lives of young Harvard men who had died in the war Higginson wrote himself. In addition, he wrote a series of local-color pieces for the *Atlantic* between 1867 and 1873, gathered under the title *Oldport Days* (1873), a work much in the vein of Harriet Beecher Stowe's *Oldtown Folks* (1869). His editing of the Harvard biographies and his correspondence with messmates kept the old army days alive. After the funeral of one of his army friends, Higginson reflected: "How like a dream it all seems. . . . That I was in it myself seems the dreamiest thing of all; I cannot put my hand upon it in the least, and if someone convinced me, in five minutes some morning, that I never was there at all, it seems as if it would all drop quietly out of my life, and I should read my own letters and think they were someone else's. This is one thing that makes it hard for me to . . . write anything about those days, though sooner or later I should do it."[26]

Later he did—in *Army Life in a Black Regiment* (1870), one of the most intriguing documents of Civil War literature, a work that Howard Mumford Jones has even called a "forgotten masterpiece."[27] Afterward, when Higginson reread *Army Life*, he was seized with surprise and interest and "with a sort of despair at the comparative emptiness of all other life after that." He felt that "those times are ever fresh and were perhaps the flower of our lives."[28]

Rejecting the Republican party in the 1880s on the ground that it had become dominated by contractors and speculators, Higginson, as a mugwump, gravitated toward the Democrats. Since suffrage was a relative right, he argued that Southern blacks had probably not been ready for the franchise. Their "lack of interest" in politics suggested that they wisely preferred to pursue education and the acquisition of property in order to elevate their social standing. Higginson now argued that a reconciliation with the South had become essential in the 1880s because radical Reconstruction had failed to help the racial situation. Thanks to what his former abolitionist allies called a retrogressive position on black rights and labor issues, he received the Democratic nomination for Congress in 1880. Higginson took the position, with respect to the Chicago Haymarket riots, that the arrested laborers were in fact murderers and, as Whittier and Lowell had argued, were well hanged for their crime. Increasingly he placed strong emphasis on the social responsibility of the business community in the age of the gospel of wealth. The labor movement and the radical antebellum reformers mounted an effective attack on Higginson's puzzling labor and race positions. Frederick Douglass dealt his candidacy the deathblow in accusing him of "having left the Republican Party," of having become a traitor, "not only to that political organization [the Republican party], but to the cause of liberty itself."[29] Needless to say, Higginson lost the election.

Yet as the racial situation in the South deteriorated, as Jim Crow legislation, race riots, and lynchings increased, Higginson's racial militancy returned in the last decade of the century. The freedom of black men had always been more important to him than their right to vote. Events in the South forced him to conclude that post-Reconstruction disorders had perhaps been caused not by carpet-baggers but by the Southerners themselves. Blacks, he argued in 1899 in the Boston *Evening Transcript*, "have a right to the freedom of civilization, the freedom of political rights, the freedom not merely to escape being held as slaves, but to have a position as free men that is worth having. The trouble is that the freedom of these people in the South is nominal, not real freedom." Higginson's anti-imperialism and his renewed racial militancy had a common basis in his growing opposition to the doctrine of white Anglo-Saxon superiority. In Higginson's view, "an essential part of Democracy is that social distinctions should be merely individual, not racial. Character is character and education is education. What social gradations exist," he told William Jennings Bryan, "should be effaced as rapidly as possible."[30]

Yet what was the solution? Siding with Booker T. Washington, he urged an accommodation of blacks to their situation in the South. "I constantly urge my colored friends to be peaceful & hopeful & leave the future to settle matters for itself, under the influence of higher education all around."[31] Higginson's faith that the status of blacks could be elevated principally through equal educational opportunities was rejected by the then-radical reformers. In 1909, at the National Negro Conference sponsored by John Dewey, Jane Addams, William Dean Howells, Oswald Garrison Villard, and W. E. B. Du Bois, the delegates repudiated Booker T. Washington's faith in patience and proposed a more militant position on civil rights.

Higginson, eighty-five at the time, was unable to attend the conference. But he remarked in an article in the Boston *Evening Transcript* that he had always "regarded the indiscriminate extension of the suffrage to an entire class as class, whether negroes or others, to be politically inexpedient; that is not conducive to the general interest, which in this particular is more important than the interest of the individual." Although he had supported the right of blacks to vote during the Reconstruction era, Higginson's final position was that the enfranchisement of the black had created "great friction between the races and an injury to the negro himself. He would better turn himself to his industrial and educational development than to strive for the establishment of a civil and political status which ... can never be effectually attained or if ever, only through a conflict of terrible consequences. ... No white community will ever consent to the political supremacy of either the black man or the colored man or the yellow man. I make this declaration philosophically and as a result of observation and reflection and absolutely without feeling of prejudice, for I have none."[32]

While Higginson's final position was remarkably conservative and, in my view, too pessimistic, there was a seed of wisdom in it that we can see only in retrospect. By that I mean that radical black militancy, after the post–World War II period, has been credited with significant gains for blacks in America. But these gains are in fact the real consequence of a temporary strategy of peaceful accommodation, higher education, and economic self-development for blacks, together with the political and moral reeducation of whites—all these creating the conditions under which positive change could (and did) occur.

III

Higginson would perhaps not enjoy a secure place in American letters had he not published, in 1870, *Army Life in a Black Regiment*, an account of his command, between 1862 and 1864, of the first regiment of freed slaves in the United States Army. The death of Robert Gould Shaw, a white officer who was killed in 1863 (while leading a black unit in a hopeless charge on Confederates at Charleston), was so heroic and poignant that Shaw has received almost all the publicity devoted to white officers of black troops in the Civil War.[33] But Higginson's contribution to military history and the forced emancipation of slaves should not be passed over lightly.

After it had become clear that the emancipation of the slaves was an actual intention of the federal government in waging the war, Higginson raised a regiment of Massachusetts volunteers in early 1862. Hardly had he begun to train his men, however, when he received a surprising invitation from General Rufus Saxton to take command of the 1st South Carolina Volunteers. Higginson was not a trained officer: he had never administered an organization of the kind; and, as a minister, he was scarcely prepared by his vocation for leading troops, of any color, into combat. Nevertheless, it is a tribute to the foresight of Lincoln's military command that this radical abolitionist and spokesman for racial equality should have been selected to command a most important enterprise for the freedmen.

Higginson's self-confidence, however, was based on his prophetic knowledge that war would come. Since "the Kansas troubles" his mind "had dwelt on military matters more or less during all that time." He felt that the best volunteer regiments "already exhibited a high standard of drill and discipline," and that the freed slaves could be brought tolerably near that standard. He had "perfect confidence" that they could be effectively trained since he knew, "by experience, the qualities of their race," and knew that they had "home and household and freedom to fight for. . . ."[34]

But suspicious that he might be slated to head "a mere plantation guard or a day-school in uniform,"[35] Higginson went to South Carolina to estimate the possibilities of this appointment. On arriving in Beaufort, he was ushered into "an old plantation, with stately magnolia avenue, decaying house, and tiny church amid the woods reminding me of Virginia; behind it stood a neat encampment of white tents, 'And there,' said my companion, 'is your future regiment.'"[36] From "the broken windows of this forlorn plantation house" Higginson could look down the "avenues of great live-oaks, with their hard shining leaves, and their branches hung with a universal drapery of soft, long moss, like fringe trees stuck with grayness." Beyond was "the sandy soil, scantly covered with coarse grass" bristling "with sharp palmettoes and aloes." He found all the vegetation to be "stiff, shining, semi-tropical, with nothing soft or delicate in its texture. Numerous plantation buildings totter around, all slovenly and unattractive," he observed, "while the interspaces are filled with all manner of wreck and refuse, pigs, fowls, dogs, and omnipresent Ethiopian infancy. All this," he was later to say, is "the universal Southern panorama. . . ."[37]

After reviewing the sea-island camp and the men, Higginson accepted the assignment. Facing him was the task of transforming eight hundred newly freed slaves into disciplined combat soldiers. *Army Life in a Black Regiment* is the fascinating record of his command of this regiment—the drill and disciplining of these men and the nature of their life in camp (including their rituals and folk songs, their religious sentiments, and their relationships among themselves and with whites). The book recounts his regiment's picket duties, its expeditions up the St. Marys, the St. Johns, and the Edisto rivers; its forays into the Southern interior to collect supplies; its invasion and occupation of Jacksonville, Florida; the Rebel ambush in which he was wounded; and his subsequent medical discharge and departure from the South.

Much of the book is written in the form of a diary, since Higginson felt that journal entries gave freshness and immediacy to the experience narrated. The sections of the book that deal with combat experiences however, are retrospective narrations, since Higginson was naturally unable to keep notes while in the field. In 1884 Higginson added a final chapter analyzing his impressions of the experience after a fourteen-year interval.

The energy, zeal, and daring of the black troops were put to the test in one of the regiment's first expeditions, up the St. Marys River in search of lumber and slaves on the interior plantations. Higginson and his ship patrol undertook a nocturnal ascent of "an unknown river" deep into the "enemy's country, where one glides in the dim moonlight between dark hills and meadows, each turn of the channel making it seem like an inland lake, and cutting you off as by a barrier from all behind,—with no sign of human life, but an occasional picket fire left glimmering beneath the bank, or the yelp of a dog from some low-lying plantation."[38] The strategy of the Confederate cavalry and the partisans was to let the federal patrol ascend the river and ambush them on their return down water. Near Reed's Bluff and Scrubby Bluff the patrol came under Rebel fire. Most of the black soldiers had been ordered below. "My men were pretty well now imprisoned below in the hot and crowded hold, and actually fought each other, the officers afterward said, for places at the open port-holes, from which to aim." Others implored Higginson to land them, exclaiming that "they 'supposed de Cunnel knew best,' but it was 'mighty mean' to be shut up down below when they might be 'fightin' de Secesh in de clar field.'"[39] Higginson's patrol boat successfully ran this gauntlet. Though the expedition was a slight one, accounts of it in the newspapers occupied a great deal of space, "so intense was the interest which then attached to the novel experiment of employing black troops."[40] Such was the uncertainty of war correspondence that, after one of these upriver expeditions, it was reported in the Northern press that Higginson and his troops "had been captured and shot." Indeed, Higginson "had afterwards the pleasure of reading my own obituary in a Northern Democratic journal. . . ."[41]

In the camp the memory of the raid up the St. Marys "was preserved . . . by many legends of adventure,—growing vaster and more incredible as time wore on,—and by morning appeals to the surgeon of some veteran invalids, who could now cut off all reproofs and suspicions with 'Doctor, I's been a sickly pusson eber since de expeditious.'"[42]

The success of the expedition up the St. Marys encouraged the Department of the South, early in 1863, to experiment further along the same line. It was proposed in Washington that Colonel Higginson's regiment undertake the invasion of Jacksonville, Florida, on the St. Johns River. Jacksonville had already been twice taken and twice evacuated by federal troops. "The present proposition was, to take and hold it with a brigade of less than a thousand men, carrying, however, arms and uniforms for twice that number, and a month's ration."[43] In a letter to the Secretary of War, dated March 14, 1863, General Saxton observed that "the object of this expedition . . . to occupy Jacksonville" was to "make it the base of operations for the arming of negroes, and securing in this way possession of the entire State of Florida." General Saxton believed that nothing could cause "greater panic throughout the whole Southern coast" than a "raid of the colored troops in Florida." The wisdom of his order was confirmed by the dismay of General Joseph Finnegan of the Confederate States Army, who reported to his superiors that the invasion would lead to "intercourse . . . between negroes on the plantations and those in the enemy's service." This infiltration, "conducted through swamps and under cover of night, . . . cannot be prevented. A few weeks will suffice to corrupt the entire slave population of east Florida."[44]

Higginson was delighted with this plan, since his men needed action in order to prove their reliability as combat soldiers. "The main objects of your expedition," General Saxton told him, "are to carry the proclamation of freedom to the enslaved; to call all loyal men into the service of the United States; to occupy as much of the State of Florida as possible with the forces under your command, and to neglect no means consistent with the usages of civilized warfare to weaken, harass, and annoy those who are in rebellion against the Government of the United States."[45] Embarking on the *John Adams*, the *Boston*, the *Burnside*, and the *Uncas*, Higginson and his troops sailed by night to Fernandina and rendezvoused near the harbor of Jacksonville. "It was 8 o'clock. We were now directly opposite the town; yet no sign of danger was seen; not a rifle shot was heard; not a shell rose hissing in the air. The *Uncas* rounded to, and dropped anchor in the stream; by previous agreement, I steamed to an upper pier of the town, Colonel Montgomery to a lower one; the little boat-howitzers were run out upon the wharfs, and presently to the angles of the chief streets; and the pretty town was ours without a shot. In spite of our detention, the surprise had been complete, and not a soul in Jacksonville had dreamed of our coming."[46] So unexpected was the invasion of this expeditionary force that the Confederate forces were totally unprepared and Jacksonville was taken without even a shot. Higginson set up temporary headquarters and thus imposed federal control on the only post on the mainland in the Department of the South.

The capture of Jacksonville, however, produced its difficulties. The chief of these was the virtual impossibility of holding it with merely nine hundred men. To deceive the enemy, Higginson deployed troops throughout the town, set up empty tents in many quarters, moved the units back and forth in the harbor in order to conceal the size of his force, and ordered white reinforcements. Meanwhile he faced the problem of disciplining some black soldiers, originally from Florida, who now had their former masters at their mercy. They were surprisingly free from vengefulness, even though they fought under the sentence of death, for a Confederate order "consigned the new colored troops and their officers to a felon's death if captured. . . . 'Dere's no flags oh truce for us,' the men would contemptuously say. 'When de Secesh fight de *Fus' Souf*' (First South Carolina), 'he fight in earnest.'"⁴⁷ Higginson also fought with the noose round his own neck, for an act of the Confederate Congress stipulated that "every white person being a commissioned officer . . . who, during the present war, shall command negroes or mulattos in arms against the Confederate States shall, if captured, be put to death or be otherwise punished at the discretion of the court."⁴⁸

Higginson felt that the success of the black regiment depended on their being treated exactly like other volunteers in the Union army. The soldiers were "constantly kidded by their families and friends with the prospect of risking their lives in the service and being paid nothing." They only half-believed they would receive "the full pay of soldiers." But "with what utter humiliation were we, their officers, obliged to confess to them, eighteen months afterwards, that it was their distrust which was wise, and our faith in the pledges of the United States Government which was foolishness! The attempt was made to put them off with half pay."⁴⁹

When the Union government reduced the pay of black soldiers by half, Higginson wrote burning letters to senators, congressmen, abolitionist friends, and the Northern newspapers, deploring the government's refusal to pay the men what they had been promised at the time of enlistment. The government's position, he told

Senator Sumner, "will be the greatest blow ever struck at successful emancipation in the Department of the South, for it will destroy all confidence in the honesty of the government." To the *New York Times* he wrote "we presume too much on the supposed ignorance of these men. I have never yet found a man in my regiment so stupid as not to know when he was cheated. If fraud proceeds from the government itself, so much the worse, for this strikes at the foundation of all rectitude, all honor, all obligation."[50] In due course, Higginson's campaign succeeded; in 1865, Congress restored full pay to the black troops.

Shortly after the occupation of Jacksonville, the military command issued an inexplicable order for Higginson's troops to evacuate the town. The men were crushed and disappointed at this turn of events. Many of the civilian residents begged to accompany Higginson and his troops on their evacuation. Their departure was something of an opera buffa since the townspeople of Jacksonville "at once developed that insane mania for aged and valueless trumpery which always seizes upon the human race . . . in moments of danger."[51] While the colonel was patiently explaining to them that their worthless furniture could not be taken aboard ship, some of the white troops under his command set fire to the town. Though perhaps no more than twenty-five buildings were burned down, the colonel was dismayed, though he was pleased that the Northern press correctly absolved the colored regiment from having had anything to do with this wanton act of barbarism.

Back in South Carolina, Higginson grew restive at the desk in regimental headquarters. Although "restricted by duty from doing many foolish things," one night he decided to collect firsthand intelligence about Confederate outposts on the other side of the river. Riding down to the causeway, he told his black sentries that he intended to go for a swim. Partly to test his powers of physical endurance and partly to satisfy his boyish love of adventure, Higginson slipped into the water and swam across the river to the spot where Rebel pickets were patrolling the shore. Fortunately he was not detected, but on the return trip, much of which he swam under water, he became disoriented when the tide turned. Swept downstream, he wound up in the marshes well below his camp. When he eventually emerged from the water, he was accosted by a black sentry from the 1st South Carolina Volunteers. It is a wonder that he was not shot as a Rebel spy as he stood there (evidently naked). Fortunately he knew the countersign, and the sentry recognized him and presented arms, despite the absence of any visible rank.

Higginson and his troops engaged in none of the "great campaigns, where a man, a regiment, a brigade, is but a pawn in the game."[52] Much of their time was spent in fighting off Rebel irregulars while liberating slaves and foraging for lumber, food, and other supplies. In due course "these upriver raids reached the dignity of a fine art."[53] Though they were relatively insignificant compared to a Vicksburg or Gettysburg, Higginson found in them "a charm" in the "more free and adventurous life of partisan warfare where, if total sphere be humbler, yet the individual has more relative importance, as the sense of action is more personal and keen."[54] His adventures with the black troops had "the same elements of picturesqueness" that belonged to the partisan skirmishes of the Revolutionary War. Their expedition up the Edisto River to destroy a bridge on the Charleston and Savannah Railway was one of these exciting raids. Liberating slaves from the upriver plantations, confiscating bales of cotton, and burning the rice houses in accordance with their orders, Higginson and his troops came under Rebel fire as they descended the river. For the first time Higginson discovered that "there were certain compensating advantages in a slightly built craft, as compared with one more substantial; the missiles never lodged in the vessel, but crashed through some thin partitions as if it were paper, to explode beyond us, or fall harmless in the water. Splintering, the chief source of wounds and death in wooden ships, was entirely avoided; the danger was that our machinery might be disabled, or that shots might strike beyond the water-line and sink us."[55]

In this attack more than fifteen cannonballs and grapeshot passed through the vessel, tearing apart rigging and shattering the pilothouse. Higginson was wounded in this attack by "a sudden blow in the side," as if some prizefighter had doubled him up. Upon examination the wound proved "to have been produced by the grazing of a ball, which, without tearing a garment, had yet made a large part of my side black and blue, leaving a sensation of paralysis which made it difficult to stand." Dazed, he remembered trying to comprehend what had happened to him and was "impressed by an odd feeling that I had now got my share, and should henceforth be a great deal safer than any of the rest."⁵⁶ Nevertheless he and the captain of the ship managed to get the craft and his men back to camp. Higginson declined to go into his "personal record of convalescence," but he was perfectly confident that his "habitual abstinence" from whiskey left "no food for peritoneal inflammation to feed upon."⁵⁷

Convalescing at Camp Shaw, he was impatient to resume active duty and indeed returned too soon, suffering a "complete prostration," compounded perhaps by malarial fever. Higginson underplayed the significance of this wound, but it was serious enough to oblige him to resign his commission in May 1864, when he was ordered home as an invalid. The expedition in which he was wounded was not a major campaign in the war, but the colonel was later to say that "the day was worth all it cost, and more."⁵⁸ Before the war ended, "the rescue of even one man from slavery" had seemed a truly great thing. Afterward how little seemed "the liberation of two hundred." Yet no one could say in 1864 how the Civil War might end. Thus the satisfaction he took at the time in the liberation of every single slave.

Much of *Army Life* is designed to correct Northern misconceptions of the character of Southern blacks. Higginson remarked that "at first, of course, they all looked just alike; the variety comes afterwards, and they are just as distinguishable . . . as so many whites."⁵⁹ At the beginning, Higginson regarded blacks as "simple, docile, and affectionate almost to the point of absurdity."⁶⁰ Living with them was "a wonderfully strange sensation," for they were "a race affectionate, enthusiastic, grotesque, and dramatic beyond all others." Higginson also found the landscape, the cuisine, and command problems different from anything in his earlier experience. He drilled his regiment by day and inspected their quarters by night, observing that they subsisted on pork and oysters and sweet potatoes and rice and hominy and cornbread and milk, mysterious griddle-cakes of corn and pumpkin, preserves made of pumpkin-chips, and "other fanciful productions of Ethiop art."⁶¹

Although their servitude had reduced them to a race of "grown-up children," these freed slaves were eager to extend the blessings of liberty to their brothers and sisters on the interior plantations. They constantly sang and exhorted one another, and one took the stump and poignantly proclaimed, "We'll neber desert de ole flag, boys, neber; we hab lib under it for *eighteen hundred sixty-two years*, and we'll die for it now." As Higginson grew more acquainted with the men, the individuality of each emerged, first their faces, then their characters, and he perceived "the desire they show to do their duty, and to improve as soldiers." Higginson noted that they evidently thought a great deal about it, for they felt that "we white men cannot stay and be their leaders always and that they must learn to depend on themselves, or else relapse into their former condition."[62]

Higginson found their "religious spirit" one of the most interesting aspects of these Southern blacks, influencing them in both negative and positive ways. On the negative side, he felt that their religion cultivated in them "the feminine virtues first," making them "patient, meek, resigned." "Imbued from childhood with the habit of submission," they could endure, he discovered, nearly everything. But he was also pleased to see that their religion strengthened them by conferring on them "zeal, energy, daring." Their religion he took to be "the highest form of mysticism"; and he quoted approvingly the regimental surgeon, who declared that they were all "natural transcendentalists."[63]

One of the great interests of *Army Life* is Higginson's transcriptions of the black spirituals of the troops. As a man of letters he had always been "a faithful student of the English and Scottish ballads," and he had even envied Sir Walter Scott for the delight he took in "tracing them out amid their own heather and of writing them down piece-meal from the lips of aged crones."[64] Set down into "the midst of a kindred world of unwritten songs, as simple and indigenous as the Border Minstrelsy, more uniformly plaintive, almost always more quaint, and often as essentially poetic," Higginson listened to and recorded the texts of some thirty-six Negro spirituals. He transcribed them "as nearly as possible, in the original dialect."[65]

Insofar as one may judge, his transcriptions are reasonably accurate and faithful in dialect. He tried, he said, to make the text easy to read, since he wished to avoid what seemed to him "the only error of Lowell's 'Biglow Papers' in respect to dialect,—the occasional use of an extreme misspelling, which merely confuses the eye without taking us any closer to the peculiarity of sound."[66]

In general, the spirituals he recorded are typical of others in that they expressed "nothing but patience for this life,—nothing but triumph in the next." Through them the slaves could "sing themselves, as had their fathers before them, out of the contemplation of their own estate into the sublime scenery of the Apocalypse."[67] Of those recorded, "I Know Moon-Rise" is one of the most moving:

> I know moon-rise, I know star-rise,
> > Lay dis body down.
>
> I walk in de moonlight, I walk in de starlight,
> > To lay dis body down.
>
> I'll walk in de graveyard, I'll walk through de graveyard,
> > To lay dis body down.
>
> I'll lie in de grave and stretch out my arms;
> > Lay dis body down.
>
> I go to de judgment in de evenin' of de day,
> > When I lay dis body down;
>
> And my soul and your soul will meet in de day
> > When I lay dis body down.

When we consider that slaves were often jailed for singing songs of freedom anticipated in the next life, because the slavemasters saw them as seditious symbolic statements, the poignancy of these lines becomes almost unbearable. There is no doubt that these spirituals were "but the vocal expression of the simplicity of their faith and the sublimity of their long resignation."[68]

Equally fascinating, in view of the contemporary debate over the oral tradition in primitive poetry, was Higginson's curiosity about "whether they had always a conscious and definite origin in some leading mind, or whether they grew by gradual accretion, in an almost unconscious way." Inquiring among those troops who were especially good singers, Higginson extracted the admission from one young man that "some good spirituals . . . are start jest out o' curiosity. I been a-raise a sing myself, once."[69] This remark convinced Higginson that spirituals tend to be invented by a single singer, whose song is picked up by other singers who, perhaps, play variations on the original invention. Thanks to Higginson's work on Negro spirituals, interest developed throughout the nation in the folksongs of the slaves. As Howard N. Meyer has suggested, Higginson "had the immediate distinction of having opened the door to the wider interest" in spirituals "and later the credit—not always assigned to him—of having been the pioneer recorder" of some of the finest of the black folksongs.[70]

Perhaps the most intriguing chapter in *Army Life in a Black Regiment* is that entitled "The Negro as a Soldier." Higginson had feared that "they might show less fibre, less tough and dogged resistance, than whites, during a prolonged trial,—a long, disastrous march, for instance, or the hopeless defense of a besieged town."[71] But the troops proved without question that they were capable of the discipline, daring, and energy of white combat troops. Moreover, they had been tested under fire and had proved the wisdom of the military command in Washington which had directed them to invade Jacksonville and to foment insurrection on the plantations in the interior.

Higginson's fears thus proved groundless. The particular assignments of his troops, moreover, proved to be "an especially favorable test" of their capacities. "They had more to fight for than the whites. Besides the flag and the Union, they had home and wife and child. They fought with ropes round their necks, and when the Confederate orders were issued that the officers of colored troops should be put to death on capture, they took a grim satisfaction. It helped their *esprit de corps* immensely. With us at least, there was to be no play-soldier."[72]

In this chapter Higginson analyzed the racial qualities of the blacks as he perceived them. On the whole, though he does not discount their individual imperfections, Higginson's attitude to them as a race was commendatory, if not idealizing. Yet he was puzzled as to why "they had not kept the land in a perpetual flame of insurrection, why, especially since the opening of the war, they had kept so still." Higginson concluded that "the answer was to be found in the peculiar temperament of the race, in their religious faith, and in the habit of patience that centuries had fortified." He noted that "the shrewder men all said substantially the same thing. What was the use of insurrection, where everything was against them? They had no knowledge, no money, no arms, no drill, no organization,—above all no mutual confidence." Higginson felt that, had he been a black, his life "would have been one long scheme of insurrection," but he learned to respect "the patient self-control of those who had waited till the course of events should open a better way."[73] He was particularly fascinated by their attitude toward their former masters, which he described as an "absence of affection" and "absence of revenge." In this moderation their religious feelings also probably played a large part.

As to personal character, Higginson found, even among the most ignorant, a frequent "child-like absence of vices," which he ascribed to both innocence and inexperience. Even the experienced he found "remarkably free from inconvenient vices," with no more or less lying or stealing "than in average white regiments."[74] Temperance was one of their virtues. But Higginson found the point of "greatest laxity in their moral habits" to be "the want of a high standard of chastity." But as their sexual habits did not affect their camp life, the colonel had little direct observation of it. Nevertheless he was sometimes asked to adjudicate problems among one of his soldiers and the man's two or three "wives." In view of the dislocating effect of slavery on family life, even Higginson attached little importance to this imputed laxity.

Higginson's greatest disappointment with blacks involved their health. He found them easily made ill by cold, damp weather, and dust, easily fatigued and lacking resilience after injuries. This should not surprise us, since lack of protein in slave diets often led to malnutrition and low resistance to infection. Higginson remarked that "their health improved . . . as they grew more familiar with military life." But he was obliged to conclude that neither their physical nor moral temperament gave them "that toughness, that obstinate purpose of living, which sustains the less excitable Anglo-Saxon."[75] This could hardly have been an intrinsic deficiency in the slaves. More probably, prolonged servile dependency had made them passive rather than active, submissive rather than aggressively individualistic. In any event they satisfied their commander as equal to whites in every other respect.

The gist of the whole experience of arming these black troops for combat is contained in Higginson's remark that they "touched the pivot of the war. Whether this vast and dusky mass should prove the weakness of the nation, or its strength" depended, "in great measure, we knew, on our efforts. Till the blacks were armed, there was no guarantee of their freedom. It was their demeanour under arms that shamed the nation into recognizing them as men."[76]

IV

Several years later Higginson revisited Jacksonville and other scenes of his Civil War experience and appended a retrospective chapter to *Army Life*. He was pleased to recognize the social progress of the blacks, many of whom were self-employed in farming their own land, working on the steamboats, fishing, or lumbering. "What more," he asked, "could be expected of any race, after fifteen years of freedom? Are the Irish voters of New York their superiors in condition, or the factory operatives of Fall River?"[77] As he spoke to some of the veterans, Higginson came to feel that if any abuses in the treatment of the blacks existed, the remedy was "not to be found in federal interference, except in case of actual insurrection, but in the voting power of the blacks, so far as they have strength or skill to assert it and, where that fails, in their power of locomotion."[78] In the decade immediately after the war's end, he believed it ungenerous, in view of the social progress made by blacks between 1865 and 1875, "to declare that the white people of the South have learned nothing by experience, and are 'incapable of change.'" Higginson believed that by 1878 the South had "reached the point where civilized methods begin to prevail," and blacks having "enlisted the laws of political economy on their side, this silent ally will be worth more than an army with banners."[79]

Unfortunately Higginson was deceived in believing that the "condition of outward peace with no conspicuous outrages" which existed in 1878 was a blessing, and he simply could not believe that there might be in the South "some covert plan for crushing or reenslaving the colored race."[80] But Jim Crow laws and other manipulations of the legal process served to institutionalize racial prejudice again and to subvert that liberty which Higginson and his black troops had fought so valiantly to achieve. Consequently, when Reconstruction failed he was obliged to take up the cause again, though in a more pacific way—as journalist, lecturer, and legislator.

The core of his final position on the future of blacks was rather like that of Booker T. Washington, who argued that through thrift, industry, education, and the Christian virtues, blacks would eventually gain full civil, political, and constitutional rights. Self-development, the cultivation of educational opportunities, hard work, and prosperity, Washington concluded, would yield blacks a quicker entry into the mainstream of American life than radical political programs like those of W. E. B. Du Bois or any of the developing black-nationalist philosophies. If Higginson's views seem conservative, hinging on the necessity of gradualism to alter the consciousness of whites, I do not think his position retrogressive, although it seemed so to some of his contemporary racial activists. Higginson was fully committed to social and educational desegregation (achieving it personally for the schools in Newport) and—astonishing for a Christian minister of the time—he was even tolerant of interracial marriage. In *Part of a Man's Life*, Higginson observed that the alleged "peril" of mixed blood "is found no longer a source of evil, this witness thinks, when concubinage has been replaced by legal marriage." He believed that "the chances are that the mingling of races will diminish, but whether this is or is not the outcome, it is, of course, better for all that this result should be legal and voluntary, rather than illegal and perhaps forced. As the memories of the slave period fade away, the mere fetich of color-phobia will cease to control our society; and marriage may come to be founded, not on the color of the skin, but upon the common courtesies of life, and upon genuine sympathies of heart and mind."[81]

Whatever may be our view of his later gradualism, *Army Life in a Black Regiment* survives the oscillation of our racial history and remains, as Howard Mumford Jones has called it, "a shrewd and sympathetic example of sociological analysis," a "forgotten masterpiece." One may disagree with Jones's assessment that "its supreme appeal is as an expression of yearning of the North for the South, for color, for warmth, for a simpler and healthier way of life than that of industrialized cities"; yet there is no doubt that "a lively humor, a fine eye for the picturesque, indignation against injustice, and real affection for his men create one of the few classics of military life in the national letters." In the case of this work, "the pen of its writer was touched with the incommunicable power that turns writing into literary art."[82]

The artistic power that informs *Army Life* was matched by a moral power in the man that generated in his troops enduring love and reverence. In a memorial tribute to him at a military reunion in the 1890s, his officers remarked: "In those brave days you were not alone our commander; you were our standard also of what is noble in character. We were young and untutored; we saw in you a model of what, deep in our hearts, we aspired to be." Howard N. Meyer rightly observes that these sentiments were shared by his enlisted men. In a letter the colonel retained until the end of his life, one of the rank-and-file privates wrote: "I meet many of the old Soldiers. I spoke of you—all hailed your name with that emotion (that become you) of the Soul when hearing of one who when in darkness burst light on their pathway."[83]

An Uncertain Abolitionist: Lincoln in Fact and Fiction

William Safire's novel *Freedom* (1987), weighing in at 1,125 pages, is a rather more imposing volume on the shelf of contemporary Civil War fiction than Gore Vidal's *Lincoln: A Novel* (1984), a book of 657 pages.[1] It is also the more formidable and historically "grounded" of the two novels, despite Vidal's risible claim that he alone, amongst American novelists, knows the American past. But both outweigh Irving Bacheller's *A Man for the Ages* (1919) and Irving Stone's *Love Is Eternal: A Novel About Mary Todd and Abraham Lincoln* (1954), which check in at a mere 416 and 468 pages, respectively. Wanting to avoid the oversimplifications that come with brevity, Safire believed that a detailed, well-written novel stood a better chance of informing the public about the Civil War than the unintelligible historical prose recently cranked out in the theory-ridden academy, where polysyllabic gobbledygook seems to be the hallmark of professional style.

Safire gave his novel a limited time span: the first two years of Lincoln's presidency, from the inauguration in 1861 (and the Confederate firing on Fort Sumter) to the Emancipation Proclamation on New Year's Day in 1863. Despite its dealing with only two years of Lincoln's first term as president, *Freedom* seems to me the best of the fictional treatments of Lincoln. It brings alive the political issues, the personal rivalries, and the battlefield tragedies that marked those critical years in Lincoln's life. Union and Confederate generals such as George B. McClellan, Ulysses S. Grant, and Robert E. Lee, cabinet members such as Salmon P. Chase, Edwin Stanton, and William Seward, and powerful Washington women such as Anna Ella Carroll, Kate Chase, and the Confederate spy "Wild Rose" Greenhow—these and an immense supporting cast are summoned to life in Safire's remarkable novel. The detective Allan Pinkerton, our first Master Spy, the battlefield photographer Mathew Brady, and the journalist Horace Greeley—these and many others play memorable minor roles. And of course there is Lincoln himself—bent on preserving the Union at all costs, usurping (if that is what he did) the war powers of Congress, proclaiming military rule, restricting the civil liberties of anti-war dissidents, and manipulating the press and public.

Walt Whitman said that the real war would never get into the books. It does not get into Vidal's *Lincoln* or Safire's *Freedom,* but the latter book is nevertheless an impressive demonstration of transformed historical research. Eight years in the making, *Freedom* gives ample evidence of Safire's having pored over the major historical documents of these critical years in Lincoln's presidency. If you wish to understand the push-pull of Civil War politics in Washington and Richmond and the personalities who pushed and pulled, Safire's novel tells more—more vividly—than Vidal's *Lincoln* and more than most narrative histories of the period. This is not merely the consequence of the novel's size. Safire has an analyst's gift for defining the political issue, linking it to the hidden calculation of the actor, and dramatizing him in action. And his battlefield scenes, at Bull Run, Antietam, and Shiloh, paint realistic pictures of the terrible carnage produced by the Secession.

But it is power politics that most absorbs Safire. In his world there is no other passion. Safire knows that the novel-reading public has an appetite for romance, and he offers us the invented love stories of Anna Carroll and Senator John Breckinridge and Kate Chase and John Hay. But it is hard to believe in Safire's affairs of the heart. Take the case of Breckinridge and Anna Carroll in bed. Safire begins a paragraph with the Senator's savoring Anna's "breasts spilling toward her arms, hands at her sides, skin luminescent." But before we can get fairly interested in what is about to happen, Safire has Breckinridge's mind wander to his "standing almost alone for the preservation of the rights in the Constitution against men who claimed to stand for the preservation of a sundered Union,"[2] and so on. Perhaps Washington politicos and their women are always thinking about politics in the sack, but for the rest of us the effect is anaphrodisiac.

Perhaps the wildest instance of the cooptation of sexual feeling by political calculation occurs in a scene where the detective Allan Pinkerton has reason to believe that Rose Greenhow, a Southern sympathizer, is getting information about troop movements from an important Union politician. Lacking a modern bugging device, Safire has Pinkerton go up to her house one night in the pouring rain, prop a ladder against the wall, climb up to the second-story bedroom window, and peer in. Pinkerton sees the whip-cracking Rose—clad only in "high-heeled shoes, black stockings, and a lace-trimmed garter belt"—and Senator Henry Wilson, naked as the day he was born. How Safire visualizes the scene is a paradigm of the treatment of "romantic" elements in the novel:

> The detective winced as the riding crop sliced through the air and caught the congressman on the side of his leg. Crawling forward, the man in thrall embraced her legs and buried his face between them. After a moment, Rose smacked him again, ordered him onto the bed on his back, and straddled him. Her breasts came into view, fuller than Pinkerton had imagined, the nipples erect and small and dark. He concluded those were the most impressive woman's breasts he had ever seen. The look on her face was a mixture of eagerness and contempt; the detective could not tell how much was sexual and how much political.[3]

Neither can the reader. But as the novel goes along it becomes pretty clear that, for Safire's characters, the sexual always *is* political. Is this credible psychology?

When I first read *Freedom* I thought (like most readers) that the Beltway contained serious people bent on serious national business. Washington always was its own special fairyland; still—momentous things, on the nation's behalf, always got done. The reality is that times have changed. William Jefferson Clinton brought us a political leadership highlighted by nonspousal telephone sex at midnight; rumors of coupling on the Great Seal; a sexual affair with an intern barely older than his college-age daughter; multiple female partners much groped in the Oval Office; the command-performance (but theologically "nonadulterous") fellatio; the use of state police and perhaps even the Secret Service for the purpose of gubernatorial and presidential pandering, and so forth. In such a milieu, no one could conceivably protest that the lubricity of Safire's politicians is exaggerated or unreal. But anticipating every possible objection, Safire slyly remarks in his "Note to the Reader": "In general, the credibility quotient is this: if the scene deals with war or politics, it is fact; if it has to do with romance, it is fiction; if it is outrageously and obviously fiction, it is fact."[4]

The challenge Safire accepts in *Freedom* is to dramatize effectively what is for him the most disturbing question of the Civil War experience: Lincoln's "usurpation" of various powers in suspending constitutional liberties. Safire's central issue is how much of the American's personal freedom must be sacrificed to maintain a free government. More specifically, he asks whether the very principles of freedom may "prevent a free government from defending itself effectively" against those who would overthrow it from within.[5] To anchor his novel in a sea of swirling facts, Safire provides the reader with a long appendix of 150 pages that he calls the "Underbook." There he presents the historical sources of his imagined scenes, confesses to what is real and what is invented, provides a bibliography of Civil War readings, and clarifies the debates of the historians over the political meaning of Civil War events.

Repeatedly, in this appendix, we are told things like this: "The interview with [Benjamin] Wade is fictional, but Lincoln's dialogue is taken from his letter to Orville Browning." Or "Some of my mind reading of [Salmon P.] Chase is fictional, and several meetings are telescoped into two, but on the whole the chapter is based on [Gideon] Welles's diary." Or this: "Fiction. This is what I think Lincoln was thinking in late May, 1862." This stratagem allows us to discriminate between the actual and the invented; it also delivers Safire from the charge of misleading readers and falsifying history for the sake of his plot. Is the result historical truth?

Since most history writing today is either unintelligible or as dull as ditchwater, a great many readers are likely to get their information about Lincoln and the Civil War from novels like *Freedom*. So there is something ethically responsible about Safire's alerting us to where he deviates from the factual into the imaginary. "My novel," he seems to say, "tells the story of Lincoln and the Civil War just as it happened—just as the history books narrate the events. And if I get fanciful here and there, I let you know it up front. So it's still a truthful narrative after all." But Safire seems grandly oblivious to the attack—within the discipline of history itself—on the adequacy of any narrative history to tell the truth about the past. For too many current historians, a historical narrative is itself a work of the imagination. An instance is the view of Hayden White, professor of historical studies at the University of California at Santa Cruz, author of *Metahistory* (1973) and *Tropics of Discourse* (1978). Another is that of Dominick LaCapra in *History and Criticism* (1985), *History, Politics, and the Novel* (1987), and *Soundings in Critical Theory* (1989). These historians complain, as *Tropics of Discourse* puts it, that people are reluctant "to consider historical narratives as what they most manifestly are: verbal fictions, the contents of which are as much *invented* as *found* and the forms of which have more in common with their counterparts in literature than they have with those in the sciences."[6] For historians such as White and LaCapra, it is naive to expect that statements about a given era or about a series of historical events will correspond to the raw facts. For them, *all* historians are novelists and all history is invented, an imaginary construction of found objects and facts. Is it any wonder that the discipline of history has now collapsed into subjective ideologies, that it is now mired in cognitive nihilism?[7]

Luckily for us, Safire is innocent of this kind of academic skepticism. He sees responsible narrative history as capable of telling a truthful story about the past of Abraham Lincoln. We may argue about the meaning of past events, but the existence of historical truth as such he never calls into question. Safire also takes it as a given that the well-researched historical novel can indeed recreate the continuity of intimate human relations, personal psychology, and public events as they occurred in Lincoln's time. Wonderfully indifferent to the inanities of current historical theory, Safire wants to get on with the task.

The task in *Freedom* is to recreate the personalities that contended, in Lincoln's administration, over the war powers of Congress and the alleged usurpations of authority by the president—issues still with us. When the Southern rebels fired on Fort Sumter, did Lincoln have the power to commit the Union troops, to suspend unilaterally the writ of *habeas corpus,* and to order the arbitrary arrest and imprisonment of anti-war dissidents? Was it then within his power to order the arrest of the individual members of the entire Maryland legislature in order to prevent them from assembling to vote on Secession? Was Lincoln in violation of our constitutional liberties when he closed down anti-war newspapers? He certainly did all these things, and he justified his actions on the ground that Congress was not in session at the outbreak of hostilities and that the Constitution required him to act immediately to preserve "the public safety." Similarly, Lincoln was elected on the promise that he had no intention of introducing the political and social equality of blacks. Did he lie? Did he experience a moral conversion to abolitionism? Or did military necessity force Lincoln to free the blacks—because General McClellan had temporized and lost major battles, and the morale of the North needed a boost? Was it within his presidential power to preempt Congress and liberate the slaves by a mere presidential *proclamation*? These are the questions—touching on the idea of the "imperial presidency"—that most intrigue William Safire, President Nixon's former speech-writer.

Freedom is divided into nine long books, each devoted to a major character (except the book called "The Negro"), each character a participant in the unfolding of political and military events that led Lincoln to propose the Emancipation Proclamation. Safire opens with John Cabell Breckinridge, the Kentucky senator who held out against Lincoln's "usurpation" of constitutional liberties until events forced him to quit Washington and don the Rebel grey. Anna Ella Carroll, who devised a brilliant military strategy for the Union army, gets a book of her own, as do Stanton, Grant, McClellan, Chase, and Lincoln. Curiously, only a handful of blacks appear in this novel: the question of their freedom is submerged in the abstract issue of the freedom of all American citizens, whose civil rights were suspended by Lincoln. Throughout each of these books, Safire superbly interconnects the Washington wheeling and dealing, the political jockeying for power, the adroit maneuvering of Lincoln to hold together the army, the government, and the country. This entry from the (fictional) diary of John Hay, Lincoln's secretary, aptly defines the president's seemingly impossible situation in September 1862:

Consider the position at this moment of the man trying to hold the country together: enemies in the field, on the march in two major offensives; enemies within the army, conniving to create a dictatorship or at least throw their weight to the Peace Democrats; enemies in the Cabinet, eager to supplant him at the next party convention; enemies in the Congress, plotting to snatch away his authority to run the war. Not to mention a wife crazy as a coot, now bringing in spiritualists to hold ghostly seances in the Mansion so she can speak to the dead [son] Willie. Sometimes it seems that the Prsdt has to fight a half-dozen wars at the same time; who can blame him for looking as if he wants to hang himself?[8]

Unfortunately Safire's novel has little of what Henry James called "solidity of specification." Settings are often vague; scenic properties are scant. We are not told enough about how rooms are furnished or given the atmosphere of specific locations. In this respect *Freedom* shares a defect with Henry Adams's *Democracy* (1880). Despite Rose Greenhow's garters, it is also difficult to visualize Safire's characters. (Some eighty photographs of the *dramatis personae,* many by Mathew Brady, illustrate the book and help to evoke a mental picture for the reader.) The style—excessively cerebral—is frankly that of a journalist and political analyst, not that of a novelist. The power struggles among Chase, Stanton, Seward, the Blair family, the generals, and others are handled not so much dramatically as by oration. Conversations quickly give way to overlong speeches which rehearse the conflicting policy positions of the antagonists. Despite Safire's mind-reading of Lincoln, the great president comes off a shadowy figure. We know that his boots hurt his feet and that he carries his notes around in his stovepipe hat, a vestige of his legal circuit-riding days. We know that he likes the cornpone jokes of Artemus Ward and Petroleum V. Nasby. But Lincoln as a magisterial presence, Lincoln as a human being, simply does not come into focus.

The reason for Lincoln's elusiveness is that Safire harbors a deep ambivalence about the president and wants to demystify the Lincoln myth. Lincoln's distrust of General McClellan, who was fired for failing to prosecute the war vigorously enough, his deviousness with the divided cabinet, his manipulation of the press—all these, together with the clamp-down on American civil liberties—make

Lincoln less the national hero, for Safire, than a president who set a disastrously bad example. But he is not content just to let the novel show us this danger. In the "Underbook" we find openly argued the political reservation that informs Safire's fictional critique of Lincoln's imperial presidency. And it is here in the appendix that the quality of Safire's mind, as a student of American history, becomes most apparent.

It is true that Lincoln adroitly exploited ambiguities in the constitutional separation of powers and the authority to conduct the war. Invoking military rule and the arbitrary arrest of dissenters, Lincoln sidestepped Congress, jailed some thirteen thousand Americans without trial (many of them merely "Peace Democrats"), ignored the Supreme Court, and closed down a number of anti-war newspapers. One effect of his proclamation of military rule was to give any army officer the right to decide on the spot who was to be evacuated as a military threat or jailed without a trial. While only individual dissidents were initially at risk, one military order put a whole group under the gun. Because certain Jewish cotton traders were evidently profiteering and "stealing the Army blind," General Grant issued a General Order (No. 11) from his headquarters at Holly Springs, Tennessee, on December 17, 1862: "The Jews, as a class violating every regulation of trade established by the Treasury Department and also department orders, are hereby expelled from the department within twenty-four hours from the receipt of this order."[9]

The role of Jews in the American Civil War is, without question, of greater interest to Safire than the role of blacks. This may be because Safire is white, Jewish, or at least absorbed with the question of the relation of American Jews to the mainstream Protestant political culture. But other causes, which I shall discuss in a moment, may be more pertinent to the strange absence of blacks in this novel and the equally strange prominence given to Jews. In any case, a great deal is made in the story of a Jewish podiatrist named Isachar Zacharie, who treated Lincoln for foot problems. As Jewish businessmen on commercial errands passed over the military lines, going both north and south, they served as useful emissaries, intermediaries, and even spies. Zacharie's inflated importance lies in a bizarre espionage mission with which he is entrusted. And, indeed, Safire makes it seem that Lincoln could not have governed as wisely as he did had not Zacharie supplied him with essential subterranean information.

It is of course ridiculous to suppose that the Jews constituted a significant political force in 1860. Their number was small (the massive immigrations from Europe and Asia came later). Compared to blacks they really had no significant role in the policies of either the Union or the Confederacy. But the attention to Zacharie is warranted, it seems to me, on this profoundly important ground: the fate of these banished Jews *as a group* perfectly symbolizes the perils that will be encountered by any minority whose civil liberties are abridged in a state of martial law or civil insurrection. What Grant did to the Jews here is a failed paradigm of state-sponsored fascism. If it had worked, any group—racial, religious, ethnic, etc.—could have been similarly brutalized. The state-sponsored abuse of blacks was widely taken for granted, in both the North and the South. But Safire's attention to Zacharie makes it plain that any of us is at risk when majority political and military action suspends the fundamental constitutional guarantees that apply to us all.

In any case, that Grant's father was in business with some of these Jewish profiteers had outraged the general. It did not matter that many Gentile merchants were profiteering or that most Jews in the area had absolutely no business dealings with the Union army. The effect of Grant's order was to expel *the Jews as a group* from the Tennessee and Mississippi areas controlled by the armies of Grant and Sherman. Luckily, Lincoln immediately countermanded the order.[10] But the episode is a pointed illustration of what happened to American citizens under military rule of the kind imposed by Lincoln.

II

In terms of significant scope, modern perspective, and genuinely trustworthy research into contemporary documents, *Freedom* is a work worth comparing with modern historical treatments of Lincoln's life. I have in mind here academic histories free of the incomprehensible jargon of postmodernism and generally readable in style—works like J. G. Randall's magisterial *Lincoln the President* (1946–1955), Benjamin Quarles's *Lincoln and the Negro* (1962), David Zarefsky's *Lincoln, Douglas, and Slavery* (1990), and David

An Uncertain Abolitionist: Lincoln in Fact and Fiction

Herbert Donald's *Lincoln* (1995).[11] These studies confront head-on Lincoln's ambivalence about slavery and set it in the context of his overriding ambition—that of preserving the Union at any cost. But an important question, given Lincoln's unswerving allegiance to preserving what the Founding Fathers had handed down—a single nation—is the way his campaigning for the presidency, during the Lincoln-Douglas debates, for instance, did (or did not) hasten the onset of the war. Lincoln's speeches and letters make plain that, long before the Civil War, it was his position that slavery was wrong "because it assumes that there CAN be MORAL RIGHT in the enslaving of one man by another." In the Lincoln-Douglas debates of 1854 he argued that the Founding Fathers, in forming the Constitution and Bill of Rights, rejected slavery in principle but were forced to tolerate it from "Necessity": it already preexisted the Constitution as a legal derivative sanctioned by the English crown and was thus protected by the law of contracts, and so forth. In his speech on the Kansas-Nebraska Act, Lincoln gave comfort to the abolitionists by enumerating, in serial order, the several legal prohibitions of the newly formed U.S. government that had increasingly narrowed the scope of slavery and prevented modes of trafficking in it or abetting its spread by expansive political means:

> In 1794, they prohibited an out-going slave-trade—that is, the taking of slaves FROM the United States to sell.
>
> In 1798, they prohibited the bringing of slaves from Africa, INTO the Mississippi Territory—this territory then comprising what are now the States of Mississippi and Alabama. This was TEN YEARS before they had the authority to do the same thing as to the States existing at the adoption of the constitution.
>
> In 1800 they prohibited AMERICAN CITIZENS from trading in slaves between foreign countries—as, for instance, from Africa to Brazil.
>
> In 1803 they passed a law in aid of one or two State laws, in restraint of the internal slave trade.
>
> In 1807, in apparent hot haste, they passed the law, nearly a year in advance, to take effect the first day of 1808—the very first day the constitution would permit—prohibiting the African slave trade by heavy pecuniary and corporal penalties.

And so on. Thus, Lincoln argued, the national government was devoted from the beginning to the constraint of slavery. It "hedged and hemmed it in to the narrowest limits of necessity." He remarked that "Less than thus our fathers COULD NOT do; and MORE they WOULD NOT do."[12] Lincoln's analysis falls short of criticizing the Founding Fathers for failing to overthrow the English acts that protected slavery. In declining to end slavery at the outset, the compromisers of 1783 planted the seeds that would later flower in the Civil War—in effect they condemned their own great-great-grandsons to be slaughtered at Chancellorsville, Antietam, and Gettysburg. But in 1783 the idea of freeing all the slaves by an act of the pen seemed to subvert the law of property, of ownership, and of contracts. The consequences of such an assault on property was too horrific even to contemplate. In 1783 more than the institution of slavery might well have collapsed.[13]

In calling his book a history for the nineties, David Herbert Donald seems to have meant that the American people no longer need great mythic figures in the national pantheon. Donald's Lincoln, like Safire's, is anything but the larger-than-life conquering hero whose sublime historical achievement was to have saved the Union and to have freed the slaves, and whose marble apotheosis was monumentally evinced in that awesome brooding Lincoln Memorial in Washington. It is of course risky to think of Lincoln as a mythic hero. Idols have clay feet, and it is probably wise not to stand too near them, as they have a way of burying their devotees as they come crashing down. Lincoln has always had a stature well in excess of his six feet four inches; and Safire and a great many other Lincoln critics have always been ready to take him down a peg or two. This president is, in my view, a troubled and troubling figure. But to do justice to Lincoln one need not mythicize him. Does Donald do him justice?

I must confess at the outset that I found Donald's Lincoln quite deflating. My reaction had nothing to do with the fullness of the book. It offers all the relevant biographical facts: Lincoln's birth in 1809 in rural Kentucky, his impoverished childhood in a makeshift log cabin in Indiana, his family's hand-to-mouth existence in Illinois, and his meager schooling but great avidity for learning. Donald takes us knowledgeably through Lincoln's early youth when he supported himself by farming, clerking, running a local mill, and doing various odd jobs to make a living. We learn of Lincoln's youthful service as a postmaster, a surveyor, an aspiring politician, and a sometime soldier (in the Illinois militia during the Black Hawk Indian War in 1832).

In the course of telling Lincoln's story, Donald also provides us with a great deal of incidental information about Lincoln's early relationships: his cultivation of the "Clary's Grove Boys," the local rowdies who assured his first election in Illinois; his friendship with Joshua Speed, the storekeeper with whom he boarded for a time; his romantic involvements with Ann Rutledge (who died at twenty-two), with Mary Owens (to whom he was briefly engaged), and with Mary Todd (whom he married in 1842). His election to the presidency in 1860 and the Civil War isolated Lincoln from family and friends, and Donald's Lincoln seems a remote, impassive figure whose only concern came to be winning the war and saving the Union. His executive actions in respect to his generals—McClellan, Halleck, Grant, Sherman, and others—were narrated with shrewd understanding. His dithering over the slave question and emancipation is sensitively handled. And Donald's account of John Wilkes Booth's shooting of Lincoln, on April 15, 1865, is affectingly narrated.

Still, I find this portrait of Lincoln rather lacking in sharp resolution. And the reason lies in Donald's decision to narrate his story wholly from within the framework of information that Lincoln had available to him at each successive point in his life:

> In tracing the life of Abraham Lincoln, I have asked at every stage of his career what he knew when he had to take critical actions, how he evaluated the evidence before him, and why he reached his decisions. It is, then, a biography written from Lincoln's point of view, using the information and ideas that were available to him. It seeks to explain rather than to judge.[14]

Presidents should not of course be judged on the basis of knowledge they did not have, that only later came to light. But the effect of Donald's self-limitation is evident in the great "gaps" in Lincoln's "life" that other biographers have already filled for us. For instance, Robert E. Lee hardly figures in this biography because Lincoln knew little about him. Yet the elusive Confederate leader who kept Lincoln and his generals guessing for four years should inexorably be one of the major players in the landscape of any Lincoln biography. But the reader of Donald's *Lincoln* is allowed to know only what Lincoln gleaned from military dispatches and the like. As Donald readily concedes, almost nothing is provided "about the internal affairs of the Confederacy, because these were matters that Lincoln could not know about."[15] Likewise, Lincoln's marriage to Mary Todd produces here a shadowy and perplexing woman because, presumably, Lincoln did not know what she was up to much of the time, and he could not understand her outbursts of weird spiritualism, her paranoia and manifest irrationalism. It could be argued, I suppose, that presidents have many unofficial sources of information. But whether or not Lincoln knew more than Donald gives us, it seems unnecessarily limiting to restrict the reader to "What did Lincoln know and when did he know it?" Most readers of history or historical biography want, I suspect, the big picture.

So far as the president's personality is concerned, much might be said about Donald's complex portrait of the man and the president and about how the presidency changed the man. But in the space available here, let me touch upon two matters that I find of most interest in Donald's portrait. The first is what he leaves out, the second what he manifestly puts in—or rather strongly emphasizes.

First, as to what Donald leaves out, there is the question of whether Lincoln was gay. Until the advent of recent Queer Nation activism, no one had ever raised such a possibility. But modern homosexuals, intent on "outing" everyone, no matter how evident their manifest heterosexuality, have been rather taken with the fact that the young bachelor Lincoln boarded for three years or so with the storekeeper Joshua Speed in Springfield, Illinois. As was quite common at the time, when private beds and bedrooms were scarce, the two heterosexual men shared the same bed. By a bizarre leap of the obsessive gay imagination, this can only have meant that the two were homosexual lovers. In fact the homosexual activist W. Scott Thompson, has recently made just this claim in "Was Abe Lincoln Gay, Too? A Divided Man to Heal a Divided Age." No responsible modern historian has supported this nonsense, but the *New York Times,* which has now become the homosexual paper of record, nevertheless continues to purvey the suggestion as if gay activists were really on to something.[16] David Herbert Donald, however, rightly ignores this contemptible calumny.

As to what Donald strongly emphasizes in Lincoln's personality, let me highlight his claim for Lincoln's essential "passivity." Attorney General Bates recorded in his diary at the end of 1861 that Lincoln showed little will or purpose and thus lacked the power to command or *lead* the nation. This was a common response to Lincoln. He drove to distraction both his friends and his enemies with the oft-repeated assertion that "My policy is to have no policy."[17] To his enemies this meant that he had no principles and so was a dangerous opportunist. But Lincoln meant that he would take matters one step at a time, make each decision as it came up, and base the new decision on the effect of the last one. He remarked that the riverboat pilots in the West steered their boats from "point to point," fixing the course no farther than they could see to the next bend, and that this method described his policy. Historian J. G. Randall in *Lincoln the President* argued that

> Though Lincoln's fatalism grew and developed while he was in the White House, it was in itself nothing new with him, not a product of his Presidential years. It may have derived from the predestinarian doctrines of his parents and of the Kentucky and Indiana communities in which he was reared. Anyhow it was firmly fixed in his mind by the time he ran for Congress in 1846.[18]

Steering from point to point and acceding to the inevitable may sound like the strategy of a native American pragmatist. But historians have usually accounted by other means for Lincoln's reluctance aggressively to define a policy in advance and then to execute it. Donald sees the president's passivity as grounded on his adherence to the "Doctrine of Necessity"—a belief that "the human mind is impelled to action, or held in rest by some power, over which the mind itself has no control."[19] This doctrine was not identical with the belief in a Higher Law espoused by Christians or even claimed by the abolitionists and transcendentalists in New England who rhapsodized over the Oversoul or the Universal Current of Being.

Lincoln was in fact a youthful prairie skeptic whose immersion in Voltaire, Volney, and Tom Paine had turned him away from his parents' Baptist fundamentalism. Condemned as a scoffer at Christianity in the 1846 campaign for Congress and periodically denounced thereafter as a "Deist," Lincoln always insisted that he had never denied the truth of the Holy Scriptures and had never spoken disrespectfully of religion or of Christianity. This reassurance to the faithful may only indicate that Lincoln was a good politician. But I mention the matter because as the Civil War carnage continued, Lincoln began to carry the Bible with him. He memorized many of its consoling passages, and he began to speak (often quite movingly) in the language of nineteenth-century religious discourse. Although Mary Lincoln was right to say that her husband was never a "technical Christian," one converted and affiliated with a particular church, Lincoln himself confessed during the Civil War that his religious ideas were undergoing a "process of crystallization."

As this crystallization occurred and as the war dragged on, Lincoln came increasingly to feel that, as Randall puts it, the war was "God's way of removing slavery and punishing the people, both North and South, for the sin that all shared on account of slavery. And he came to look upon himself, humbly, as God's man, God's human agent in the working out of His mysterious providence."[20] In other words, it was not he and Jefferson Davis and their governments and generals who were killing these boys but God himself. God evidently did not want the swift end of the Civil War. God did not want it ended until some obscure purpose had been worked out. He told Mrs. Eliza P. Gurney that

> The purposes of the Almighty are perfect, and must prevail, though we erring mortals may fail to accurately perceive them in advance. We hoped for a happy termination of this terrible war long before this; but God knows best, and has ruled otherwise. . . . We must work earnestly in the best light He gives us, trusting that so working still conduces to the great ends He ordains. Surely He intends some great good to follow this mighty convulsion, which no mortal could make, and no mortal could stay.[21]

And to the editor of the *Frankfort Commonwealth* in Kentucky he said, "I claim not to have controlled events, but confess plainly that events have controlled me." He observed that "at the end of three years of struggle the nation's condition is not what either party, or any man devised, or expected. God alone can claim it."[22]

This fatalist resignation found its decisive expression in the second inaugural address, where Lincoln confronted the paradox that the Civil War, which at its outbreak was supposed to end after only a few months, had in reality dragged on for years, to the ruination of both the North and the South, and was still going on! Neither section

> anticipated that the *cause* of the conflict might cease with, or even before, the conflict itself should cease. Each looked for an easier triumph, and a result less fundamental and astounding. Both [sides] read the same Bible, and pray to the same God; and each invokes His aid against the other. It may seem strange that any men should dare to ask a just God's assistance in wringing their bread from the sweat of other men's faces; but let us judge not that we be not judged. The prayers of both could not be answered; that of neither has been answered fully. The Almighty has his own purposes. "Woe unto the world because of offences! for it must needs be that offences come; but woe to that man by whom the offence cometh!" If offences which, in the providence of God, must needs come, but which, having continued through His appointed time, He now wills to remove, and that He gives to both North and South, this terrible war, as the woe due to those by whom the offence came, shall we discern therein any departure from those divine attributes which the believers in a Living God always ascribe to Him?[23]

Donald suggests that this fatalism was Lincoln's mode of escape from the moral burden it was his to bear, a projection onto God of a responsibility for unbearable slaughter that was actually a human responsibility—that of Lincoln, his cabinet and his generals, that of Jefferson Davis and the flesh-and-blood powers of the Confederacy. Shelby Foote has made a similar observation in suggesting that Americans in both the North and the South, during the Civil War, allowed the stupefying carnage to go on because they could not find a way *not* to fight each other. He holds that the genius of our political system is the political leaders' capacity to negotiate and to compromise on initally divisive issues. Even though Americans beguile themselves in the belief that they are quite *un*compromising when it comes to principles, our real strength, the true genius of our governmental system, he believes, is the capacity to compromise, and, in this case, it failed us.

The conclusion of these historians seems implicitly utopian to me. Both Donald and Foote assume that history can be controlled by rational thought and manipulated and directed by actions issuing therefrom. To the secular rationalist, differences can always be defused through negotiated compromise. But, in my view, while conflict resolution *is* sometimes possible, often it is not. That historical developments are beyond the capacity of man to control should not be so surprising. Men can barely control themselves. How, then, can they "dominate history"? The simple fact is that neither historian can tolerate the idea that the unfolding of history may have a purpose that is nonhuman, providential, or divine. Lincoln had begun to think otherwise. Repeatedly he recurred to those familiar lines in Shakespeare's tragedy: "There's a divinity that shapes our ends, / Rough-hew them how we will." Only a railsplitter like Lincoln, a man familiar with the blunt edge of the axe, could have fully appreciated *Hamlet*'s figure of one's "rough-hewn" destiny ultimately and more finely shaped by a Divinity beyond human comprehension.

Did he have a clear sense of his own destiny? He had been elected, he thought, to preserve the Union, not to free the slaves. And he told Horace Greeley, editor of the *New York Tribune*:

> My paramount object in this struggle *is* to save the Union, and is *not* either to save or to destroy slavery. If I could save it by freeing *all* the slaves I would do it; and if I could save it by freeing some and leaving others alone I would also do that. What I do about slavery, and the colored race, I do because I believe it helps to save the Union: and what I forbear, I forbear because I do *not* believe it would help to save the Union.[24]

But the irresistible feeling that a higher power was moving him from point to point in the twisting river of time evidently persuaded Lincoln that the freeing of the slaves must be *the key* to the salvation of the Union and to the hidden purposes of history. And so he issued the Emancipation Proclamation on January 1, 1863.

III

For historian J. G. Randall, the Civil War was undesirable, unnecessary, and deplorable. It was caused, he thought, by a blundering generation of radical abolitionists, firebrand slaveholders, and newspaper propagandists who seized control of the issues and warped the national agenda. They thus drained Lincoln's presidency of the genius it might have exhibited. Donald's Lincoln, though "one of the least experienced and most poorly prepared men ever elected to high office," is also given high marks.[25] He is one of the most memorable presidents of the Republic. Nevertheless, one comes away from Lincoln's life in fact and fiction troubled by many aspects of the man and his administration. Basically a case lawyer experienced in routine litigation, Lincoln had no theoretical understanding of the law. Inexperienced, ill organized, lacking in forcefulness, he was full of contradictions that confused and disabled his administrations. Moreover, while the Civil War that erupted during his administration required extraordinary measures for the safety of the Union, we have the duty to question whether some of his decisions were really warranted by the actual peril: Lincoln's harsh invocation of martial law, his suspension of the writ of *habeas corpus*, his ignoring the decisions and orders of the Supreme Court, his arbitrary arrest of dissenters, and his closing down of anti-war newspapers. We think of these matters as involving the sacred constitutional rights of our citizens. Indeed, the Ohio congressman Clement L. Vallandigham—who had been arrested for speaking out against the government—charged that Lincoln's approval of the repeated arrest of civilians, his suspension of the right of *habeas corpus*, his interference with the freedom of the mails, his authorization of the invasion of private houses, his suppression of the free press and freedom of speech, and other such enormities had transformed the United States into a heinous despotism. Was Lincoln a tyrant? Was a native fascism aborning?

Safire's *Freedom* is inclined to this view. He cannot agree with the claim, frequently expressed by patriotic historians, that Lincoln acted with reasonable restraint in abridging the constitutional freedoms enjoyed by our citizens in peacetime: "I disagree. The argument that times were tough, and a few thousand dissenters clapped in jail were no big deal in the midst of insurrection, misses the point of democracy under stress: insofar as a nation departs from its guarantees of civil liberty, it is less of a democracy."[26] Libertarian generalizations are always appealing. But one must protest to Safire that a civil rebellion was under way, that McClellan was dithering, that the capture of Washington seemed imminent, and that Lee was moving into Pennsylvania. For Safire, the suspension of *habeas corpus* and the proclamation of military rule were never really necessary and did nothing to help win the war; and Lincoln should never have taken radical steps that other presidents (e.g., Wilson, FDR, and Lyndon B. Johnson), even in time of war and civil disorder, managed to avoid. As Safire remarks in the "Underbook":

> Lincoln cannot be above criticism because he meant well, or because he freed the slaves while he was at the business of saving the Union, or he was lenient in applying his usurpation of the rights of the people. The purpose of hindsight is to draw a lesson. The lesson in this most extreme of cases is that it is never a proper time to ignore the Constitution in the name of saving the Constitution. To be tolerant of Lincoln's excesses is to encourage future abuses of power.

Safire takes some satisfaction in the fact that the Supreme Court, in 1866, struck down as unconstitutional Lincoln's proclamation of military rule: "martyred heroes come and go, but the rule of law wins in the end."[27]

This is a respectable position, and many historians endorse it. The question comes right down to how much disorder, how much anarchy, how much plain subversion a democracy can tolerate while a civil war is going on within its borders. Not a great deal, if the country is to survive. Attorney General Edward Bates made the case to Lincoln's contemporaries, and it retains its force today:

> The power to do these things [suspend the *habeas corpus* privilege, etc.] is in the hand of the President, placed there by the Constitution and the statute law as a sacred trust to be used by him in his best discretion in the performance of his great first duty—to preserve, protect and defend the Constitution. . . . He is the chief civil magistrate of the nation and being such *and because he is such* [author's italics] he is the constitutional Commander in Chief of the Army and Navy, and thus within the limits of the Constitution he rules in peace and commands in war and at this moment he is in the full exercise of all the functions belonging to both those characters.[28]

This is essentially the argument that Safire's sexy female character Anna Carroll makes in defense of Lincoln's exercise of extraordinary war powers in the face of the Southern insurrection. Lincoln's best spokesman in this novel, she in fact offers a well-articulated political rationalization for the president's unprecedented abrogation of our civil rights. Quoting Jefferson, who had also lived through both war, revolution, and internal disorder, she remarks: "A strict observance of the written law is doubtless one of the highest duties of a good citizen, but it is not *the highest*. The laws of necessity, of self-preservation, of saving our country when in danger, are of higher obligation."[29] This famous position Jefferson had expressed in his letter to J. B. Colvin in December 1810, long after the military disorder attending independence had ended: "To lose our country by scrupulous adherence to written law would be to lose the law itself, with life, liberty, property, and all those who are enjoying them with us, thus absurdly sacrificing the end to the means."[30]

Lincoln, a lawyer, knew that in suspending *habeas corpus* and in proclaiming military rule he was putting postwar constitutional government at risk, supplying, in theory, a precedent for a later tyrant. But as Safire presents him, Lincoln wished to preserve the Union at all costs, and the emancipation of blacks—proclaimed at just the right political moment—was an astute maneuver to reanimate the abolitionists and to mobilize flagging Northern support for the war. Lincoln felt that the judgment of thoughtful men would be forgiving and that future thinkers would affirm his decisions. His actions are certainly approved by David Herbert Donald. Although this biography undertakes to demystify Lincoln, he is still, for Donald, "the greatest American President,"[31] a man whose extraordinary executive measures, when the government of the country was under assault, seemed finally warranted. Safire, however, thinks that Lincoln was wrong about the judgment of the future; his criticism indeed illustrates the point that we have not yet reached consensus on the extreme measures that Lincoln invoked. It is easy for a president—say, a Jefferson or a Jackson or a Franklin D. Roosevelt—to approve of Lincoln's desperate remedies. But presidents are privileged, habituated to command, and think themselves virtuous in their conduct. The powerless, whether as individuals (like Vallandigham) or as a class (like the Jews), may have a different view when constitutional liberties are suspended. Safire's is thus a sobering political lesson in fictional form.

Lincoln's Generals: Grant and Sherman in Their Memoirs

During the lazy New York summer of 1990—in which the only other major cultural issue seemed to be why the NEA was still supporting pornography with the taxpayers' money—a minor flap developed at the Grand Army Plaza, at Fifth Avenue and Central Park South, in Manhattan. This dustup involved the restoration, by a coalition of benefactors working with the city's Art Commission, of an equestrian statue of General William Tecumseh Sherman. It was erected in 1903 by Augustus Saint-Gaudens and is one of the principal equestrian memorials of the Civil War. What caused the flap—mostly played out in articles and letters to the *New York Times*—was the restoration of a layer of bright yellow gilding that lighted up the dingy statue like a New York City taxicab. Garish and vulgar, said some. No, said others, the golden statue now perfectly duplicates the finish that Saint-Gaudens specified: three layers of thin gold, against a background of green trees. Others insisted that Saint-Gaudens had the color toned down before the installation of the work. Never mind, their opponents said, New York City air pollution would tone it down rapidly enough. Not so, according to one of the benefactors: a heavy coat of protective gelatin would cover the gold patina of the Sherman statue, which would be maintained, in perpetuity, in all of its aureate splendor.

Whether the tourists in the park or the lounging office workers at lunch by the statue's pedestal could identify William Tecumseh Sherman, or explain what the Grand Army of the Republic was, is anyone's guess. But with the publication of *The Memoirs of General W. T. Sherman* and *Ulysses S. Grant: Memoirs and Selected Letters,* we now have in a convenient format two of the most important historical documents touching the American Civil War.[1] If anyone wants to know who these superb generals were or what they accomplished as military leaders, there could be no better introduction to their lives than these volumes. Apropos of the genre, each memoir deals mainly with public events and the role of each general in the design of the strategy and the command and deployment of Northern troops. Little of personal sensibility, private thought, or subjective feeling is revealed. Nevertheless, the mind and character of both men, their courage and conviction, their strengths and weaknesses, come through in these volumes.

II

William Tecumseh Sherman (1820–1891) was descended of English immigrants who arrived in 1634 and settled in Connecticut; the family line included Roger Sherman, the signer of the Declaration of Independence. Sherman's father Charles, a lawyer, saw an opportunity in the West and moved his family to Ohio, where he was eventually appointed judge of the Supreme Court. Taken by the exploits of the great chief of the Shawnees, Charles gave his son that remarkable middle name, Tecumseh. Sherman thus grew up with a sense of the nation's history and its destiny and of his family's role in it. While the death of his father left the family quite impoverished, the family's social prominence made it possible for Sherman to enter West Point and for his abolitionist brother Charles to succeed as a senator from Ohio, a post he held throughout the Civil War.

Sherman graduated in 1840, sixth in a class of forty-three, and was commissioned as a second lieutenant. In his youth he had various assignments: capturing and removing Florida Seminoles to the Indian territory in what is now Oklahoma; taking legal depositions of various kinds throughout many parts of the South; scouting the West with the explorer General John C. Frémont; and reporting on the gold discoveries in California. His service in the

Far West, however, meant that Sherman missed the Mexican War, a sure route to military advancement. Thinking his service career blighted, he resigned his commission in 1853 and became a successful bank agent in California. Later, when the bank closed in 1857, Sherman opened a law firm in Kansas, then went into farming in Ohio, and finally, in 1859, accepted the superintendency of the newly created Louisiana Seminary of Learning and Military Academy. This institution, with five instructors, sixty cadets, and no furniture, was meant to become a Southern West Point; in fact, it later evolved into Louisiana State University. During 1859–1860, as the South was mobilizing for secession, Colonel Sherman advised Louisiana state officials that, in his judgment, "secession was treason, was *war*."[2] It was therefore no surprise that, when Louisiana militiamen seized the federal arsenal in Baton Rouge on January 10, 1861, months before the attack on Fort Sumter, Sherman resigned his academic post in the South and volunteered for Union service.

Ulysses S. Grant (1822–1885) was born at Point Pleasant, Ohio, to a much less distinguished family. His father operated a tannery and sold cut wood. Grant attended various schools and seminaries before matriculating at West Point in 1839. He graduated in 1843, twenty-first in a class of 223. With the outbreak of the Mexican War he was assigned to the army of General Zachary Taylor and fought with distinction at Palo Alto, Resaca de la Palma, and Monterey. Later, under General Winfield Scott, Grant took part in the siege of Veracruz and Mexico City. After this war Grant served in various parts of the country, rising to the rank of captain before resigning his commission in 1854. His career between 1854 and 1861 was checkered and abysmally unsuccessful. He farmed for a while, sold cut wood, dabbled in real estate, and clerked in his father's leather goods store. With the outbreak of the Civil War, Grant was appointed commander of an Illinois regiment by Governor Richard Yates. In the first year of the war he organized and led troops in several places in Missouri, Illinois, and Kentucky. In early 1862 he distinguished himself by taking Fort Henry and Fort Donelson. Unlike so many vacillating Union generals, he captured the attention of the nation by telling the Confederates at Donelson that, barring a quick and unconditional surrender, he intended to move immediately upon their works. But Grant unfortunately fell afoul of his superior, General Henry W. Halleck. While Grant was on raids up the Tennessee River to disrupt the Confederate railroad, Halleck sent him several dispatches demanding to know his whereabouts and strength. Although neither Halleck's dispatches nor Grant's own reports were received by the other, the furious (and perhaps jealous) Halleck simply relieved Grant of his command, condemned his performance at the battle of Shiloh (at Pittsburg Landing), and took personal command of the Army of Tennessee. All these Union generals were under tremendous political as well as military pressure to succeed. Back home, "after every [Northern] military defeat, it was natural for radical Republicans to call for more harshness, and for radical Democrats to protest that the nation's only salvation lay in conciliation."[3] A general who was not afraid to engage the enemy was—or at least seemed to be—a comparative rarity in the early years of the war. In any case, when McClellan was relieved as commander of the Union armies in 1862, Halleck succeeded him in the post and was obliged to restore Grant to his command. It was Sherman's view that "General Halleck was a man of great capacity," but his "extreme caution" led to miscalculations that prolonged the war.[4] Lincoln also sensed this deficiency; and, after Grant's victories at Corinth, Vicksburg, and Chattanooga, Grant replaced Halleck as the military commander of the Union armies.

III

Sherman's military experience before the Civil War meant that he already knew many of the officers, both Northern and Southern, who would play a major role in the conflict—especially O. C. Ord, H. W. Halleck, Braxton Bragg, Pierre G. T. Beauregard, and D. C. Buell.[5] Moreover, his various assignments in the South enabled him, as he remarked, "to traverse on horse-back the very ground where in after-years I had to conduct vast armies and fight great battles."[6] He was thus perhaps as well informed as any other Union officer about the capability of the Southern armies. What he knew was that the Confederacy would not be a military pushover, a fact that Washington was not, at first, disposed to hear. Although the disastrous defeat of federal forces at Bull Run on July 21, 1861, should have convinced Washington that this would not be a ninety-day war, Sherman's dire predictions went largely unheeded. And when he told General McClellan in Washington that he would need up to 200,000 men to expel the Confederates from Kentucky, he was denounced in the *Cincinnati Commercial* as insane. His immediate superior, General Halleck, put Sherman on medical leave for twenty days and told McClellan that Sherman was unfit for duty.

Reassigned to support the assault on Fort Donelson in the Cumberlands, Sherman met up with Grant and thus began one of the most effective military combinations in this or any other American war. Grant took Donelson on February 16, 1862, and moved immediately against Corinth and Vicksburg, Mississippi. Vicksburg was well defended and geographically impregnable. But Grant, the commanding general, and Sherman, his right hand, finally took the city on July 4, 1863. This victory effectively split the Confederacy in half. Moving eastward to reinforce the Army of the Cumberland after its defeat at the Battle of Chickamauga, Sherman and his army then linked up with General George H. Thomas to defeat Braxton Bragg's Rebel army at the Battle of Chattanooga in late 1863. Thereafter, Sherman relieved the army of General Burnside, which was besieged at Knoxville by Confederate General James Longstreet.

Could the war have been averted? Lincoln, as we have seen, thought not. It says nothing to the superiority of political leadership in our own miserable time that the antebellum period lacked great political figures who might have resolved the ongoing conflicts over states' rights and abolition. Too much absolutism, despite the constitutional checks and balances of political and social power, permeated American society, North and South. The war began and, once begun, took on a horrific life of its own. And it did not end. As the war dragged on, political considerations made it imperative that Lincoln relieve General McClellan from overall command of the Union armies. The simple fact was that McClellan was dithering in Washington, unwilling to leave the city unprotected and take the field against Robert E. Lee's armies. The successes of the Western armies, under Grant, led to Grant's being made general-in-chief on March 17, 1863. Grant and Sherman planned the spring 1864 offensive: it involved Grant's direct engagement with Lee's Army of Northern Virginia with a view to the capture of Richmond, the most important city in the eastern Confederacy; and, further South, Sherman's all-out assault on Atlanta, which was defended by the Confederate generals John B. Hood and William J. Hardee. Atlanta was taken on September 2, 1864, evacuated of civilians, and largely burned, making it unfit for Confederate army support. The destruction of this city, as visualized in the movie *Gone with the Wind*, remains vivid in the American mind.

IV

Military strategy before Grant favored constantly protecting an army's rearguard lifeline that supplied the food and ammunition needed for the troops' survival. Napoleon had said that an army marched on its stomach; and it is true that an army's ability to provision its troops is a key to its success. Much of military history is therefore a tedious record of flanking movements to cut off an enemy army's supply line, to destroy railroads, to burn supply wagons, ammunition trains, and provisions. Quartermasters were constantly provisioning the army from the rear. Grant had learned at Fort Donelson, however, that his army could subsist off provisions taken directly from the surrounding farms. The South was so fertile an agricultural area that importing food from the North, by Union railroads and wagon trains, came to be seen as unnecessary. Consequently Grant approved Sherman's plan to strike out eastward toward the sea, Sherman's armies living off the crops and livestock of Georgia and the Carolinas, so as to come up behind Lee and the Army of Northern Virginia, which was defending Richmond. The significance of Richmond, at this stage of the war, has been accurately defined by Emory M. Thomas:

> The capital was crucial, not only as a center of war industry and a base of supply for the army, but also as the last hope for faltering Southern national morale. Richmond had served as a military magnet before, luring enemy armies onto killing grounds in 1861, 1862, and 1863. In 1864, though, Richmond was a military millstone around Lee's neck. The Army of Northern Virginia and indeed the Confederacy could not live without the city. But every day the Confederates remained in their trenches, they were accepting a war of attrition—and such a war they could not hope to win.[7]

Sherman's "March to the Sea" was one of the most controversial strategies of the Civil War, inasmuch as his army of 65,000 men devastated a wide area of the South as it moved to join Grant at Richmond. Southern newspapers and politicians raged at Sherman as an infamous barbarian who had "changed the rules of war," asserting, as Sherman put it, that

> we respected neither age nor sex; that we burned every thing we came across—barns, stables, cotton-gins, and even dwelling-houses; that we ravished the women and killed the men, and perpetrated all manner of outrages on the inhabitants. Therefore it struck me as strange that [Confederate] Generals Hardee and Smith should commit their families to our custody [when Savannah was taken], and even bespeak our personal care and attention. These officers knew well that these reports were exaggerated in the extreme, and yet tacitly assented to these publications, to arouse the drooping energies of the people of the South.[8]

In Dixie mythography, Sherman's March to the Sea is called a holocaust that laid waste an "already defeated" South. The claim is nonsense. While there was some violence against civilians by some disorderly Union troops—who were spread out on a march fifty miles wide, foraging as they went along—the brutalization of civilians was not the aim of Union policy. "War is cruelty and you cannot refine it," Sherman told the Atlantans, who had just been expelled from the city. He told Halleck that "we are not only fighting hostile armies, but a hostile people, and must make old and young, rich and poor, feel the hard hand of war."[9] The destruction of barns, stables, gins, and mills, and the sacking of munitions factories, gasworks, and railyards were solely directed to making the Southern economic infrastructure incapable of supporting Confederate armies that might at any time fall back and regroup for supplies and reinforcements in the deep South. An Alabaman on Sherman's staff, Henry Hitchcock, bothered by the vandalism of some of the Union troops on the March to the Sea, nevertheless justified it by saying that "while I deplore this necessity daily and cannot bear to see the soldiers swarm as they do through fields and yards . . . nothing *can* end this war but some demonstration of their helplessness." He declared that "this Union and its Government must be sustained, at any and every cost; to sustain it, we must war upon and destroy the organized rebel forces,—must cut off their supplies, destroy their communications . . . [and] produce among the people of Georgia a thorough conviction of the personal misery which attends war, and the utter helplessness and inability of their 'rulers,' State or Confederate, to protect them. . . . If that terror and grief and even want shall help to paralyze their husbands and fathers who are fighting us . . . it is mercy in the end."[10]

V

Yet, even though there was ample justification for a Sherman military maneuver that might shorten the war and thus save both Union and Confederate lives, some post-Vietnam writers and historians have transmogrified Union policy into something perilously close to the butchery of civilians and have in fact "criminalized" Sherman as some kind of Nuremberg monster. Needless to say, all of these critics are white. Mary McCarthy, for instance, with her usual gift for getting everything wrong, described Sherman's March to the Sea as a "war crime." And Charles Royster has described Sherman and rebel Stonewall Jackson as generals deranged by their religious belief and philosophical convictions. For Royster, who evidently knows nothing about Christian faith or religious conviction, these generals and the American people of the Civil War era were given to finding, of all things, "uplifting emotion in the violence" of war. Here is Royster on Sherman:

> His victories and his methods won widespread acclaim in the North. To large numbers of people his public character embodied the severity needed for crushing the rebellion; his name became synonymous with war that punished all rebels. He owed his notoriety not only to his destructive marches through the South but also to his pungent letters and reports. Widely reprinted and often praised, these documents made him the clearest exponent of winning by a willingness to use any means. However, Sherman did not advocate this policy early in the war. He came to it through experience, after civilians long had urged it on the government.[11]

But did Sherman advocate *winning by a willingness to use any means?* Hardly. There is incontrovertible evidence that Sherman knew—and imposed on his troops—Article I, Paragraph 52 of the

American Articles of War (1806): "Any officer or soldier who shall quit his post or colors to plunder and pillage shall suffer death or other such punishment as shall be ordered by sentence of a general court martial." But the rules of land war do permit an army to requisition from civilians—if payment or receipts are given—whatever it needs to sustain a military operation. (Rebel soldiers readily took Southerners' food, horses, and cattle—frequently paying with worthless Confederate currency.) While there was indeed random Union looting and pillaging, Sherman regularly denounced it, ordered that civilians not be molested, and frequently had the fires put out.

What is implicit in such attacks seems to be a veiled dislike of Amerika, a wish to locate the origin of twentieth-century holocausts here, even to find their source in Sherman. Southern journalist James Reston, Jr., puts it this way:

> If [Sherman] widened the license of war dramatically, his sins lay in the wanton destruction of property, rather than the wanton destruction of life. But where does barbarism begin? How does the process start? Once undertaken on a wide scale in one war, especially one that results in victory, does it not become accepted practice in the next war? And is the gulf between property and life so great? Does it not become easier to destroy the latter if the despoilment of the former has been widely practiced, especially if practiced without success?[12]

Reston poses these as questions rather than assertions, but they appear to be rhetorical formulations intended to convince us that, if Sherman destroyed cotton mills, Hitler and General William Westmoreland learned from that wantonly to destroy civilians. The logical gaps in the reasoning that undertakes to link these matters are breathtaking. The military destruction of property need not and usually does not automatically lead to the destruction of innocent civilian life. Most American soldiers, even in combat, have regarded the gulf between property and life as immeasurably great. Nor does victory in war have anything to do with the barbaric behavior that overcomes deranged soldiers. At Saltville, Virginia, on October 2, 1864, Confederate troops murdered one hundred Northern prisoners, many of them black and quite a few of them wounded. They were not following Sherman's orders.[13] Such behavior had nothing to do with the example of Sherman. Nor were they following the policy of Robert E. Lee. The rules of engagement and the *American Articles of War* constrain military behavior, or should. But in the chaos and carnage of war all restraints can fail.

The burden of anti-Sherman sentiment appears to hinge on the idea that there is a "national American bloodlust" that was first manifest in the Civil War. The barbaric practices of Civil War generals like Sherman are supposed to have led naturally to Nazi Germany and, circling back again, thence to Vietnam—so that from armies fighting each other we modern Americans have descended to the wholesale murder of civilian ethnic groups, to "search and destroy" missions, to "free fire zones" in which innocent noncombatants are routinely butchered—in short, to Lieutenant William Calley and the My Lai massacre.[14] But in my view, for which I think there is abundant historical and anthropological evidence, bloodlust runs deep in human nature. Far from being a modern phenomenon, it is a primitive quality that tribalism ignites, fans, and makes at times uncontrollable. If we look over the long vista of the past—at various nations, states, racial populations, ethnic or religious groups—the bloodlust that has led one tribe to slaughter the warriors of another has invariably led to the imprisonment, enslavement, or butchery of the innocents—women, children, the old.

There is really nothing modern in the warfare that victimizes civilians. What is modern is the extent to which, in *American* wars, political efforts have been made to contain the all-too-human bloodlust that war always evokes, not only through the rules of engagement but through formulations like the *Articles of War* and the *Uniform Code of Military Justice*. Yet we need a devil. We need a demon, some satanic figure who can be blamed for the evil that men may do in combat. Charles Royster, who knows as much about Sherman as anybody, has summarized the tendency as follows: "Kitchener's devastations in the Transvaal, the German policy of *Schrecklichkeit* or 'frightfulness,' the bombing of Coventry and London, the fire-bombing of Dresden and Tokyo, the atomic bombing of Hiroshima and Nagasaki—all went back, along 'a straight line of logic,' to Sherman." The logic of this backward-looking search for a scapegoat is of course faulty, and it is to his great credit that Royster concludes: "Sherman the creator of modern war has been largely a rhetorical rather than a historical figure." He is right to observe that "The common purpose in these formulations of Sherman's responsibility was not so much to offer a historical argument about causation as to condemn war in which destruction lost contact with its rationale. For this moral argument Sherman served as an evocative symbol—a sinister genius, a Machiavelli, a Napoleon, whose reputation took on a life of its own."[15]

No one can deny that war is both an expression of and a provocation to the savagery of human beings, including Americans. Yet there is a great difference between the savagery of an individual soldier who goes haywire in a combat situation and the policy of his government that forbids such conduct. As Winston Churchill remarked,

> "War is hell," [Sherman] said, and certainly he made it so. But no one must suppose that his depredations and pillage were comparable to the atrocities which were committed during the World Wars of the twentieth century or to the barbarities of the Middle Ages. Searching investigation has discovered hardly a case of murder or rape.[16]

In fact, when one contemplates governments that have implemented a *policy* of butchery, murder, rape, and genocide, or that have condoned it, Americans are nowhere to be seen. We have only to mention Serbia, Bosnia, Nazi Germany, Lebanon, Idi Amin's Uganda, Rwanda, Zaire, Afghanistan, Syria, Iraq, and Azerbaijan to bring to mind recent civil wars where genocide was either government policy or a condoned practice as governments collapsed. If the American people and their government were indeed the bloodthirsty descendants of the old Civil War butchers, Generals Colin Powell and Norman Schwartzkopf would have annihilated Iraq, massacred her people, and put Saddam Hussein to the sword. Instead, in a mere hundred hours, the imperial designs of Iraq were set at naught, Kuwait was liberated, and the U.S. withdrew its troops. Are our soldiers moral monsters? It is worth remembering that Lieutenant Calley *was,* after all, court-martialed, convicted of the premeditated murder of civilians, dismissed from service, ordered to forfeit all pay and allowances, and sentenced to confinement at hard labor for life. And, as James Reston has reminded us, although there are a great many Georgia ladies who nowadays will assure you that Sherman laid waste the town and burnt it to the ground, they will, after tea, take you out to see the grand plantations and the lovely antebellum homes that somehow survived intact.

Sherman's stratagem—living off the land while he marched to the sea—worked. As Grant besieged Richmond, Robert E. Lee was thus faced with a dilemma: to stand and fight Grant's army or to withdraw southward, intercept Sherman, and try to crush his army. As the siege of Richmond continued, many Southern troops became demoralized and deserted. Grant was relentless in his maneuvering to capture the Confederate stronghold. To Lee, from a Confederate military point of view, Richmond was a burden to defend that prevented him from taking the offensive and dealing Grant a decisive counterblow. Lee hesitated and held his ground, preventing Grant from having his way with Richmond. But then, when the position of his army became untenable, he withdrew from the city. Nothing now stood between Grant and the capital of the Confederacy, and the population naturally bolted. The evacuation of the city produced a chaos reminiscent of that in Atlanta. A Richmond *Times* reporter observed that "crowds of men, women and children traversed the streets, rushing from one storehouse to another, loading themselves with all kinds of supplies. . . . After midnight [the] . . . straggling [Confederate] soldiers made their appearance on the streets and immediately set about robbing the principal stores on Main Street. . . . Soldiers roamed from store to store, followed by a reckless crowd, drunk as they."[17] As Richmond dissolved into chaos, General Phil Sheridan meanwhile sent Grant a dispatch indicating that

> the Whole of Lee's army is at or near Amelia Court House, and on the right side of it. General Davis, whom I sent out to Painesville on their right flank, has just captured six pieces of artillery and some wagons. We can capture the Army of Northern Virginia if force enough can be thrown to this point, and then advance upon it. My cavalry was at Burkesville yesterday, and six miles beyond, on the Danville Road, last night. General Lee is at Amelia Court House in person. They are out of rations, or nearly so. They were advancing up the railroad towards Burkesville yesterday, when we intercepted them at this point.[18]

Since Lee seemed to be moving South to join forces with Confederate General Johnston, so as to intercept Sherman, Grant rode up to the battle site, reconnoitered the positions of his army, and ordered a rapid pursuit. Lee was so wily an antagonist, and he had escaped the Union net so many times, that Grant was determined he should not escape this time. Consequently the Union commanding general was totally unprepared for the note he received from Lee dated April 9, 1865, proposing a discussion of the surrender of his army at the Appomattox Court House.

Grant recollected that General Lee rode into the meeting wearing "a full uniform which was entirely new, and . . . a sword of considerable value."[19] Grant had not expected the capitulation and was bespattered from riding up and down the lines. He lacked a sword and happened to be wearing only the shoulder straps of a lieutenant general to indicate his rank. (Of course his enemies said that he had once again been drinking; but modern historians have cast doubt on Grant's legendary bibulation.) Of the scene of Lee's surrender, Grant wrote:

> What General Lee's feelings were I do not know. As he was a man of much dignity, with an impassible face, it was impossible to say whether he felt inwardly glad that the end had finally come, or felt sad over the result, and was too manly to show it. Whatever his feelings, they were entirely concealed from my observation; but my own feelings, which had been quite jubilant on the receipt of his letter, were sad and depressed. I felt like anything rather than rejoicing at the downfall of a foe who had fought so long and valiantly, and had suffered so much for a cause, though that cause was, I believe, one of the worst for which a people ever fought, and one for which there was the least excuse.[20]

Grant's surrender terms were generous, as befitting Lincoln's wish to bind up the wounds of war, and Lee's men were sent home with their horses to begin the spring planting.

Lee's surrender found Sherman moving up through North Carolina, and he was immediately redirected to find the Confederate army of Joe Johnston and destroy it. But, knowing the end was at hand, Johnston moved to surrender his troops. In view of Sherman's reputation for merciless punition, we should note that the terms he offered Johnston were even more generous than

Grant's to Lee. In fact they were too generous. Although Sherman's terms were submitted to Washington for approval, they were immediately denounced by President Andrew Johnson and Secretary Stanton. (The situation in Washington was confused: Lincoln had just been assassinated.) Sherman was vilified through press leaks planted by the jealous Stanton, and ordered to offer only what Grant had offered Lee. Stanton denounced in public Sherman's overgenerous terms and, stupefyingly, insinuations were made about Sherman's loyalty to the Union. This reading of Sherman seems incredible today, but such were the passions of war and of political preferment that for some weeks Sherman's reputation was under a cloud. Grant and other defenders eventually redeemed it, but Sherman was ever thereafter to regard Stanton—whose desire to be president was overweening—as a mortal enemy. Later, of course, Grant went on to become president, a task for which he was largely unfitted, and Sherman followed him as commanding general of all the United States armies.

VI

The style of these two memoirs is better than we have a right to expect, coming as they do from two such men of action. Both works detail at great length the relentless sequence of skirmishes, battles, sieges, and other military engagements. Both volumes illustrate the text with battlefield orders, maps, command rosters, body counts, and the like. Sherman's memoir is perhaps the livelier of the two, expressing certainty, self-confidence, and *joie de vivre*. Both men give due credit to the other. Grant, whose taciturnity was legendary, was a mystery to most of his subordinates, but he makes it plain in his memoir that he owed much of his success to Sherman. Sherman, for his part, claimed never to have understood U. S. Grant: "I knew him as a cadet at West Point, as a lieutenant of the Fourth Infantry, as a citizen of St. Louis, and as a growing general all through a bloody civil war. Yet to me he is a mystery, and I believe he is a mystery to himself."[21] Even Sherman exhibits a remarkable modesty about some aspects of his battlefield experience. He does not tell us some things that we have to go to Grant's memoir to learn. Here is Grant on Sherman at the Battle of Shiloh (April 6, 1862):

A casualty to Sherman that would have taken him from the field that day would have been a sad one for the troops engaged at Shiloh. And how near we came to this! On the 6th Sherman was shot twice, once in the hand, once in the shoulder, the ball cutting his coat and making a slight wound, and a third ball passed through his hat. In addition to this he had several horses shot during the day.[22]

Of the two books, Grant's is the better. In fact it holds its own with every other military history written by a commanding general, going back to Caesar's Gallic wars, so far as I have read them. Matthew Arnold sniffed at Grant's bad grammar and so drove Mark Twain wild, for Twain idolized the general and arranged the book's publication. But Edmund Wilson was more nearly right in praising Grants's *Memoirs,* in *Patriotic Gore,* as a striking instance of the transition from a flowery Victorian style into a style of direct, straightforward realism. Perhaps no passage will illustrate this style more clearly than Grant's account of the Battle of the Wilderness, fought in May 1864:

> At 4:15 in the afternoon Lee attacked our left. His line moved up to within a hundred yards of ours and opened a heavy fire. This status was maintained for about half an hour. Then a part of Mott's division and Ward's brigade of Birney's division gave way and retired in disorder. The enemy under R. H. Anderson took advantage of this and pushed through our line, planting their flags on a part of the intrenchments not on fire. But owing to the efforts of Hancock, their success was but temporary. Carroll, of Gibbon's division, moved at a double quick with his brigade and drove back the enemy, inflicting great loss. Fighting had continued from five in the morning sometimes along the whole line, at other times only in places. The ground fought over had varied in width, but averaged three-quarters of a mile. The killed, and many of the severely wounded, of both armies, lay within this belt where it was impossible to reach them. The woods were set on fire by the bursting shells, and the conflagration raged. The wounded who had not strength to move themselves were either suffocated or burned to death. Finally the fire communicated with our breastworks, in places. Being constructed of wood, they burned with great fury. But

the battle still raged, our men firing through the flames until it became too hot to remain longer.[23]

William McFeely, in his excellent biography of the general, has remarked that, while it does not have Sherman's "flashes of fire" or Mary Chestnut's "lavish social detail," Grant's memoir is "wonderfully clear": "There is conciseness, totality, and strength, but what is perhaps most striking is the timeless quality of the prose. It has classical force."[24]

In any case, this Battle of the Wilderness might have been another Chancellorsville, that is, another Union defeat in which a superior Northern force had been hamstrung by a dense forest, blinding smoke, and superb Confederate fighting. As it was, the first day of battle was so chaotic that neither side was entitled to claim victory or could acknowledge defeat. In the burning woods, as Bruce Catton has observed,

> there was hardly one brigadier who could really control his own line, because there was hardly one brigadier who could put his hand on more than a fraction of his own command. The lines had been jumbled as they had never been jumbled before. Divisions and brigades were all divided. Along the zone of the heaviest fighting there was not a single regiment which had on either flank a regiment which so much as belonged to its own army corps.[25]

Grant spent most of the first day of the battle in the rear, at headquarters, whittling, trying to make sense of the confused reports reaching him and issuing commands that for one reason or another could not always be executed. Nobody could see for the smoke and dense woods. The number of Union dead and wounded was horrifying. The Confederate numbers were hardly better; and rebel General Longstreet had mistakenly been shot by his own troops. When Lee withdrew and Grant counted his casualties, he took to his tent and wept. He had every reason to see this disaster as the end of his career and the occasion for which Peace Democrats had been waiting, the pretext for an armistice that would give the Rebels the slaves and the political separation for which they had originally gone to war.[26]

Mary Chestnut, whose Civil War diary is a mine of Confederate information, wrote that "Grant don't care a snap if men fall like the leaves fall; he fights to win, that chap does. . . . He has the disagreeable habit of not retreating before irresistible veterans."[27] She was wrong about his concern for the wounded and the rebel veterans, but her remark about his refusal to retreat was right. Grant had learned at the battle of Fort Donelson, and again at Shiloh, that after a day of horrible fighting "both sides seemed defeated, and whoever assumed the offensive was sure to win."[28] After the first engagements of the Battle of the Wilderness, instead of withdrawing the Army of the Potomac into the North, as had been done after Chancellorsville, Grant roused his dispirited troops, took the offensive, turned them South, marched them toward another attack on Lee, and dealt the rebels a crushing blow. His dogged persistence had the effect of transforming defeat into a mere stage in the accomplishment of a telling victory.

Grant's victories not only saved the Union and preserved the unity of the United States as a political entity. They enforced in the most decisive way possible the authority of Lincoln's Emancipation Proclamation and permanently secured the freedom of American blacks. He would probably never have written the memoirs that describe these victories had not disastrous investments, later in life, threatened to ruin his family. The memoirs were completed as he was dying, facing the specter of bankruptcy, and the writing shows, toward the end, traces of his pain, his fatigue, and the morphine he was taking. But the work remains an essential record of Union military history. Grant died in 1885, shortly after completing it, and was eventually interred north of the Grand Army Plaza in New York City, in a marble tomb overlooking the Hudson River. William Tecumseh Sherman died six years later. At his funeral procession in New York City, attended by President Harrison and former presidents Hayes and Cleveland, one of the pallbearers was Confederate General Joseph E. Johnston. Although eighty-four years old, General Johnston refused to cover his head, as a mark of respect for Sherman, his old foe. He said that he knew Sherman would have done the same for him. A month later Johnston died of pneumonia. Sherman was buried in St. Louis, at the Calvary Cemetery, near his family.

Twain's Huck: Fresh Tears and Race Flapdoodle

> Persons attempting to find a motive in this narrative will be prosecuted; persons attempting to find a moral in it will be banished; persons attempting to find a plot in it will be shot. — BY ORDER OF THE AUTHOR PER G. G., CHIEF OF ORDNANCE.
> —Mark Twain, *Adventures of Huckleberry Finn*

Although Twain—or was it first-person narrator Huck?— issued the edict above, protesting (with remarkable prescience) the follies of the litcrit crowd, the discovery in 1991 of the lost half of the manuscript of *Adventures of Huckleberry Finn*—some 665 holograph pages in the hand of Samuel L. Clemens—has resulted in a flurry of new criminal activity. I shall have more to say about our current critical crimes and misdemeanors a bit later, since they deserve the punitive attention of G. G. For the moment, though, let me say that the manuscript discovery was one of those chance events in the literary world that electrify scholars who are always waiting for a big find. These recovered leaves represent an important new index to the operation of Twain's literary genius and a signal element in the genesis of an American classic. Even so, the patient work of scholarship is likely to be immediately eclipsed by the academic ideologists who are ingenious at finding new ways to falsify a literary work while beating the drum for some form of political correctness.

First, the manuscript. The always-known part of the manuscript of *Huck Finn* has since 1885 reposed in the Buffalo and Erie County Public Library in upstate New York. It was donated to the library by its then curator, James Fraser Gluck, who had asked Twain for the manuscript, much as we ask for autographs today. The author was quite flattered by the request and obliged by sending Gluck all the handwritten leaves he could find—the text of the last half of the novel. "I have hunted the house over, and that is all I can find," he told Gluck. The first half, he said, was probably "sent to the printers, who never returned it."[1]

Later Twain found the rest and sent it on. Gluck took it home to read and evidently forgot all about attaching it to the other half. In any case, the last half went to the library, and the delayed first half went into a trunk, which was passed down the family line and eventually inherited by two of Gluck's granddaughters in Los Angeles. It was they who recognized the find and asked Sotheby's to authenticate the manuscript and find a buyer and publisher. Library officials in Buffalo immediately objected to the sale of the fragment, claiming that the library was the true owner of the holograph and that, as the beneficiary of Gluck's gift, they were owed in effect an "overdue book." The Gluck heirs demurred. Then the Mark Twain Foundation, which holds rights to the intellectual content of Twain's writing and which has sponsored the impressive University of California edition of Twain's complete works, raised an objection to any infringement of *its* legal rights to the contents of the manuscript. Thanks to some some complicated negotiations, litigation over ownership rights was finally averted, and the two parts of the manuscript of *Huck Finn* have been reunited at the upstate library. Now the full manuscript text of the novel, newly published by Random House,[2] is ready for analysis. What does it tell us?

II

First, it indicates what we have always known—that Twain had poor judgment about good taste and felt obliged, in revision, to emend or to cancel some unsatisfactory scenes, sentences, and usages that were, or would have been, offensive to the readership he sought. Such blemishes he regarded as defects in the art of the novel, and he wanted them excised or changed. Some of the manuscript revisions are minor—such as the portrait of an overweight black woman at the Holy Roller camp meeting who, rapt in religious ecstasy, wants to smother whites with kisses but is repelled by them. Another involves the "House of Death" scene, where Huck and Jim find the murdered Pap in a house that has collapsed into the Mississippi River and is drifting southward. Victor Doyno, a Twain scholar at SUNY-Buffalo, wants us to believe that the manuscript indicates that Pap died in a one-woman brothel; but the argument is unconvincing. Another difference involves an episode about some raftsmen which Twain deleted from *Huck* and shifted to another book, *Life on the Mississippi*.

But the most striking difference between the new manuscript section and the novel as originally published is a three-page scene in which, during a storm of thunder and lightning, Huck and Jim leave the river and take cover in a cave. During the storm Jim tells Huck about his encounter with a true ghost. As Jim tells it, at the age of sixteen he had been ordered by his master, a young medical student, to go to the college and warm up a cadaver so that it could be dissected. Jim goes to the examining room in the dead of night, in a storm, to get the body ready, only to see the stiff begin to move its toes. Jim panics, the clammy corpse falls on him, and he bolts from the room, convinced that a ghost has assaulted him. Later the medical student dismembers the cadaver and derides Jim for his fear and superstition. The scene, in part, reads as follows:

> "Well, thinks I, I wisht I was out'n dis; what *is* gwyne to become er me?—en dis feller's a-movin' his toes, I *knows* it—I kin *see* 'em move—en I kin jis' feel dem eyes er his'n en see dat ole dumplin'head done up in de sheet, en—"
>
> "Well, sir, jis' at dat minute, *down he comes*, right a-straddle er my neck wid his cold laigs, en kicked de candle out!"
>
> "My! What did you do, Jim?"
>
> "Do? Well I never done nuffin'; only I jis' got up en heeled it in de dark. *I* warn't gwyne to wait to fine out what he wanted. No sir; I jis' split down stairs en linked it home a-yelpin' every jump."

"What did your Mars. William say?"

"He said I was a fool. He went dah en found de dead man on de flo' all comfortable, en took en chopped him up. Dod rot him, I wisht I'd a had a hack at him."[3]

Grisly and gothic, the tale is an instance of how the morbid and funereal could tickle Twain's dark humor. The scene adds nothing to the novel, which is really about Huck's adventures. In fact, it is an inset; it is an episodic digression—a vice common in Twain's tales. It deserved excision from the manuscript, and Twain rightly canceled it. But, against Twain's wishes, Random House has put it back.

One of the lawyers involved in the negotiations over the manuscript encouraged Daniel Menaker, an editor then at *The New Yorker*, to publish this ghost story in the issue of June 26, 1995. After Menaker moved to Random House, he struck a deal with the sometime litigants to publish both parts of the manuscript as *Adventures of Huckleberry Finn: A Comprehensive Edition*. Poor reproductions of some thirty pages of the manuscript illustrate the book; Justin Kaplan has provided a preface; and Victor Doyno has provided a running commentary on what the revisions seem to indicate.[4]

In my judgment this "comprehensive edition" should never have been published—at least with this subtitle. A facsimile of the manuscript would have been preferable. Failing that, a transcription of the manuscript, properly designated as such, so as to distinguish it from the 1885 authorized printed text of the novel, would have been acceptable. But the makers of this book—heirs, lawyers, foundation executives, publishers, and editors—were out for a quick buck, and in the process they were not above corrupting the text of an American classic—the novel that Twain approved and ushered into print. Before the book was published, Menaker remarked that "we could publish a revised standard edition of Huckleberry Finn that would also be sound and interesting from a scholarly viewpoint. . . . And we could subsequently use our Modern Library imprint to make a revised standard edition less expensively available."[5] Indeed they could have, but they did not. In presenting the new book Random House violated the principles of modern textual scholarship in editing. The canceled passages should have been relegated to an appendix as Twain's rejected substantives. They should not have been reinserted into the text—where there is only the slightest of typographical indications, a Scotch rule, to signal the insertions. In any case, the book cannot be substituted for the authorized 1885 edition; it cannot be used as the basis of sound literary criticism; and its release to the reading public could create a serious misunderstanding about what Twain finally intended to give us in *Huck Finn*. Moreover, if this text is later pirated or inexpensively reprinted without the foreword and afterword, readers will have no idea that what they are reading is not the text Twain authorized. In reinserting canceled readings into the text of the novel and calling the novel a "comprehensive edition," the makers of this book suggest that the novel we have always known is defective or partial. It is not. As a violation of Twain's aesthetic intention, it deserves the *oubliette*.[6]

To grasp the motive for this "modernization" of Twain's novel it is worthwhile to follow a little further the thinking of editor Daniel Menaker:

> ... when Twain set out to write this book he had something even darker and more satirical in mind: something that I now think of as the book he would have published if he were alive now—a *Huckleberry Finn* for the nineties, so to speak—because the constraints and limits that operated upon him when he was composing the book no longer exist in public discourse and publishing today. He could have shown a slave woman embracing whites. He could have made it more evident that Huck's father, pap Finn, died in a one-woman brothel. Both of these intentions, among many others, are clear in the manuscript and are presented and discussed in the new and comprehensive edition of the novel.[7]

Menaker's comments make it plain that the Random House edition of *Huck Finn* is to be preferred because it is supposedly more in harmony with the liberated sexual mores of the 1990s. The implication is that, in the 1880s, a false gentility prevented Twain from mentioning such things as bordellos or interracial sex, and so he was obliged to eliminate them from *Huck*. We of course are liberated, Menaker seems to say, and we can take more daring descriptions. This is nonsense. As a prospector and journalist in the West, Twain made it plain in books like *Roughing It* (1871) that frontier life thrived on the towns' ubiquitous saloons, gambling halls, and whorehouses. Furthermore, Twain's *Pudd'nhead Wilson* (1894) is a fully developed study of Southern miscegenation and its effects on the boys Tom and Chambers, one white and one black, who were switched in the cradle by the vengeful slave mother Roxy. Blood, race, sex, revenge—it is all there in Dawson's Landing.[8]

However, Twain knew that he needed—and indeed he regularly solicited—editorial advice about his manuscripts. As a result of his upbringing in the Old Southwest and his years lived out on the Nevada and California frontier, he grew up frankly coarse, sometimes irreverent, often profane, and occasionally beyond the pale of civilized discourse. He had what psychiatrists call poor impulse control and at times had little capacity for self-criticism. In the heat of composition he could go overboard without any thought of what a reader's response might be. He knew he was occasionally gross, did not want to be, and begged his wife Olivia and others to save him from his own lapses of taste and aesthetic judgment. Twain asked Mrs. Mary Fairbanks, a woman he had met on his expedition to the Holy Land, to point out offensive or overwrought passages in his manuscripts. William Dean Howells, his friend and editor at the *Atlantic*, was also enlisted to read and critique nearly every story in manuscript.[9]

Toward the beginning of his career he wrote to Olivia: "If you and Mother Fairbanks will only scold and upbraid me now and then, I shall fight my way through the world, never fear."[10] Livy was a sympathetic (yet critical) reader of his work. As Twain told F. M. White: "Ever since we have been married, I have been dependent on my wife to go over and revise my manuscript. . . . Not but that I can do the spelling and grammar alone—if I have a spelling-book and grammar with me—but I don't always know just where to draw the line in matters of taste. Mrs. Clemens has kept a lot of things from getting into print that might have given me a reputation I wouldn't care to have, and that I wouldn't have known any better than to have published."[11]

Is Menaker giving Twain a reputation that he did not care to have? I believe so. Twain needed editing, solicited it, and concurred with it whenever he crossed the line. Did this censorship (or rather self-censorship) repress his genius? Menaker thinks so, echoing Van Wyck Brooks, a young radical of the 1920s. Brooks reduced the

Victorian age to a Freudian nightmare of sexual repression, blasted Twain's America, and denounced Livy for her polished sense of propriety and decorum. Livy's motive in helping her husband was, Brooks argued, "to further him, not as an artist but as a popular success, and especially as a candidate for gentility. . . ."[12] There is no need to rehearse here the already familiar evidence adduced by Bernard DeVoto in *Mark Twain's America* (and by others) that simply demolished Brooks's extravagant claims.[13] The help that Mrs. Fairbanks, Howells, and Olivia gave to Twain hardly repressed his genius or suppressed his wit but was often, in fact, the playful occasion of it. Early on he confessed to his fiancée Livy, "I have got mother Fairbanks in a stew again. I named that lecture ['The American Vandal Abroad'] just for her benefit. And I sent her an absurd synopsis of it that I knew would provoke her wrath—& intimated that I was idling somewhat. I like to tease her because I like her so."[14] This, we should note, is bad-boy acting-out, just for the fun of it. But he continually clowned in even more engaging ways. Before I get to them, however, the reader must forgive me if I digress for a moment to discuss Twain's meticulous revisionary process in going over his manuscripts and his correction of printed page proofs. This digression will, I believe, make clear why Twain's so-called repression is misunderstood and why the Random House edition of the *Huck Finn* manuscript must be consigned to the wastebasket.

III

Early in his writing career, Twain's beloved daughter Susy wrote a biographical sketch of her father when she was about twelve, a sketch that—misspellings and all—gives a child's description of her father and mother's handling of "outrageous" scenes:

> Papa read *Huckleberry Finn* to us in manuscript, just before it came out, and then he would leave parts of it with mama to expergate, while he went off to the study to work, and sometimes [sister] Clara and I would be sitting with mama while she was looking the manuscript over, and I remember so well, with what pangs of regret we used to see her turn down the leaves of the pages, which meant that some delightfully terrible part must be scratched out. And I

remember one part pertickularly which was perfectly fascinating it was so terrible, that Clara and I used to delight in and oh, with what despair we saw mama turn down the leaf on which it was written, we thought the book would almost be ruined without it. But we gradually came to think as mama did.[15]

Susy was Twain's eldest daughter, his favorite. She was to die at age twenty-four of spinal meningitis, a death from which neither he nor Livy ever recovered. In his old age, with this passage before him and reflecting on what Livy and the children had meant to him while they were all young, Twain remarked on how the revisionary process had often devolved into a game. Here is Twain in his *Autobiography* commenting on Olivia's editorial "excisions."

> The children always helped their mother to edit my books in manuscript. She would sit on the porch at the farm and read aloud, with her pencil in her hand, and the children would keep an alert and suspicious eye upon her right along, for the belief was well grounded in them that whenever she came across a particularly satisfactory passage she would strike it out. . . . The passages which were so satisfactory to them always had an element of strength in them which sorely needed modification or expurgation, and was always sure to get it at their mother's hand. For my own entertainment, and to enjoy the protests of the children, I often abused my editor's innocent confidence. I often interlarded remarks of a studied and felicitously atrocious character purposely to achieve the children's delight to see the pencil do its fatal work. I often joined my supplications to the children's for mercy, and strung the argument out and pretended to be in earnest. . . . Now and then we gained the victory and there was much rejoicing. Then I privately struck the passage out myself. . . .[16]

Far from abandoning his creative intuition or sacrificing his art on the altar of Genteel Era respectability, Twain learned both to please himself and to please his reading audience. He accepted (or rejected) others' advice as he saw fit. Some works, like *Letters from the Earth* (1962), he withheld from publication as too irreligious and explosive. But once Twain had completed his text the way he wanted it, he was ruthless about anyone else's changing it. He grew up as a printer's devil, made a youthful living by setting type, and had inflexible ideas about the composition of the printed page. Extant instructions to his typesetters show that Twain would tolerate absolutely no printhouse changes in the setting copy—not even a change in a comma or semicolon. And he rained down some rather colorful curses and wild maledictions on any publisher or printer who tried to alter his text without his approval.

Further consideration of Twain's insistent and demanding conformity to the composition of his books may help us to put the Random House edition in its proper light and sustain the argument that copies of the book should be sent to the shredder as soon as possible. An instance of Twain's animosity to "inventive" or careless typesetters and to arrogant publishers is his complaint to his publisher Elisha Bliss, arguing that Bliss ought to take over the proofreading of *Innocents Abroad* because his recalcitrant compositor was "spiteful" and "infernally unreliable" in persistently misspelling words that Twain had corrected. "He never yet has acceded to a request of mine made in the margin, in the matter of spelling and punctuation, that I know of."[17] *The Prince and the Pauper* was so badly set and poorly corrected that Twain complained that "the proof-reading on the P & P cost me the last rags of my religion."[18] The typesetting of *Huck Finn*, however, at first seemed better than that of previous books, largely because Howells prepared two typescripts from the manuscript, and the compositors at J. J. Little's in New York City had an easier time in reading it. "Most of this proof" for *Huck Finn*, Twain told his nephew Charles Webster, the publisher, is "clean & beautiful, & a pleasure to read; but the rest of it was read by that blind idiot whom I have cursed so much, & is a disgraceful mess." Furthermore, he added, "If all the proofs had been as well read [by the proofreader] as the first 2 or 3 chapters were, I should not have needed to see the revises at all. On the contrary it was the worst & silliest proof-reading I have ever seen. It was never read by copy at all—not a single galley of it."[19]

Referring to the early packets of proof, Twain told Howells that the printers "don't make a very great many mistakes, but those that do occur are of a nature to make a man curse his teeth loose."[20] Eventually he exploded to Howells: "I am sending you these infernal Huck Finn proofs—but the very last vestige of my patience has gone to the devil, & I cannot bear the sight of another slip of them. My hair turns white with rage, at sight of the mere outside of the package."[21] Still, he kept on reading the proof-slips—correcting and revising, emending and perfecting the novel that we have heretofore so admired.

The point of these citations is that Twain gave close attention to his manuscript and to the proof-slips of *Huck Finn*. Given his rage at even the slightest deviation from the copy he had authorized for typesetting, there is really every reason to reject the Random House "improvement" of the novel and to continue to read the book in the 1885 text that Twain authorized.

IV

If not the Random House text, what edition of this novel should we read? The "standard version" of *Adventures of Huckleberry Finn* ought to have been volume eight of *The Works and Papers of Mark Twain*, edited by Walter Blair and Victor Fischer in 1985 for the University of California Press. (This edition was reprinted in an identical handy paperback volume in the Mark Twain Library, a series intended to saturate the market with scrupulously established texts of Twain's works.) Blair and Fischer were both experts in Twainiana, and this California edition promised to be the definitive edition forever. Unfortunately this text too is not without flaws. And its most egregious flaw involves—you guessed it!—the raftsmen passage. Like Bernard DeVoto in his 1942 edition of the novel, editor Fischer wrongly restored the canceled raftsmen passage on the ground that, in deleting the section, Twain "changed his mind *only* to accommodate the publisher's convenience—a decision roughly akin to accepting the publisher's censorship."[22] This argument won't do.

Twain's publisher (his nephew Charles Webster) recommended that *Huck* be shortened so that it could be sold by subscription in a matched set with *Adventures of Tom Sawyer*. (The title page of *Huck* describes him as "Tom Sawyer's Comrade.") This sales consideration was not a negligible matter to Twain. He had often been vitriolic about previous publishers' efforts to sell his books. He had even gone into the publishing business himself, with Webster, to minimize costs and maximize his sales. This was, in effect, a family business. With respect to subscription publishing, Twain knew what selling points were useful to his canvassers, or door-to-door salesmen, and he understood what appealed to homeowners who bought his books from such traveling agents. Producing a paired set of novels of matching length was a brilliant commercial suggestion that presented Twain with an engaging formal problem. He solved it by deleting the raftsmen passage. Doing so was hardly akin to suffering censorship, especially since the Webster publishing company was in effect Twain's own creation. Twain thus assented wholeheartedly to his nephew's suggestion. And since the raftsmen passage was merely a dispensable inset episode, he shifted it to *Life on the Mississippi* (1883), where it now belongs. Fischer's editorial decision is therefore open to serious objection. In fact the general editor of the Mark Twain Project, Robert H. Hirst, was obliged to remark that, since there is no evidence to document Fischer's supposition, it is "always possible that Mark Twain's intentions for his text just happened to coincide with his publisher's needs. . . ."[23] In my judgment they did indeed; they coincided in fact with Twain's own perceived needs. We stick, then, to the 1885 edition.

The help of advisers such as "Mother" Fairbanks, Olivia, and Howells, by the way, did not always save Twain from criticism on the ground of bad taste and vulgarity. When the novel was published, it was banned from the Concord, Massachusetts, library on the ground of its being "trash suitable only for the slums": "It deals with a series of adventures of a very low grade of morality; it is couched in the language of a rough dialect, and all through its pages there is a systematic use of bad grammar and an employment of rough, coarse, inelegant expressions."[24] All of this is quite true, but the complaint pales before the sheer imaginative power and linguistic genius of the writer.

V

But a more important question is whether *Huck Finn* should be read in any edition today. A great many of *our* contemporaries *also* say no. The ground of the complaint, however, has shifted. It is not bad grammar or inelegant expression that perturbs. Given the imperative of political correctness in racial matters now obtaining, the novel is nowadays regularly denounced as "racist trash." Every year brings one or another account of a school board or a library effort to ban it. As Peaches Henry has remarked, "Black protestors, offended by the repetitions of 'nigger' in the mouths of white and black characters, Twain's minstrel-like portrayal of the escaped slave Jim and of black characters in general, and the negative traits assigned to blacks, [have] objected to the use of *Huck Finn* in English courses."[25] The black teacher John Wallace has even called the novel "the most grotesque example of racist trash ever given our children to read. . . . Any teacher caught trying to use that piece of trash with our children should be fired on the spot, for he or she is either racist, insensitive, naive, incompetent or all of the above."[26]

No doubt some blacks *have* been wounded by the word "nigger" in *Huck Finn*. It is a term that, used as a slur, is patently racist and is meant to offer insult. During the O. J. Simpson murder case, the defense lawyers spent hours in impeaching the testimony of white Detective Mark Fuhrman, who claimed he had never used the word. The implication of the defense team was that anyone who had ever used the "N-word" (most of the lawyers were unwilling to say the word aloud in public) was not above planting evidence and framing a national sports hero.

But there is, it seems to me, a problem in the effort to banish "nigger" from the English language. Derived from *niger*, the Latin word for black entered Spanish and Portuguese (and thence English) as merely a word for a black person. In the long history of racial relations in this country, Southerners—with their customary difficulty in pronouncing the terminal *-er* sound, transposed it into a schwa and pronounced it "nigguh." (In this, their terminal phoneme perfectly corresponded to the Latin spelling.) This was, I believe, the universal Southern pronunciation of the word—certainly it was in my boyhood in the South a half-century ago. Other terms used by whites included "darkies" and, by both groups, "colored folks." After the post–World War II civil rights movement got under way and "nigger" was declared totally offensive, a great many educated Southern whites who wanted to be accommodating to blacks produced a genteel term supposedly more literate and inoffensive. It was pronounced something like "Nigra." Black activists were still not satisfied, however, and by the 1970s this too had to be scrapped for the then more inoffensive term "black." (We were, at that point, back to the etymological meaning of "Negro," but the source of the term had been lost to the activists, if they ever knew it.) Somewhat later, in the 1980s, perhaps to achieve linguistic parity with other ethnic groups like Franco- or Italo-Americans, the term "black" too had to be abandoned for "Afro-American." But by the 1990s this too had somehow come to seem demeaning and had to be scrapped—as Jesse Jackson insisted—for "African American."

I understand the bid for respect and the role of ethnic pride in this effort to control what whites call blacks. But the problematic element arises when we observe that "nigger" is a term commonly used amongst blacks in referring to each other, and it often expresses the deepest affection. I know the usual arguments about the self-hatred that ethnic minorities sometimes manifest in the presence of majority prejudice, but I do not believe that black use of the term is a case of a people's adopting the language of the oppressor—except, perhaps, when it is used as an insult. (In adopting its name, the black rap group Niggaz with Attitude has evidently embraced the insulting connotation as a badge of in-your-face defiance of white racism. The same may be said of the second album title of the recently murdered "gangsta rapper" Tupac Shakur: *Strictly 4 My N.I.G.G.A.Z.*)

Here it may be useful to remember the distinction made many years ago by the semanticist S. I. Hayakawa. In his persuasive analysis of linguistic usage in *Language in Action*, Hayakawa pointed out that some words can function either as an insult or an endearment. He called these words "snarl words" and "purr words." It is not their denotative content that is communicated but rather an attitude toward the hearer or reader.[27] "Nigger," when used in anger, derision, or contempt, is clearly an insult; but when used with affection or affability—as it has often been used by many blacks and whites over the years—it is a purr word. Twain knew this and used the term both ways. Blacks want to eliminate the term as an insult but preserve it (for themselves) as an endearment. But language—a powerful emotive instrument, for good or ill—simply does not yield to any group's ideological fiat. Ask the French Academy about *franglais*.

Was Twain a racist? For some black activists perhaps every white Southerner is a racist. And it is true that Twain's father and uncle owned slaves in Hannibal and Florida, Missouri. As a boy, Twain later wrote,

> I was not aware that there was anything wrong about it. No one arraigned it in my hearing; the local papers said nothing against it; the local pulpit taught us that God approved it, that it was a holy thing, and that the doubter need only look to the Bible to settle his mind—and then the texts were read aloud to us to make the matter sure; if the slaves themselves had any aversion to slavery, they were wise and said nothing. In Hannibal we seldom saw a slave misused, on the farm, never.²⁸

In his childhood he no doubt absorbed unconsciously the values of adults, and in maturity they were sometimes manifest as prejudice. Twain was no more consistent than most men and probably a good deal less, and, given his explosive temper, he was even capable of dismissing some blacks as "human vermin." This seems to be what Julius Lester resents in "Morality and *Adventures of Huckleberry Finn*." For him Hannibal was then and is now a racist town, and Twain's novel "demeans blacks and insults history." Lester even sympathizes with "those who want the book banned, or at least removed from required reading lists in schools."

But the reality is that the mature Twain's letters and notebooks, as well as the memoirs of those who knew him, show an ever-enlarging liberalism and a complete commitment to the well-being of blacks, even as he came to the point of railing at whites as "human muck," the scum of the earth. In his *Autobiography* he even said that, as a boy, he preferred the company of blacks to that of "the elect."

> All the negroes were friends of ours and with those of our own age we were in effect comrades. I say in effect, using the phrase as a modification. We were comrades; color and condition interposed a subtle line which both parties were conscious of and which rendered complete fusion impossible. . . . It was on the farm that I got my strong liking for his race [that of Uncle Dan'l, the model of Jim] and my appreciation of certain of its fine qualities. This feeling and this estimate have stood the test of sixty years and more, and have suffered no impairment. The black face is as welcome to me now as it was then.²⁹

Not only was *Huck Finn* a sustained attack on slavery, the portrait of Jim was also charged with personal affection and friendship. In fact the black critic Sterling Brown has said that, compared to other white authors' stereotypes of the black, Twain's Jim is a believable instance of the ordinary Negro slave in nineteenth-century fiction—illiterate, superstitious, yet hoping to be free, and full of love for his own people.[30] After the war Twain sponsored black students at Northern and Southern colleges because he held himself "responsible for the wrong which the white race had done the black race in slavery." Doing it was, he said, "part of the reparation due from every white to every black man."[31] His outrage at postwar Jim Crow racism equaled his detestation of prewar slavery, as essays like "Only a Nigger" (1869) and "The United States of Lyncherdom" (1901) will show. In fact Clemens's sympathy for blacks came to be so strong that Mrs. Clemens gave her husband a convenient rule of thumb for saving his temper—"Consider every man colored till he is proved white."[32]

One recent critical effort that ought to give some comfort to those who have been wounded by *Huck Finn* or who are dissatisfied with Twain's view of race is Shelley Fisher Fishkin's *Was Huck Black?* (1993). This is an engaging critical study that undertakes to explore the impact of black English on the novel. Professor Fishkin argues that "the model for Huck Finn's voice was a black child instead of a white one and that this child's speech sparked in Twain a sense of the possibilities of a vernacular narrator."[33] Is Huck's speech really "black English"? The idea deserves exploration, especially since Twain included in the novel an "Explanatory" making a claim, it is sometimes said, for his own dialectal versatility:

> In this book a number of dialects are used, to wit: the Missouri negro dialect; the extremest form of the backwoods South-Western dialect; the ordinary "Pike-County" dialect; and four modified varieties of this last. The shadings have not been done in a haphazard fashion, or by guess-work; but pains-takingly, and with the trustworthy guidance and support of personal familiarity with these several forms of speech.

Twain concludes: "I make this explanation for the reason that without it many readers would suppose that all these characters were trying to talk alike and not succeeding." Twain's comic "explanation" is part of the general hilarity of his satire on book-derived writing in a monotone style in which the human voice cannot be heard. But it has started a number of wild hares—mostly humorless professors of American speech and dialectology trying to demonstrate where each linguistic isogloss may be drawn.

Such efforts are of course doomed, but the "Missouri negro dialect" of Jim, and Professor Fishkin's claim for the formative effect of black English on *Huck Finn* raise another question newly relevant to the novel. And that is whether Jim's speech is a dialect of English, as Twain suggests, or whether black speech is even English at all. I raise this point because some black activists are now claiming that black English is a separate language. According to the Oakland, California, school board, in fact, black speech is really "Ebonics"—a language distinct from English.[34] The claim for this "genetically based" Ebonics language is its supposed origin in the syntax of Congo and West African languages. All of this might seem to be a joke, but Carolyn M. Getridge, the black Oakland school system superintendent, has put it decisively: "African Americans have a different language system."[35]

Where she got that notion has never been disclosed to linguistic science, and no student of languages has ever made such a claim. Needless to say, black students are stunned at being robbed of English, which they have heretofore regarded as their own language. The superintendent's evidence for "Ebonics" largely rests on some distinctive pronoun shifts, pronunciation variants in black English, alternate plurals, and deleted or nonstandard copulative or other verbs: *My brother he bigger than you mens. I axed him a question, but sometime he be too busy to answer. But he have a bike wif handlebars.* None of these usages, in fact, adds up to a distinctive non-English language. In fact, every one of these "black" locutions may be traced back to white Southern American (often mountain) speech. Even further back, they are traceable to the speech patterns of the English provincial counties in the sixteenth century, whence they and the American settlers who reflected them actually originated. Most of the cited instances of "Ebonics," in fact, are conservative (that is, old-fashioned and now outdated) oral-tradition noun or verb selections—e.g., those that once alternated between the Old English *beon* (be) and *wesan* (am, were). The Wessex novels of Thomas Hardy, for instance, suggest how common such usages have remained in the illiterate provincial speech of English farmers down to the twentieth century. The stylistic features of "black English" are in fact little different from the speech patterns (or language problems) of white farm boys I taught fifty years ago in South Carolina. Where did blacks learn such usages except from listening to their ill-read white coevals? And where indeed did such whites learn them, if not from black mammies, or nurses, housekeepers, and black playmates who had already picked them up? The claim that "Ebonics" is a separate language system is frankly nonsense perpetuated by militant race activists who have no knowledge of the historical development of the English language — a subject that, like linguistics, semantics, phonemics, and American dialects, is no longer required, it seems, of aspiring English teachers or school administrators. In other words, know-nothings in the educational system are now running the show.[36]

In any case, the black child who, according to Professor Fishkin, was the model for Huck was the "Sociable Jimmy," a very talkative and colorful black child about whom Twain wrote a sketch for the *New York Times* in 1874. This Jimmy was not, of course, the real model for Huck, for as Twain remarked in his *Autobiography*,

> In *Huckleberry Finn* I have drawn Tom Blankenship exactly as he was. He was ignorant, unwashed, insufficiently fed; but he had as good a heart as any boy had. His liberties were totally unrestricted. He was the only really independent person—boy or man—in the community, and by consequence he was tranquilly and continuously happy, and was envied by all the rest of us. We liked him, we enjoyed his society. And as his society was forbidden us by our parents, the prohibition trebled and quadrupled its value, and therefore we sought and got more of his society than of any other boy's.[37]

Professor Fishkin knows that Blankenship was the model, so her claim for black Jimmy is a transparent exaggeration. But she has something else in mind. She wishes to conduct an extended argument—an unimpeachable one, in my view—that the language in *Huck* and other vernacular novels of white American writers has in fact been shaped and formed by black speech. Indeed it has. The speech of all who speak or write English has been changed by the influence of black English. And her book is a splendid scholarly elaboration of the evidence that, as Ralph Ellison once put it, "the black man [was] a co-creator of the language that Mark Twain raised to the level of literary eloquence."[38] But the satisfaction of *Huckleberry Finn*'s having been co-created out of the richness of black English is unlikely to pacify race militants, who have a natural interest in perpetuating white guilt while eradicating the last vestiges of racism. Nor will it content those whose feelings are automatically wounded by the word "nigger," even if blacks themselves frequently use it in forms of affectionate address. As long as this situation continues to be the case, *Adventures of Huckleberry Finn* will remain controversial.

VI

The substitution of controversy—any controversy—for questions of style and form, art and method, is a sign of the time. Hence it is no surprise that Gerald Graff has now popped up again to beat the dead horse of ideological criticism. Graff is that hopelessly PC academic who is always urging teachers to give up teaching literature and instead substitute "teaching the conflicts about literature."[39] In the present case, Graff has prepared a new classroom edition of *Huck Finn* for the sole purpose of smothering it—and the students—with a collection of argumentative essays by academic critics on a variety of sociological issues applied to the novel.[40] Only a few of these essays deal with the novel as such, and these old chestnuts—some readings by T. S. Eliot, Lionel Trilling, and Leo Marx—are devoted only to the ending of the book. They are a sop to readers who might be interested in the art of fiction, but they are so out of date that one assumes that there is nothing original to be said about Twain's art in our time.

Graff's real objective is indicated in section headings such as "The Controversy over Race: Does *Huckleberry Finn* Combat or Reinforce Racist Attitudes?" and "The Controversy over Gender and Sexuality: Are Twain's Sexual Politics Progressive, Regressive, or Beside the Point?" Both of these rubrics and nearly all the essays published under them are extraliterary and therefore beside the point, but Graff's book is additional evidence that classrooms, curricula, conventions, and textbooks have now been taken over by the proponents of one or another radical ideology. The purpose of this series—despite the editors' apparent stance of disinterested observation—is not to elicit student discussion of *Huck Finn* as a work of art (which is the only reason for being interested in it). The series is really intended to help teachers flush out and condemn crypto-aesthetic, racist, patriarchal, sexist, or homophobic elements in literature, criticism, and student thought. The intent is thus to inculcate in students a "progressive" viewpoint. This much becomes evident in the editors' admission that

> Teaching by controversy accords in spirit with the revisionist impulses underlying attempts both to create a broader and more inclusive canon and to develop new theoretical approaches to literature. We identify ourselves with those working to revise the canon, and we regard the new approaches to literature—approaches that stress issues of race, gender, class, sexuality, and power—as a very positive force, not least because they have aroused controversy.[41]

In consequence of this politicization of letters, the editors give transparent prominence to arguments about the evils of patriarchal culture, gender as a social construction, the insensitivities of the Victorian past, and the friendship of Huck and Jim as a manifestation of homosexual attraction.

Readers of this "boy's book"—which has very few women characters (Miss Watson, Aunt Polly, the Wilks girls, and Mrs. Phelps among them)—will be surprised at how *Huck Finn* too can be ransacked to manufacture the usual feminist complaints against men. Nancy A. Walker, in "Reformers and Young Maidens: Women and Virtue in *Adventures of Huckleberry Finn*," complains that "the women in *Huck Finn*, viewed from the male perspective of the novel, are finally powerless—as Aunt Sally Phelps demonstrates—to change the adolescent dreams of the American male." This, in a word, seems to be what feminist literature teachers are up to nowadays—trying to alter the young American male. (I, for one, hope that the young American male will continue to dream his own dreams and resist any such coercive social engineering.) But Ms. Walker goes further. She remarks that "by accepting the limited roles for women that his culture promoted, Twain effectively limits the extent to which Huck Finn can be a moral force in his society."[42]

Huck—a moral force in his society? The bad boy who smokes, skips school, scoffs at religion, lies prodigiously, and lifts the occasional chicken that warn't roostin' comf'tably? The notion is risible but not to the earnest and humorless Ms. Walker. Such a view of *Huck Finn* requires yet another digression, this time on the subject of Twain's moral intention.

Trying to turn Huck into a moral exemplar of the kind proposed by Ms. Walker has misled a great many inattentive critics. Some years ago, in "Why *Huckleberry Finn* Is a Great World Novel," Lauriat Lane put the best case for Huck's moral function.

> *Huckleberry Finn* also gains its place as a world novel by its treatment of one of the most important events of life, the passage from youth into maturity. The novel is a novel of education. Its school is the school of life rather than of books, but Huck's education is all the more complete for that reason. Huck, like so many other great heroes of fiction—Candide, Tom Jones, Stephen Dedalus, to mention only a few—goes forth into life that he may learn. One of the central patterns of the novel is the progress of his learning.[43]

But does Huck indeed learn? Does he morally develop? Does he pass from youth into maturity? And is his education really the more complete because he cannot read books? And is he really a moral force? Is he the spokesman, for example, for the right moral position on slavery? Lane said yes, but he and other such readers do not seem to notice that, in declining to turn in Jim and go to hell instead, Huck does the right thing but for the wrong reason. He explains his decision as in fact the morally wrong thing to do, the consequence of *his* being evil, not those who perpetuate or justify slavery, of *his* not a-goin' to church, of his consorting with low-down abolitionists and nigger-stealers:

> It was awful thoughts, and awful words [his saying "All right, then, I'll go to hell"], but they was said. And I let them stay said; and never thought no more about reforming. I shoved the whole thing out of my head; and said I would take up wickedness again, which was in my line, being brung up to it, and the other warn't.[44]

Huck himself, as this passage makes plain, has little capacity for moral reflection. He is in fact less a plausible moral agent than a narrative device for transparently reflecting social evils that youth and inexperience cannot intellectually or morally grasp. Critics like Lane also made much of Huck's wish to light out for the territories, as if he were a sixties existential hero, say, Susan Sontag, in moral reaction against "the barbarity of white American civilization." Huck is hardly that. Twain has created here a perpetual *naif* who cannot even tell when he is being conned by a circus "drunk" or by the Duke of Bilgewater. At the end of the novel Huck wants to go west with Tom and Jim, but what for? To escape, a la Rousseau, the corruptions of civilization? Hardly. Resistance to "sivilization," for Huck, comes down to a protest against getting his ears washed and his hair combed all to hell, getting sent to school, and told not to smoke or lie around in filthy hogsheads. His are *infantile* registers of protest. What Tom and Huck, perennial bad boys, really long for is "howling adventures amongst the Injuns, over in the Territory, for a couple of weeks or two"[45] — adventures like "ambuscading" the Sunday School picnic in Chapter 1. That the boys never mature as moral beings, never in fact grow up, is shown by Twain's continual recycling of them in *Tom Sawyer Abroad* (1894), *Tom Sawyer, Detective* (1896), and the posthumously published *Huck Finn and Tom Sawyer among the Indians and Other Unfinished Stories* (1989). The comedy of these stories, in fact, usually arises from Huck's *not* understanding what the reader can see through.

In any case, let us return to the feminist argument. In the Judith Loftus episode, where Huck dresses like a girl to get some news about the slave catchers pursuing them, Twain creates broad comedy out of the farce of cross-dressing. The spectacle of males in female clothing or females in male clothing has been the source of guffaws since the days of Aristophanes. And why not? It is patently *contra naturam*, and all such aberrations from the norms of sexual difference between men and women are grist for satire. But for the humorless Myra Jehlen in "Reading Gender in *Adventures of Huckleberry Finn*," the Loftus episode is made to prove—guess what?— that a girl *is* what a girl *does*, that gender is a matter of nurture, not nature. Twain is even said to have attained "a clear understanding that gender is a matter of ideology."[46] If so, this realization must put Twain at least a century before his time and will make him the true contemporary of Bella Abzug, a congressperson he would have found infinitely amusing.

The fact is that scenes of sexual impersonation are ancient comic devices and can hardly be used as evidence of Twain's lucubrations on gender. Twain in reality pinched the Loftus scene from Chapter 65 of his friend Charles Reade's *The Cloister and the Hearth* (1861), where the medieval libertine Gerard brings aboard ship on the Tiber a beauty introduced as "Marcia," who is really a man in drag. Suspicious, another woman tosses some almonds into the lap of Marcia, who claps her knees together: "Aha! you are caught, my lad. . . . 'Tis a man; or a boy. A woman still parteth her knees to catch the nuts the surer in her apron; but a man closeth his for fear them shall fall between his hose." Twain probably also knew G. P. R. James's *One in a Thousand* (1836), as Walter Blair has remarked, in which a girl masquerading as a page is discovered when she spreads her knees to catch a jackknife tossed into her lap.[47]

But even more egregious than a feminism that produces the same old complaints against men—this time using *Huck Finn* as the stick to beat them—is the identity politics of the new homosexual activists. This brand of sexual politics is positively commended by editors Graff and Phelan, who choose to print in their collection Christopher Looby's "'Innocent Homosexuality': The Fiedler Thesis in Retrospect." Older readers may remember that in 1948 Leslie Fiedler—in a provocatively entitled essay—advanced the then-revolutionary (if really ridiculous) idea that the friendship of Huck and Jim expressed a latent (and therefore "innocent") biracial homosexuality.[48] That is, although the boy and the slave never engaged in sodomy, fellatio, "fisting," or other perverse homosexual acts, Huck and Jim are claimed to be "homoerotic" in feeling for one another. Are they? Only someone with a Freudian bee in his bonnet could think so. The Fiedler thesis sexualized mere friendship and largely ignored the fact that Huck is prepubescent and Jim a married man who grieved at the slavemaster's separation of him from his wife and who mourned the death of his little girl. But Freudian Fiedler was nothing if not totalizing. He in fact called *all* classic American literature not merely averse to representations of heterosexuality but predisposed to embody true affectional feeling in latent homosexuals of different races. Aside from Huck and Jim, Fiedler instanced Leatherstocking and Chingachgook and Ishmael and Queequeg. I cannot remember whether he also "outed" the Lone Ranger and Tonto or Cosby and Culp.[49]

But time has caught up with poor Fiedler, once the sexual revolutionary and all-time bad boy of American literary criticism.

In the Graff–Phelan collection he is now savaged by Looby as a gay-baiting homophobe whose use of the phrase "innocent homosexuality" implies that genital homosexuality isn't. Of course it isn't. But Looby is one of those academic propagandists who wants readers to think that homosexuality—rather than a sexual perversion (and in many places still a crime)—is simply a different "lifestyle choice," like a preference for Clairol shampoo and black leather pants. Despite deep transcultural taboos against homosexuality extending over many millennia, not to speak of moral prohibitions expressed in every major religion, for Looby homosexuality is by its very nature "innocent." Others will regard it as degradingly compulsive, an instrument of suicidal contagion, and, especially when it involves a child the age of Huck, a moral monstrosity. I should imagine that black readers who are well disposed toward *Huck Finn* would be incensed at the claim that Jim is really a pederast after all.

In any case, Fiedler called the friendship "innocent" and so is accused of "dishonesty," "incoherence," "queer-hating," and "paranoia." But it gets even worse. Looby even has the pertinacity to revive the discredited claim that, because some prospectors in the West often had to share a room or even a bed, "Twain's relationships with his intimate male friends may well have had an erotic dimension."[50] For such a claim there is zero evidence, and it is stupefying to see it advanced in an academic book from St. Martin's Press. But there is much counterevidence that Twain was fully heterosexual, loved his wife Livy, enjoyed their sex life with exuberant gusto, and thought less of the Christian idea of heaven because souls there are bodiless and are not given in marriage. The coarse propagandists for homosexuality that have tried to "out" Twain have been thoroughly ridiculed by Twain scholars steeped in the biographical record.[51] But it is a measure of the publishing world and the academic scene today that, if Graff and Phelan have their way, students will now be obliged to read (and then discuss aloud in class) the dubious claims made by the apologists for homosexual perversion, radical feminism, and other politically correct ideologies rather than concentrating on the art of the novel.

Is this an overreaction to Gerald Graff's wanting to manufacture a controversy so as to inculcate gay values in the classroom? I do not think so. As homosexual activist Michael Swift has promised,

"We will sodomize your sons, and seduce them in your schools. [They] will become our minions and be recast in our image," for "we are the natural aristocrats of the human race. We shall conquer the world, and live according to the dictates of pure imagination." Swift promises that "Our exquisite society will be governed by an elite who will indulge the Greek passion," and "the family unit, which only dampens the imagination, will be eliminated."[52] Of course this is all gay twaddle, the merest perversity self-exposed by its own ridiculous rhetorical posturing. It is also a travesty to human intelligence. But university classrooms today are full of such teachers, suggesting that it is time, after all, to call in G. G.—not Gerald Graff but rather Twain's G. G.

VII

While we await G. G.'s arrival, we can sit back with *Adventures of Huckleberry Finn* itself, a wonderful boy's book of hair-raising adventure that still appeals even in maturity. The earliest attraction evolves into the adult appeal when life makes it clear to us that interwoven into the broad comedy is a stinging satire on everything that properly roused Twain's ire. If the novel has trouble keeping its focus on the friendship of Huck and Jim, the reason is Twain's preference for a structure of changing satirical episodes, each a chapter or two long, that are strung together, in no particular order, like beads on a string. The episodic structure allowed Twain to jump from folly to folly in exposing what he would later come to call the "damned human race" living along the river. One of these follies was religious sentimentality and ignorant superstition of the kind seen at the camp meeting. Another was mob cowardice. Yet another folly was the Victorian appetite for romance literature —the kind of man-in-the-iron-mask fiction that Tom reads in order to spring Jim from busted-heart captivity, or the kind of sentimental verse that Emmeline Grangerford writes in funereal poems like "Ode to Stephen Dowling Bots, Dec'd." *Huck Finn* is in fact an all-round guffaw at the vice, folly, gullibility, and pretension of vain human beings.

Juxtaposed against the ranting illiteracy and racism of the underclass such as Pap Finn, the blind social complacency of Miss Watson and such middling families as the Thatchers, and the bogus aristocracy of well-to-do Southerners such as Colonel Grangerford and the Shepherdsons is the friendship of the white boy and the black slave. The novel's central movement is not their drift southward into deep slave territory but the oscillation of Huck and Jim between the raft and the shore. It is an oscillation between a world of violence—represented by the bounty hunters, slave catchers, con men, fake preachers, roving gangs, and feuding families—and a world of peace, freedom, and friendship—represented, for these two outcasts, by the river and the raft.[53]

Twain could not hold on to the pastoral simplicity of this interracial friendship because he was too indignant at other aspects of human folly, and, as a professional humorist, he would always sacrifice anything solemn if he thought he could get a good laugh. But just for a moment at the center of that book, and flickeringly if not fully realized, *Adventures of Huckleberry Finn* called into being a dream of personal virtue and human possibility that makes all academic palaver about literary controversies an inessential distraction—what Huck calls mere "tears and flapdoodle."

Pride and Shame: The Winning of the West

Ken Burns's several films for television—*The Civil War, Baseball*, and, most recently, *Lewis and Clark: The Corps of Discovery*—have evidently reignited interest in the film documentary as a genre and turned our history into the stuff of public television. In making these films, Burns has given the National Endowment for the Arts something to cheer about, and PBS stations can now offer something more substantial than lavish adaptations of British novels of manners or Agatha Christie mysteries. There have of course been other American historical documentaries devoted to the West, for instance *In Search of the Oregon Trail*, narrated by Stacy Keach and recently aired by a number of PBS stations. But it is my impression that these are relatively low-budget items, at least insofar as publicity and advertisement are concerned. Burns, however, knows how to write grants and raise money, to use arresting photographic images, and to merchandise and advertise successful film productions about the American historical experience.

In producing these television programs, Burns assembled a talented crew of filmmakers, and one of them, the director Stephen Ives, launched out on his own and in 1996 offered his own TV production called *The West*.[1] This program was a set of TV shows, totaling more than twelve and a half hours of video, exploring the American West through diaries, letters, journals of exploration,

Pride and Shame: The Winning of the West

newspaper records, government documents, and first-person narratives of what it was like to venture into, explore, and try to settle the American West. Not omitted from these programs was an account of the oral testimony of some of the Native Americans who were here at the time and who tried without success to repulse the white immigrant settlers. Its distinction is such that *The West* will doubtless be shown on cable TV for many years to come and will probably even be picked up for in-school instruction. A book, based on its script, is already in print.[2]

Ken Burns's *Lewis and Clark: The Corps of Discovery* is less voluminous: its subject—the Western expedition of Meriwether Lewis and William Clark (1804–1806)—fills only two cassettes. But this is partly to be explained by the fact that there are no photographs or movies of the West from the time of the great exploration—and no moving pictures! Still, the series exhibits a great many original manuscripts; oil paintings of important personae; photographs of the still spectacular landscape; drawings of vast herds of buffalo and longhorn cattle; interesting examples of Indian regalia; and many other such artifacts. These are also conveniently complemented by the book that accompanies the cinematic production.[3]

"The West" is a flexible notion that has meant different areas at different times and places in the colonial and federal history of this nation. The early Puritans in the sixteenth century thought of points beyond the Connecticut River Valley as the West. Further south (and somewhat later on), the West meant anything beyond the Alleghenies. But by "the West" these videos signify that area of more than two million square miles west of the Mississippi, much of it acquired through Jefferson's purchase of the Louisiana Territory from France, and the rest, like Texas and California, acquired from Spain or, like the Oregon Territory, from Great Britain. This is the region first explored by Lewis and Clark, who were commissioned by President Thomas Jefferson in 1803 to traverse the region and to report back to the nation about the vast tract of the unknown that stretched all the way to the Pacific Ocean.

Although Burns's *The Corps of Discovery* (1997) was filmed after Ives's *The West* (1996), it will be useful to discuss it first since the Lewis and Clark expedition was really a preliminary to everything that later happened in the settlement of the West. Burns deals with the West as it was between 1804 and 1806; Ives's *The West* covers the region from about 1820 to 1890, when the frontier was officially closed. Moreover, since these two directors worked so closely together and even shared a scriptwriter, there is a harmony of viewpoints, perspectives, and cinematic techniques that makes these different film treatments virtually interchangeable. Much could be said, by the way, about the brilliance of their film methods, the sequence and pacing of the narratives, the stunning use of color, camera angles, juxtapositions, montage effects, and so on. But it is their politically correct conception of Western American history that most interests me. For this is the view of the West that will be perpetuated in the popular culture, on cable TV, and in public-school history classes for some time to come.

II

The first deep probe by American whites into the interior of the West was the Lewis and Clark expedition of 1804–1806. Jefferson had commissioned these captains to map the region, to note its topography, mountains, rivers, lakes, streams, soil, flora and fauna, mineral ores, volcanic activity, climate, and the like. He also wanted them to make an ethnographic record of the various Indian tribes they encountered, to record their languages, laws, customs, domestic accommodations, and their occupations in respect to hunting, fishing, and agriculture. Jefferson urged them "to acquire what knolege you can of the state of morality, religion & information among them, as it may better enable those who endeavor to civilize & instruct them, to adapt their measures to the existing notions & practices of those on whom they are to operate."[4] Manifest in Jefferson's charge was the belief that there really did exist a navigable waterway, or a "Northwest Passage," to the Pacific that would open up to America the trading wealth of the Orient. The dream of Columbus, in other words, was still alive.

Heading out with a party of nearly fifty men, a river barge, and several small vessels, Lewis and Clark left St. Louis in May 1804. By the time they reached Fort Mandan, Meriwether Lewis observed in his journal:

> This little fleet altho' not quite so rispectable as those of Columbus or Capt. Cook, were still viewed by us with as much pleasure as

those deservedly famed adventurers ever beheld theirs; and I dare say with quite as much anxiety for their safety and preservation. we were now about to penetrate a country at least two thousand miles in width, on which the foot of civilized man had never trodden; the good or evil it had in store for us was for experiment yet to determine, and these little vessels contained every article which we were to expect to subsist or defend ourselves. however, as the state of mind in which we are, generally gives the colouring to events, when the immagination is suffered to wander into futurity, the picture which now presented itself to me was a most pleasing one. enterta[in]ing as I do, the most confident hope of succeeding in a voyage which had formed a da[r]ing project of departure as among the most happy of my life. The party are in excellent health and sperits, zealously attached to the enterprise, and anxious to proceed; not a whisper of murmur or discontent to be heard among them, but all act in unison, and with the most perfict harmony.[5]

Following the Missouri River westward to what is now the state line separating Missouri and Kansas, Lewis and Clark then paddled northward, ascending the Missouri as far as the confluence of the Platte River and Council Bluffs. They then proceeded upward along what is now the Iowa-Nebraska state line. Continuing to follow the Missouri northwestward, Lewis and Clark then reached the plains of what is now South Dakota and then moved northward, passing along the route (and sometimes naming) waterways such as the White, Teton, Cheyenne, Cannonball, and Heart rivers. Bad weather and subzero temperatures obliged them to dig in near the site of present-day Bismarck, North Dakota, where they built a fort and wintered alongside the Mandan Indian tribe. In the spring of 1805 they resumed their westward course, following the Missouri to its headwaters, then crossing over the Rocky Mountains, traversing the Cascade range, and finally descending the Salmon, Snake, and Columbia rivers to the Pacific Ocean.

In the course of the journey, Lewis and Clark and their men endured perilous encounters with unforgiving nature in the wild rapids that sometimes overturned their boats and occasionally ruined their supplies. All too often they had to resort to portage, that is, carrying their boats and supplies around sections of a river that were too shallow, rocky, or obstructed by debris. Obliged to hunt for food, they also risked death in unknown forests filled with wildcats and fearfully huge, virtually unkillable grizzlies. They sometimes were at risk on vast plains swept by hundreds of thousands of thundering buffalo or raging prairie wildfires. They were caught out in brutal hailstorms or sudden blizzards, and they suffered inhumanly cold temperatures theretofore unknown in Europe or America. The exploration party suffered near-starvation, dysentery, various viral and bacterial infections, hunting accidents, dental abscesses, rashes, boils, cancers, and broken bones. These they treated as well as they could. Finally, they had many a dangerous confrontation with savage Indian tribes well known for treacherous behavior, river piracy, and territorial belligerence. There was simply no ignoring the scalps that hung from the belts of the Indians they encountered. But the expedition survived —with the loss of only one man, a victim of illness.

Lewis and Clark finally arrived at the Pacific near Haley's Bay in what is now Washington State in November 1805, some eighteen months after their departure from St. Louis. Clark recorded the happiness of his men in his journal: "Great joy in camp we are in *view* of the *Ocian*, this great Pacific Octean which we have been so long anxious to See. and the roreing or noise made by the waves brakeing on the rockey Shores (as I suppose) may be heard disti[n]ctly." But, as happy as they were, they still had to get back home. And in 1806 they commenced their return to St. Louis. Although they came back by a somewhat different route, they ran the same risks and suffered some of the same ailments and illnesses that had afflicted them before. Needless to say, those back East who first encountered Lewis and Clark and their men "acknowledged themselves much astonished in seeing us return. they informed us that we were supposed to have been lost long since, and were entirely given out by every person &c."[6] Theirs was a heroic enterprise in physical exploration that turned these men into national heroes. On the journey they discovered some 178 plants and 122 New World animals never before known to science. And their account of the geography, weather, natural resources, and modes of Indian life opened a door to westward migration that forever changed the character of the American nation.

Permeating *The West* and *Lewis and Clark* is a nostalgia for the

Pride and Shame: The Winning of the West

simplicities of primitive life that strikes a distinctive anti-Western ideological note. Burns, for instance, complains that

> to our great disappointment, much of what Lewis and Clark saw we can no longer see. Progress has eliminated or diminished or obscured many of the pristine views that had challenged the vocabularies of the awestruck explorers as they struggled to describe the sublime works of nature they stumbled across at every bend in the river.[7]

Progress, Burns makes clear, is a doubtful commodity. This is apparent in his aesthetic complaint at a loss of photographic opportunities because power lines ruined the camera image, or a hydroelectric dam uglified the scene, or a "homesteader's attempt at Manifest Destiny" spoiled the virgin world Lewis and Clark knew. And if there are not a lot of modern people around to muck it up, Burns finds the alternative even more sinister: "Often our only company out on the dusty dirt tracks of the prairie were the ominous black vehicles of the military men who service the hundreds of missile sites now dotting the land Lewis and Clark had first claimed for the United States."[8] Another observer might have seen the discovery, exploration, and development of America—and her forthright intention to defend herself—as something to be grateful for. But not Burns. The fact is that the individual is now much safer in the West than at any previous time known to man. This is thanks to the advent of civilization, which brought with it the rule of law. The rule of law eventually came to replace the rule of force—the law of the jungle that had since time immemorial characterized Native American life in the West. As to the so-called "claim" of the American nation to the land, the claim was perfectly legal: the land was acquired by purchase from France. But Burns always panders to the politically correct sentiments of the moment: Green is in; industrial development is out. Pacifism is in; nuclear self-defense is out. Indian squatters are in; legal purchase by contract is out. Burns even goes so far as to pander to Native American superstitions in suggesting that "the grandfather spirit" of the landscape was what "pulled us along and gave us images of great beauty and experiences and emotions we will never forget."[9] Since the journals of the expedition of Lewis and Clark rank very high in the literature of exploration before the advent of Western civilization, I commend them as an essential counterweight to the distinctly romantic and slanted book and film productions that are my subject here.

Two of the most reprehensible forms of political correctness in public discourse today involve ethnicity and gender. Women, accordingly, must always be claimed as equal to men (if not superior to them), despite any evidence to the contrary; and each minority group must be celebrated as equal in every respect to every other group, even if gross exaggeration or falsehood is required to sustain the fiction. The film of *Lewis and Clark: The Corps of Discovery*, as well as its book, shamelessly exaggerates the role of women in the expedition, and it hopelessly distorts the reality of Native American life in the West during the nineteenth century. The gross falsification begins with Dayton Duncan's "Introduction" to the book:

> They [Lewis and Clark] carried the most modern weapons of their time, but in their two moments of greatest need, women would intervene on their behalf; and time and time again, they would be saved by the kindness of strangers.
>
> They told people who had been occupying the land for hundreds of generations that the West now belonged to someone else; yet they would meet more as friends than enemies, and only once fire their guns in anger.[10]

These paragraphs contain some of the most striking perversions of fact in the Lewis and Clark materials. Let us discuss, first of all, "the kindness of strangers." This remark suggests that Native Americans were all a pacific and kindly people, perhaps like "the gentle Tasadays."[11] The fact is quite otherwise. Each Indian tribe was an insular and territorial group devoted to maintaining itself through the destruction (or at least the pacification by threat and intimidation) of its enemies. A tribe's enemies were other Native American tribes. Wealth, power, and glory were conferred as a result of prowess in battle. The most successful killers secured the admiration of the tribe. Battle trophies, in the form of human scalps, were worn at the belt or were mounted as tepee decorations. Human heads, those of defeated enemies, were routinely impaled on poles around the Indian campsite. Whites were simply one more enemy tribe, one with a lighter skin.

It is quite true that most of the Indians encountered by Lewis and Clark did not offer them violence. There are three reasons for this. The first is the skin color of the explorers. Whites were an oddity, especially as Lewis and Clark went deeper into the continent. Yet, paradoxically, the skin color of the one black man on the expedition—Clark's personal servant York—commanded more Indian puzzlement than the white man's. The journals show the bemused Indians trying to wash off York's black skin, convinced that he was covered with bear grease, dye, or war paint. And I am afraid that the whites told the Indians a number of whoppers about York's violent capacities in order to keep them in line. Clark observed at one point: "These Indians wer much astonished at my Servent, they never Saw a black man before, he Carried on the joke and made himself more turribal than we wished him to doe."[12] But whites were not an absolute rarity, except in the Rockies area. Various white trappers had ascended the major Midwestern rivers in the decades preceding Lewis and Clark. They were mostly French Canadian or Spanish, so some of the Indians knew some things about white men. Moreover, along the Pacific Coast, Indians knew a few white seamen from vessels that had landed and traded along the coastline and in the immediate interior regions. This was at least inferred by Lewis and Clark from the tattoos and trinkets that the Indians proudly showed off. Yet it was not so much the rarity of white men or their pale skins that intrigued the Indians; it was their powerful "medicine." Whites brought a superior knowledge of how things worked and how to live in the world. So superior were explorers to the locals that natives often thought of them as gods. Indians regularly took their sick to Lewis and Clark in the full confidence they would get superior medical treatment. And, although primitive by modern standards, it worked.

The second reason for treating Lewis and Clark and their men peacefully is that Indians were traders and wanted the material goods that white men would bring—fabric for clothing, tobacco, weapons, metals, unusual seeds, even mirrors and gewgaws, and so forth. Most of the chiefs did not want to kill the goose that laid the golden egg, even if some of their braves did.

The third reason for the tolerance of Lewis and Clark is that they made it perfectly clear that they were superior *warriors*. These whites were dealing with violent societies, with tribes that regularly undertook to destroy each other. Only the winter weather prevented war parties from their incursions. Once it warmed up, in April and May, armed groups regularly went out in search of each other with genocide in mind. The women and children of slain enemies were either killed or taken captive. If taken captive, they were usually tortured, always enslaved, and frequently sold as slaves to others. Violence was a natural way of life with Native Americans, and it is a shameless lie to present them as friendly and pacific to the white strangers. This is Rousseauist nonsense. As historian Francis Parkman dryly remarks in *A Half-Century of Conflict* (1892), "the benevolent and philanthropic view of the American savage is for those who are beyond his reach. It has never yet been held by any whose wives and children have lived in danger of his scalping-knife."[13]

Lewis and Clark made it apparent to these Indians that if any violence was offered to them, the consequences would be dreadful. Each time the whites came upon a new tribe, whether they were threatened or not, they immediately brought out their weapons. They made plain to these Native American warriors their own superior firepower. Especially convincing was their demonstration of cannon. Firing off a few rounds of cannon, the swivel gun, or the "pop gun" was usually sufficient to show Indians that it would be folly to threaten or take up arms against these whites, who otherwise had perfectly peaceful intentions. Nothing restrains the temptation to violence—even in Indians taught to go on the warpath and kill their enemies—so much as the certain knowledge of their own death. Of course the tribes could, at any time, have destroyed all the whites who ever came into the West—if only they had joined forces to do so. But they were too busy killing one another.

It must be recognized, however, that the temptation to violence was always present in Native Americans, and theft was the usual way of life. Especially important to some of the more aggressive tribes was the control of river trading; and they were willing to butcher whites in order to control (and take profit from) the cargoes that were allowed to pass or be shipped upstream. In the passage I have quoted above, alluding to the whites' firing their guns in anger, the episode involved a shootout initiated by Blackfeet Indians who undertook to steal the white men's guns and horses. While visiting the Lewis and Clark camp, these Blackfeet availed themselves of the whites' hospitality. But at night, when everyone had gone to sleep, they tried to rob the whites of their rifles and horses. Roused by the cries of the man on watch, who was struggling with an Indian who wanted his rifle, the men of the corps awoke. One group of Indians was simultaneously trying to steal the horses. In the melee, one Indian was stabbed, others scattered, and the whites gave chase. Clark pursued two of them into a gulley. As he described it in his journal,

> being nearly out of breath I could pursue no further, I called to them as I had done several times before that I would shoot them if they did not give me my horse and raised my gun, one of them jumped behind a rock and spoke to the other who turned around and stoped at the distance of 30 steps from me and I shot him through the belly, he fell to his knees and on his wright elbow from which position he partly raised himself up and fired at me, and turning himself about crawled in behind a rock which was a few feet from him. he overshot me, being bearheaded I felt the wind of his bullet very distinctly.[14]

Stealing another tribe's horses, kidnaping an enemy's women, slaughtering their children, stealing their property—these were the rule rather than the exception in the West before the advent of civilization, the commonplace kind of behavior traditionally praised by the Native American elders and chiefs.

The passage from Duncan that I quoted above implies that Lewis and Clark owed their lives and the success of the expedition to the Indians who assisted them. This is a modern view typical of politically correct ideologists who have a political agenda in mind. Among other things, they wish to curry favor with contemporary Native American activists by confessing that a grievous wrong was done to Native Americans in generations past. Confessions of this kind supposedly reduce hostility to whites and make more tolerable to Indians the fact of their defeat long ago in the pitched battles for control of the land. Perhaps the most well-known spokesman for this liberal viewpoint today is the historian Stephen E. Ambrose.[15] Ambrose takes the position that "Lewis and Clark 'never could have made it across the continent without the Indians.'" That is a doubtful inference: the expedition was fully equipped for every peril they confronted. They could not, of course, have withstood an especially large Indian war party intent on destroying them. But they did not encounter such a group. Ambrose believes that the approaching 200th anniversary of the Lewis and Clark expedition (especially white plans for its reenactment) will doubtless provoke "a lot of hard feelings among American Indians." It is his view that "We're going to have Native Americans saying things we're going to have to deal with, we're going to have to face."[16] This is no doubt true. Some Native Americans resent it that they lost out in the battle over the land and will try to spoil the celebration. But it is not true that the success of the Lewis and Clark expedition was owed to the Indians. As hired local guides, they were of course useful in directing the party through passes in the mountains. They were also useful in supplying horses, dogs, local foodstuffs, and information. But in my view, Lewis and Clark and their men were exceptionally competent in wilderness survival techniques and would have arrived at the Pacific even without the supplies and information provided by Native Americans. In fact, if a moral reckoning is in order, Native American activists will themselves have a great deal to explain in respect to the violent and unethical character of their ancestors' tribal way of life.

The passage from Duncan quoted above follows Ambrose slavishly in attributing the success of the expedition not merely to Native Americans but to Native American women, to the "female interventions" that saved the explorers. The interventions allude to two episodes on the journey. In one, a Nez Percé woman persuaded her tribe not to destroy the whites. What Duncan does not mention is that she spoke up for them because, after she had been captured and enslaved by Blackfeet, she was sold to a white Canadian trapper who had treated her well. Perhaps she had a higher opinion of whites than of other Indians.

The other episode, much more ideologically useful to the left because no nice white men are involved, concerns Sacagawea, an Indian woman who was present on the Lewis and Clark expedition as an interpreter. Ambrose has said that "The expedition owed its success to Indian women . . . and to other things—luck being big, big, big. . . . But if the captains were aware they owed something to Sacajawea, they never said so."[17] Did Lewis and Clark owe their

Pride and Shame: The Winning of the West

success to her? It certainly pacifies feminists to say so, but the evidence does not support the claim. A Shoshone, Sacagawea (her name meant "Bird Woman") had earlier been captured by the Hidatsas in a raid and was subsequently sold as a slave to Touissant Charbonneau, a French Canadian trapper hired by Lewis and Clark to guide them up the Missouri. Her being the wife of the guide Charbonneau accounts for her presence in the party. The horrendousness of her capture, enslavement, and sale (common enough in Indian life) is hardly mentioned by Ambrose or Duncan. Instead it is swiftly masked by inflating Sacagawea's importance to the expedition. Now, no one would wish to diminish Sacagawea's honorable place in the history of the West. But there is no point in hiding the facts of how she came to be with these Americans or in exaggerating what she did after she had joined them.

Sacagawea is mentioned in the eight volumes of the journals only about thirty-five or forty times. Mostly the references are fleeting and insignificant. Two or three times she *did* elicit a commendation from the captains. On one occasion she acted promptly to salvage some of their supplies lost overboard and was praised for her quickness. Her act is all the more remarkable in that she was the mother of a child still young enough to be carried. On another occasion her mere presence becalmed some devastated Indians who mistakenly thought they had been captured by an Indian war party and were about to be executed. Clark remarked that as "Soon as they Saw the Squar wife of the interpreter they pointed to her and . . . they immediately all came out and appeared to assume new life, the sight of This Indian woman . . . confirmed those people of our friendly intentions, as no woman ever accompanies a war party of Indians in this quarter."[18] Finally, because Sacagawea knew the Shoshone territory where she was born and was good at Indian sign language, she was useful to the captains in their plan to purchase and trade horses necessary for the Rocky Mountain crossing. This was quite fortuitous: the first Shoshone chief they encountered was Sacagawea's brother—one of the most extraordinary accidental encounters in the literature of wilderness exploration.

There is no reason to believe that the Lewis and Clark expedition would have turned out any different had Sacagawea not been amongst the party. Yet Duncan's *Lewis and Clark* grossly exaggerates her importance. This is very easy to do since our knowledge of her is sketchy. And because she left no journal herself (the Western tribes were illiterate) and because the few facts about her are scant, Duncan devotes a whole chapter of the book, "Finding Sacagawea," to the speculative fantasies of one Erica Funkhouser, poet, who supplies us with an invented account of Sacagawea's life, in other words, a gross supposition about what history does not give us.

But it is not just Sacagawea whose existence is distorted. Both *Lewis and Clark* and *The West* frankly equivocate about the real situation of all Indian women in the West. In commanding this expedition, the captains ordered their men to respect Native American women and to avoid sexual encounters with them. This was, in the first instance, a matter of Christian morality. But as a similarly important matter, the captains also wished to avoid health risks and venereal infections, for which at the time there were no effective cures. It is of course naive to suppose that the crew were all chaste throughout the long expedition, especially in view of the voluptuousness of the Indian women, who loved to pet the men, and the Indian men's readiness to offer the sexual services of their squaws. Duncan dignifies the lasciviousness of the tribes by turning their sexual practices into an expression of spiritual values:

> Among The Arikaras—and many other northern Plains tribes—sexual relations were sometimes imbued with ritual meanings. Through sex with a young man's wife, the wisdom and special power, usually called "medicine," of older men in the tribe (or of important strangers) could be transferred to the younger husbands. Many tribes practiced polygamy, and the offer of a wife for an evening to a visitor was also a sign of hospitality.[19]

Is this putting the best face possible on a shrewd con by which dirty old men ever got to enjoy the tender flesh of nubile young women? It is better than the ruse of John Humphrey Noyes, founder of the Oneida Community, who conned his flock into believing that young females, if they wished to be saved, were required to have sex with their elders (especially with Noyes). Here is how Clark describes the sexual practices of the Plains Indians in his journals:

> a curious Custom the old men arrange themselves in a circle & after

Pride and Shame: The Winning of the West

Smoke[ing] a pipe which is handed them by a young man, Dress[ed] up for the purpose, the young men who have their wives back of the Circle go [each] to one of the old men with a whining tone and request the old man to take his wife (who presents [herself] necked except a robe) and—(or Sleep with her) the Girl then takes the Old Man (who verry often can scarcely walk) and leades him to a convenient place for the business, after which they return to the lodge; if the old man (or a white man) returns to the lodge without gratifying the Man & his wife, he offers her again and again; it is often the Case that after the 2d time without Kissing the Husband throws a new robe over the old man &c. and begs him not to dispise him & his wife (We Sent a man to this Medisan Dance last night, they gave him 4 Girls) all this is to cause the buffalow to Come near So that they may Kill them.[20]

Ah, inducing the buffalo to come near! That's why the old men of the tribe commanded the practice.

What comes through in the journals of Lewis and Clark, but not explicitly in the videos, is that the Indian women were continually brutalized. They "do all their laborious work & [are] I may Say perfect Slaves to the Men, as all Squars of Nations much at War, or where the Womin are more noumerous than the men."[21] Most tribes were like the Clatsops, Chinnooks, and Killamucks in respect to "the servile manner in which they treat their women": "they do not hold the virtue of their women in high estimation, and will even prostitute their wives and daughters for a fishinghook or a strand of beads. in common with other nations they make their women perform every species of drudgery. but in almost every species of this drudgery the men also participate, their women are also compelled to geather the roots, and assist them in taking fish, which articles form the greatest part of their subsistence."[22] The proper inference to be drawn from such eyewitness accounts is that civilized whites were always in fact much more generous and caring and gentlemanly in their treatment of the weaker sex than the red man.

Thus far I have been highly critical of the political slant of *Lewis and Clark* and *The West*. But it must be admitted that the photography in these videos is indeed spectacular. I find the landscape of the region to be breathtaking in its immensity and variety—including the near unimaginable vastness of the endless rolling prairies; the majestic rivers, cascades, geysers, and deep canyons; the towering snow-crested Rocky Mountains, and the sometimes arid, sometimes beautiful, and very often lethal Western deserts. Ives gives us vivid panoramas of this majestic landscape in living color, as well as in black-and-white still photos of the place as it was when nineteenth-century settlers, after the era of Lewis and Clark, pushed into the West. Infused into these programs is that remarkable land mystique about the West frequently to be found—from Frederick Jackson Turner onward—in romantic American thought. According to this view, it is the landscape itself that generated American democratic values and high-minded social ideals; and it is the greatness of the land that inspires Americans to a comparable moral greatness. Hence the very landscape itself is a therapeutic and beneficent agency.

In my view no landscape can mean anything in the absence of people to inhabit it. Think of the aridity of the moonscape without the presence of Neil Armstrong or Buzz Aldrin. The story of the West is a story of largely open, uninhabited space. Lewis and Clark, we remember, often went weeks or months without seeing a human face. But its regions were never empty of people. In fact the West came to boast its share of some of the most colorful personalities ever to have festooned the pages of the national biography. Ives presents brief biographical accounts of Kit Carson, Coronado, Sitting Bull, Wyatt Earp, Buffalo Bill Cody, John Sutter, Chief Joseph, Leland Stanford, General Custer, Brigham Young, Mark Twain, Red Cloud, and a host of others whose stories made the West a place of fantastic myth and international symbolism.

One of the familiar myths perpetuated in this series is that the Westerner is somehow more authentic than other Americans, that he is in fact the *essential* American. Of course this is nonsense, as the region is so vast as to have sustained a great diversity of peoples of all races and types, precluding a convincing definition of *the* Westerner, much less *the* American. Still, these TV programs give a rich iconography of Western portraits. The invention of the daguerreotype and the camera made available to us some of the most striking weathered faces ever photographed. Of course, for some of these Westerners, the necessity of holding still for several minutes during the long exposures gave the eyes a fixed and glassy, even a demented, look. Sometimes the look corresponds to what we know of their actions.

What were those actions? Some, like those of John Brown in Kansas, *were* demented, even if they are sometimes called heroic. Others were unquestionably heroic, and others everything in between. Their actions were as various as the people. Ives in *The West* gives us brief chronicles of the some of the most important historical events in the region: hair-raising exploratory ventures into the uncharted geographical wilderness, such as the 1533 Spanish explorations northward into unknown California, or the long Lewis and Clark expedition in search of the Northwest Passage that found instead the majestic Rockies. The great cattle drives of the old Texas cowboys were fascinating for me to follow. And I was struck with the stupendous economic revolution produced by the 1849 discovery of gold at Sutter's Mill in California and silver in Nevada. Ives is especially good at showing the anti-slavery skirmishing in the Missouri-Kansas border raids as abolitionists fought the confederates who wanted to extend slavery clear to the Pacific.

Ives quite rightly notes that the story of the West is a story of conquest. At times it is the conquest of man over the harshest conditions of Nature—fire and flood, blizzard and drought. But more importantly it is about warfare. Noteworthy are his narrative accounts of epic battles like that at the Alamo (1836), where Davy Crockett, Jim Bowie, and a small band of Texans held off Santa Anna and his much superior Mexican army. Equally striking is Ives's account of the battle of Little Big Horn, where in 1876 Sitting Bull wiped out General Custer and his men. Everyone bellicose is given something to feel proud of in Ives's historical record.

We are also given historical accounts of remarkably positive social ventures such as the establishment of the Mormon colony in the Utah territory, and the passing of the Homestead Act of 1862, which made free land available to millions of eager settlers. I was struck with Ives's account of the great technological and engineering feats, such as the completion of the transcontinental railroad in 1869, and the 1913 diversion of the entire Owens River into the Los Angeles reservoirs. One of the most important historical events was of course the slow disappearance of the Indian tribes in the face of the continuous, relentless migration of millions of Easterners, Europeans, Mexicans, and Chinese into the region.

III

In presenting his gallery of Western personalities and in recording the historical events that shaped the West, Ives has eschewed a straightforward, linear, continuous narrative. He proceeds by what I can only call the snippet method. A typical program begins with the dissonance of an Indian chant, then an aerial overview of the Western landscape, then a shot of three buffalo (the only ones left?) being chased by a helicopter, or an introductory comment by one of the "talking heads." These are usually American historians, often ethnic studies experts, or even descendants of those who lived in the region back then. Then we have a few minutes on Brigham Young and the Mormon settlement, a few frames on polygamy, then a quick cut to the diminishing supply of deer and antelope, with a shift to the delusional missionaries who thought they could Christianize the Indian, and then a cut to the sudden blizzards that buried the wagon trains. And the program ends with some prospectors scrabbling in the California gold fields.

Ives's scattered themes are picked up and carried from program to program. The defect of his method is a surprising degree of repetition if the nine cassettes are watched in quick succession. But to bring the biographies alive, Ives quotes extensively from the letters and journals, the newspapers and government documents that illuminate his pioneer subjects. A great many celebrities were drafted to read these documents. Among those listed as "Voices" in *The West* were Jimmy Smits, Eli Wallach, Blythe Danner, Julie Harris, Derek Jacobi, George Plimpton, John Lithgow, and Arthur Miller. Many are excellent readers, though Arthur Miller's speech has a tang of New Yorkese; and Plimpton's suave delivery discordantly suggests an Eastern aristocracy of great wealth and privilege. No one, it seems to me, reads as well as the series narrator, Peter Coyote, whose accent and delivery (even his name!) are perfect for this Western material.

Mostly implicit but sometimes explicit in Ives's work is the notion that one cannot understand the West as an actual entity in the national experience. For Ives the matter of the West has no essence or center. Instead there are just stories or myths about Western experiences. There are as many different stories as there are Western-

Pride and Shame: The Winning of the West

ers with a tale to tell. For Ives, all these stories are in competition with each other. In order to decenter the narrative of the West and to make sure that no one group gets to tell the story or dominate its transmission, Ives employs the snippet method. Every minority group, every "marginalized" voice, gets heard. The vanishing Indians, the dispossessed Mexicans in California, the sisterhood of Mormon women violently deprived of polygamous marriage by Washington, the underpaid Chinese railway workers, the aggrieved Southern freedmen stranded in Kansas—are all given ample time to voice their complaint about how the nation—that is, how white Americans—have oppressed them. The idea that the past is a babel of contending voices and that all must be given equal time really prevents a clear grasp of the major tendencies and larger historical developments of the region. But this notion of "empowering marginal voices" dominates the academy nowadays and has evidently—through the writers and historians who appear on camera (T. H. Watkins, J. S. Holliday, Richard White, Jack Chen, Ronald Takaki, Martin Ridge, Ricardo Romo, Marc Reisner, and Bill Gwaltney among them)—shaped the thinking of Stephen Ives.

Instead of multiple narratives, however, what we really have in *The West* is a single underlying master narrative about the illegitimacy of the expansion of the American peoples into the West and the shame that all Americans must feel about our treatment, throughout the history of the West, of various minority groups—blacks, Mexicans, Chinese, Indians, and so forth. This motif is not developed at length; it is broken up into hundreds of small vignettes, expressed in scores of stray asides, and delivered in a great many offhand comments. There is so much shame-mongering infused into the nine programs that I cannot give a full accounting of it here. But some comment about Ives's presentation of the fate of the American Indian will have to serve for the whole.

The theme of the illegitimate American appropriation of the West is announced at the outset in the claim of Chief Joseph, of the Nez Percé tribe of Oregon, that the Indian has a right to the land. The hospitality of various Indian tribes to early explorers is often touched on. Appreciative accounts are given of the richness of Indian culture, the freedom of Indian life, the spirituality of their religion, and Indian reverence for nature. For all of this there is ample documented evidence. Native American culture has much of fascination, interest, and worth—to all peoples, whatever their backgrounds. The American Indian writer N. Scott Momaday tries to suggest some of these considerations in his masterly interpretations of Indian legends and myths. But his voice is charged with rueful melancholy. Pathos is in fact the dominating affect in the whole video series: the Western past was so sad. In any case, there is so much that is positive about American Indian culture that it will seem inconceivable to the innocent viewer that white Americans could have wished to be protected from Indians by federal troops, or have urged that Indians be restricted to reservations, or have sought to abrogate lawful treaties, or have wanted war to be waged upon them. How could the point have eventually been reached where the *Eureka Herald* called for the extermination of the Indian?

The answer to this question involves both the nature of Indian character and life and the prior history of Indian-white relations in the East. Well before the West was ever explored, colonial Americans had an informed knowledge of Indian character. One aspect of it—a trait only lightly touched on in *The West*—emerges in the admission that war was the highest calling of the Indian peoples. In the narrow Indian tribal view, all outsiders were enemies, and they were ripe for the war party and the hatchet. We hardly hear, in Ives's account, that the Apaches hated the Navajos, that both hated the Pueblos, and that Comanches and Kiowas lusted for each other's scalps. Savage hatred for these new white men was nothing special.

The idea that "whites took their lands" also needs, I think, to be reexamined. Individual tribes regularly went to war with each other over who controlled what hunting grounds. The tribes moved hundreds of miles north or south, east or west, following game, battling with other tribes along the way. Might actually made for Indian right. Hence I do not see how one can invoke the question of ownership when Indians were predisposed to decide such matters as the result of pitched battles. No one, in fact, owned the Western land, although, at different times and places, after they had been dislodged by whites, various tribal leaders claimed it by a verbal declaration. But *The West* seems to suggest that Indians were a homogeneous people whose primordial presence on the land was the mystical equivalent of a constitutional theory of property, real estate, ownership, and contract law. In fact the continual shifting about of Indian peoples and the transience of settled tribal centers makes the whole property question a doubtful one at best. Even so, government actions were from time to time frankly shameless and, by our own law, illegal.

The lack of a settled existence on the plains and the nomadic character of Indian life (as they followed the game from region to region) become most apparent in relation to questions of Indian hygiene and health. Whites are often accused of having destroyed the Native Americans by introducing to them diseases that they could not withstand. I find it hard to assign blame for the transmission of diseases which occurred quite readily in the case of nomadic people with poor hygiene, like the Plains Indians. In fact, well before the advent of the white man, Indian tribes in North America were dying out in huge numbers because of the contagious diseases they kept inflicting on one another. In inquiring about what had happened to the Omahas, a tribe of notorious river pirates that had regularly preyed upon many weaker tribes in the region, Lewis and Clark learned in 1804 that the tribe had just disappeared.

> The ravages of the Small Pox (which Swept off 400 men & children in perpopotion) has reduced this nation not exceeding 300 men and left them to the insults of their weaker neighbours, which before was glad to be on friendly turms with them. I am told when this fatal malady was among them they Carried their franzey to verry extroadinary length, not only of burning their Village, but they put their *wives* & children to Death with a view of their all going together to some better Countrey. they burry their Dead on the top of high hills and rais Mounds on the top of them. The cause or way those people took the Small Pox is uncertain, the most Probable, from Some other nation by means of a warparty.[23]

In 1804 whites could hardly have been responsible for the destruction of the Omahas. Except for Lewis and Clark, it would be many years before whites reached so far into the interior. What these remarks make plain is that, while going on the warpath did a great deal to kill off the tribes, disease was perhaps even more lethal.

The West presents a great deal of Indian mysticism, a great many tales of what the animals tell us, and a lot of drum and breathy flute music. But here and there a stray reference makes vividly plain why whites found it impossible to coexist peacefully with Indians. It lay in the Indian lust for war—a constant factor in tribal life stretching back into prehistory. Especially revealing is the brief reference in the second program to the ongoing savage battles amongst the Kiowas, Cheyennes, and Lakotas for control of the Black Hills hunting ground. Charlotte Black Elk, a Lakota descendant, gives the game away in her rather proud recollection that her ancestors formed a warrior society and that it was a badge of tribal honor to be feared and hated by the other tribes and by whites. Any young man who did not kill and scalp in war was ridiculed in the tribe as effeminate. Indeed, no young woman would have a brave who had not proved himself in war.

Of the dismal history of intertribal savagery, which "had existed time out of mind," the historian Francis Parkman observed in *A Half-Century of Conflict* (1892):

> There is a disposition to assume that [such] events . . . were a consequence of contact of white men with red; but the primitive Indian was quite able to enact such tragedies without the help of Europeans. Before French or English influence had been felt in the interior of the continent, a great part of North America was the frequent witness of scenes still more lurid in coloring, and on a larger scale of horror. In the first half of the seventeenth century, the whole country, from Lake Superior to the Tennessee, and from the Alleghenies to the Mississippi, was ravaged by wars of extermination, in which tribes, large and powerful, by Indian standards, perished, dwindled into feeble remnants, or were absorbed by other tribes and vanished from sight. French pioneers were sometimes involved in the carnage, but neither they nor other Europeans were answerable for it.[24]

The Parkman book I have cited here is a study of North American Indian tribes north of the Canadian border, yet migrating seasonally as they descended southward into the great Midwestern prairies, where they continually fought with local tribes over the existing game. There was, at that time, no national boundary between New France and the British colonies observed by the tribes. In any case, one cannot help noting that a comparable level of savage intertribal violence was then occurring amongst the Plains

Indians themselves, as a great many other historians have rightly shown.[25] In any case, it cannot be doubted that what prevented peaceable relations between Indian and Indian, and Indian and white, was the sanguinary imperative of a primitive warrior culture.

In consequence of Indian bellicosity—something *The West* is too pusillanimous to criticize—whites who passed too close to the tepees often suffered the horrors of the savage scalping party. But only once or twice do we hear of the farmers who were butchered, their noses slit, genitals hacked, bodies mutilated. Only once or twice in twelve and a half hours do we hear of the assaulted wagon trains, the raped and kidnaped women, or the many homesteads burnt to the ground. In one telling section called "This Guilty Land," U.S. Senator Ben Nighthorse Campbell inadvertently reveals that successive peace treaties negotiated between whites and peacemaking Indian chiefs had to fail—had to fail because, to the younger braves, the making of peace by the elders represented a denial of their manhood, and they were not about to be feminized by the circulation of a peace pipe.

Yet Ives and his politically correct historians make no effort to reach a moral judgment about the bloodlust that animated the Indian people, who were in fact still living in the Stone Age. Instead we find a great many stray sentences like this one from the episode called "Death Runs Riot": "A Cheyenne chief who wanted nothing but peace would find no escape as time and again his unsuspecting village became a battlefield." Like as not it became a battlefield because some kidnaped white women or children were imprisoned in the camp, as hostages held for ransom. In fact the Cheyenne wanted peace only after defeat in battle or after their bloodlust had been temporarily slaked.

IV

I have been sharply criticized in the past for using the word "savage" and for alluding to Native Americans as a Stone Age people. This, I am told, is simply not politically correct or permissible. Ours is a time when tender sensibilities must be protected. The feelings of our contemporaries—wounded by the outcome of historical events occurring long ago—must, I am advised, still be soothed. One cannot be critical of the ancestors of another group.

I confess that I am not up to the task of silencing myself about the difference between savagery and civilization. Perhaps it is my age. As a child I was an avid reader of the literature of world exploration. I grew up studying the *National Geographic* at an impressionable time, a time when anthropological exploration of foreign cultures was turning up a great many interesting savage peoples in the interior of Africa, in the Brazilian rain forests, in the remote islands of the South Pacific. Anthropologists in those days had no problem with the designation of some cultures as primitive or savage. One could identify savages by the rudeness of their way of life and by certain practices that civilized humanity had left behind. I mean such things as ritual scarification and tattooing, body piercing, cannibalism, human sacrifice, the impaling of enemy heads on spears, totemic identifications, animistic rites, and so forth. During World War II, the naval and armed forces, moving through the remoter islands of New Guinea, came upon primitive tribes that existed on an inconceivably prehistoric time scale. Such peoples in my youth were frankly designated as savages.

Unfortunately anthropologists subsequently surrendered to the preposterous notion that all cultures are "equal," "authentic," and "valuable." It was considered elitist and even smug to privilege "civilization" over "savagery." To call Western civilization and its way of life superior to the primitive order of disadvantaged peoples of color was supposedly "racist" and "imperialistic." Doubtful interpreters like Malinowski and Mead, Lévi-Strauss and Foucault, became our contemporary gurus. We were told that people supposedly primitive really had values superior to that of civilized men and women. The shameless sexual attitudes and practices of Samoan youth were held out by Mead as superior to those of the Judeo-Christian West; and Foucault announced that sexual repression was evil.

Of course it later turned out that Mead was conned by her Samoan informants; and Foucault turns out to have been sunk in obsessive sexual perversions. But these were supposedly intellectual giants giving us a serious interpretation of the meaning of differing cultures. What folly! To sum it up, I have witnessed since my childhood the elevation of primitive cultures to a level of the cultures of France or England or the United States. But I regard this shift in attitude as a mark of intellectual and moral decadence.

Simultaneous with the elevation of primitivism in my time there has occurred a devastating devaluation of civilization as such. It has been said that Europeans, pretending to be civilized, have butchered one another by the millions in our century. This is indeed the case. The Armenian massacre, Lenin's destruction of the kulaks, Stalin's mass murders, World Wars I and II, the holocaust of the Jews under Nazism, the use of the atomic bomb, the recent collapse of Bosnia into horrific civil war—can any culture be called civilized in our time? I too am appalled by these instances of violence in peoples pretending to have attained the very highest state of civilization.

But what these events actually show is that civilization does not go very deep. Civilization, in my view, is substantially a matter of individuals; occasionally it is an attribute of societies; once in a while it is a term that can be attributed to a state or nation. But barbarism is barbarism, whether acted out by an individual, an Apache raiding party, or the Third Reich. Moreover, the dismal ethnic history of the twentieth century also suggests to me that, once attained (after great labor), civilization is easily lost. There are people walking the streets of New York City today who have hardly emerged from a savagery like that of the old American West. I am convinced that it would take little to provoke in them an immediate regression to barbarism. The daily headlines prove it to me. Freud even suggested in *Civilization and Its Discontents* that a hostility to civilization is built into the psyche of each one of us because it has been purchased at the price of the suppression of the libido—including the savage wish to kill one's enemies right now. If he is right, this discontent with civilization must be frankly faced and suppressed. Civilization is too precious an achievement where it exists, and too fragile an attainment for those lucky enough to have it, to surrender to its alternative, social chaos.

In any case, it is clear that we live in an age when the horrific acts of civilized societies have made "simple primitive life" attractive to urban dwellers. Hence abandoned practices are making a return. There is now a good deal of tattooing going on, even the tattooing of women. It has started out slowly, with an occasional rose on the shoulder or a butterfly on the bum, but now women seem fascinated by how extensive body decoration might become. (Some members of the Hell's Angels suggest the freak-show extent to which complete body tattooing might go.) Tattooing used to be thought a heathen practice unfit for Jewish or Christian people who regarded the body as a temple of the divine spirit, but who thinks this way anymore?

Body-piercing has also made its return in metropolitan areas. Now rings of different sizes and various metals are regularly stuck into noses, lips, eyebrows, nipples, and even—pornographic cable TV makes this plain—the genitalia. Infections, of course, are rampant, and not only bacterial. I have not seen any actual bones in the nose, as used to be common in *National Geographic* photographs. (No immigrant Africans in New York, where I live, engage in such practices: they evidently wish to modernize as rapidly as possible.) But amongst whites I expect pendulous earlobes to make a return —descending from the the jaw to the shoulder down toward the waistline, as heavier and heavier artifacts, preferably primitive, are suspended from them. Nor have I seen evidence of a return to the elongation of the female neck, through the insertion of more and more neck-coils. But even that cannot be far behind. One way of expressing hatred for civilization and its imperialism, one way of expressing solidarity with the victims of civilization, is to go native.

Even so, there is no use blinking the fact that the Indians of the American West were a Stone Age people. They had no smelting or metalwork, no alphabet, no written records, no sustainable system of law. They had not yet invented the wheel. Their social institutions were few and rudimentary. Their agriculture was primitive and founded on meteorological superstitions. Although it was a warrior culture, Indian weapons were limited: arrows were made of wood, bits of feather, chipped stone; lances were sharpened tree poles; axes had stone heads strapped to a handle of wood by deerskin strips or thongs of buffalo hide. Existence was primitive by contemporaneous civilized standards. This is no special discredit to the Indian peoples, but it suggests how late in the process of civilization's expansion they came to know a more advanced way of life. Despite the Greco-Roman contribution, it took northern Europe perhaps fifteen hundred years to attain something that we could call a civilized way of life. It took only about two hundred or so in America.

A great many perfectly civilized, modern American Indian activists are now intent on trying to obscure the bloody record of

Indian atrocity so as to make their peaceful forefathers the victims of brutal Western civilization. Guilt-films like *Dances with Wolves* or *The West* are quite useful propaganda. But the past being over, the West having been settled, the historical record is clear; and the problem is how we—Indians and whites—live together now. Sympathy and compassion are due those in distress, but I do not believe that the historical record should be distorted to protect the sensibilities or to enhance the self-esteem of minority groups. If I called the Indian great-great-grandfathers savages, it is the case that we are all descended from savages. My father was English and Scots-Irish. I note that the northern Picts in primordial Scotland painted themselves blue and liked to bathe in enemy blood. I think along the same lines about that strain of Irish ancestry on my mother's father's side: many of the Northern Irish today—whether pretending to be Protestants or Catholics—are savages. Needless to say, the society of my German great-grandfather gives me a lot to think about in relation to the Wehrmacht.

I am descended, on my mother's mother's side, from the Cherokee Nation in Missouri. I lived for a time in Wyoming, where in school I was an honorary Bannock. I am proud of my Indian descent, though clear-sighted enough, I hope, to see that descent for what it was—in both its strengths and weaknesses. It is precisely because I regard myself as an authentic American—that is, someone of mixed background—that I feel bold enough to express contempt for the bogus primitivism and politically correct twaddle that nowadays distorts American history. We are already a multicultural people, but we are not going to get along any better if we do not effect daily reconciliations based on the reality of how it really was—on both sides—and on mutual forgiveness.

V

The most striking viewpoints espoused in *The West* are not in fact those of the PC historians. There are a great many interviews worth quoting, but I found especially worth reflection three comments, one by Stewart L. Udall, former secretary of the interior; one by (of all people) Ann Richards, former governor of Texas; and one by Albert White Hat, a contemporary Lakota. None of the comments is felicitous in style and some are downright ungrammatical, but I find in them a certain wisdom. Udall, descended from persecuted Mormon settlers, argues convincingly that "the settlers are the real heroes, yes, yes, indeed. In this harsh country, much of it harsh and forbidding and demanding, a tough country, the fact that people could go there and establish communities and make a living for themselves and build up societies, I think that was a real triumph." Udall rightly puts the emphasis on the creation of communities, on the development of society and the westward march of an American civilization, a Western civilization, with shared values and noble ideals.

The settlement of the West involved a poignant price for both the winners and the losers, but I think that Ann Richards, descended from those original rowdy Texas cowboys, was wise in remarking:

> Prejudice and destruction as a consequence of war and destruction is not a pretty picture. But it is the story of all places, all nations. No matter where in the world, it is the story of conquering, great sacrifice, great loss, and a lot of times the taking away of things belonging to somebody else. But even knowing all of that, and wishing that part of it were not there cannot take away the spirit and idealism and excitement that people felt that actually did it and that we still feel when we think about them doing it.

Indeed, it would take a dour pessimist not to admit that out of the great drama of Western settlement has evolved a nation of the highest moral and social ideals, however imperfect Americans may be in fulfilling them. The fact of our ongoing dialogue about these matters is a sign that we have advanced from the days of having at each other with hatchet and gun.

In this respect, toward the end of the television series, Albert White Hat, a Lakota trained in youth in the Christian schools, speaks a kind of wisdom gained of his own tormented experience. In the 1960s, when he decided to reappropriate his Indian identity, he let his hair grow, took up tribal ways, and brooded long on the massacre of Indians at Wounded Knee and Sand Creek and on the tragic fate of his people. His anger made him want to get out his rifle, go on a rampage, and kill all the whites he could find. But the lust for revenge, he came to discover, was too tall an order for any individual Indian nowadays and could only lead to self-destruction or drunkenness. The only way to come to terms with the history of his people, said Albert White Hat, is forgiveness. The same must be said for all of us, whether we are white, Mexican American, Chinese American, or whatever. It is this notion of forgiveness and reconciliation, an idea at the very heart of a culture that still has a claim to be called Judeo-Christian, that makes it possible for us to live amicably together today under the rule of law.

Ethnic Blues and All That Multicultural Jazz

We can get along. —Rodney King.
Why can't we all just get along? —Jack Nicholson
as the president in the sci-fi film *Mars Attacks*

For many years now we have been treated to various studies in "American ethnic history"—narrative accounts, that is, of the experience of immigrant groups that have come to (or been forcibly brought to) this country for varying reasons. Among such books, Albert Camarillo's *Chicanos in a Changing Society*, Irving Howe's *World of Our Fathers: The Journey of East European Jews to America*, and Kerby A. Miller's *Emigrants and Exiles: Ireland and the Irish Exodus to North America* have usefully suggested the processes by which immigrant peoples have integrated themselves into American society. But many others—Dee Brown's *Bury My Heart at Wounded Knee: An Indian History of the American West*, Yuji Ichioka's *The Issei: The World of the First Generation Japanese Immigrants*, and Lawrence Levine's *Black Culture and Black Consciousness*—have stressed the *dissimilar* in the ethnic or migrational experience of our various immigrant groups. Sometimes, but not always, "racial difference" has been called decisive in impeding assimilation. However, such narrowly focused studies of individual ethnic groups will not—in this "post–Rodney King era"—do any longer.

That, at least, is the viewpoint of Ronald Takaki, professor of ethnic studies at the University of California and author of several well-known studies of immigrant experience, including *Strangers from a Different Shore: A History of Asian Americans* and *A Different Mirror: A History of Multicultural America*.[1] This last book was intended to avoid the earlier "fragmenting" of America, which occurred when Howe and others studied "each group separately, in isolation from the other groups and the whole." What Takaki wants, and what *A Different Mirror* gives us, is an interwoven history of the Puritans and the Indians, the Indians and Southern whites, the Southern whites and black slaves, the wild Irish in the North and the South, the blacks and the Jews, the Mexicans and Anglos, and the Chinese and the Japanese, mainly in California. In its temporal and geographical scope it is a big book; it aspires to be the text of choice in the multicultural courses now mandated across the country; and it has provoked in me a great many reflections, some that the author might not have intended.

First, let it be said that Professor Takaki has handled, very adroitly, the problem of moving into and away from the experience of specific ethnic groups while yet developing—over the long chronological continuum of the American past—an ongoing central narrative about the development of the United States as a whole. Readable and fluent, *A Different Mirror* is also timely in addressing issues that have come to be known as the rainbow curriculum. It reflects wide research into immigrant history and demographics; and it evinces a definite point of view. It does not flinch at what it sees in the ethnic history of America, and it has an agenda for the days ahead. Professor Takaki believes that our vision of the future will be dictated by the image of the past that is victorious. And he is intent on seeing that his view of our past will win out. That view may be summarized in the sentence: "America does not belong to one race or one group."[2]

That is fair enough. In fact, America belongs to a great many more groups than Professor Takaki pays attention to. I wish that he had given some significant consideration to the Dutch in early New York, the French in Creole Louisiana, the Swedes in Wisconsin and Minnesota, and the current Jamaicans in Queens. Since I live close to the World Trade Center, which was bombed a few years back, I would like to know more about fundamentalist Muslims in Jersey City; and, given the recent Bosnian debacle, some information about Serbs in New York City would be useful. But why quibble? We are so diverse a nation that even *A Different Mirror* cannot reflect all of us—especially since a good many of us are here illegally, a fact that does not seem to concern the U.S. Immigration and Naturalization Service, even though certain states like California are being bankrupted by unfunded congressional welfare mandates.

The fact that recent ethnic historians tend to concentrate on minorities of color—ignoring the Swedes, Finns, Scots, Danes, and so forth—has already begun to bear poisonous fruit. That is, minorities that successfully Americanized long ago are now beginning to see the advantages of victim status and are now *retroactively* claiming it for themselves. In 1996, for instance, the New York state legislature, in its infinite ignorance, passed a law requiring that all students now be taught that the Irish famine of the mid-nineteenth century was *"deliberately caused by the British."* For years historians have attributed the famine to the potato fungus *Phytophthora infestans*, but no longer. According to the new Irish-American historical revisionism, not the potato blight but rather the British administrations of Sir Robert Peel and Lord John Russell were responsible for the starvation of the Irish. As one spokesman for the new law put it,

> History teaches us that the great Irish Hunger was not the result of a massive failure of the Irish potato crop but rather was the result of a deliberate campaign by the British to deny the Irish people the food they needed to survive.

That this is arrant nonsense has been ably demonstrated by Roger Kimball in his analysis of the *bona fide* English effort—admittedly insufficient in view of the intractability of the infestation—to avert the growing famine.[3] In any case, thanks to the power of the Irish in New York City ethnic politics, the state legislature and the public schools have now become an unwitting tool of IRA policy—to get the Brits out of Northern Ireland—and current New Yorkers of Irish descent can now claim that they were as anciently victimized as Holocaust Jews or the enslaved blacks.

Is it mere quibbling to complain of the distinct left-wing bias that animates much of ethnic history nowadays? The American historical past reflects a national development that, for most Americans, generates great patriotic pride. But ethnic historians tend to reduce our history to the history of ethnic victimization—one group after another 'buked and scorned, hustled, manipulated, and exploited, invariably dumped on by the white American power structure.

Over the two centuries of our national existence there is, of course, a great deal of evidence to back up ethnic complaints. No one can blink the fate of the American Indian—rousted from the land he roamed and claimed as his own, his tribal treaties abrogated, and finally his people rounded up and sent to remote reservations. By way of explanation, it must be said that, of all ethnic groups in America, the American Indian has been the most violent and the least assimilable to the forces of modernization that have developed in Western civilization. Savagery and civilization simply cannot coexist. But we are reluctant to acknowledge that savagery existed here and is still a factor in ethnic identification in various parts of the world. Doubtless, to acknowledge that the old Native Americans were savages would hurt the feelings of some tribal descendants, and nowadays we are fanatical about building ethnic self-esteem, even if we have to falsify past racial or ethnic interrelations. But go back far enough and we all of us discover a wild ancestry. These are matters noted in "Pride and Shame: The Winning of the West."

But American Indians are only part of the story. The history of black slavery is likewise a blot upon the national character. "No Irish need apply" tells *its* story, as does the to-let placard *"Keine Juden, und keine Hunde."* "When I first came," wrote Andrew Kwan, a Chinese immigrant to California, "Chinese treated worse than dog. . . . The hoodlums, roughnecks and young boys pull your queue, slap your face, throw all kind of old vegetables and rotten eggs at you."+The Mexicans who stayed in the old Southwest and California after the Mexican-American War, both grandees and peons, found themselves spurned as "foreigners in their own land." And a good many American citizens who happened to be of Japanese descent were illegally interned during World War II. (In a special flourish of political correctness, Professor Takaki offers subsections, in very nearly each chapter, indicating how much *worse* it was for the women of each particular ethnic group.)

And yet, with the exception of kidnaped blacks on slave ships, how eagerly and willingly ethnics have come and kept on coming to these shores. "Over in Ireland people marry for riches," one Irishwoman wrote in Philadelphia, "but here in America we marry for love and work for riches." A Chinese worker in nineteenth-century California could make ten times what he could in China. He still can. The Japanese created the national market for California farm produce: "Much of what you call willow forests then," a Japanese farmer rightly boasted in 1924, "Japanese took that land, cleared it and made it fine farming land." Pablo Mares of Jalisco came to Estados Unidos, he said, "because it was impossible to live down there with so many revolutions." Another testimony: "The day begins with my pushcart full of fruit, and the day never ends before I count up at least two dollars' profit—that means . . . four rubles a day, twenty-four rubles a week!" So says one of Anzia Yezierska's Jewish pedlars. "[W]hite bread and meat I eat every day just like the millionaires."[5]

It is rather difficult to square such enthusiasm about American economic opportunity, peace, and political stability with the rather dismal account of the unremitting brutalization of ethnics at the hands of already established Americans, a brutalization regularly presented in college ethnic studies classes as if it were the whole story of the immigrant experience. There is, of course, a substantial amount of testimony about discrimination of this kind. Simply by being different, immigrants could be demonized or discriminated against. Race, language, and skin color are always decisive factors. Even taking this into account, however, I do not believe that discrimination of this type is particularly American or particularly white. Tribalism, or hostility to outsiders, and xenophobia, or suspicion of foreigners, are endemic in humankind and appear wherever racial or cultural differences become apparent. Consider the appalling carnage mutually inflicted on each other by the Tutsi and Hutu tribes of Rwanda and Zaire (who to outsiders will seem indistinguishable) or the savage animosity between the Serbs and Croats and their mutual detestation of Bosnian Muslims. Japan, the homeland of Professor Takaki's ancestors, is one of the most insular, racist, and xenophobic cultures in the world—as anyone can tell you who has spent more than a week in the country. But of course it is easier to blame "America" than human nature.

In fact, much of the indictment of America in ethnic protests often involves trivial things such as "rotten landlords" who insist on getting paid their rents, or harsh "capitalist bloodsuckers" who want a day's good work out of the socialists, syndicalists, and Communists they have employed. In the litany of immigrant grievances, no established Americans are exempt. Government officials, white corporation officers, railroad managers, agricultural overseers, even union figures have it in— in many ethnic histories— for the immigrant. They do not give the Mexican a job; or if they do hire him, the labor market is "deliberately oversupplied" in order to force him to work for peanuts. If Japanese laborers are hired, the white bosses also hire Koreans so as to pit ethnic enemies against each other, prevent union solidarity, and get maximum productivity. Naturally, if the ethnics strike, scabs are hired. If ethnics are given jobs, they will be denounced for having them. But Takaki quotes one protest that, in my view, undermines his whole complaint against ethnic discrimination without his even realizing it: "Isn't it a pretty sight to see men, brawny American men with callouses on their hands and empty stomachs—sitting idly on benches in the plaza," complained the American Federation of Labor's organ, the *Advocate*, "while slim-legged peons with tortillas in their stomachs, work in the tall building across the way?"[6] Indeed, if Mexicans were so employed, as the protest suggests, surely they cannot all have been discriminated against in hiring. But Takaki wants it both ways and so seizes upon immigrants' work success as further evidence of American discrimination against them.

Are only WASPs prejudiced against the newcomer? Hardly. Those already here, of whatever background, have always taken a singular pleasure in trying to flummox or control the new arrivals. Howe's *World of Our Fathers*, for instance, is rich in tales of greenhorn victimization at the hands of their own *landsmen*. But there is certainly no point in trying to waive away the racial and ethnic prejudice of already established white Americans who have been in a position to govern, hire, or otherwise direct the lives of new immigrants. And for quite a while it was widely believed that the U.S. government ought to define the American way as the white or

Anglo-Saxon way. As one nativist congressman put it, "This continent was intended by Providence as a vast theatre on which to work out the grand experiment of Republican government, under the auspices of the Anglo-Saxon race."[7] There is a high degree of presumption in this congressman's proposing to understand the intent of Providence; but there is no denying that America is and has been the stage on which transplanted Anglo-Saxons, mostly, created and managed this American experiment in republican government. Naturally, protecting and enlarging this idea has involved resistance to a great many native or imported ideas for changing it for the worse—hence national opposition to socialism, communism, syndicalism, anarchism, and a great many other isms that immigrants or natives may have concocted or imported.

Moreover, despite notions of Manifest Destiny, it will be plain from the historical record that most ethnic prejudice was transported here in steerage. If Americans of Irish and of English descent cannot get along, you won't find the explanation in *American* social conditions. Further, if the Korean Americans and Japanese Americans are at swords' point, the reasons are rooted in their oriental past, not in Anglo-Saxon deviousness. Most sons of the Old Sod opposed black emancipation as "setting the Niggers high" at the expense of the Irish workingman. And most Mexican and Japanese farm workers resent the Portuguese and Filipinos for depriving them of work—in taking jobs at what used to be called "coolie wages." Come to think about it, long before Anglo-Saxons got to these shores, the Iroquois hated the Algonquins, and the Senecas butchered the Delawares. Ethnic cleansing has had a long history, even in this country, and precedes the arrival of the WASPs.

At one point in a *A Different Mirror* light dawns, and Professor Takaki seems alarmed by his own accumulating evidence: "What is the nature of malevolence? Is there a deep, perhaps primordial, need for group identity rooted in hatred for the other?"[8] He has no answer to this question, which runs against his romantic liberal optimism, but the historical evidence seems decisive. Very little separates America from, say, Bosnia—except that structure of interconnected cultural institutions (in law, government, religion, economics, and education) that distinguishes America from many other countries. Unfortunately many ethnic historians do not seem to be able to connect this structure of institutions, which is Eurocentric in origin, with the very appeal of America for ethnics. Yet it is fair to say that the national identity of the United States was founded on Anglo-Saxon cultural attitudes, Christian religious and moral values, and egalitarian Enlightenment politics. The distinctive national qualities arising from these influences are precisely those that attract ethnics to America; they attract because the social conditions thus created here are best calculated to afford ethnics the opportunity to live the good life, however they may choose to define it. Americans, for their part, have always been open to immigrant peoples who wish to melt into the pot.

Melting into the pot used to be the American ideal. When that ideal prevailed—until the 1920s, I should think—the immigrant's racial or ethnic heritage was always secondary to the more important fact of his taking on a grand American national identity. There is a great deal of vivid testimony, in older immigrant literature, to the pleasure ethnics took in becoming "an American!" And even today, at any citizenship swearing-in ceremony, such enthusiasm is still evident. For the Americanization process means for most newcomers a leaving behind of a great many different sources of oppression and impoverishment and the flowering of hope for a better future.

But of course we now live in an age when identity politics is more important than the national unity. Self-appointed race leaders or ethnic spokesmen feel there is more to gain by stressing their group's difference from other ethnics or from the "hegemonic culture"—and stressing not only their difference from but their superiority to the others. Ethnic alienation has become a permanent way of life. Cries of victimization are continuous in the press and on TV. Public protests over welfare benefits, job quotas, educational preferences, affirmative-action entitlements, and so on are organized at the drop of a hat if some group does not feel it is getting its way. The American system is organized in order to accommodate a great deal of factionalism in politics, and, given the always built-in legal protections of minority rights, serious issues seem to work out well enough. But the dominant tone of our politics now alternates between a whine and a threat.

I have suggested that the older historical record shows a great deal of immigrant pleasure in the process of Americanization. But the idea of pleasure is no more understood—in ethnic studies courses—than the affect of rage latent in the psychology of a great many immigrants. The journals, letters, and memoirs of ethnics reveal a great deal of what I can only call undirected anger. To abandon one's homeland—even for a rational cause like escaping starvation, a revolution, or a pogrom—is likely to produce rage at what fate has compelled. An immense injustice has been visited upon the innocent, who must now uproot himself and his family. On top of that, even America, with her "streets of gold," cannot live up to immigrant expectations. There is, amongst many ethnics, a deep sense of failure, a great deal of felt worthlessness, and a simmering rage. It is now convenient to ventilate it at white Anglo-Saxon Protestants. Things are regularly said about WASPs that, if said about blacks or Jews, would mobilize the Reverend Al Sharpton or bring out the Jewish Defense League. The present generation of WASPs seems to understand that they have been elected to be scapegoats for the disappointment that immigration creates and for the failure of past ethnic harmony. These WASPs seem self-confident enough to live with this role imposed on them, or else they see it as a harmless way to defuse a potentially dangerous ethnic rage. On the other hand, while all ethnics seem to agree that WASPs are hogging the streets of gold, it is mainly on each other that ethnics turn. Very nearly every ethnic group seems ready to denounce all the others. Life in the United States, in this ghetto mentality, comes down to a competition of my ghetto turf with all the other ghettos.

In this competition for a slice of the American pie, by the way, ethnic rage is reassuringly constrained by a remarkable combination of civil rights laws that punish gross forms of discrimination. (On the whole, it should be remarked, civil rights legislation in this country—from the ratification of the Constitution to whatever our current leaders may have in mind—is mainly the work of Eurocentric white politicians well grounded in Roman law, English common law, and American constitutional history. Some of the most recent decisive actions intended to break down discrimination against ethnics—the integration of blacks into mainstream American life, the Immigration Act of 1965 that abolished ethnic quotas, the liberalization of naturalization procedures, the prohibition of prejudice in public matters based on sex, age, handicaps, ethnic background, and so forth—were the work of WASP politicians such as Harry Truman, Dwight D. Eisenhower, and Lyndon Baines Johnson.)[9]

Yet it seems to be evident that—despite remarkable progress in the area of civil rights and discrimination against persons or ethnic groups—there is plenty of prejudice to go around, and it does not all come from the Anglos. What accounts for it? Racism is continually thrown around as the answer. But obviously we cannot go on blaming ethnic discrimination for all America's ills, especially when the post–World War II civil rights laws, vigilantly enforced, do a fairly good job in eliminating at least its overt forms. Professor Takaki is uncomfortable with the idea that, despite wonderful civil rights laws, ethnic hostility still abounds. Thus he plays the game that all liberals do. He switches from the problem of endemic tribal or ethnic hostility to the problem of income levels. WASPs are nasty to the welfare class, and ethnic groups are hostile to each other because of their relative status on the economic ladder. And if we could only eliminate poverty, all the ethnic groups, now at one another's throats, would get along wonderfully. Harmony would at last prevail. Would it?

I don't think there is any doubt that Japanese Americans and Korean Americans have earned the respect of a sizable majority of the American people. They have done so by becoming "model minorities." They have proved that by thrift, hard work, a respect for the law, and the prudential virtues, members of an ethnic group—with a colored skin, a different culture, and another language—can pull themselves up by their own bootstraps, attain education, succeed economically, and so obviate the need for ethnic affirmative-action quotas and welfare giveaways. These groups illustrate, for most Americans, what the American dream has always meant; and they prove that it remains a fulfillable possibility. Professor Takaki is uneasy because he believes that the praise of model minorities is a white political stratagem really directed at blacks. And to celebrate their success will expose Asian Americans to black rage. Indeed, in the wake of the Rodney King trial, some ghetto blacks in Los Angeles openly targeted Korean businesses, while the police, outrageously, stood around and for days did nothing. Similarly, under the mayoralty of black politician David Dinkins in New York City, a confrontation between Hasidic Jews and blacks in Crown Heights in Brooklyn—a situation that could have been controlled—was permitted to escalate into a riot. During the Dinkins administration, the police likewise turned a blind eye to black violence against Korean storefront merchants in the Bronx.

Professor Takaki does not want Asian-American success highlighted. He even wants to deny that Asian Americans have succeeded. If they have more spending money, better housing, finer cars, he does not want it known. He stands for inconspicuous consumption in their case. Like most other ethnic historians, he wants in fact a rainbow coalition of liberal politicians who will put unemployed men onto the government payroll and disadvantaged mothers onto welfare. His book appeared at a time when liberals were under the delusion that, the cold war having ended, there would be a peace dividend of billions to be distributed to the ethnic poor, and with poverty eliminated the peaceable kingdom would at last have arrived. Any critique of the uselessness of long-term government patronage Takaki decried as a manifestation of a "cultural war" against ethnics, a reflection of "a traditional Eurocentrism that remains culturally hegemonic." To the liberal mind, any resistance to the multicultural agenda of big-government patronage of ethnics will fuel what Arthur Schlesinger, Jr., has called the "disuniting of America."[10] In this viewpoint, ethnics must be bribed to keep the peace. I for one am appalled at this reading of the low character of our immigrant peoples.

In her memoir *A Backward Glance* (1934), the WASP American novelist Edith Wharton remarked that the "really vital change" between the 1870s and the 1930s, between the Age of Innocence and the Depression Era, was that

> in my youth, the Americans of the original States, who in moments of crisis still shaped the national point of view, were the heirs of an old tradition of European culture which the country has now totally rejected. This rejection (which Mr. Walter Lippmann regards as the chief cause of the country's present moral impoverishment) has opened a gulf between those days and these.[11]

Mrs. Wharton thought that the European tradition had been totally abandoned; and so, in the political turmoil of the Depression, it might have seemed to people of her class and background. But in fact ours still is a European inheritance of constitutional law and a respect for civil rights. It is a European tradition continually modified and transformed by changing American political and social actualities, especially in dealing with immigrant groups—a tradition that distinguishes the United States from other nations and in part attracts foreign groups to our shores. By now this European tradition has been so modified by native experience that it must be deemed thoroughly American. But it is this inherited tradition, continually enlightened and modified by our immigration experience, that has substantially prevented the kind of "ethnic cleansing" that we see in so many places—the tribal warfare going on all over black Africa, the savagery of the Armenians and Azerbaijanis, the Kurds and the Iraqis, the Palestinians and Israelis, the Sikhs and the Hindus, the Hindus and the Muslims, the Serbs and the Croats, and so on and on.

By the middle of the next century more than half the American people will trace their ancestry to somewhere in the Third World.[12] They or their ancestors will have been attracted here because of our relative freedom from state controls, because of our open economic opportunity and our religious freedom, and especially because of a constitutional system that can protect them from gross forms of discrimination, not to speak of the genocide, that have readily been practiced elsewhere. The vast majority of immigrants do not come here in order to replicate the culture they left behind, and they want the future of America to be for them what it has been for others in the past—yet a future in some way improved by reason of their own willing contribution. If we turn our backs on the structure of religious, social, and political ideas that constitutes our Western inheritance, which has been so attractive to so many immigrants from far-flung nations, if we reject it in favor of some Third World model, we will not be living in America as it has been given to us. It will be some version of Guatemala, Bosnia, or Rwanda.

Loathing Western Civilization: Christianity and Race in America

The relation of civilized men to savages has had a long, deep-seated, quite complicated fascination for Western intellectuals. It clearly antecedes even Jean-Jacques Rousseau and his modernist claim for the superiority of a free life lived in "the state of nature." This relation arose concomitant with the development of shipbuilding, nautical science, and astronomy. These made possible the trade contacts following on the Europeans' coasting of Africa, the Asian subcontinent, and, after Columbus, the Western Hemisphere. There were of course overland contacts with underdeveloped peoples; but these (apart from highly exaggerated tales by travelers in the Marco Polo school) yielded less knowledge about savages than the information brought home by the great navigators and those who followed them.

Before real contacts were definitively established, wild tales circulated about strange varieties of hybrid humanoid types: the offspring of the divine and the human (like Minos, fathered by the god Zeus on the maiden Europa); or the issue of the human and the animal (like the Minotaur, fathered by a bull upon Pasiphaë); or even the divine and the inanimate (like the *centauri*, half man and half horse, the offspring of Ixion and, of all things, a cloud). Many accounts of unknown lands turned their savage inhabitants into something manifestly less than human. I mean books such as Pliny's *Natural History*, which makes a claim for the existence of such creatures as the Cyclops, who have but a single eye in the middle of the forehead; or the Sciopodes, who have but a single leg with two feet; or the Hermaphrodites, who are half man, half woman. In *Othello* the Moor attains his success in wooing Desdemona by defeating not just "the Cannibals that each other eat" but

> The Anthropophagi, and men whose heads
> Do grow beneath their shoulders.[1]

Actual contact with the distant unknown, with what is now tediously generalized as "The Other,"[2] eliminated the mythic: centaurs faded from consciousness; satyrs disappeared; the demigods vanished in smoke. But the constant surprise created by the real experience of the primitive, whose world was newly accessible thanks to the triumph of modern navigational methods, raised afresh the issue of "the savage" and made natural a comparison between primitive and civilized ways of life. To some of the Spanish and Portuguese mariners in the Renaissance, African blacks looked human, but—given to cannibalism, infanticide, and human sacrifice—they had "evidently" no souls. One of the great tasks of Christian education in Europe was to overcome the widespread prejudice amongst people there that primitive man was less than human because he had not been endowed with a soul. St. Augustine (354–430) and other church fathers had repeatedly tried to show that this notion was incompatible with Christian doctrine. But this argument was not widely enough believed, even in "Christian" nations. The French philosopher Etienne Gilson remarks in his foreword to *The City of God* that

> the anti-racism of St. Augustine embraces all men whatsoever their state, even the pygmies, if there are such creatures; St. Augustine was not sure that there were. He even includes the Sciopodes, who shelter themselves from the sun in the shade of one foot, and the Cynocephali, who had dogs' heads and barked. Whoever is rational and mortal, regardless of color or shape or sound of voice, is certainly of the stock of Adam. None of the faithful (*nullus fidelium*) is to doubt that all of the above originated from the first creation. God knew how to beautify the universe through the diversity of its parts.

In the process of trying to educate navigators and emigrants about the complete spiritual equality of the natives, the Dominican friar Francisco de Vitoria (as James Brown Scott has shown in *The Spanish Origin of International Law*), provided the irrefutable arguments that ground the treatment of primitive peoples in the law of nations. Vitoria stipulated that

> —Every Indian is a man and thus capable of attaining salvation or damnation.
> —The Indians may not be deprived of their goods or power on account of their social backwardness, nor on account of their cultural inferiority or political disorganization.
> —Every man has the right to truth, to education, and to all that forms part of his cultural and spiritual development and advancement.
> —By natural law, every man has the right to his own life and to physical and mental integrity.
> —The Indians have the right not to be baptized and not to be forced to convert to Christianity against their will.

As Robert Royal has remarked, "these principles may seem of little significance in light of what happened to native territories. But failure to live up to principles does not mean that they are themselves meaningless."[3] Indeed not. We owe to Augustine, Vitoria, Bishop Las Casas, and many other such churchmen the elucidation of a moral law and the exposition of a Christian theology according to which the Arawaks, Caribs, Aztecs, Incas, and other such primitive New World tribes were indeed fully human, possessed of a soul, and therefore children of God for whom salvation was a desirable outcome of the complex cross-cultural process.

But the attraction of civilized men to primitive modes of being cannot fully be understood nowadays apart from the claims made by Freud in *Civilization and Its Discontents*. In that work Freud postulates that men have a built-in aversion to civilization because of the high price it exacts from us in the form of the repression of desire. In the state of nature, he remarks, primitive men—if they are strong enough and cunning enough—act immediately to gratify impulse and desire. They eat when they are hungry; they seize a weaker man's stone axe if it is better; they take a woman sexually whenever lust arises; and they will even kill the father or his kingly surrogate whenever external authority unbearably frustrates the will to power. For Freud, primitive man is a savage because he has not yet been socialized: that complex of impulses and instincts (called the id or the libido) has not been brought under the control of the ego and the superego.

Freud took it as a given that no civil society could be possible if men and women continuously acted on libidinal impulses. The result of doing so would be a social existence marked by continuous strife—an existence in which incest, rape, theft, and murder would be the common experience. Freud's theory of our social origin is thus a somber alternative to the happy glorification of our original freedom in nature as Rousseau had envisioned it. If Freud's account of primitive life reduced existence to the "nasty, short, and brutish," we can only say that Darwinism had provided him a ready-made set of arguments which could be adopted in the firm confidence that this new interpretation of civilization was grounded on empirical evidence.

Freud, then, superimposed on Darwin a psychoanalytical reading of the processes of becoming civilized. Civil society arose, as he imagined it, when (after constant civil strife) people agreed to repress or sublimate their libidinous drives for the sake of peace and mutual security. With such a social contract put in force, men were free to search for the rational and ethical bases of behavior and to develop those institutions—in law, religion, the schools, and so forth—that make for peace and that protect life. Nevertheless these achievements of the ego and the superego are purchased at the expense of the repression of the instinctual life. That libidinal energy may become etiolated, but it will never completely disappear. It is the frustration of the libido that makes for human dissatisfaction with civilization, that causes eruptive attacks upon it, and that creates the modern regressive attraction to primitive culture. Whichever group is locally regarded as more primitive, more native, or less civilized (historically, blacks, Mexicans, Indians, Asiatics) is likely to be romanticized as somehow more "in touch" with the "primordial self," with "fundamental human appetites," or with what D. H. Lawrence grandly called "blood consciousness."

For the past century, intellectuals have given themselves over to Darwin, Marx, and Freud with a wild abandon. And the disastrous consequence of their influence—in defining human origins as bestial, in encouraging the rejection of repression (especially sexual repression), and in affirming the "holiness of impulse" and the "authenticity of instinct"—has manifested itself in a growing hostility to the structures and institutions that constrain violence and socialize men and women in their group relations.[+] If "Man is born free, but is everywhere in chains," as Jean-Jacques opined; if the chain linking us to our simian ancestors has only a single missing link, as Darwinism solemnly intones; if you ought to destroy (capitalist) civilization, as Marx and Engels advised, because "You have nothing to lose but your chains"; if all of this is true, then why not go all the way and assent to the fantasy of the superiority of primitive cultures? Why not romanticize native groups like "the gentle Tasadays"? Why not attack the Christianized West for trying to civilize primitive cultures that practiced cannibalism and human sacrifice? Why not flaunt one's own tattoos and body-piercing and act out atavistic (call it bestial) social behavior? The Stanford University student chant "Hey, hey, ho, ho, Western Civ's gotta go" expresses perfectly the ignorance of the young whose professors really had no coherent idea of what Western civilization was and the horror that would attend a real regression into the savage heart of darkness.

The intent of the following pages is to hold out, for inspection, two recent histories by white males, both university professors, who undertake to comment on the origin and character of Western civilization and particularly to assess the role of Christianity in the shaping of the West. Both exemplify perfectly the hatred of civilization that arises out of the secular rationalism deriving from Darwin, Marx, and Freud (with a dose of Nietzsche thrown in); and both illustrate that hostility to the traditions of the mind and spirit that one finds so frequently now in the University, where the "tenured radicals" (to borrow Roger Kimball's definitive phrase) have now taken command of the education of our youth.

The first book, *The Founding Legend of Western Civilization*,[5] is by Richard Waswo, a professor of English at the University of Geneva. Waswo undertakes nothing less than to bring to light the hidden monomyth that underlies the development of Western civilization in its entirety. This would be a tall order even for a sociologist or a historian. But as the disciplines of sociology and history have become bankrupt, nowadays anybody can pretend to be either, or both. Or, to put it somewhat differently, since avant-garde intellectuals in the academy now pretend there is no longer a set of intellectual disciplines, anybody can "discourse" about any area he pleases. The upshot is that we now have college and university professors claiming expertise in all kinds of disciplines for which they are not trained. My own field, American literature, is typical of the bankruptcy of the disciplines. For not only has a complete mastery of American literature been abandoned as a curricular objective of graduate study, but extraneous courses in the arcane theory of various social scientists are regularly substituted for literature, on the assumption that poetry is not intelligible without an understanding of Bakhtin, Derrida, or Jacques Lacan. Walk into any college literature class nowadays and you are likely to hear Foucault's theory of sado-masochism advanced as the real explanation of romanticism; Marx's *Das Kapital* as the key to fictive naturalism; "queer theory" as the the only avenue to understanding Faulkner, and so on. Professor Waswo has spent a great deal of time reading about anthropology, narratology, myths, monomyths; and he believes that an archetypal legend he has found not only originated culture in the West as we know it but that even today it surreptitiously directs our civilization in terrible ways.

To understand the story of culture, Professor Waswo claims that we must understand the stories cultures tell. The West has only a single important story, for him, and it is contained in the *Aeneid*. Professor Waswo finds it significant that Virgil locates the origin of the Roman Empire not in the greatness of primordial Latium but in the sack of Troy by the Greeks. The destruction of this once-great civilization resulted in the exile of Aeneas and his men, who wandered away, bearing their culture with them. As they moved, they vanquished the savages who fought with them, finally settling on the Tiber and founding Rome. From this hub, Virgil says, all subsequent civilization radiated outward. The later western European mythographers tended, like Virgil, to locate their national origins in the culture and the greatness of these exiles from Troy. That is, the cultures of Italy, Spain, France, and even Great Britain—as we learn from Geoffrey of Monmouth—imagined themselves as all descended from Trojans bearing the gifts of civilization. The Rome they founded was the great center of the West.

Most of us think that the bringing of law, art, architecture, literature, city planning, and government administration into the anarchic tribal disorder of middle and northern Europe, in the Dark Ages, was a good thing. This was the *translatio imperii et studii*—the transmission of empire and learning into benighted regions where only savagery had prevailed. But for Professor Waswo, the process of creating Western civilization was—and still is—an unacceptably brutal and violent one. The introduction of Western civilization, wherever it has occurred, means for him the "unfounding" of whatever primitive society might happen to have been there at the time. He has taken his text from the Marxist critic Walter Benjamin, who claimed in "Theses on the Philosophy of History" that "There is no document of civilization which is not at the same time a document of barbarism." Whatever may be the value of the great achievements of Western civilization—let us say the Parthenon, the Sistine Chapel, *The Portrait of a Lady*, the polio vaccine, Wagner's *Ring*, the telephone, the odes of John Keats— these have been purchased at the price of the destruction of the poor, the primitive, the dispossessed, "those without a history" who vanished in the process by which culture was brought into the place where they had lived.

To support this reading of Western civilization—as a process of butchery bought with the blood of vanished primitives—Waswo summons the usual suspects—Michel Foucault, Jurgen Habermas, Raymond Williams, and Clifford Geertz among them. These romantic radicals are adduced to prop up a jerry-built historical argument—evidently made up of bits and pieces of Waswo's lecture notes on poetry and fiction—that condemns the whole of Western civilization.

After an opening discussion of Virgil and Latium, Waswo hopscotches to the Middle Ages and thence to the Renaissance (the latter evidently his academic specialization). The iniquity of civilization is then pursued relentlessly in chapters on (of all people) Spenser and Donne, Pope and Richardson. These writers soon give way to other chapters advancing the manifestly bankrupt argument that, since the Renaissance, it has been capitalism that has fueled the destruction of indigenes in the name of civilization. All forms of colonialism are declared to be wicked. "It has been the destiny of savages in our founding legend since Virgil: they join civilization or it rolls over them. In the world today joining civilization still means what it has meant since Columbus: producing for our money economy."

In glorifying the primitive, in romanticizing a barbaric way of life which sensible men deplore as entailing disease, filth, illiteracy, superstition, and violence, Professor Waswo pretty much exhibits what is wrong with English departments today. Although he is a professor of literature, it is evident that he has no feeling for the felicities of art or for aesthetic considerations of any kind. One would never guess from his discussion of Joseph Conrad's *Heart of Darkness* that Conrad is anything but a racist and an imperialist—instead of one of the most brilliant and complex artists of his or any time. Waswo is one of those misplaced sixties radicals who use their academic lecterns to propagandize for the new identity politics. The beneficiaries of Waswo's ideological obsession are the "traditional societies," the "tribal peoples," and "helpless primitives" who are passing out of existence even now: "To us, people who roam forests and build no walls are not *quite* people; our legend, mediated through all kinds of discourses in all our languages, thus defines them as some sub-, pre-, or proto-humanity not *quite* entitled to whatever full measure of compassion we are presumably obliged to bestow on others more like ourselves."

With his uncritical compassion for the nomads and the forest peoples of the world, Professor Waswo is naturally a supporter of Survival International. He gives us a long list of the endangered tribes, much of the material derived from *The Gaia Atlas of First Peoples* and other such sources. In South America, to name only one continent, he finds on the endangered list the Wayapi, the Palikur, the Akawaio, the Pemon, the Waiwai, and so forth. He sees Western-style governments, the World Bank, and the UN agencies as instrumental in their destruction. He wants your money to go toward their protection, in their natural habitat. No practical particulars are given, but it is clear that this professor wants the tribes left alone—alone with their malnutrition, disease, ignorance, and despair. (Unfortunately for him, they want powerboats, nylon fishing nets, portable radios, and electric generators.)

In the end, Professor Waswo traces the looming extinction of these native peoples back to the Trojans who founded Rome and inaugurated the transmission of empire and learning. He thinks the *story* itself of their culture-bearing actually directed and controlled human behavior in subsequent interethnic encounters. He believes that the legend as such dictated how civilized men and savages engaged with each other over the centuries. Only a Marxist English teacher, impervious to political and economic reality, could so exalt mere storytelling at the expense of sociological reality and thus dismiss the manifest benefits of a civilization that has made the West the envy of the Orient and the Third World.

Because he feels "discourse" to be more powerful than historical events and even empirical facts, Waswo concludes by arguing that a different story or founding legend would have changed Western history. He would have preferred a cultural mythology founded on—of all things—Homer's *Odyssey*. Having recently reread it in the light of the televised film version starring Armand Assante and Isabella Rossellini, I frankly doubt it. It is not civilization that turns men into swine but rather gross appetite freely indulged; libidinal excess justified as conducive to mental health; the rejection of the moral law and the conscience that calls us to account for our human imperfections; and the absence of those social and material conditions that permit men and women to form the institutions of society that civilize us. Books like *The Founding Legend of Western Civilization* do not merely give cultural history and English studies a bad name; they libel the process by which superior cultures have helped to lift those less fortunate.

II

We owe to Nietzsche perhaps the most withering intellectual attack yet mounted on Christianity as a religious belief system. In *Beyond Good and Evil* and scattered throughout his writings elsewhere, Nietzsche expresses nothing but contempt for the way in which Christianity teaches "even the lowliest how to place themselves through piety in an illusory higher order of things and thus to maintain their contentment with the real order, in which their life is hard enough—and precisely this hardness is necessary." He wants nothing less than to annihilate the Christian ethic—which he contemptuously dismisses as a psychology of "devotion, self-sacrifice for one's neighbor, the whole morality of self-denial. . . ."

Of course Nietzsche wants the weak sent to the wall so that the heroic man can arise. He is the man who will not deny himself, for he frankly acknowledges the will to power that drives him. It is he who will dictate the values by which the mass of men, contemptuous lot, are to live their lives. Only if the *Sklaven-moral,* or slave morality, is replaced by the *Herren-moral,* or the morality of the master, can the *Ubermensch,* or the Superman, evolve. Christianity Nietzsche saw as an impediment to the development of this Superman. He wrote:

> Christianity has been the most calamitous kind of arrogance yet. Men, not high and hard enough to have any right to try to form man as artists; men, not strong and far-sighted enough to *let* the foreground law of thousandfold failure and ruin prevail, though it cost them sublime self-conquest; men, not noble enough to see the abysmally different order of rank, chasm of rank, between man and man—*such* men have so far held sway over the fate of Europe with their "equal before God," until finally a smaller, almost ridiculous type, a herd animal, something eager to please, sickly, mediocre has been bred, the European of today.

The central emphasis in the Christian faith—self-sacrifice in the service of God and man—was for Nietzsche "a sacrifice of all freedom, all pride, all self-confidence of the spirit; at the same time, enslavement and self-mockery, self-mutilation."

Nietzsche's designation of Christianity as an "arrogant" faith, yet the religion of "slaves," will inevitably be recalled by anyone reading Forrest G. Wood's *The Arrogance of Faith: Christianity and Race in America from the Colonial Era to the Twentieth Century.*[6] It may seem unfair to single out Wood's dubious lucubrations as exemplary of the contemporary attack on religious faith—specifically on Christianity. But I cannot think of another book that so perfectly illustrates the "Christian-bashing" that has become the stock-in-trade of the media, the film and television industry, impious "homosexual artists," and certain liberal politicians on the national level.[7] Wood attempts nothing less than a full-scale assault on the "Christian view" of blacks. But, unlike Nietzsche (who, by the way, is never mentioned in this derivative screed), Wood sees Christianity as a religion of the *Herren-moral,* the faith of vicious and hypocritical bigots who are driven by racism alone.

That the Christian churches in America, like almost every other public institution, have had a troubled history in relation to questions of slavery and race will come as no surprise to anyone broadly familiar with the course of our national development, especially in the years preceding and after the Civil War. American church history unfolded as it did in part because most American Christians accepted literally the teachings of the Hebrew Bible and the New Testament as the divinely inspired Word of God, the texts constituting God's formal covenants with mankind. While nearly every Christian denomination in America, in the years that followed the Revolution, denounced slavery as an evil, there was an absolute failure of racial discussion in the immediate antebellum years. Great Britain, which abolished slavery not long after the American Revolution, might have constituted a model of enlightened political emancipation—and should have. But the emergence of ill-educated raging hotheads and smug moral authoritarians on both sides prevented sensible men from commanding the debate and so negotiating a peaceful resolution that would have preserved the Union while abolishing slavery.

Because of their belief in the inspiration of the Bible, then, many Southern Christians found their authority for the maintenance of slavery in scriptural texts. Leviticus 25:44–46, although it established the law only for the ancient Israelites, was often taken as a warrant for the permissible forms of American slaveholding:

> Both thy bondmen, and thy bondmaids, which thou shalt have, shall be of the heathen that are round about you; of them shall ye buy bondmen and bondmaids. Moreover of the children of the strangers that do sojourn among you, of them shall ye buy, and of their families that are with you, which they begat in your land: and they shall be your possession. And ye shall take them as an inheritance for your children after you, to inherit them for a possession; they shall be your bondmen for ever: but over your brethren the children of Israel, ye shall not rule one over another with rigour.

Of course, New Testament practice incorporated and superseded, for Christians, the Mosaic law, but even the New Testament acknowledged slavery, which was endemic in the Roman Empire, the Near East, and Africa. Given the existence of an institution that was taken for granted everywhere in antiquity, it is not surprising that the authors of the Epistles felt obliged to stipulate the moral conventions that ought to govern it. St. Paul, in Ephesians 6:5–8, admonishes those who are enslaved:

> Servants, be obedient to them that are your masters according to the flesh, with fear and trembling, in singleness of your heart, as unto Christ; Not with eyeservice, as men-pleasers, but as the servants of Christ, doing the will of God from the heart; With good will doing service, as to the Lord, and not to men: Knowing that whatsoever good thing any man doeth, the same shall he receive of the Lord, whether he be bond or free.

Likewise the epistle to the Colossians counsels: "Masters, provide your slaves with what is right and fair, because you know that you also have a Master in heaven." In fact, it is just to say that in Matthew 20:26–28 Christ commanded all believers henceforth to regard themselves as slaves, as individuals dedicated to service: "Whoever wants to become great among you must be your servant, and whoever wants to be first must be your slave—just as the Son of Man did not come to be served, but to serve, and to give his life as a ransom for many." In this respect Nietzsche is right about the Christian ethic of self-sacrifice, and Wood is misinformed. The latter wants us to think that slavery somehow originated inside the institution of the Christian church. But slaves already existed in every society to which Christianity was carried.

These biblical texts acknowledge slavery and express the Christian's subordination to the civil and military power of the state that enforces it. The early church fathers did not absolutely condemn slavery since they inferred that it must in some way express the will of God. Slavery, for instance, could be seen as the just outcome of sinful behavior. When a nation rose up and made war against its neighbor and its soldiers were taken prisoner in battle and enslaved, their servitude could be deemed an appropriate punishment for wrongful warmongering. Even in the case of victory by a warmongering nation, those enslaved must nevertheless be suffering a just punishment of some kind. In the fallen condition, as Augustine makes plain, "sin is the primary cause of servitude." If this seems harsh, no one can claim to be innocent, as *The City of God* makes plain:

> But, as men once were, when their nature was as God created it, no

man was a slave either to man or to sin. However, slavery is now penal in character and planned by that law which commands the preservation of the natural order and forbids its disturbance. If no crime had ever been perpetrated against this law, there would be no crime to repress with the penalty of enslavement.[8]

Given the function of slavery as punition for some kind of sinful behavior that God in his unknowable design wishes to punish, the question for mankind is what ethic ought to govern one's own relation to the slave. Hence there arose the biblical precepts defining the Christian slave's duties and the obligations of the Christian slavemaster.

If early Christianity assumed the existence of slavery, there are of course other biblical texts that command a charity toward others that is incompatible with slaveholding. If one is to love his neighbor as if he were oneself, that central commandment alone would imply an equality that implicitly subverts the institution of slavery. More directly to the point, St. Paul, in the epistle to Philemon, celebrates the devoted service of the slave Onesimus, whose actual equality in Christ is made plain to his earthly master Philemon.

St. Paul's preoccupation with the status of the slave actually derives from a paradox implicit in the Incarnation. As he sets it forth in the epistle to the Philippians (2:5–11), although Christ is one with God, he must be understood as having emptied himself of his Divine selfhood in order completely to have realized his full humanity:

> Have this mind among yourselves, which you have in Christ Jesus, who, though he was in the form of God, did not count equality with God a thing to be grasped, but emptied himself, taking the form of a slave, being born in the likeness of men. And being found in human form he humbled himself and became obedient unto death, even death on a cross. Therefore God has highly exalted him and bestowed on him the name which is above every name, that at the name of Jesus every knee should bow, in heaven and on earth and under the earth, and every tongue confess that Jesus Christ is Lord, to the glory of God the Father.

Further on in *The City of God*, St. Augustine remarks that central to this Pauline emphasis on the slave is the very selfsameness of service and servitude. Christ is a slave in that he performs the particular service of mediating between God and man, the human and divine:

> Christ Jesus, Himself man, is the true Mediator, for, inasmuch as He took the "form of a slave," He became the "Mediator between God and men." In His character as God, He receives sacrifices in union with the Father, with whom He is one God; yet He chose, in His character as a slave, to be Himself the Sacrifice, rather than to receive it, lest any one might take occasion to think that sacrifice could be rendered to a creature. Thus it is that He is both the Priest who offers and the Oblation that is offered.[9]

Slavery may represent servitude of various kinds. Such sayings of Jesus as "Truly, truly, I say to you, every one who commits sin is a slave to sin" (John 8:34), or St. Peter's remark that "whatever overcomes a man, to that he is enslaved" (2 Peter 2:19) define forms of spiritual servitude. But it was opposition to the physical enslavement of blacks that constituted the basis for the Northern Christian abolitionist movement and inaugurated the interpretive battles that divided Christians until the midcentury antebellum era, when a number of Southern denominations split off from their Northern brethren and formed separate branches supporting slavery.

If the Bible led some nineteenth-century Christians to acquiesce in or tolerate the existence of slavery, yet another source of Christian passivity toward slavery was the view of the body versus the soul and the view of this life versus the next. Wood is quite right to note Christian belief in a Pauline dualism, according to which body and soul are distinct entities. Whatever the politics of the state one lived in, true freedom came—as Presbyterian James Henley Thornwell (among others) argued—from "the emancipation of the will from the power of sin." Until the *fin-de-siècle* rise of the Social Gospel, salvation always was an individual matter, *not a project for the reformation of society as a whole*. The Christian renders unto Caesar what he must, but he is in fact a citizen of the City of God. Perhaps the most striking formulation of this position is that by the Reverend Jacobus Elisa Joannes Capitein of the Dutch Reformed Church, who, in the *Dissertatio Politico-Theologica de Servitute, Libertati Christianae, non Contraria* (1742), confidently preached that slavery was "not contrary to Christian freedom," a declaration all the more forceful because his parents were native-born African slaves. Spiritual freedom in Christ is frankly always more desirable than bodily freedom (which is an illusion in any case), and therein lies the salvation of the soul.

Professor Wood has no use for belief in the inspired utterance of the Bible or for this Pauline dualism of body and soul. Nor can he entertain the possible sincerity of any nineteenth-century Christian who assented to the arguments for defending this peculiar institution. In fact he has no use for Christianity at all, since he sees it not as the faith of slaves but the religion of their racist slavemasters:

> The central thesis of this book is that Christianity, in the five centuries since its message was first carried to the peoples of the New World—and, in particular, to the natives and the transplanted Africans of English North America and the United States—has been fundamentally racist in its ideology, organization, and practice. While popes, bishops, preachers, evangelists, and missionaries proclaimed Christianity to be the ultimate solution to all of the world's problems, their celebration of that belief created and maintained one of the worst of those problems, a problem so pervasive but insidious that for a very long time many observers thought the cause of the disease was its cure.

In Wood's view the enormity of racism and slaveholding was not the result of the moral blindness of Southern or Northern bigots, not the shortcoming of immoral American men and women. The criminality lay in "not just churches and communicants but, more fundamentally, [in] Christianity as a belief system." Again: "Christianity was a cornerstone of modern slavery and, *ergo,* modern racism." Finally: "English North Americans embraced slavery *because* they were Christians, not in spite of it." These are frankly the absurd expostulations of one who has lost complete touch with reality.

Such preposterous claims, advanced by a professor of history at California State University, speak ill for the profession of history in the academy today. But, as Gertrude Himmelfarb, Keith Windschuttle, and many others have lamented, academic history today has dissolved into fiction-writing, ideological posturing, and pointless counterfactual imaginings. Wood justifies his smug moral superiority by invoking "the requirements of scholarship":

Since I was obliged to observe the canons of scholarship I did not have the luxury of accepting on faith an inerrant Bible and thus was left only with the premise that Christianity itself, the Way and the Word, was man-created—that man created God in his image, or, as Voltaire put it, *Si Dieu n'existait pas, il faudrait l'inventer*—and, accordingly, was the source of many of the evils that Christians insisted were human corruptions.

But the canons of historical scholarship hardly lead to the tendentious conclusion of which Wood is here so confident—and in any case these canons are not at all observed in his polemical diatribe. I shall not repeat here Eugene Genovese's *New Republic* exposé of Wood's many egregious "embarrassing errors, some of them really dumb." These "howlers," as Genovese called them, may be briefly classified as misinterpreting Christian doctrine; misrepresenting historical documents; falsifying the position on slavery of many Christian ministers; caricaturing the views of other historians; getting wrong the denomination, sectional loyalty, and even nationality of historical figures; and so on. Wood's *The Arrogance of Faith* stands, for Genovese, as "a testimonial to the standards that have been reigning in the historical profession since its establishment capitulated to the demands for political and ideological conformity that were introduced by the McCarthyists of the 1950s and have been carried forward by radical leftists ever since." In addition, Wood's "sundry other atrocities" enumerated by Genovese, whose knowledge of slavery in this historical period is beyond cavil, are enough to land Wood's book in the dustbin of botched historical scholarship.[10]

Genovese's comment on the dismal fate of the profession of history is inescapably evident. But Wood's work is also a symptom of the manifest deficiencies of the liberal mind at the present moment in our history. In particular one notes the contempt he evinces for Western civilization and the role of Christianity in its development. Likewise one notes Wood's readiness to sentimentalize blacks and to exalt African culture at any price. It must be said at the outset that the African slaves brought by force to this country by the slavetraders had been living in a Stone Age culture. They believed in various forms of animism, practiced a superstitious magic, and organized themselves according to a warrior code that made for more or less continuous African tribal conflict. This is still the case today in many nations. One would never get the idea from Wood's study that *they conquered and bought and sold each other into slavery*—long before they were introduced to Christianity.[11] If the social organization of African tribes was simple by Western standards, its science was virtually nonexistent, its art and architecture rudimentary, its educational system primitive by any standard. Wood quotes with smug approval the African writer Okot p'Bitek, who complains of the readiness of Westerners to characterize Africans as "barbarian, primitive, pagan, savage, idolatrous, heathen, and superstitious."

But such they seemed, it must be said, to the English and Americans who bought them from the African slavetraders. Given their condition, the enslaved—as the historical record often discloses—exhibited a belief in the superiority of Europeans or Americans, thanks to their remarkable science, technology, and educated understanding. The earliest records of exploration and colonization suggest that the Spanish *conquistadores* and French Canadian Jesuits were often regarded as gods and worshiped as superior beings. In any case, because of the barbaric conditions of the slaves' existence in America there arose a fervent wish on the part of many American ministers and missionaries to educate, civilize, and convert them to the faith.

Nothing could be more risible, from the point of view of comparative cultural analysis, than Wood's attempt to exalt non-Western forms of social organization or behavior at the expense of Christian America. Some of the following material has nothing to do with the South African and West African tribes who came as slaves to America, and thus its pertinence to an argument about the origin of slavery in Christianity is tenuous at best. Nevertheless Wood goes rather far afield to note that

> the ancestors of the modern Sudanese had devised artificial streetlighting facilities. Two thousand years ago, the forefathers of the Haya people of modern Tanzania produced medium-carbon steel in preheated, forced-draft furnaces, a technique not developed in the West until the nineteenth century. The Moche people of ancient Peru, whose society flourished from A.D. 100 to 700, were wonderful architects and craftsmen who developed sophisticated metal-

plating techniques fourteen centuries before the Europeans were to perfect similar skills.

To this Wood adds the "dazzling" accomplishment that "Twenty centuries before Christ, the citizens of Mohenjo-Daro on the Indus river in what is today Pakistan had developed an effective sewerage system." Wood wants us to think it an advantage over the Christian West that some early peoples in Asia knew enough not to befoul their villages. He also evidently believes that some kind of moral superiority arises from the fact that "The Bushmen of the Kalahari Desert did not even have a word in their language for 'guilt.'" And he quotes approvingly Geoffrey Parrinder's *West African Religions* to the effect that the distinction between good and evil is unknown to the people of West Africa.

These are stupefying remarks—mind-boggling in their credulity. No word for "guilt"? No capacity to distinguish between good and evil? And this Wood holds out to us as a mode of being that is ethically superior to the ethical vision offered by Christianity? One wonders how (without a vocabulary based on moral distinctions and categories) West Africans can have expressed their opposition to being taken as slaves! Non-Western accomplishments in drainage, metallurgy, and architecture surely deserve their due in the history of human struggle and endeavor. And we are all richer for the surviving attainments of these cultures. But what really lies beneath Wood's glorification of these non-Western accomplishments is a detestation of the West, which in Wood's view suffers from "ethnocentric shackles," a "cultural myopia, and its taproot was Christianity."

This detestation of his culture—or of the religion that has shaped it—makes Wood stretch for any scrap of information that will assist him in caricaturing Christianity. He makes Islam, with its tradition of slavetrading and the *jihad* or "holy war," look positively beatific by comparison. If Southern clergymen sought admission to the plantations to educate, civilize, and convert blacks to Christianity—knowing that slaveholders would deny them all access if they preached against slavery—the pastors, to Wood, were *ipso facto* trimmers and hypocrites. If Catholic priests and Protestant ministers inveighed against slavery by warning of its corrupting effects and of God's wrath to come, Wood dismisses them as only concerned with the moral health of slavemasters and as without compassion for the slaves themselves. Wood argues, against a mass of overwhelming evidence, that the institutional involvement of Northern churches in the abolition movement was "virtually nonexistent"—this despite the anti-slavery evangelism of Theodore Dwight Weld and Thomas Wentworth Higginson, the Presbyterians Charles Grandison Finney, Henry Ward Beecher, and Arthur and Lewis Tappan, the Quaker Grimké sisters, and many, many others. Moreover, if the Christian churches *did* attack slavery, Wood then shifts his ground and claims that the attack actually "obfuscated the more fundamental issue of *racism.*"

Perhaps the most significant omission of this book is Wood's failure to discuss the black's relation to Christianity. He does take note of the development of separate wings of some Protestant denominations, such as the African Methodist Episcopal church and its white counterpart. And he sees the formation of black congregations as a response to the prejudice of whites who did not wish to worship with blacks, even after the Emancipation Proclamation. Many blacks, for varying reasons, also wanted their own congregations. It is possible that black racism may account for the evolution of some of these congregations, but I doubt it: racism was the very evil that black Christianity sought to eradicate, and segregation was preeminently an imposition of the white man. Still, Wood's view of Christianity is such that he has no way of explaining why many nineteenth-century congregations did have mixed audiences, or why white Christians—especially in many Presbyterian and Baptist congregations—not only allowed blacks to become ministers but sat in the pews and consented to be preached to by them. There is a long tradition of churchly satisfaction in whites' being preached to by African blacks whose ministry represents the successful fruition of white missionary work abroad. Wood seems to have no conception of this history.

But, more decisively, Wood's hostility to Christianity makes it utterly incomprehensible why blacks should have yielded to conversion at all or have consented to bind themselves to the doctrine and practice of this faith. Any Christian can understand (though Wood cannot) the slave poet Phyllis Wheatley's poem "On Being Brought from Africa to America":

> 'Twas mercy brought me from my pagan land,
> Taught my benighted soul to understand
> That there's a God, that there's a Saviour too;
> Once I redemption neither sought nor knew.

If American blacks have a special relation to Christianity, it lies in the recognition that even a slave passage to America brought with it such spiritual and economic benefits that it can only be understood as a form of divine mercy. This affirmation has turned the black church into one of the most vital manifestations of Christianity in America. I do not mean the views espoused by the Reverend Jesse Jackson or the Reverend Al Sharpton, for whom the pulpit is a mere ladder to political power, but rather the thousands of local congregations where blacks regularly engage with issues of the soul, sin, and salvation.[12] If it were true—as Wood claims—that "Christianity was a cornerstone of modern slavery and, *ergo,* modern racism," what modern black could profess this faith? Wood must think that black Christians are gullible fools for practicing this religion; and his implied contempt for them is appalling to contemplate. But then the preaching of Christ crucified, as Saint Paul reminded the Corinthians, *is* foolishness to those who place their faith in mere reason, science, history, or mass politics. Anyone who thinks to save his soul through these is in for a real letdown.

That said, white American Christians can take absolutely no comfort in the churches' response to racism. Antebellum enslavement, civil war, and segregated life generated admirable instances of Christian devotion, in both the North and the South, to black need. But the Christian record is also appallingly disfigured by the racist hate-mongering of ignorant preachers, self-ordained bishops, and prejudiced congregants. Wood gleefully records their abominations in *The Arrogance of Faith*; and it is well to have them gathered into one place for moral reflection on the Christian's readiness, in relation to others, to do that which he ought not to do and to fail to do that which he knows he should. The lesson of humility that it ought to teach would make even Nietzsche smile.

Countee Cullen at "The Heights"

This essay undertakes to describe the undergraduate career of Countee Cullen at New York University between 1922 and 1925 and to present an edited text of his most significant surviving piece of undergraduate critical prose, the senior honors thesis he presented to the Department of English on May 1, 1925: "The Poetry of Edna St. Vincent Millay: An Appreciation." In both biographical and critical treatments of Cullen, these years have received scant attention, although they were immensely formative in his experience as a poet. In fact the thesis presented here is largely unknown to Cullen's readers or to students of the Harlem Renaissance.

The mind of a poet, the poetic influences to which he is exposed at an impressionable moment in his life, the critical context in which these influences are received, and the personalities of those having a decisive effect on the shaping of his perceptions and values—all of these are essential in understanding his originality, his development, and his reception. In the case of Countee Cullen, an adequate account of these varying influences—including the impact of Millay's cynicism, ennui, and world-weariness, together with her love lyrics and ballad forms—would require a full-length biography, one more devoted to the facts and their critical meaning than is the case with Blanche E. Ferguson's *Countee Cullen and the Negro Renaissance* (1966). In the space available here, no such full account is possible. But something of a start may be made by presenting his essay on Millay and by bringing to light some of the facts—hitherto unknown or forgotten—of this remarkable poet's education at New York University.

As will be evident to anyone reading this thesis, Countee Cullen, though only twenty-one years old when he wrote the work, was an accomplished and subtle student of poetry. The essay reflects a sensitive understanding of the varied generic and metrical gifts of Millay. And it is passionately responsive to her sense of the fragility and transience of beauty and love in a world where all must change and die. Students of Cullen's poetry have sometimes noted, without demonstrating at any length, the impact on him of Millay's lyric verse. (An exception is Margaret Perry's suggestive comparison of "The Shroud of Color" with Millay's "Renascence.") The present thesis offers, I believe, the critical ground on which a fuller influence study and a more informed comparative evaluation can be based. For here, in Cullen's "appreciation," will be found a description of the thematic and technical features of Millay's art that Cullen most admired, as well as a commentary on those defects of her performance of which he was most critical.

I am not of course the first to note the relation of Cullen's art to that of Millay. Walter White, for example, linked Cullen to a poetic tradition "of which A. E. Housman and Edna St. Vincent Millay are the bright stars."[1] Perry herself has remarked that "Countee Cullen's poetry also bears a close resemblance to both the poetry of Edward Arlington Robinson (whom Cullen considered to be America's finest poet) and of Edna St. Vincent Millay."[2] But Perry was apparently not aware that Cullen had written this thesis—it is not listed among the "Unpublished Works" in her bibliography —so that the ground for a more extensive comparison was not available to her.

I shall perhaps go further than White and Perry. I shall argue that, if in 1930 Cullen gave to Robinson the laurel as the best American poet, in 1925—when he wrote his thesis and published *Color*—Millay was foremost in his mind. Further, while granting that some of the following themes may also be found in Housman and Keats, I shall argue that common to both Cullen and Millay are these thematic elements: 1) a profound recognition of the transience of life; 2) a sense of the world as the vale of inexplicable agony and suffering; 3) an awareness of the inadequacy of the usual Christian explanation of why God permits, if he does not inflict, human suffering; 4) the impulse, therefore, to seize the day, to indulge in and celebrate poetically the pleasures of life—especially love in its erotic character and sensuous beauty in all its forms. I would call this a frank aesthetic and sexual paganism, typical of the disillusioned youth of the 1920s; 5) nevertheless, a recognition that love is transient and sexual pleasure is fleeting—a recognition conveyed in both poets in wry, flip, cynical, and anguished tones; 6) yet the implied wish that it might be otherwise, that the order of existence might fulfill the heart's desire, especially in relation to love and sexuality, together with an occasional affirmation, sometimes like resignation, that there is a providential ordering, somehow, of human affairs.

All this is perhaps just another way of saying what Countee Cullen himself said, namely, that one of his chief difficulties had always been "reconciling a Christian upbringing with a pagan inclination."[3] This aesthetic and sexual hedonism, or paganism, in Millay was one of the chief appeals of her work. To these six thematic elements that link Millay and Cullen I would add a seventh, technical parallel: both poets' preference for the conventional forms of the poetic tradition—in relation to rhythms, rhyme schemes, stanzaic structures, and genres—especially the sonnet and the ballad.

II

Cullen's thesis, "The Poetry of Edna St. Vincent Millay," exists in a typescript of nine numbered pages, plus an unnumbered title page and an unnumbered final page listing Cullen's references and bibliography. It is contained in a brown cardboard cover marked in black ink "Cullen" and "1925" (perhaps in Cullen's hand). Stamped on the title page is "Library/N.Y. Univ." Between 1925 and 1972 this thesis was shelved in the English House Library at University College in the Bronx. When this college at "The Heights" was merged with Washington Square College in Greenwich Village, Cullen's thesis was transported, with others, to the downtown English Department storage room, where, after a flood in the building in 1976, I identified and salvaged it. The thesis is now located in the Cullen papers of the New York University Archives. Xeroxed copies of it have also been deposited in the Fales Collection of the Elmer

Holmes Bobst Library at New York University, in the Cullen papers on deposit at Fisk University, and at the Amistad Research Center at Tulane University in New Orleans. A copy of the thesis was also presented to the late Mrs. Ida Mae Cullen, who graciously granted permission to publish it here.

The essay is typed on plain white bond, 8½ x 11-inch typing paper, now yellowed, with the watermark "Whiting's Mutual Bond," and a logo of a capital W within which rests an acorn. The title page, now marked with smudged fingerprints, lists title and author as well as Professor Hyder E. Rollins's evaluation. The nine-page typescript of the text has margins of about 1¾ inches on the left and 1 inch on the top, right, and bottom. The text is paginated in type at top center. The footnotes, entered in black ink at the bottom, are not numbered consecutively throughout the paper but begin on each new page with "(1)"; they are also entered by hand in the text. Since the brand of typewriter is unknown, it cannot be calculated whether the text is double-spaced or set at 1½ line spaces.

By modern standards it has the look of the latter. Throughout, evident typing errors are sometimes corrected in black ink in Cullen's hand or through typewriter strikeovers. I make no effort to present a facsimile of the text. Strikeovers, hand corrections, misspacings, misspellings, and other features of imperfect student typing and orthography are here silently corrected. Cullen's occasional errors in the transcription of Millay's poetry are also corrected. (Possibly he quoted from memory or used a corrupt popular reprint of Millay's poems rather than the standard edition.) Professor Rollins, to whom Cullen submitted the paper, did not assign it a letter grade. Instead this handwritten assessment appears on the title page: "Approved (after some mental reservations!) Hyder E. Rollins, May 6, 1925." His mental reservations are specified only in his underlining the word *immortal* in the sentence of Cullen's essay beginning "But in 'The Poet and His Book' Miss Millay rises to immortal heights. . . ."

Perhaps it is best now to let the thesis speak for itself. At its conclusion I shall try to set it in the fuller context of Cullen's life and work as an undergraduate at New York University:

THE POETRY OF EDNA ST. VINCENT MILLAY

An Appreciation

by

Countee Cullen

We are forever searching for the hand behind the picture, for the physical embodiment that wrought the mighty symphony and the majestic poem; and we are forever being disappointed and disillusioned. Curiosity is, however, a mortal ailment, and idols must continue to fall. I remember absenting myself from classes one day last summer, and dispensing with my last dollar, unterrified by certain retribution in the form of a lunchless week, in order to hear Edna St. Vincent Millay read her poems at Union Theological Seminary! My idol did not fall, but surely she wobbled dangerously. After the manner of the great, she was tardy. She made a *grande entrée*, half an hour after her scheduled time, amid a flutter of applause, half-resentful, half joyfully anticipatory. She was attired, most conspicuously, in a brilliant yellow-and-red Spanish shawl, the effect of which she must have appreciated, since she consumed a full five minutes in languidly divesting herself of it. She read in a calm, even voice; she deprecated our applause, and her grey-green eyes had a far away look that usurped one's attention from her poetry. Once when a poem was called for from the floor, she had to consider whether she had written it. I thought this rather astounding, but admissible under the caption of "temperament," an indispensable concomitant of artistic endowment.

To this rather shadowy picture of Edna Millay may be appended, with more clarifying results, this portrait by the anonymous person who sketched her for the BOOKMAN's "Literary Spotlight":[4] "Edna St. Vincent Millay is a slim young person with chestnut-brown hair shot with glints of bronze and copper, so that sometimes it seems auburn and sometimes golden; a slightly snub nose, and freckles; a child mouth; a cool, grave voice; and grey-green eyes."

"With these materials she achieves a startling variety of appearances. When she is reading her poetry, she will seem to the awed spectator a fragile little girl with apple blossom face. When she is picnicking in the country she will be, with her snub nose, freckles, carrot hair, and boyish grin, an Irish 'newsy.' When she is meeting the bourgeoisie in its lairs, she is likely to be a highly artificial and very affected young lady with an exaggerated Vassar accent and abominably overdone manners. In the basement of the Brevoort, or in the Cafe de la Rotonde in Paris, or in the Cafe Royal in London, she will appear a languid creature of a decadent civilization, looking wearily out of ambiguous eyes and smiling faintly with her doll's mouth, exquisite and morbid. A New England nun; a chorus girl on a holiday; the Botticelli Venus of the Uffizi gallery. . . ."[5]

Most people, faithful to the faulty memory of humankind, will remember Edna Millay's "Renascence" as a poem which was submitted in a prize-poem contest, and published, among other poems, in the "Lyric Year" for 1912; so far, so good, but in the light of succeeding days, they will also be prone to remember that the poem won the prize. In fact, this poem, which is now one of the marvels of present-day poetry, received none of the three awards. It excited a measure of interest and admiration in the breasts of a few of the more discerning critics and poetry-lovers. But, according to Louis Untermeyer:[6] "Its author, totally unknown at the time, was little more than a child living on the sea-coast of Maine, and it was not until her first book was published five years later that it became possible to appraise the work of Edna St. Vincent Millay."

With the publication of "Renascence" by Mitchell Kennerley in 1917, Edna Millay took her place as one of the giants of Parnassus. She did not, however, immediately create the Edna St. Vincent Millay vogue, nor establish the legend which now surrounds her. That is another story. Yet "Renascence," which still continues to be the most favored of her books, contains, to a greater or less degree, all the ear-marks which accentuate or limit her powers. One finds in it her marked inclination toward form, her superb mastery of word-marriage, her simplicity, which, in less capable hands, would degenerate into banality, her sudden flourishes of frivolity which mar many fine poems worthy of a happier termination. "Renascence" is too well known and too much of a unit in its mystic grandeur to permit dissection; but mighty as it is, and as extensive as is its scope, the briefer "God's World," with its heart-break and its anguish at the revelation of beauty, is no less expressive, and lends itself more readily to quotation:

GOD'S WORLD

O world, I cannot hold thee close enough!
Thy winds, thy wide grey skies!
Thy mists, that roll and rise!
Thy woods, this autumn day, that ache and sag
And all but cry with colour! That gaunt crag
To crush! To lift the lean of that black bluff
World, World I cannot get thee close enough!
Long have I known a glory in it all,
But never knew I this:
Here such a passion is
As stretcheth me apart,—Lord, I do fear
Thou'st made the world too beautiful this year;
My soul is all but out of me,—let fall
No burning leaf; prithee, let no bird call.

Louis Untermeyer, in speaking of Miss Millay's lyric genius in "Renascence," says,[7] "This lyrical mastery is manifest on all except a few pages (such as 'Interim' and 'Ashes of Life' which lisp as uncertainly as the hundreds of poems to which they are too closely related)." One must respect expert criticism; but it seems to me that "Ashes of Life" is one of Miss Millay's best lyrics, exemplifying a simplicity which is at once so acute and yet so expressive that it approaches legerdemain, and which in its last stanza executes an audacity of monotony that only a genius would have dared perpetrate. What other poet, having written so effective a stanza as this, with its courageous third line, would have allowed it to stand:

> Love has gone and left me,—and the neighbours
>   knock and borrow,
> And life goes on forever like the gnawing of a mouse,—
> And tomorrow and tomorrow and tomorrow
>   and tomorrow,
> There's this little street and this little house?

Although Miss Millay's first book contained only six sonnets, these were enough to mark her as a master-craftsman in that form. Under her command the medium accomplishes a Shakespearean rejuvenation; octave and sestet are no longer compromised; each has its beginning and its ending, and their mating is the sonnet as it has rarely been written before, and as no one else writes it today. One critic writes of her,[8] "Her sonnets, with the phrasing cut down to the glowing core, exhibit the same sensitive parsimony that one finds in the best of the Imagist poets, plus a far richer sense of human values." That such an encomium is justified is borne out by a survey of almost any one of her sonnets. The manner in which she adds image to image unto the perfect whole, the rush with which her words flow on, with no one word able to be dispensed with, is an astonishing feat, to put it mildly. With her there is no padding for the sake of rhyme or rhythm, truly nothing but the "glowing core." Let the following octave be a more vivid testament than I:

>   Time does not bring relief; you all have lied
>   Who told me time would ease me of my pain!
>   I miss him in the weeping of the rain;
>   I want him at the shrinking of the tide;
>   The old snows melt from every mountain-side,
>   And last year's leaves are smoke in every land;
>   But last year's bitter loving must remain
>   Heaped on my heart, and my old thoughts abide.

Or consider the perfect unity of this:

>   Pity me not because the light of day
>   At close of day no longer walks the sky;
>   Pity me not for beauties passed away
>   From field and thicket as the year goes by;
>   Pity me not the waning of the moon,
>   Nor that the ebbing tide goes out to sea,
>   Nor that a man's desire is hushed so soon,
>   And you no longer look with love on me.

Miss Millay's anonymous biographer in "The Literary Spotlight" says, "In the last few years there has grown up an Edna St. Vincent Millay legend, a sort of Byronic legend, which the younger generation is pleased to believe in. . . . The Edna St. Vincent Millay legend is based on her poems—or, to speak more exactly, upon one particular book of poems, the one entitled 'A Few Figs From Thistles.'[9] With the publication of 'Figs From Thistles' (Frank Shay, 1920), she became the poet laureate of the younger generation."

And why should the younger generation not pin its faith on a poet who writes:

> My candle burns at both ends;
> It will not last the night;
> But ah, my foes, and oh, my friends—
> It gives a lovely light!

Does she not say, with a more articulate clarity, what youth has cried out since the world began, when she sings:

> Safe upon the solid rock the ugly houses stand:
> Come and see my shining palace built upon the sand!

Some persons who have passed the rainbow romantic stage complain that with these poems Miss Millay has exchanged her birthright for a mess of pottage. But her young admirers are of a different opinion; for they love her for these kindred utterances, as many of the Rev. Robert Herrick's parishioners must have loved him less for his sermons than for his worldly advice to gather rosebuds while they might.

In 1921, when she published "Second April" through Mitchell Kennerley, Miss Millay showed that she could eat her mess of pottage, and yet retrieve her birthright. A treasure-trove of beauty— "Second April. Death," the grave concern of most young poets, plays an important part in this book, and is the butt of the poet's many moods. In "Spring," overwhelmed with the vitality of "little leaves opening stickily," and of "the spikes of the crocus," she is intrigued into the belief that "it is apparent that there is no death." But recollection brings this reaction:

> But what does that signify?
> Not only under ground are the brains of men
> Eaten by maggots.
> Life in itself

> Is nothing,
> An empty cup, a flight of uncarpeted stairs.
> It is not enough that yearly, down this hill,
> April
> Comes like an idiot, babbling and strewing flowers.

In "Passer Mortuus Est" she speaks of death's finality in all things, in love as well as in life, with a resignation that is also flippant:

> Death devours all lovely things:
> Lesbia with her sparrow
> Shares the darkness,—presently
> Every bed is narrow.
> ....
> After all, my erstwhile dear,
> My no longer cherished,
> Need we say it was not love,
> Just because it perished?

In "Alms" she accepts the death of love with a listlessness that is extremely bitter in its passivity:

> There was a time I stood and watched
> The small, ill-natured sparrows' fray;
> I loved the beggar that I fed,
> I cared for what he had to say, . . .
> But it is winter with your love;
> I scatter crumbs upon the sill,
> And close the window,—and the birds
> May take or leave them, as they will.

"Mariposa" accepts the fact of death neither bitterly nor flippantly, but as an inevitability that makes it logical to say:

> Suffer me to take your hand.
> Suffer me to cherish you
> Till the dawn is in the sky.
> Whether I be false or true,
> Death comes in a day or two.

But in "The Poet and His Book" Miss Millay rises to immortal heights,[10] and, relying on the strength of her work, cries out

> Down, you mongrel, Death!
> Back into your kennel!
> I have stolen breath
> In a stalk of fennel!
> You shall scratch and you shall whine
> Many a night, and you shall worry
> Many a bone, before you bury
> One sweet bone of mine!

And surely while love of beauty and sincerity persist, "The Poet and His Book" shall give the lie to death.

"The Ballad of the Harp Weaver and Other Poems" (Harper and Brothers, 1923) is a combination of the finer artist and her legendary self, with the legendary too much in evidence. It is this book which makes evident the force of the following remark by Carl Van Doren: "What sets Miss Millay's poems apart from all those written in English by women is the full pulse which . . . beats through them. . . Rarely has a woman since Sappho written as outspokenly as this."[11] Indeed, this is a book of the utmost candor, almost to the point of indiscretion. There are persons who, knowing nothing else that Miss Millay has written, can quote with startling accuracy her sonnet beginning:

> I, being born a woman and distressed
> By all the needs and notions of my kind,

and whose opinion of her takes such a sonnet as its guide. Yet, another poem equally confessional, can be expressed so lyrically that one accepts the circumstance as vindicated by the poem:

> What my lips have kissed, and where, and why,
> I have forgotten, and what arms have lain
> Under my head till morning; but the rain
> Is full of ghosts tonight, that tap and sigh
> Upon the glass and listen for reply,

> And in my heart there stirs a quiet pain
> For unremembered lads that not again
> Will turn to me at midnight with a cry.

The title poem of this last volume, telling the tragic story of maternal sacrifice, is one of the finest literary ballads in the language, an actual *tour de force*. But the author's efforts to tell a story in sonnet form in her "Sonnets From an Ungrafted Tree" are less happy. Not even she is able to make a form which is so complete in itself the means of narrative continuation. And her substitution of a hexameter last line in these sonnets for the accustomed pentameter line jars because of its unexpectedness, which was probably meant to be its virtue. Moreover, the language of this sequence is less Miss Millay's than the cryptic word arrangement of Edwin Arlington Robinson, without his peculiar magic.

No appraisal of Miss Millay's poetry can omit to mention her two most important plays: "The Lamp and the Bell" (Frank Shay, 1921), and "Aria da Capo" (Mitchell Kennerley). Both plays show her marvelous control over the stringent, uncompromising blank-verse form. Most poets have recognized, not losing sight of its beauty and serenity, the restrictions of blank-verse, and have chafed under the restraint. But generally, where they have come out in open rebellion, their quarrel has been too boisterous; the reader finds himself stumbling, tripping upon miscast beats, and foundering upon extra syllables maladroitly placed. But Edna Millay is a tamer of words; beneath the soft sleeking of her hands the most recalcitrant becomes docile and dutiful. Some poets ply Pegasus with lash and spur, and are nine days in falling from their perch; but she talks to him, flatters him, cajoles him, and subdues him with her patience. When we come to that sardonic tragedy "Aria da Capo," to the premier appearance of which an entire edition of Harold Munro's CHAPBOOK was devoted, and which is now an inevitable part of the repertoire of every Little Theatre movement in the country, we see the fruition of her patience and the triumph of her subtlety in such a passage as this:

> I find no jewels . . . but I wonder what
> The root of this black weed would do to a man
> If he should taste it . . . I have seen a sheep die,

> With half the stalk still drooling from its mouth.
> 'Twould be a speedy remedy, I should think,
> For a festered pride and a feverish ambition.
> It has a curious root. I think I'll hack it
> In little pieces.... First I'll get me a drink;
> And then I'll hack that root in little pieces
> As small as dust, and see what the color is
> Inside.

In such a passage we find the noblest vehicle of English versification not made ignoble in being shorn of its rhetoric, nor rendered unpleasing to the ear because its arbitrary cadences have been shifted and modified to meet the exigencies of situation and the demands of genius. "Aria da Capo" and "The Lamp and the Bell" afford numerous instances of such control. The latter play also contains three of Miss Millay's most exquisite lyrics, significant for their beauty and expressive of their maker's attitude toward life. Those to whom she is high priestess surely bring richer homage to her altars, when they find their sluggish blood rekindled by lines like these:

> Oh, little rose tree, bloom!
> Summer is nearly over.
> The dahlias bleed, and the phlox is seed.
> Nothing's left of the clover,
> And the path of the poppy no one knows.
> I would blossom if I were a rose.

Such a gospel needs must win its adherents, as surely as the plainness of the following bit of truth needs must assume a sad significance conducive to a "Carpe diem!" reaction, when couched in terms so simple and direct:

> Beat me a crown of bluer metal;
> Fret it with stones of a foreign style:
> The heart grows weary after a little
> Of what it loved for a little while.

Few poets writing today seem more destined than she to escape the treachery of the world's unremembering mind. Time is the truest connoisseur of wisdom and beauty; constrained to careful selection lest any new endeavor suffer in comparison with what has already been voted "immortal," the years will perhaps reject the legendary Edna Millay, who gestures prettily, snaps her fingers at convention, and laughs at life and death and love; they may pass her candor by as a lamentable indiscretion, but surely they will find a separate, enduring niche for her exaltation and for the golden felicity of language which is hers. "Renascence," "God's World," "The Ballad of the Harp Weaver," many of her sonnets,—all are reasons enough for this poignant utterance, too true to savor of conceit, in "The Poet and His Book":

> Sexton, play your trade!
> In a shower of gravel
> Stamp upon your spade!
> Many a rose shall ravel,
>
> Many a metal wreath shall rust
> In the rain, and I go singing
> Through the lots where you are flinging
> Yellow Clay on dust!

Countee Cullen
May 1, 1925

References

"The New Era in American Poetry," Louis Untermeyer, Holt, 1919.
"Miss Millay's Poems," Padraic Column in the "Freeman"
    for November 2, 1921.
"Taking the Literary Pulse," Joseph Collins, Doran, 1924.
"The Literary Spotlight," Doran, 1924.
"American Poetry Since 1900," Louis Untermeyer, Holt, 1923.

Bibliography

"Renascence," Mitchell Kennerley, 1917.
"A Few Figs From Thistles," Frank Shay, 1920.
"The Lamp and the Bell," Frank Shay, 1921.
"Aria da Capo," Mitchell Kennerley, 1921.
"The Harp-Weaver and Other Poems," Harper and Brothers, 1923.

III

Now let us set this senior honors thesis in the context of Countee Cullen's undergraduate studies at New York University. Cullen matriculated at University College of Arts and Pure Science in February 1922 and was graduated on June 10, 1925, with a B.A. degree. This college, familiarly called "The Heights," was one of two undergraduate liberal arts colleges of New York University at that time; it was located at University Heights, overlooking the Harlem River in the Bronx. There Cullen majored in English and took a first minor in French and a second minor in philosophy. Since there has been, as yet, no detailed account of Cullen's educational development, and since he was a poet, it will perhaps be of value to future students of his life and art if I discuss his coursework at "The Heights." However, as a biographical preliminary, I wish to present some information, derived from his University College transcript, that will perhaps serve to clarify other aspects of his background and development.

First, since there is some uncertainty as to his place of birth, it is worth noting that his birth data are given as "5/30/03 Louisville, Ky." If, as seems likely, Cullen filled out his own application forms in 1922, he was giving his birthplace as Louisville rather than New York. His religious denomination is listed as "Protestant." Penciled in is the registrar's handwritten notation "Negro." Such notations were common in American colleges of the time, usually as a way of determining quotas of admission for minority applicants—whether black, Jewish, Hispanic—or of otherwise singling them out. I have been unable to confirm that there was such a quota for admission of blacks at New York University in the 1920s. But a review of the yearbooks during Cullen's undergraduate period suggests that a black student was indeed a rarity at "The Heights." Still, it should be remarked that New York University was founded for and was open to ethnic, immigrant, and working-class minorities; and there is no evidence that Cullen experienced significant prejudice at the college. In fact the memoirs of his white classmates acknowledge Cullen with admiration and affection.

In the transcript, Frederick Asbury Cullen, his adoptive father, is given as his parent, and his address is listed as "234 West 131st Street, NYC." This is the parsonage of the African Methodist Episcopal Church in Harlem, where the Reverend Cullen served for forty-two years as pastor. Countee Cullen was admitted without entrance conditions, by diploma, as a graduate of De Witt Clinton High School. He is noted as having matriculated on 2/2/22 in the class of 1925. It would appear that he had a state scholarship in 1924–1925. His special adviser was listed as Professor Thorne, but this name is then crossed out and "Borgman" replaces it. (This change doubtless occurred when Cullen declared an English major, for Albert S. Borgman was a member of the English Department.) The registrar's handwritten entries indicate that Cullen was elected to Phi Beta Kappa in March 1925. The records of his election by the Phi Beta Kappa association at "The Heights" indicate that Cullen stood thirteenth in a class of 102 students, with an average of 88.2. Although only nine seniors were elected, some of those with higher averages did not receive the necessary three-fourths approval of the voting faculty members. Cullen did, and so was inducted into Phi Beta Kappa on March 11, 1925. He is recorded as having requested copies of this transcript on October 17, 1924; on June 23, 1925 (for his application to graduate study at Harvard); on November 5, 1927 (for a Guggenheim Fellowship application); and in September 1928 (for reasons unknown).

The transcript itself indicates that Cullen began his classwork in the spring of 1922 and took a summer program that year so as to catch up with the other freshmen. (Thereafter he did not attend summer school.) In the first two years his curriculum involved a wide array of courses in introductory English, French, Latin (always with *cum laude* grades), math, physics, geology, philosophy, Greek, physical science, and (as a holdover from the World War I years) military science. As an upperclassman he concentrated on intermediate and advanced English and French, picked up German, and took additional courses in history and philosophy. And, as a senior, he took a number of courses in education that prepared him for certification as a teacher in the public school system of New York City, in which he served with great distinction in later years.

Cullen's program and his manifest distinction as a student, then, indicate that he received a solid liberal arts education with a strong emphasis on languages and literature, history and philosophy. He was well prepared for graduate study at Harvard in either English or French, both of which he later taught in New York City. But even more important, this undergraduate education—although just the foundation of his career as a poet—acquainted him with a wide range of literary forms, styles, and techniques; it educated him about the culture of writers in several national traditions; and it helped him understand the literary heritage in its historical and philosophical contexts. This much, of course, can be inferred from the poems alone, for his engagement with the literary heritage is implicit in all his characteristic themes and subjects, in his literary allusions, and in his strategies of versification and language use.

When one studies the transcript information against the college bulletins for the years 1922–1925, one particular facet of Cullen's program appears remarkable. Although the English Department boasted a faculty of between fifteen and twenty professors during these years—including such local eminences as Dean Archibald L. Bouton, Francis Henry Stoddard, Vernon Loggins, Arthur Huntington Nason, and Homer Watt—almost all of Cullen's English coursework was taken with one man, Professor Hyder E. Rollins.

The major required that Cullen take the prerequisite English 10–20, *Rhetoric and Composition*; this multisection course was taught by Professors Rollins, Allen, Borgman, *et al*. It cannot be determined that Rollins was his instructor here, but it is possible. Certainly in English 30–40, *Advanced Composition,* Rollins was his teacher. Professor Borgman taught the required introductory course, English 31–41, *History of English Literature.* But thereafter all of Cullen's English courses were taught by Rollins: English 52–62, *English Poetry of the Nineteenth Century*; and English 53–63, *English Prose Fiction.* Cullen could have taken a wide array of other courses—*Shakespeare, American Literature, Types of Literature,* and so forth. But he appears to have elected only those courses that Rollins offered, even though, as the transcript makes plain, Rollins was a hard grader who gave him quite a number of Bs. I shall later return to the influence of Rollins on Countee Cullen's development. But it should be noted that Cullen's apprenticeship as a poet was not limited to the classrooms at "The Heights." For he was deeply involved in the extracurricular literary life of the university—in ways that are not evident in the published biographies and bibliographies of his work.

For one thing, Cullen was published in the university literary magazines as early as 1922; and in his junior and senior years he was in fact the poetry editor of *The Arch: The Literary Magazine of New York University*. The issues of November 1924 and January, March, and May 1925 list him on the masthead. In this role Cullen corresponded and conferred with other student writers, selected verse for publication, and oversaw the printing of this department of the magazine, which incidentally served students of every college of the university. Even more important, Cullen's own verse appeared in *The Arch*. Neither his poetry editorship nor his publications in *The Arch* have been noted in previous bibliographies of his work. This is worth stressing because critical treatments of volumes such as *Color* (1925) and *Copper Sun* (1927) sometimes suggest that the poems in these volumes appeared only in such national publications as *Harper's, The Nation, Poetry,* and *Vanity Fair*. But some verses in these volumes first appeared in *The Arch*. For the sake of clarifying the record, therefore, some attention to his extracurricular work in *The Arch* and its relation to other sites of publication seems warranted.

In Volume I, Number 8 of *The Arch* (June 1922), page 13, there appears a "Triolet" beginning "I did not know she'd take it so"; this "Triolet" had first appeared in *The Magpie* (Christmas 1921), the literary magazine of the De Witt Clinton High School. It was renamed "Under the Mistletoe" and republished in *Copper Sun*.

In Volume II (misprinted Volume I), Number 1 of *The Arch* (November 1923), page 8, appear two poems. The first is "To—" beginning "Whatever I have loved has wounded me"; this poem is retitled "A Poem Once Significant, Now Happily Not," and is reprinted in *Copper Sun*. The second is "Triolet," beginning "I have wrapped my dreams in a silken cloth"; this poem, retitled "For a Poet," was dedicated to John Gaston Edgar and was republished in

Harper's (December 1924) and in *Color*. In Volume II, Number 2 of *The Arch* (January 1924), pages 40–42, appeared one of Cullen's best-known poems, "The Ballad of the Brown Girl." This was the second-prize poem in the Witter Bynner Intercollegiate Poetry Contest. Bynner thought it should have won and advised Cullen to send it for republication to *Palms,* where it appeared in the Early Summer Issue of 1924. Finally, it was republished in book form by Harper and Brothers in 1927. In Volume II, Number 3 of *The Arch* (March 1924), page 88, appeared "The Love Tree," which was reprinted in *Copper Sun*. And in Volume II, Number 4 (May 1924), page 122, appeared "Sacrament," which was reprinted in *Color*.

Finally, in Volume III, Number 1 of *The Arch* (November 1924), page 17, appeared "Variations on a Theme," which was reprinted in *Copper Sun*; and in the March 1925 issue appeared "The Poet" (page 14), also reprinted in *Copper Sun*. (This very early poem first appeared in *The Magpie* in November 1920.)

This record of Cullen's student publications suggests several things: first, some of the poems appearing in national periodicals were first tried out in *The Arch*; second, a number of his other poems in the *published volumes* first appeared in the NYU student literary magazine; and third, some of the poems reprinted in *Copper Sun* as "juvenilia" were indeed the work of either his high school or undergraduate years, poems that he had not deemed worth including in *Color*. The pressure to publish his second volume led him to recycle them in order to expand *Copper Sun* to book length.

Let us turn now to Cullen's senior honors thesis and set it in the context of his academic program. In addition to required and elective courses in the English major, the regulations of University College between 1894 and 1925 required that each student submit to the college faculty a "satisfactory thesis" related to the student's major. After 1925 this college requirement for graduation was abandoned, but several humanities disciplines immediately instituted departmental honors programs. To be graduated with honors in English required, in addition to an overall grade of B, with an even higher average in the major, the submission of an acceptable thesis. It would appear that, since Cullen graduated in the year that the college thesis requirement was abandoned, his essay is a senior honors thesis, submitted to the Department of English. It was hand-dated and signed "Countee Cullen May 1, 1925."

The genteel English Department faculty naturally stressed the classic writers, most of whom were safely dead. But Professor Hyder E. Rollins (to whom Cullen submitted the thesis for reading) was perhaps exceptional: he was not averse to essay topics involving living writers. Most of his colleagues would probably have looked askance at Millay, but such was Rollins's personal authority that his acquiescence in the subject carried the day.

The English Department's tolerance for the subject of Edna St. Vincent Millay, however, is surprising in view of her scandalous reputation in 1925. Although Millay was only ten years older than Cullen, she had already incurred a notoriety, in the eyes of the older generation, owing to her highly publicized sexual escapades, about which she wrote with unaccustomed frankness. However liberated her behavior, though, Millay's distinction as a lyric poet and ballad writer had become widely acknowledged; it was confirmed by the award of a Pulitzer Prize just two years earlier in 1923. And, since 1925 saw "Flaming Youth" in full rebellion against the oldsters' genteel values, the New York University English Department seems to have allowed its talented majors to pay attention to literary incarnations of this revolution. Still, as the essay makes plain, Countee Cullen felt an obligation to his instructor, Professor Rollins, to rescue Millay from the excesses of her own behavior in order to salvage her reputation as a poet.

As I have noted, Countee Cullen took at least three and perhaps four of his five two-term English courses with Rollins: possibly *Rhetoric and Composition*, and certainly *Advanced Composition, English Prose Fiction*, and *English Poetry of the Nineteenth Century*. What was the magic appeal of this instructor? Because I believe Hyder Rollins to have been a major influence on Countee Cullen, some attention to this extraordinary scholar and teacher seems warranted here.

Hyder E. Rollins (1889–1958), a Texan by birth, had been educated at Southwestern University and Harvard, where he took his doctorate in 1917, under the supervision of George Lyman Kittredge, one of the greatest American scholars of the Middle Ages and Renaissance. Upon completing his doctorate, Rollins was recommended to NYU by Kittredge, but, World War I intervening, Rollins entered the army as a lieutenant in the 313th Field Signal Batalion of the AEF and served in France until the Armistice. After demobilization he spent 1919 in London at the British Museum, where he began amassing a collection of unpublished English and Scottish broadside ballads of the Renaissance. During this research year his salary was renegotiated upward with Dean A. L. Bouton so that he could return to England each summer in order to collect more ballads. In a letter to Bouton of October 13, 1919, he writes, "I meet a new Harvard Ph.D. every day [at the British Museum]: not War, Pestilence, or Sudden Death can stop them." Even so, that research year was, for Rollins, a difficult one. On February 12, 1920, he wrote to the Dean: "England is starving me to death, and withal I'm working too hard." Nonetheless, out of this work came his first magisterial book, an edition called *Old English Ballads, 1553–1625* (1920).

During World War I the enrollment in the German Department at "The Heights" had collapsed, and German professors were assigned to English Department courses. Consequently Rollins was offered a program that was not his specialty. To Dean Bouton he expressed the wish that he could be assigned a ballad course or one in the Restoration drama; and he complained that the short story was not his field. It appears, he wrote to Dean Bouton on February 12, 1920, that "everything I really know—everything for which I am competent—has been staked out already; and as a new-comer I do not want to arouse commotion and prejudice by infringing on the fields of colleagues." If he was to be assigned something outside his field, "if it must be poetry, please drag in Keats and Tennyson!—and I shall do my best with them. It will be a splendid thing for me to be obliged to study something 'out of my line.' I have been in nothing but a line, or perhaps it's a trench, for many a day."[12]

Once he had arrived on campus, Rollins quickly distinguished himself as one of the most erudite and challenging professors on the faculty. Accepting an assistant professorship in 1920, he rose rapidly through the ranks to full professor in just four years. In 1926 he left NYU to accept a professorship at Harvard, where he taught until his retirement in 1956. Although Rollins's professional career is nowadays wholly identified with the Harvard English Department, where (following Kittredge in the Guerney Professorship of English Literature) he is remembered for his great scholarly distinction, Rollins actually attained international recognition while yet at University College. His meteoric rise in university teaching is largely owing to definitive publications like *A Pepysian Garland* (1922), *Cavalier and Puritan: Ballads and Broadsides* (1924), *A Handful of Pleasant Delights* (1924), and *An Analytical Index of Ballad-Entries in the Registers of the Company of Stationers in London* (1924)—all books appearing during Cullen's undergraduate years.[13]

In one respect, the assignment of a course in which Keats was "dragged in" had a permanent influence on Rollins's future career—and on Cullen's as well. For Rollins became enchanted with Keats and devoted to his life and work. Out of this ardor came, after Cullen's graduation, several of Rollins's major publications: *Keats' Reputation in America to 1848* (1946), the two-volume *The Keats Circle: Letters and Papers, 1816–1878* (1948), *Keats and the Bostonians* (1951), *More Letters and Poems of the Keats Circle* (1955), and the magisterial two-volume edition of *The Letters of John Keats, 1814–1821* (1958). In my judgment, the many Keatsian thematic and technical characteristics of Cullen's verse—not to speak of the encomia in "To John Keats, Poet. At Springtime" and "To Endymion"—are directly attributable to Rollins's impassioned lectures on Keats in *English Poets of the Nineteenth Century* during Cullen's junior year, in 1923–1924.[14]

Rollins's devotion to Keats and the departmental processes by which essay topics were devised by the English Department staff are suggested by a letter in the NYU Archives in which Rollins writes to Dean Bouton about the subjects to be assigned for a prize essay. The topics Rollins proposes are "Permanent Qualities of the Poetry of John Keats," "John Keats and John Gould Fletcher: A Study of Imagery," and "The Sensuous Appeal of Keats' Poetry." Then, as if this too much reflected his own ardor for Keats, he adds "Originality in the Love Songs of Sara Teasdale," "Portrait-Painting in the Poems of Edgar Lee Masters," "The Narrative Art of John Masefield's Poems," "A Study of Thomas Hardy's *Dynasts*," and "Drinkwater's *Abraham Lincoln* and Shakespeare's *Henry IV*: A Study in the Technique and Matter of the Historical Play." These last topics suggest that Rollins was perhaps exceptional among the English staff in inviting attention to modern writers, such as Millay, about whom Cullen eventually wrote his thesis. To Dean Bouton, Rollins remarked that he found the subjects for the English prize essay "very difficult to decide on, for my mind runs along the line of 'problems.'" He noted that "All these subjects, save the first three, are ultra-modern. Possibly it might be wiser simply to assign as a subject 'The Poetry of John Keats.' The average undergraduate needs something broad. But whatever subject is assigned, I shall do my best to get my own students interested in it."[15] Needless to say, Countee Cullen was not an average undergraduate. Although he came to revere Keats as Rollins did, he selected his own topic for the senior honors thesis, an ultra-modern writer conspicuously absent from Rollins's list for Dean Bouton.

Setting aside Keats for the moment, Rollins's mind was also profoundly oriented toward the Renaissance, where his research involved the compilation of an immense collection of popular broadside ballads. On these ballads he worked assiduously during Cullen's undergraduate years. There must have been many occasions when Cullen went to Rollins's office, perhaps to discuss a paper or an assignment, and noted piles of photocopied ballad manuscripts, just arrived from the British Museum or another repository. Rollins worked over these manuscripts meticulously, comparing them with variant ballads in the Scottish, Irish, and other north European literatures, readying his next edition. Cullen left no account of this teacher, to my knowledge, but a letter in the NYU Archives from Chancellor Elmer Ellsworth Brown to the Guggenheim Foundation describes Rollins as "a comparatively silent man, and works night and day, week in and week out. Nevertheless, he is personally liked by his classes."[16] This seems to have been the case, for in one of Rollins's letters to the chancellor (dated January 15, 1924), Rollins grandly remarks that three of his books have been published in one month. This must have seemed proof of the University's wisdom in promoting him up the ladder. But Rollins goes on to say: "Meanwhile, two admiring classes have given me a huge quantity of cigarettes—and with this tangible honor to boast of, I think it certain that research isn't injuring my teaching!"[17] Sitting there in that office, perhaps with a magnifying glass, Rollins must have communicated his immense enthusiasm for the old popular ballads to his young black student.

But if Rollins communicated enthusiasm for ballads to Countee Cullen, behind Rollins—forming a link with Cullen—was Rollins's own mentor, George Lyman Kittredge, who lectured on the ballad form at Harvard and inspired students such as Rollins to carry on the work. Kittredge was a man of formidable erudition whose knowledge of the English ballad was founded on the work of his Harvard master, F. J. Child. The five-volume *The English and Scottish Popular Ballads,* edited by Francis James Child (to which the young Kittredge had supplied notes and annotations), was the groundwork upon which the work of Kittredge and thereafter Rollins was based. Ultimately, it was also the source of Cullen's ballad poems. Kittredge's one-volume edition of *The English and Scottish Popular Ballads* (1904) also served as the introduction to these poems for generations of Harvard students such as Rollins. But Rollins went even beyond his mentor Kittredge and rivaled Child's monumental work in preparing the original collections I have already named, as well as others published after Cullen's graduation.

Is it any wonder, then, that Cullen's first three volumes, *Color* (1925), *Copper Sun* (1927), and *The Ballad of the Brown Girl* (1927), are full of ballad settings, characters, and stylistic features? Or that he wrote his thesis on a woman poet who, in "The Ballad of the Harp Weaver," had established her claim to eminence with a Pulitzer Prize? Such lines as Cullen's "He rode across like a cavalier, / Spurs clicking hard and loud" ("Two Who Crossed a Line") are unimaginable except under the influence of Rollins's *Cavalier and Puritan: Ballads and Broadsides.* Cullen's portrait of his parents in "Fruit of the Flower" is a reflection of Rollins's influence: "My mother's life is puritan, / No hint of cavalier. . . . " Such narrative poems as "Judas Iscariot," as well as Cullen's recurrent use of the *abcb* quatrain, culminate in "The Ballad of the Brown Girl," published in *The Arch* in 1924. This is not the place to offer a full critique of that remarkable poem, which grew directly out of Millay's experiments and out of Rollins's lectures on the ballad tradition and his editing of four volumes of ballads during Cullen's undergraduate years. Yet some observations and clarifications of fact may perhaps be offered here. First, it is very unlikely that Cullen found the source for the ballad in *The Oxford Book of Ballads* or *The Ballad Book,* as Alan R. Shucard has suggested in *Countee Cullen.*[18] In view of Rollins's intimate involvement with Kittredge, with whom he continually corresponded about his ballad work, and in view of Kittredge's connection to F. J. Child, it is more likely that Rollins steered Cullen to the source in Child's edition of "Lord

Thomas and Fair Annet" and its variants like "The Nut-Brown Bride," "The Brown Bride and Lord Thomas," "Lord Thomas and Fair Elinor," or "Sweet Willie and Fair Annie."[19] These Child versions of the ballad give the full dramatis personae of Cullen's poem, as the abbreviated versions in the *Oxford* and *The Ballad Book* collections do not. Further, it is beside the point to criticize Cullen for verboseness in expanding the ballad from ten (*Oxford* version) or fifteen (*Ballad Book*) stanzas to fifty.[20] Cullen's poem is only slightly longer than the "E" version of the ballad ("Sweet Willie and Fair Annie"), which runs to forty-two stanzas. Nor is there any point in faulting Cullen, as Houston A. Baker, Jr., does in *A Many-Colored Coat of Dreams: The Poetry of Countee Cullen,* for making Lord Thomas dependent on his mother, since this aspect of Lord Thomas is found in the originals.[21]

Blanche E. Ferguson has reported that it was only after Cullen had written *The Ballad of the Brown Girl* that he discovered that her color did not refer to race: "The term was merely used to identify her as a peasant."[22] I do not know the source of Ferguson's remark here. But it will be evident to anyone reading the originals that the nut-brown maid was dark-complexioned and, in view of her wealth, no peasant. I doubt seriously that Cullen, who worked so extensively with Rollins, would not have known precisely what a nut-brown maid, as a recurrent type-character, meant in these old ballads. Alan Shucard has also called "a surprising piece of information"[23] the report that Blanche E. Ferguson gives of Kittredge's reaction to the poem. Ferguson remarks that the ballad "also prompted the writing of one of the most highly prized letters that Countee had ever received. This letter came from the outstanding authority on ballads, Professor Lyman Kittredge of Harvard. Countee found it hard to believe Dr. Kittredge had written that 'Ballad of the Brown Girl' was the finest literary ballad he had ever read."[24]

This *is* surprising, and I cannot find the published source of the claim. But in the Amistad Research Center collection of Cullen correspondence is a Hyder Rollins letter to Cullen, dated December 7, 1923, thanking Cullen for a copy of "The Ballad of the Brown Girl" (probably in *The Arch* version). "Your ballad seems to me charming—even if, in spots, a bit too literary to be a genuine ballad. Many thanks for the copy, which I forwarded to Mr. Kittredge (the G.L.K. whose initials appear below). I shall let you see Mr. Kittredge's acknowledgment. Meanwhile, it occurs to me that even this bare note will interest you." Attached to Rollins's letter is a note from Kittredge: "Dear Rollins, I see that a Negro student at N.Y.U. has won a prize for a ballad. May I have a copy? Yours ever, G.L.K." Kittredge received the copy Rollins sent him and responded directly to Cullen on December 8, 1923: "Professor Rollins, in response to my request, has kindly sent me a copy of your 'Brown Girl,' which I am very glad to have. It will stand me in good stead as an unusually successful example of poetical composition in the style of the 'popular ballad.' Allow me to congratulate you on your achievement."[25] However commendatory, this letter does not suggest that Kittredge thought the poem to be "the finest literary ballad he had ever read," as Ferguson suggests. It is, however, a literary ballad of great distinction.

In 1925, the year that *Color* was published and Cullen submitted his senior honors thesis to Professor Rollins, the NYU faculty and students showered Cullen with compliments. Rollins, for example, wrote, "We are proud of you, we New York University people, and we hope that Harvard, with its erudition, won't ruin you."[26] Even the chancellor of NYU, Dr. Elmer Ellsworth Brown, sent Cullen this handwritten note: "I happened on a copy of your book, *Color*, at the University book store down town to-day, brought it home, and have read it this evening. I want to tell you how deeply I am stirred by the terrible singing sincerity of your words."[27] Chancellor Brown is even recorded as having committed "For Joseph Conrad" to memory and quoting it in the august precincts of the Century Club of New York City.[28] Later Brown recommended Cullen for the Guggenheim Fellowship he won, as did Dean Bouton at University College. In a gesture of thanks, Cullen sent Bouton *The Black Christ, and Other Poems*. Bouton responded on October 28, 1929, that it was "a profoundly significant piece of work" that would continue "to be heard from after the printing press is dry and your first edition is long exhausted." Dean Bouton told Cullen:

> I certainly foresee splendid things ahead of you and am glad to have been present, even if only in a very slight way, at the time when you were in the making, so to speak. It is particularly gratifying that the Guggenheim Foundation should be so broad in the interpretation

of its functions that they have seen their way clear to give you a fellowship for creative work. That, of course, is rather a novel thing in American education and you are doing much for the future, I think, of many deserving young men by what you are now accomplishing under the fellowship which you hold.[29]

This praise from Cullen's professors was matched by the comments of some of his classmates. The undergraduate poet Charles Norman, when he came to write of their college days in retrospect, in *Poets and People* (1972), remarked:

> I think I can honestly say that the only poet I ever envied was Countee Cullen, who had been my schoolmate. One day, when I praised his work, he told me that there was nothing of his already published work that he could not have improved if he wanted to. I received an impression of immense talent which I would be unable to overtake or match. He said it without vanity, without self-consciousness, in his soft, sincere, melodious voice.[30]

Perhaps for this reason Norman turned his attention to biography and is remembered for his lives of Ezra Pound and e. e. cummings. This sense of undergraduate rivalry among the NYU college poets is rather softened, however, in Martin Russak's recollection in the NYU literary publication, *The Critical Review*, for March 1928:

> When Countee Cullen was a junior at New York University, I was a freshman and therefore came into contact with him only rarely. But I remember how proud we all were that he was our school-mate. That was a banner year for our campus; Charles Norman was there, and there was a whole group of young poets. Though we were all good friends, there were, of course, minor jealousies; but Cullen had our complete admiration and was our chief pride. Always a quiet, modest, retiring fellow, he could nevertheless seldom be seen walking across the campus without two or three of us chattering and gesticulating around him. It was not his poems or his intercollegiate poetry prize that captured our imaginations; it was the air about him and his name—the air of one who is unmistakably marked out for achievement, the indefinable air of one who carries within him, deliberately, some very precious burden entrusted to his particular safekeeping.

For Russak, *Color* and *Copper Sun* fulfilled the bright promise of Cullen's undergraduate years, justifying their faith in him so that "Today [1928] Countee Cullen stands as without a doubt the most important and distinguished young poet before the public."[31]

In 1926 Professor A. H. Nason, a member of "The Heights" English Department and the director of the NYU Press, had accepted Hyder Rollins's recommendation that the press publish *Some Recent New York University Verse*, edited by David L. Blum. In the collection, Cullen's "Heritage," "To John Keats, Poet. At Springtime," "Love in Ruins," and "The Poet" were reprinted. In his introduction, James B. Munn, dean of the Washington Square College, remarked:

> What will be the future achievement of these young poets, we cannot tell. Some may lose the vision; others may seek a different medium of artistic expression. Will there be one or two who will pursue the search until the end? If so, what will the search bring? There is always a chance that such a volume may presage some great achievement.

Munn felt that "all those whose work appears here have been subjected to academic influence and have apparently withstood whatever effects it may have to eradicate individualism." This is an odd remark, especially for an educator at Cullen's school. Academic influence is evident in the careers of a great many twentieth-century poets. But it points to issues implicated in Cullen's alleged failure to fulfill his promise as a poet, a failure cited more often by black than white critics. Was his individualism, as a black, "eradicated" by the program of English studies he undertook with Rollins and others? Was it inhibited by his turning to the wrong models—to Keats, Millay, Housman, Robinson, the ballad, the white English literary tradition—rather than to the literature of rising black consciousness represented by Dunbar, McKay, Hughes, and others in Harlem? Or should his models have been the literary modernists then bursting on the scene—Pound, Eliot, cummings, and Hart Crane?[32] Whatever the case, Dean Munn improbably remarked that "If the poetry of youth be ardently sincere, its promise frequently makes its very imperfections insignificant. Let the young poet not fear the critic who, Jeffrey-like, says 'This will never do.'"[33]

One New York University critic who was not afraid to say what would not do was Professor Eda Lou Walton, who taught English at the Washington Square campus. (I have found no information on whether Cullen knew the playwright and future novelist Thomas Wolfe, who also taught at the Square.) She and Cullen sometimes read or listened to other poets. In *The Critical Review* issue in which Martin Russak fondly remembered his freshman awe of Cullen, Professor Walton undertook to criticize the negative effects on individualism of the "Teasdale-Millay school" then so popular in colleges. In view of the defensive tone of Cullen's thesis on Millay, Walton's comments in "The Undergraduate Poet" deserve serious attention. Speaking of the impact of Teasdale and Millay on youthful writers, Walton remarked:

> These young poets upon first falling in love begin to sing sweetly and tritely of their hearts and souls, of longing and yearning, and burning. If they confuse their hearts and souls with trees and stars, with moons and seas, so much the better. They lift and fall with the tides; they are swept by storms, they are lonely as clouds. They are safe in the uniqueness of their emotion and blind, for the most part, to its amusing commonplaceness. Then comes the first disillusionment. They begin "burning the candle at both ends" and pretending that "it makes a lovely light," although often they do not believe a word of it. They turn a bit cleverly cynical and can never end a lyric without some ironical fillip. They announce stridently the uselessness and stupidity of the opposite sex. They try to pick out figs, but are more intent on thistles.[34]

For Walton, the "Teasdale-Millays" had little to say, in contrast to another camp of undergraduate poets, whom she identified as the "Cerebrals," whose masters were T. S. Eliot, Hart Crane, cummings, and Marianne Moore. In characterizing these two camps, Walton was of course implicitly highlighting—and condemning—the conventional academic romanticism of the kind of poetry Cullen was writing, although she never mentions Cullen by name. Cullen's indifference to those currents of poetic modernism, developing on the campus as well as in the international literary culture, has indeed been a constant factor in the definition of his work as "minor."

Whatever one may claim to have been the proper model for Cullen's art, there is no doubt that for Hyder Rollins the English tradition from the Middle Ages onward was the right foundation for a poet. His hope that Harvard's erudition would not ruin Cullen was largely facetious, an in-joke, for Rollins himself was on the eve of departure for Harvard, where he joined Kittredge on the English faculty. On May 15, 1926, Rollins wrote to Cullen: "No doubt you already know that I am going abroad on June 12, thanks to a Guggenheim Fellowship, and that, accordingly, I shan't reach Harvard until September, 1927. That means you'll have to stay on for two more years! I shall certainly hope to see you in either Cambridge or New York."³⁵ In fact Cullen did not study with Rollins at Harvard; he completed his M.A. work in one year, studying instead with Irving Babbitt, Bliss Perry, Robert Hillyer, Kittredge, and others. Nevertheless, Rollins and Cullen continued to correspond throughout the 1920s. When Cullen sent his mentor a copy of *The Black Christ,* Rollins replied on October 28, 1929, that he had "read it with genuine interest and enjoyment. There's no denying that you're a poet, and a good one, and I am proud of your successes and achievements." He commended Cullen's choice of Paris for Cullen's Guggenheim year and remarked that "the weather of London is so devilish that, after three winters' experience of it [collecting ballads], I fear I shall never be courageous enough to face it again." In a final allusion to their time together at NYU, Rollins concluded: "Life seems rather dull on the Charles. Next week I'm going to N.Y.U. to see if it is also dull on the Harlem [River, which "The Heights" overlooked] or whether I'm the dull one!" And he closed, "Every good wish forever. Your sincere friend."³⁶

This overview of Countee Cullen's undergraduate years at "The Heights" suggests several conclusions. First, Cullen was a highly popular and academically successful student who attained an impressive celebrity with his classmates and professors. Trained in a conventional academic program that emphasized the classic writers of the white English tradition, Cullen naturally gravitated to the work of Keats, Robinson, Millay, Masters, and the old ballad writers. Essentially shaped by Hyder E. Rollins, an international scholar with a deep affinity for Keats and the ballad forms, Cullen supplemented his studies by extracurricular activities such as publishing in the student literary periodical, *The Arch,* even editing the magazine in his last two years, and by attending and giving readings of poetry on campus and throughout the country. His achievement was thus an inspiration to other young poets. Some have suggested that Harvard, with its erudition, may have "ruined" Cullen for the task of elevating the quality of down-home, right-on black poetry in the twentieth century. But for better or worse, Cullen's direction was set well before he got to Harvard: the route was fixed at "The Heights."

There is no doubt that his work would have benefited from deeper immersion in the modernist poets who were then attaining fame—writers such as Eliot, Pound, Stevens, and Williams. And it is highly probable that the application of modernist techniques to problems of racial identity and experience would have deepened the impact of such poems as "Heritage," "The Black Christ," and others that express his sense of the meaning of blackness in white America, thereby allying him more intimately with the poetic projects of Claude McKay, Langston Hughes, and other figures of the Harlem Renaissance. But Cullen was the product of the forces that shaped him and of the choices and models he selected. Within those terms and limits, he attained exceptional distinction as a lyric poet with an impassioned romantic sensibility. If he failed to scale the highest point of Parnassus, he did reach the lesser heights.

The Negro Writer as Spokesman (1969)

> It is quite possible that much potential fiction by Negro Americans fails precisely at this point: through the writers' refusal (often through provincialism or lack of courage or opportunism) to achieve a vision of life and a resourcefulness of craft commensurate with the complexity of their actual situation. Too often they fear to leave the uneasy sanctuary of race to take their chances in the world of art.
> —Ralph Ellison, *Shadow and Act*

From Crispus Attucks to Malcolm X and Martin Luther King, Jr., the American black, speaking for himself, has rarely been heard above the din and babble of white voices speaking for him. Some of the white voices have spoken not so much for the black as for a reactionary social order in which the black would find himself subordinated through race, caste, and color. The apologists of reaction—from Calhoun, Tilman, Vardaman, and Bilbo to Ross Barnett, Leander Perez, and George Wallace—have assumed an arbitrary right, throughout the agonizing racial history of the United States, to speak for the black, down to him, at him, and about him. Few large-minded students of the American social order have accorded any merit to the dogmas of reactionary racism. But such has been the power of conservatism in the United States that for most of our history, reactionary racism has been institutionalized, through law and custom, in many features of our public life.

But equally obnoxious to the American black is the voice of white liberalism speaking in his behalf. Before the advent of black-power militancy, white liberals were necessary to the emancipation and progress of the American black. Without the army of lawyers, politicians, professors, social workers, clergymen, editors, and like public forces for change, the black would doubtless be more socially and institutionally enslaved than he now is. And to a great extent, white liberals are still necessary. But white liberals, like their conservative counterparts, often speak not so much for the black as for their own version of an ideal American social order. And in frequently looking at the black as merely a white man with a black face, and in surrendering to the self-complacency of their own radical rhetoric, white liberals have often permitted distinctively black interests, aims, and aspirations to become warped or lost. The treatment of the black by the American Communist party is a conspicuous case in point.

In 1965, disturbed by the fact that most midcentury voices speaking for the black seemed to be white voices, Robert Penn Warren published *Who Speaks for the Negro?* In a series of taped interviews Warren sought to put on record the voice of the black speaking for himself. *Who Speaks for the Negro?* was an attempt "to find out something, first hand, about the people, some of them anyway, who are making the Negro Revolution what it is—one of the dramatic events of the American story." What Warren found out—in talking to simple sharecroppers, yardmen, manual laborers, black editors, union leaders, college presidents, and others—was that beyond the non-negotiable demand (in unison) for respect and recognition, no single voice spoke for the black. Individual blacks spoke for themselves and articulated many similar and dissimilar, harmonious and contradictory views with respect to major issues that concerned them: the nature of integration, the relationship between black power and political power, the role of the black as "redeemer" of American society, nonviolence versus militancy as a strategy of black progress, the "specialness" of the black "personality" and "culture," the debt or reparations owed the black by white society, the relationship between black art and propaganda, the rate of historical process versus Freedom Now urgencies, and so on.

The dilemma of the black—that there is no consensus as to what should be done, in what order of priorities, or by what means—is uniquely the dilemma of the black writer. For he, preeminently, is expected to be, in some sense or other, a "spokesman" for his race. He experiences, perhaps more sensitively than his brothers, that psychological doubleness which W. E. B. Du Bois described, a "double consciousness," that "sense of always looking at one's self through the eyes of others, of measuring one's soul by the tape of a world that looks on in amused contempt and pity. One ever feels the two-ness,—an American, a Negro; two souls, two thoughts, two unreconciled strivings, two warring ideals in one dark body, whose dogged strength alone keeps it from being torn asunder."[2] If the black writer suffers a cultural schizophrenia, he also experiences the daily humiliation that is the lot of his black brethren. He shares the sense of rage and outrage that burns in the heart of every sensitive black man. He is constrained, like them, to protest against the conditions in which he finds himself, to give vent in action to the pressures of rebellion within him. But to throw himself into the life of politics, direct action, agitation-confrontation, is to surrender his role as spectator, mediator, and artist, to manipulate his imaginative energies, to dissipate and perhaps to damage his literary gifts. And if, in his role as writer, he is seduced by the overtures of the militant sociologist, he sacrifices the autonomy of his imagination to the services of a social cause: he becomes the racial apologist, the polemicist, the black propagandist—and forfeits thereby the "permanence," "artistry," and "universality" that are the presumed aim of every writer. What is he to do?

II

For every black writer the example of Richard Wright bears on his dilemma. Mississippi-born, ghetto educated, Richard Wright was appalled by the harsh realities of black life in America, organized and expressed his rage in *Native Son* (1940), *12 Million Black Voices* (1941), and *Black Boy* (1945), despaired of seeing any changes in the conditions of that life, and left the United States for Paris in sorrow, anger, and deep anguish. The example Wright offers to other black writers is the literature of social protest. In the portrait of Bigger Thomas and his family in their filthy, one-room, rat-infested tenement; in the vision of Bigger's hatred and fear; in the dramatization of his mindless impulses to violence against the whites who oppress him; in the narrative of the murder of Mary Dalton and Bigger's trial, Wright sought in *Native Son* to protest, through the mode of naturalism, the sociological conditions determining the lives of urban blacks and to put on record precise notations of the inner though inarticulate psychology and intense emotionalism of the black man in America. Though *Native Son* is marred by overt courtroom Marxist propagandizing, the novel was a black bombshell in white America: it exposed to unconscious whites everywhere the barely suppressed wrath and rage of what had seemed merely docile, servile, shuffling, psalm-singing darkies. But "no American Negro exists," as James Baldwin has written, "who does not have his private Bigger Thomas living in the skull. . . ."[3]

Native Son, for the would-be writer, for the black intending fabulist, was a dead end. Or so it seemed, at any rate, to Baldwin. In "Everybody's Protest Novel," "Many Thousands Gone" (reprinted in *Notes of a Native Son*), and "Alas, Poor Richard" (reprinted in *Nobody Knows My Name*), Baldwin took Richard Wright to task for his naturalistic reduction of the complex black experience to that of racial victim. Where was Bigger's "discernible relationship to himself, to his own life, to his own people, . . . to any other people"?[4] Where was the sense of shared experience among blacks? Wright did not provide it. He eliminated several layers of black experience in order to create a stereotype of black martyrdom, a stereotype no more revealing of rich black humanity than Uncle Tom or Aunt Jemima. Such falsifications of complex experience are the mark of the social protest novel. Baldwin urged upon black writers a fuller, more complex approach to characterization in which, whatever the quantum of racial agony, the whole vision would be rounded, balanced, and purified in the alembic of the artist's imagination and therefore successful in aesthetic terms.

This is not the place to rehearse the quarrel between Wright and Baldwin over what Wright called "all that art for art's sake crap."[5] The argument is self-evident in Baldwin's essays and has been adequately described in Maurice Charney's "James Baldwin's Quarrel with Richard Wright."[6] Nor is it germane to the point to observe, with Irving Howe, that Baldwin did not succeed in composing the kind of novel he counterposed to the work of Richard Wright.[7] It is not even relevant that Baldwin, after Wright's death, performed a *volte-face* and began to write essays and novels of social protest—although it may make it appear that Wright was right all along and that Baldwin eventually came to his senses. Baldwin's change of mind is not relevant because the issue of the danger to the writer who is urged to become a spokesman for social protest is still a live issue. The risks for the writer as artist are still very real. His talents, his imaginative vision, the sources of his artistic energy—all may be perverted or dissipated if his writing does not spring instinctively and intuitively from that well of inspiration that is personal and unique to him. What could be clearer than the waste of great imaginative talents conspicuous in propagandistic works like Hemingway's *To Have and Have Not,* Faulkner's *Intruder in the Dust,* even Baldwin's *Another Country*?

III

If Baldwin never wrote the kind of novel he counterposed to *Native Son,* perhaps Ralph Ellison has in *Invisible Man* (1952). (The aspiration to high art is a particularly taxing one for the black writer with any kind of artistic conscience: Ellison has not yet been able to complete a second novel.) *Invisible Man* is still the best American novel written by a black because of Ellison's great imaginative gifts and his well-nigh religious devotion to craft. In its way it is a more powerful articulation of black protest than *Native Son* (and all of Baldwin's work) because of the richness of Ellison's language, the extravagant inventiveness of his imagination, the fullness of scene, episode, and character, the careful control of structure and symbolism, and the depth and complexity of his racial, social, and political reference. All these put *Invisible Man* virtually in a class by itself. But it is a vexing work for the radical militant critic because it does not make an explicit protest like the work of Richard Wright.

Invisible Man was of course bitterly attacked for abandoning Wright's "black anger" and "clenched militancy," for Ellison's refusal, as Robert Bone has put it, "to enlist his image-making powers in the service of the cause."[8] But while Ellison and every other black writer seems condemned to play off the black experience against the white world, or the black's interpretation of it, the postures of despair, alienation, and feverish militancy need not be, and probably should not be, the only stance or strategy for the black writer to take. Yet these are the postures black critics insistently urge upon black writers. Baldwin and Ellison are now called passé because they are too keyed on the white world, on Western cultural values.

IV

The understandable impulses to black political separatism in this country have given rise to a mystique of black aesthetic separatism. A new racial psychology is currently developing in the United States, and according to black critics a new literature is called for to accurately reflect and express the new black sensibility. Warning black writers from trying to enter the "mainstream" of American letters, black critics have begun to assert a new "black aesthetic." Based on Frantz Fanon's view that "in the time of revolutionary struggle, the traditional Western liberal ideals are not merely irrelevant but they must be assiduously opposed," young separatist black authors "have set out in search of a black aesthetic, a system of isolating and evaluating the artistic works of black people which reflect the special character and imperatives of black experience."[9]

Negro Digest in fact devoted an issue to the opinions of thirty-eight black writers on issues like the "black aesthetic." While no unanimity was evident, some of their views throw light on the literary separatism now fashionable. Larry Neal, for example, argued:

> There is no need to establish a black aesthetic. Rather, it is important to understand that one already exists. The question is: where does it exist?. . . To explore the black experience means that we do not deny the reality and the power of the slave culture; the culture that produced the blues, spirituals, folk songs, work songs, and "jazz." It means that Afro-American life and its myriad of styles are expressed and examined in the fullest, most truthful manner pos-

sible. The models for what Black literature should be are found primarily in our folk culture, especially in the blues and jazz....

Strictly speaking it is not a matter of whether we write protest literature or not. I have written "love" poems that act to liberate the soul as much as any "war" poem I have written. No, it can't simply be about protest as such. Protest literature assumes that the people we are talking to do not understand the nature of their condition. In this narrow context, protest literature is finally a plea to white America for our human dignity. We cannot get it that way. We must address each other. We must touch each other's beauty, wonder, and pain.[10]

Central to this rejection of the white world as audience, central to this rejection of Western liberal political and social ideals, has been the repudiation of the test of a work of art in terms of its *universal* application. This rejection strikes to the heart of aesthetics, as it is conventionally subsumed under the category of metaphysics dealing with the definition, creation, and experience of beauty in the world. Universality as a norm of values has heretofore always been defended as a criterion for judging art. But it is now rejected by the militant critic because it is the test by which a good deal of black literature has been dismissed as inferior. As a substitute for norms of value based on the conventional canons of aesthetics, the Organization of Black American Culture has tried to formulate a definition of this "black aesthetic" that is expressive of the mystique of Negritude currently fashionable. The substance of this aesthetic is apparently (and I say "apparently" because none of the definitions is adequately precise) the extent to which and the accuracy with which black writing incorporates and expresses the uniquely black elements of American life—the folklore, the music (spirituals, blues, work songs, and jazz), the distinctive idiom of black cats, the special cuisine (soul food), the dance, dramaturgy, and religion of the American black. These elements are viewed as materials to be organized with the purpose not merely of protesting the black's degradation but of asserting his virtue and beauty and condemning the white race. As LeRoi Jones has put it, the black writer's role in America

> is to aid in the destruction of America as he knows it. His role is to report and reflect so precisely the nature of the society, and of him-

self in that society, that other men will be moved by the exactness of his rendering and, if they are black men, grow strong through this moving, having seen their own strength, and weakness; and if they are white men, tremble, curse, and go mad, because they will be drenched with the filth of their evil."[11]

There is more than an echo of black magic in all of this: Jones is reaching back for the strongest racial power his heritage affords him. In this way the role of the black writer is to ritualize the race's fundamental myths, ideals, and values. As Larry Neal has put it: "The oldest, most important arts, have always made their practitioners stronger. Here I refer to the Black Arts, ju-ju, voodoo, and the Holy Ghost of the Black Church. . . . We are Black writers (priests), the bearers of the ancient tribal tradition. . . . As writers, one of our sacred functions is to reconstruct our ancient tradition and to give that tradition meaning in light of the manner in which history has moved."[12]

V

On a less mystical, more political level, this revolutionary aesthetic of destruction has been succinctly defined by Ron Karenga: "Black art must expose the enemy, praise the people, and support the revolution."[13] In *The New Black Poetry* (Karenga's statement is its epigraph and manifesto), Clarence Major, the editor, observes in his introduction that many of the poets chosen are "full-time militant activists" because "droopy concepts of western ideology are already obsolete": "The capitalist imperialist Euro-American cultural sensibility has proven itself to be essentially anti-human and is being rejected not only by black poets—black people—but also by the white radical activist."[14]

An example of this aesthetic of destruction is offered by Harry Edwards's poem "How to Change the U.S.A.":[15]

> For openers, the Federal Government
> the honkies, the pigs in blue
> must go down South
> and take those crackers out of bed,
> the crackers who blew up
> those four little girls

> in that Birmingham church
> those crackers who murdered
> Medgar Evars [sic] and killed
> the three civil rights workers—
> they must pull them out of bed
> and kill them with axes
> in the middle of the street.
> Chop them up with dull axes.
> Slowly.
> At high noon.
> With everybody watching
> on television.
> Just as a gesture
> of good faith.

Well structured and well paced in its parallelism, tightly organized and carefully controlled, vigorous in diction and rich in ironic emotional effects, this poem expresses an attitude as vicious, bloodlustful for revenge, and as anti-human as any expression of the "Euro-American cultural sensibility" I am familiar with.

Like nearly all racial protest works by blacks, it is obsessed by race victimization, though here the general fate of black brutalization is given precise concretization in the catalogue of the black martyrs. (Two of the unnamed civil rights workers were of course whites.) What is suggestive, from the point of view of the psychic genesis of these hate emotions, is that the poet or narrator would make other whites the instruments of black revenge. This kind of poem is distressing to contemplate because calls for revenge-assassinations as "gestures of good faith" do not seem likely to effect that revolution of consciousness, to create that transcendent "new man," that "new humanism," which the poet S. E. Anderson has called the purpose of the black aesthetic revolution.[16] One is hesitant to say this because it exposes one to the counterclaim of white racism, and because apologists for the new black aesthetics have condemned in advance whatever negative responses to it the white critic may experience: "The movement," Hoyt Fuller has claimed in "Towards a Black Aesthetic," "will be reviled as 'racism-in-reverse,' and its writers labeled as 'racists,' opprobrious terms which are flung lightly at black people now that the piper is being paid for all the long years of rejection and abuse which black people have experienced at the hands of white people...."[17] 'Buked and scorned blacks have been at the hands of whites, but this kind of writing—I do not fling the term lightly—is patently racist.

It seems to me that black critics and writers would do well to contemplate the quality and humanity of their protests against the social order that has degraded them. Apologists of black revolutionary aesthetics may complain about "the effrontery of white critics in presuming to sit in judgment on the quality of black life and on the character of the literary expression which grows organically out of that life experience."[18] But the white critic *must* judge the moral and aesthetic character of black writing as well as that of every other kind of writing that falls within his purview. It is his function and duty to do so—both as a man concerned about the quality of human life reflected in his culture, and as a critic, aware that literature has consequences and concerned about the quality of writing that bears upon the literary traditions he cherishes and wishes to preserve. For it is the critic who is able to bring to bear upon a literary work the full range of aesthetic, moral, social, historical, and psychological implications that illuminate the literary work.

Thus the critic, black or white, must not only understand the poet Larry Neal when he says, "Culturally and artistically, the West is dead. We must understand that we are what's happening."[19] But he must also qualify and correct the statement by defining the extraliterary purposes of this kind of rhetorical exaggeration, by setting the poems of writers like Neal, Claude McKay, Langston Hughes, and Gwendolyn Brooks into a context of works including those of Eliot, Auden, Pound, Yeats, and Lowell. Understanding is also demanded of the critic who ponders the views of the black poet Etheridge Knight:

> The Caucasian has separated the aesthetic dimension from all others, in order that undesirable conclusions might be avoided. The artist is encouraged to speak only of the beautiful . . . his task is to edify the listener, to make him see the *beauty* of the world. And this is the trick bag that Black Artists must avoid, because the red of this aesthetic rose got its color from the blood of black slaves, exterminated Indians, napalmed Vietnamese children, etc., ad nauseum.

> ... When the white aesthetic does permit the artist to speak of ugliness and evil—and this is the biggest trick in the whole bag—the ugliness and evil must be a "universal human condition," a flimflam justification for the continuous enslavement of the world's colored peoples. The white aesthetic would tell the Black Artist that all men have the same problems, that they all try to find their dignity and identity.[20]

When the critic contemplates such indictments, while acknowledging the dismal and bloody history of white colonial exploitation, he must insist that there is a fundamental ground of humanity on which men do experience the same problems. And he must balance the view of Fuller and Knight with the counterclaim of writers like Saunders Redding and Robert Hayden that there can be no such thing as a black aesthetic. As Redding has observed, "Aesthetics has no racial, national or geographic boundaries."[21] The struggle of the individual with an oppressive society is only one angle of a triad—the others being the individual's struggle with himself and his struggle with nature. Arriving at a full measure of one's identity and dignity is a colorblind, universal problem—at all times and in all places. It is an optimistic, groupthink black who can reduce the ubiquity of human evil to the forms of white racism. And it is a cynical black writer who can exploit the agony of the black by reducing the tragic conditions of human life to the manipulations of sociology and politics: "what an easy con-game for ambitious, publicity-hungry Negroes this stance of 'militancy' has become," Ralph Ellison has lamented.[22]

Yet this kind of reduction is precisely what underlies the militancy of some of our current black critics. Thus in the Introduction to his anthology *Black Expression,* Addison Gayle, Jr., dismisses, as inappropriate material for black artists, age-old metaphysical quests. "Who am I? What is my identity? What is my relationship to the universe, to God, to the existential other? is of no value to a black community daily confronted by the horrors of the urban ghetto, the threat to sanity and life in the rural areas of the South, and the continual hostility of the overwhelming majority of its fellow citizens."[23]

The vision of black American life implied in this dismissal of psychological, theological, and existential questions is shuddering to contemplate. It reduces the black to the role of merely victim of white brutality. It conceives of all blacks as Bigger Thomases—mindless, inarticulate, totally determined, subhuman creatures incapable of experiencing creative freedom, intellectual curiosity, or liberating self-consciousness. The spectacle of the black critic thus circumscribing the range of black writing is full of pathos indeed, for it lulls the black writer into believing that any kind of careless, undisciplined craftsmanship is acceptable—as long as it voices the outraged black sensibility. Thus the hysterical emotionalism of much of LeRoi Jones's recent work, or the anarchic rant of Yusuf Rahman in "Transcendental Blues," recently published in an anthology called *Black Fire*,[24] edited by LeRoi Jones and Larry Neal:

> White maggots will not military your
> babies down dead
> again
> White maggots will not mercenary
> your fertile Nile to ache with pus
> again
> My spears shall rain
> I-can't-give-them-anything-but-drops-of-hate
> erasing them
> exterminating them
> so humanity can have a clear slate
> Just keep me constant
> ebony lady
> LOVE ME EBONY LADY
> LOVE ME EBONY LADY.

VI

The truth is, of course, that as appalling as the conditions of black life in America generally are, the black writer may be a spokesman for joy, not rage. There is no necessary reason why this should be so, but his blackness may be the very force within him making for his acceptance of the world, his affirmation of it in spite of all the pain it affords him, in his struggle with nature, society, and himself, in his effort to achieve a sense of his own dignity and identity.

Thus, after reciting the material deprivations of her tenement childhood in relation to the warmth and love among her family, Nikki Giovanni concludes in "Nikki-Roasa":

> ... I really hope no white person ever has cause to write about me because they never understand Black love is Black wealth and they'll probably talk about my hard childhood and never understand that all the while I was quite happy.[25]

It is precisely possible to understand in a general way the childhood of this young woman because of the way in which she has dramatized the transcendence of poverty and pain through the redemptive power of love.

To the avenues of transcendence I wish to return in a moment. But in the meantime I believe it is worth pointing out that the sensitive white can understand the way in which family love, soul-brotherly love, and erotic love can constitute "Black wealth." For beyond the accident of race, such manifestations of love are common to all men and are expressions of a "universal" kind of experience. The judgments of white critics are no doubt irritating to black militants: the novelist John O. Killens has asserted that "White critics are totally—and I mean totally—incapable of criticizing the black writer. . . . They don't understand Afro-Americanese."[26] But whatever the subtleties and nuances of the black idiom, it is merely a variant of our mother tongue. And the view that the white critic cannot dig it—cannot experience, enter into, understand, criticize, and judge the work of blacks—is a gross exaggeration intended to humble white critics, minister to black fraternity and solidarity, and focus the efforts of young writers like Neal, Rahman, and Lawrence Benford toward the revolutionary social goals of the so-called black aesthetic.

If the black writer aspires to be a spokesman for his race, even to be a militant-activist dedicated to the emancipation of his people, he must learn the strategy by which moral and aesthetic purpose may be fused in the transformation of private experience into the public ritual of art, a ritual that affirms and celebrates the mystery of human life. That strategy Hemingway described in *Death in the Afternoon*. Paraphrasing it, Ralph Ellison has written:

> For I found the greatest difficulty for a Negro writer was the

problem of revealing what he truly felt, rather than serving up what Negroes were supposed to feel, and were encouraged to feel. And likened to this was the difficulty, based upon our long habit of deception and evasion, of depicting what really happened within our areas of American life, and putting down with honesty and without bowing to ideological expediencies the attitudes and values which give Negro American life its sense of wholeness and which renders it bearable and human and, when measured by our own terms, desirable.[27]

A moment ago I spoke of how Nikki Giovanni's little poem asserted the possibility, on the day-to-day level, of transcending pain through the redemptive power of love. For the black writer, another way of transcendence is open. It lies in his recognition that the conditions of one's fate may be transformed and transcended not only by the power of love but also through the power of the artist's imagination. Literature has power—the word serving both to liberate and to destroy. But to liberate, the word must be an expression of the writer's creative freedom and must be brought somehow into relation with the literary traditions it can extend and express. Whatever may be the vestiges of an African tradition available in the United States, blacks here are, willy-nilly, Americans and share in as well as contribute to the "Western" cultural tradition. This may be galling to some black militants, but it can be a source of enrichment to the black artist who can establish himself in relation to it. Addison Gayle, Jr., has asserted that "the Negro critic must demand that the Negro writer articulate the grievances of the Negro,"[28] but grief is not the only emotion the black experiences and must not be the only luxury permitted him. Black humanity is fuller in its range than this inadequate term of self-definition. I am not arguing here an art-for-art's-sake attitude. But I am arguing for a creative use of the freedom and of the tradition available to whoever would write works men would not willingly let die.

To get into relation with this tradition, to discover this way of transcendence, is to be released from the extrinsically imposed obligation to be merely a propagandist, merely a protester, merely a voicer of black fire, black rage. It frees him, the writer, from the illusion, commonest among whites, that race has a positive value. It frees him to explore, appropriate, and transform the Western cultural and literary tradition which is his birthright as well as the birthright of white writers. To engage with this tradition is not to ignore the viability of sociological realities as the material of black art. Once again, the insights of Ralph Ellison provide a valuable touchstone for the black writer: "I've never pretended for one minute that the injustices and limitations of Negro life do not exist. On the other hand, I think it's important to recognize that Negroes have achieved a very rich humanity despite these restrictive conditions. I wish to be free not so that I can be less Negro American but so that I can make the term mean something even richer. Now, if I can't recognize this or if recognizing this makes me an Uncle Tom, then heaven help us all."[29]

The Problematic Texts of Richard Wright

❦ It is an event of great cultural importance to have, at last, the best of Richard Wright now available in the Library of America series.[1] By 1992, with respect to black writers, only W. E. B. Du Bois had been represented in the collection, although it is only fair to the Library to remark that some of the best black writers are modern, and considerations of copyright and high royalty fees have delayed the appearance of many twentieth-century writers, both white and black. In a manner of speaking, the reprint of a writer's work in the Library of America may be perceived as a sign of greatness, even an admission to the "canon of classic texts." At the very least it is a great honor, for most readers probably assent to the Library's claim of offering us "the only definitive collection of America's greatest writers." *Definitive* is a loaded word, about which I shall say more later, but whatever his flaws, Richard Wright belongs, in my judgment, in this distinguished group—which includes, at least in the Library series, such familiars as Twain, Crane, Parkman, William and Henry James, Lincoln, Cather, Wharton, Cooper, and Franklin, among others.

Native Son is, without question, Wright's best novel. Ralph Ellison has rightly remarked that "*Native Son* was one of the major literary events in the history of American literature." And Irving Howe has even gone so far as to say that "the day *Native Son* appeared, American culture was changed forever."[2] A new work of great imaginative power rearranged the tradition of American fiction; and, in respect to black protest writing, it made previous black novelists like Charles Chestnutt, Du Bois, Nella Larsen, and Rudolph Fisher seem gentle by comparison. Younger black writers also found a new model for the naturalistic representation of their experience; and in quick order new grim portraits of black life appeared in Chester Himes's *If He Hollers Let Him Go* (1945), Ann Petry's *The Street* (1946), Curtis Lucas's *Third Ward Newark* (1946), and Willard Motley's *Knock on Any Door* (1947).[3] Equally as important, after *Native Son* white readers no longer found it possible to luxuriate in an illusion of black docility, passivity, and contentment.

II

Richard Wright, the grandchild of slaves and the child of an illiterate sharecropper and a backcountry schoolteacher, was born in 1908 on Rucker's Plantation near Roxie, Mississippi. He had all the disadvantages of being black in the Jim Crow Mississippi of that time; and the bitter effects of racial animosity toward blacks and legal segregation were compounded by a grinding poverty that would have stunted nearly anyone's development. Making ends meet required the family to split up from time to time, and Richard and his brother were placed for a while with their grandparents in Natchez while the parents searched for work. Eventually his father, a brutal man, abandoned the family, and his mother moved the boys about continually—to Memphis, Tennessee; Jackson, Mississippi; and Elaine and West Helena, Arkansas—as she shifted from job to job, laboring as a cook or cleaning woman for white families. A dominant motif of Wright's autobiography—surely exaggerated, like much else—is the constant hunger he suffered. But it appears to be the case that there was never enough money for rent or food. For a time Wright was placed in a Methodist orphanage in Memphis; and for a while he lived with his uncle Silas Hoskins. (Hoskins was lynched in 1917 in Elaine—only because, it seems, he had a successful business coveted by whites.)

It would be tedious to rehearse the family's many moves, or Wright's chronic hunger as a child, his makeshift schooling in one town or another, or the menial labor and odd jobs—as delivery boy, sales clerk, dishwasher, and bellboy—by which the growing boy tried to help out his mother and grandmother, who were in continual ill health. *Black Boy* offers a compelling account of these experiences. For his family the strict fundamentalism of Methodist and Seventh-day Adventist Christianity was completely sustaining, but the religious prohibitions of his family, their moral strictness, and the manifest hypocrisy of Southern racial relations alienated and estranged the boy, even while he was filled with a lifelong sense of anxiety and dread. Great curiosity and omnivorous reading—in thrown-away issues of the *Atlantic Monthly, Harper's,* and *American Mercury*—saved him from the common fate. Mencken's iconoclastic *Prejudices* and *A Book of Prefaces* taught him to see "words as weapons"; he began to haunt the public libraries and to cultivate a burning ambition to write.

Black poverty in the rural South is horrific enough in Wright's account of it in *Black Boy*. The North, with its more liberal racial attitudes and industrial capacity, beckoned to the Wrights, as it did to thousands of rural blacks. But the Wrights' move to Chicago in 1927 plunged young Richard into evils almost as great as those he had left behind. And the urban poverty he experienced, particularly after the Crash of 1929, was equally as appalling. But he eked out a life of sorts, supporting his mother and aunt as a dishwasher, ditchdigger, postal clerk, and insurance agent. He read extensively in Conrad, Twain, James, Proust, Dostoevsky, and others. But, as he told an interviewer for *L'Express* in 1960, "Theodore Dreiser first revealed to me the nature of American life, and for that service, I place him at the pinnacle of American literature."[4]

The Communist organizers in the League of Struggle for Negro Rights captured Wright's attention in the 1930s, and he became an active member of the local John Reed Club. Joining the Communist party in 1934, he developed friendships with many proletarian writers and social critics—including Nelson Algren, Jack Conroy, Arna Bontemps, and James T. Farrell. His literary talent opened opportunities for him in *Left Front, Anvil,* and *New Masses,* and between 1934 and 1937, Wright was an impassioned activist at writers' congresses and in Midwest literary groups. Wherever he went he argued for racial equality and espoused his Communist faith. Yet he cooled to the Chicago branch of the party in 1937 when it tried to infringe on his freedom as a writer. Moving in that year to New York, he pursued his literary career as the Harlem editor of the *Daily Worker*, to which he contributed more than two hundred articles. His first breakthrough came with the publication of *Uncle Tom's Children* in 1938. *Native Son*, a Book-of-the-Month Club selection, followed in 1940, and, with the many accolades it earned him, his career took off. For the Chicago phase of his development, *American Hunger* is indispensable.

Wright's subsequent life seemed foreordained by his popular success in America. His works were translated into French, Italian, German, Dutch, and other languages. The power of the novel made him in constant demand as a spokesman for racial equality, and he toured the country as a platform speaker and panelist. His distinction as a portrayer of black life in America led naturally in 1941 to *12 Million Black Voices: A Folk History of the Negro in the United States*; and, after some disagreements over its content, his best-selling autobiography appeared in 1945 as *Black Boy: A Record of Childhood and Youth*.

Toward the close of the 1930s, Wright was becoming estranged from the Communist party theoreticians, who were dictating to sympathetic writers what they could and could not write about. Authors such as Wright were told to stick to the canons of Socialist Realism and advance the cause of the imminent proletarian revolution. Wright chafed at this infringement on his freedom as a writer, and in May 1940, on the eve of World War II, Wright asked Mike Gold, "Are we Communist writers to be confined merely to the political and economic spheres of reality and leave the dark and hidden places of the human personality to the Hitlers and Goebbels? I refuse to believe such." Disillusionment with communism and Socialist Realism was turning him more toward the psychology of poverty and race. Sociological protest fiction had sustained him throughout the 1930s, but now he seemed ready for something more subjective. He said that

> Not to plunge into the complex jungle of human relationships and analyze them is to leave the field to the fascists and I won't and can't do that. If I should follow Ben Davis's advice and write of Negroes through the lens of how the Party views them in terms of political theory, I'd abandon the Bigger Thomases. I'd be tacitly admitting that they are lost to us, that fascism will triumph, because it alone

can enlist the allegiance of those millions whom capitalism has crushed and maimed. No! I say, wherever the fascists go with their rot and noise, I, too, make my claim.⁵

Objecting to the Communists' view of how to represent the race question, Wright quietly broke with the party in 1942, but his political views had brought him under government surveillance, which continued throughout most of his lifetime, and he had constant passport difficulties in traveling abroad. In 1946 he took a month-long trip to France, at the invitation of Jean-Paul Sartre and Claude Lévi-Strauss, where he formed friendships with Gertrude Stein, Simone de Beauvoir, André Gide, and many others. In Paris he was introduced to the *Négritude* movement sponsored by Léopold Sédar Senghor and Aimé Césaire. What particularly pleased him about France was its greater racial tolerance and openness to new ideas. In 1947 racial prejudice in the Greenwich Village housing scene provoked his ire, and he decided to move permanently to France, taking with him his white wife Ellen, a onetime Polish Communist, and his daughter Julia. Wright was to tell Ralph Ellison that his "exile" in Paris arose because of the rupture with the party—that "after I broke with the Communist party I had nowhere else to go. . . ."⁶

Whatever may have been the full complex of his motives, this expatriation raised a new critical issue: whether or not Wright's Paris life deracinated him from his natural subjects and settings, from black American character and language, and was therefore damaging to his art. This issue—which has been raised about nearly *every* American expatriate—is much too complicated to address here, but, it should be noted, Wright's severest critics on this point were black. James Baldwin bluntly asserted that Wright got "out of touch" with American blacks, and he insinuated that Wright came to think of himself as *"white."* And Cecil Brown concluded that Wright expatriated because "his definition of 'Negro life' was too narrow, too confining, too puny, and too dependent on White Society."⁷ What seems obvious in such remarks is the sense of racial betrayal or abandonment, the sense that the United States was really the proper arena for Wright to have pursued his career and that the final thirteen years in Paris vitiated his art.

In Paris, Wright became a spokesman for the American colony of blacks (and for African blacks in Paris), and he founded and joined many literary and liberal political organizations. The existentialism of Sartre and Camus was then all the rage, and Wright began to read in the philosophy of Heidegger, Husserl, and Jaspers. (This existentialism, in ill-digested clumps, unfortunately mars his novel *The Outsider* [1953].)[8] At the same time his friendship with George Padmore (the Trinidadian author of *Pan-Africanism or Communism?*) had the effect of heightening his interest in Africa, and in 1953 he toured Ghana, Sierra Leone, and other countries—producing in 1954, out of this experience, *Black Power: A Record of Reactions in a Land of Pathos*. As fascinated as he was by black Africa, it must be said that his reactions are those of a Western Marxist intellectual sharply critical of the tribal mentality.

During this period Wright's political, cultural, and philosophic interests interfered with his imaginative work. And it is hard to disagree with Saunders Redding, who remarked that the late work "turns precious and arty; honesty deserts him; dedication wilts; passion chills."[9] *Savage Holiday* (1954), a novel about a white psychopathic murderer, was a weak performance. Harper rejected it, and he was obliged to bring it out as an original paperback by Avon. Somewhat like the later Faulkner, Wright saw himself as an important public spokesman on national and international issues, and he began to play up the part. As a cultural reporter for the Congress of Cultural Freedom, he attended the Bandung (Indonesia) Conference of nonaligned nations and listened to Nehru, Sukarno, Nasser, and others declaim on the state of international relations in the cold war era. *The Color Curtain: A Report on the Bandung Conference* appeared in 1956. *Pagan Spain* (1957), a travel book, *White Man, Listen!* (1957), a collection of essays based on his lectures about race, and *The Long Dream* (1958), a novel set in Mississippi, represent the final phase of his declining career. He was in ill health in the last years of his life, probably as a result of amoebic dysentery picked up in Africa, but he died in fact of a heart attack in Paris in 1960, as he was completing the proofs of *Eight Men* (1961), his last collection of stories.

III

Richard Wright: Early Works, in the Library of America edition, begins with *Lawd Today!* This is a work not very well known, principally because it was not published in Wright's lifetime. Completed in 1935 and originally entitled *Cesspool,* the novel was rejected by several publishers. An account of one day—an anniversary of Lincoln's birthday—in the life of a black postal worker, it portrays in Jake Jackson an arrogant, irresponsible, vain, and cruel member of the *lumpenproletariat* who begins the day by beating up his wife (the section is called "Commonplace"); and he ends it, in a drunken rage, by nearly killing her (in "Rats' Alley"). In between, Jake is shown hanging out at Doc Higgins' Tonsorial Palace, borrowing from a loan shark, malingering at the post office (the "Squirrel Cage" section), and drinking himself into a violent rage at a ghetto whorehouse, where he is rolled of the $100 he has just borrowed. Not without its defects, *Lawd Today!* failed to interest a publisher in 1936, and it languished in manuscript until it posthumously appeared in 1963. The editor, Arnold Rampersad, has thought it important enough to include here; and indeed its structural form, rhythmic dialogue, contrapuntal themes, and suggestive symbolism give a clear foreshadowing of the Wright who would emerge, fully matured, in *Native Son.* As a reflection of the social and moral inferno in which these hollow men live, *Lawd Today!* is Wright's version of Eliot's *The Waste Land,* construed as the bitter end of Lincoln's dream of black emancipation.

Uncle Tom's Children, a fully achieved work of fiction, contains five long stories preceded by an autobiographical sketch, "The Ethics of Living Jim Crow." Wright was a dedicated Communist at the time he wrote these tales, and each introduces, more or less, the Marxist viewpoint. But they are by no means mere propaganda, which is no doubt why Wright got into trouble with the Chicago branch of the party, which hinted, ominously, of purging the "bastard intellectuals" and "incipient Trotskyites" in their midst. Wright's troubles with party orthodoxy are recounted in his essay "I Tried to Be a Communist" (1944), which was reprinted in *The God That Failed.* As an account of how the Soviets and the Communist party in this country betrayed the American people, and especially blacks, it is eye-opening. But Wright's essay does not fully admit his extensive work for the party. Russell Carl Brignano points out that *The God That Failed* essay "describes events only until Wright departed Chicago for New York in 1937," but that Wright actually worked as a reporter "for the Party organ in New York, *The Daily Worker,*" and that "Marxist content" is apparent in all of Wright's work published between 1937 and 1941.[10] But "I Tried to Be a Communist" does have the merit of indicating how ruthlessly the party theoreticians wished to eradicate traces of individualism in authors such as Wright.

Each of these stories focuses on a black protagonist who reacts against brutalization by whites not so much on the basis of ideology as on an instinctive desire for freedom from social oppression and on the intuition of a better way of life. As the children of Uncle Tom, each of them has learned "to lie, to steal, to dissemble," to "play that dual role which every Negro must play if he wants to eat and live."[11] In "Big Boy Leaves Home," a group of trespassing boys, swimming naked in a Mississippi stream, are surprised by a white woman who begins screaming when they approach to retrieve their clothes. Her husband, alerted by the screams, shoots at them and is, in turn, killed by Big Boy in self-defense. The tale ends with his friend Bobo lynched and Big Boy escaping to the North. In "Down by the Riverside," a black named Mann steals a boat—during a flood emergency—in order to row his pregnant wife to the hospital. He is caught in the act by the owner, whom he kills in self-defense. Though he tries to get his wife to the hospital, the boat is commandeered by white soldiers intent on rescuing those trapped in the inundated and floating houses. Although Mann's conduct throughout the flood is heroic (he even saves his victim's wife and son), he is identified by the dead man's family and—trying to escape—is shot down. "Long Black Song" narrates the rape of a black woman by a white traveling salesman, her husband's revenge killing of the rapist, and the inevitable lynching that follows.

"Fire and Cloud" is, in my view, the most upbeat of the five tales. It tells the depression story of a black minister, Reverend Taylor, whose people are starving but who cannot persuade the white power structure to provide relief in the form of food. When the Communist organizers urge a demonstration, the mayor and police chief warn Reverend Taylor to discourage his people from attending. He is a Christian, has always been a "good nigger," and is rightly worried that if he leads his people into the town square, a bloodbath will await them. But before he can decide what to do, he is seized by Klan rednecks, taken out into the country, and horse-whipped until he is unconscious. On the following morning, having had a "vision," he walks with most of the town's ten thousand blacks into the square—a multitude so numerous that the mayor and the police back down, capitulate, and agree to provide food for the starving. While the story is meant to be an illustration of Lenin's slogan—that *"Freedom belongs to the strong!"*—its literary power inheres in Wright's masterly presentation of the poignant helplessness of those who have nowhere else to turn.[12] All of the tales suggest a complex grasp of racist social relations in the pre–World War II South, yet Wright's command of the nuances of emotion in his inarticulate characters, their blind impulses and bewildered striving, is equally compelling. His ear was true to the dialect of Mississippi blacks, at least as I knew it fifty years ago, and his expert use of biblical symbolism and Christian allusion is richly counterpointed with his own idiosyncratic Marxist perspective.

In the writing of *Uncle Tom's Children,* Wright was later to claim that he had

> made an awfully naïve mistake. I found that I had written a book which even bankers' daughters could read and weep over and feel good about. I swore to myself that if I ever wrote another book, no one would weep over it; that it would be so hard and deep that they would have to face it without the consolation of tears. It was this that made me get to work in dead earnest.[13]

The reader's affect of sympathy for his characters meant less to Wright than administering a shock that would stun white readers into an amelioration of the conditions of black existence. In *Native Son,* he exploded a bomb.

IV

Native Son's narrative of a deprived black boy living in a rat-infested tenement, a boy who commits two more or less unintended but brutal murders, naturalizes Dostoevsky in a Chicago tenement setting. It is preeminently a novel of crime and punishment. Bigger Thomas becomes the chauffeur for a rich white man and is sexually attracted to his promiscuous daughter. After a night on the town, when Mary Dalton and her Communist boyfriend Jan Erlone get drunk and make love in the back seat of the car, Bigger Thomas has to put the comatose Mary to bed. When Mary's blind mother enters the bedroom, Bigger, in trying to keep Mary quiet, accidentally smothers her, and, to cover up his crime, stuffs her body into the furnace. Framing Erlone, Bigger then fakes a kidnap note to mislead the police, but—when he is discovered—he runs. During the manhunt, he hides out in several abandoned buildings, murders his girlfriend Bessie to prevent betrayal, but is nevertheless caught and brought to trial.

Modeling his narrative on *An American Tragedy,* Wright constructed the novel so as to interpret the meaning of Bigger's experience from a Communist perspective. This was not difficult to do in passages of dialogue and expository narration. Wright's literary problem, however, was that Bigger is too inarticulate and unintellectual to understand his own experiences, much less to communicate a Marxist interpretation of class and race. Hence the account of Bigger's life and the explanation of his crimes are given through the speeches presented by the defense lawyer, a Communist attorney named Boris A. Max. Needless to say, Bigger is turned into a symbol of all blacks, and the sociological conditions of black urban poverty and white racism are invoked as the proximate cause of the murder of these two women. Thus white society is put on trial,[14] and Bigger Thomas is made out to be the victim of the social forces of capitalism and racism conspiring to diminish black life in America. Furthermore the inarticulate and homicidal rage of Bigger Thomas is asserted to be typical of virtually every black in America—as the following passage from Max's defense suggests:

> Multiply Bigger Thomas twelve million times, allowing for environmental and temperamental variations, and for those Negroes who are completely under the influence of the church, and you have the psychology of the Negro people. But once you see them as a whole, once your eyes leave the individual and encompass the mass, a new quality comes into the picture. Taken collectively, they are not simply twelve million people; in reality they constitute a separate nation, stunted, stripped, and held captive *within* this nation, devoid of political, social, economic, and property rights.[15]

But is Bigger typical of *all* secular blacks? Are their lives, like his, without *any* self-esteem, family love, professional or vocational gratification, or social fulfillment? No laughter and no love—even when white folks aren't around? No intimacy, happy jiving, or the experience of inner wholeness? No intellectual passion or artistic purpose? Of course not. In making this subhuman figure a symbol of all blacks, Wright really reflected "those hopeless assumptions about Negro life which elicited its rage, and its protagonist's sense of his own identity is formed by just that image of himself which, as it lives in the larger culture, has caused his despair."[16]

It is no wonder that James Baldwin complained that "a necessary dimension has been cut away; this dimension being the relationship that Negroes bear to one another, that depth of involvement and unspoken recognition of shared experience which creates a way of life." For Baldwin, "Bigger has no discernible relationship to himself, to his own life, to his own people, nor to any other people—in this respect, perhaps, he is most American—and his force comes, not from his significance as a social (or anti-social) unit, but from his significance as the incarnation of a myth."[17] (The myth is of course a stereotype—the worst nightmare of white racial anxiety.) Likewise, Ellison complained that protest literature of Wright's kind is so reductive of black experience, of any kind of *human* experience, that the effect is grotesque; and, for all his friendship for Wright and admiration of *Native Son*, he deplored a fiction that fails "to explore the full range of American Negro humanity and to affirm those qualities which are of value beyond any question of segregation, economics or previous condition of servitude. The obligation was always there and there is much to affirm."[18] But affirming black life is a more complex task than writing a protest novel. What *Native Son* finally offers us, then, as Nathan Scott remarks, is "a depraved and inhuman beast as the comprehensive archetypal image of the American Negro."[19]

But these objections, which go to the heart of the *representativeness* of *Native Son* as a portrait of black life, are really reflections of the reception-history of the work. At present, other critical issues seem paramount. It is now unfashionable to remind readers of Wright's naturalistic reduction of Bigger Thomas to a victim shaped by the supposed determinism of his racist society. It is also assumed to be unfair to point out that Wright was a sucker for the dehumanizing Marxist ideology that underlies this reductive literary determinism. On the first point, contemporary critics are likely to grant that Dreiser and other naturalists had an influence on Wright but to argue that Wright's work transcends the doctrinaire determinism of heredity and environment usually implied in the ideology of literary naturalism. Hakutani notes this trend in posing a question for criticism today:

> In *Native Son*, for instance, does he [Wright] subscribe to the novel's implicit assumption that American social conditions are directly responsible for the degradation of blacks? Recent criticism has modified or refuted this assumption, suggesting that Wright went beyond naturalism.

Hakutani claims that Wright's "existentialism taught him how to liberate man from the strictures imposed on him."[20] This, it seems to me, is both true and false. None of the recent criticism has really refuted the idea that Wright initially subscribed to a theory of sociological determinism. Yet it is also true that Wright went beyond naturalistic determinism. But this is true of the *later* Richard Wright, the Wright of Paris and Sartre and Camus, not the Wright of *Native Son* in 1940. At the time he composed this novel, Wright's agenda was focused, intense, and clear: to eliminate from Bigger's life any dimension of human freedom, to project his character as the pure victim of a malicious racism fueled by capitalism, so as to indict white society. And Boris Max is the voice of that indictment.

Some of Wright's current defenders have also tried to deflect attention away from the proletarian dimension of his Communist protest fiction, probably because, as Nathan Scott has remarked, we find proletarian novelists today to be "writers with whom it is virtually impossible any longer to have a genuinely reciprocal relation, for the simple fact is that the rhetoric of what once used to be called 'reportage' proves itself, with the passage of time, to be a language lacking in the kind of amplitude and resonance that lasts."[21] Houston A. Baker is one of those who wish to repress our memory of Wright's ideology and of *Native Son* as an expression of it: "Wright's most significant niche is scarcely to be found in the Proletarian school." But if not there, where? Baker can come up with only "the folk tradition": Bigger is "a conscious literary projection of the folk hero who embodies the survival values of a culture."[22] The "survival values" of black culture? Hardly. Rinehart, in Ralph Ellison's *Invisible Man,* is such a folk character. We have only to compare him with Bigger to see that Wright's character, who does *not* survive, is no incarnation of survival values. He is, however, to judge from Baker's other examples, a figure who responds to his situation by murdering. Baker's attempt to paper over Wright's seduction by the left and to call Bigger an incarnation of folk wisdom and survival techniques trivializes the novel. In fact, the emotive energy of the work inheres in the intensity with which everything is seen through the Marxist lens.[23] Keneth Kinnamon has, as usual, got it right:

> As a fervent party member, Wright maintained a thoroughly communistic point of view in *Native Son.* The courtroom arguments of Max in the final section, of course, are patently leftist. He equates racial and class prejudice, both being based on economic exploitation. He repeats the basic party concept of the times regarding the collective status of Negroes in America. . . . He discerns in Bigger a revolutionary potentiality. Not all of Max's courtroom speech reflects so directly communist doctrine, but none of it is inconsistent with the party line on racial matters.[24]

The novel is thus a distinctive work of Communist social protest, condemning American racism through the method of a Marxist sociological determinism. In the history of the American novel, the book was customarily regarded as a "proletarian" novel—that is, a fictional leftwing attack on the "class structure" and "capitalist exploitations" of the American underclass. Like most novels with this ideological bias, however, the motivation of the action is a problem. Still, setting aside Wright's unconvincing explanation of why Bigger is a murderer, and setting aside the courtroom defense it elicits in Max's prolix courtroom speech, the novel is still a work of horrifying and sobering import.[25] Wright was later to say, in "How 'Bigger' Was Born," that while his "contact with the labor movement and its ideology" (his euphemism for communism) made him feel "the pinch and pressure of the environment" that produced a Bigger Thomas, he did not mean to say that "environment *makes* consciousness."[26] But Bigger has little enough consciousness to have any comprehensible view of why he is a murderer. Like Dreiser, Wright constructed his novel out of newspaper accounts of the trial of one Robert Nixon, who had murdered a white woman. Nixon was defended by two black lawyers. In the novel, Wright changes the defense to a leftist white lawyer, for no black attorney would have mounted the sociological defense of Bigger that Max provides.[27] Yet Wright's attention to Bigger's shapeless inner life and the prolixity and dubiety of Max's courtroom speechifying have led some of Wright's defenders to suggest that Wright really *wasn't* writing a novel of social protest, that Wright *saw through* the dubious argument advanced by Max, and that the book is really a psychological novel of sorts. This stratagem, in my view, deflects attention from the novel's Marxist message, robs the novel of its force as a document of social protest, and misrepresents Wright's ideological sympathies in the late thirties.[28] The Marxist solution Wright espoused, as incarnated in the Soviet Union and Eastern Europe, was productive of immense evil, and if it had been tried in the United States, the result would have been a like disaster—especially for blacks. Wright was therefore wrong in subscribing to this political ideology. Still, despite his dangerous political views, he was a remarkable novelist. Since we must take him as he was, there is no use in denying the doubtful views that he espoused. *Native Son,* for all its defect of political understanding, survives its own ideology, thanks to its *literary* power. And it is this literary power that makes him worth reading today.

In understanding Wright's development into a Communist, his autobiography *Black Boy (American Hunger)* is immensely illuminating, for its portrait of abject poverty and of racial prejudice in the South produced such smoldering rage that not even the ministrations of family or the consolations of religion could overcome. In this self-life he does very nearly what he did in *Native Son*: in recording the ways in which he was brutalized, he completely strips out of the life any positive experience. This gross exaggeration has led many to wonder how—if Wright's life were so unremittingly cruel a victimization—he could have developed into the talented and literate author that he was. The answer can only be that Wright did not wish to record the forms of nurturing and help that account for his escape from the bondage of poverty and racism; he wished only to arraign the Jim Crow South and the hellhole tenement world of Chicago that his conversion to communism helped him understand. In 1943, when he completed the manuscript, he intended to call his autobiography *American Hunger*. In the draft he sent to his agent, Paul Reynolds, the manuscript contained two sections: "Southern Night," dealing with his life in the South; and "The Horror and the Glory," dealing with his Chicago life and membership in the party. The Book-of-the-Month Club was interested in it, but they recommended to Wright's editor at Harper, Edward Aswell, that only the first part be published. Wright agreed and renamed the autobiography *Black Boy*; it dealt with only his Southern years. Not until 1977 was the second part published, by Harper and Row, under the title *American Hunger*. In the Library of America text, we now have the whole of Wright's original manuscript—presented under the title *Black Boy (American Hunger)*.

V

As rich as is the content of Wright's autobiography (not to speak of *The Outsider*), and as deserving as both books are of critical attention here, I must turn away from the problematic *content* of Wright's work toward its problematic *form*. That is, some of the textual decisions by the Library of America demand comment. As a first principle of professional editing, it ought to be the publisher's objective *to present that form of the text that represents the author's final intention*. According to this principle, a text editor should incorporate any changes on the manuscript leaves, galleys, and page proofs (and pages of already published editions) that reflect the last wish of the author with respect to the form in which his work should appear. This description of editorial procedures reflects the copy-text rationale demanded by the Center for Scholarly Editions, an agency of the Modern Language Association that certifies the accuracy of newly edited literary texts. In the past the Library of America has endorsed this rationale and promised to use CSE certified texts wherever possible. In fact at least one eminent bibliographer involved in establishing the Center's editorial procedures, Thomas Tanselle of the John Simon Guggenheim Foundation, serves as an adviser to the Library, identifying those writers for whom certified texts already exist. The Library's policy—at least as explained to me some years ago, when I edited a Washington Irving volume in the series—has been that where no certified text exists, as in the case of Richard Wright, an authoritative published edition of the text will simply be reprinted. Only typographical errors or gross misreadings of the setting copy by a compositor would be corrected. Hence there is rarely any serious "editorial intervention" into Library of America texts. But this wise policy, as the discussion below indicates, has not been followed in the case of Wright. For one thing, *Black Boy (American Hunger),* in the Library of America edition, is not a form of the text of his autobiography that Wright ever approved. As I have remarked, to get it published he assented to cutting the manuscript in half, publishing his Southern chapters as *Black Boy* and dropping *"American Hunger,"* with its record of his Communist life in Chicago.

Now, an argument *could* be made, I suppose, that Wright merely acquiesced, under pressure from Harper and the Book-of-the-Month Club, in a change to his autobiography that otherwise he would not have made. He wanted, after all, to get his autobiography published. And in fact Wright did privately complain in his journal, I have been told, that "pressure from Communists" had induced the Club to request deletion of the second part. (I have seen no documented evidence for this belief that the Communists, from whom he had become estranged, did not want his Chicago story to come out. Frankly, it is a scandal that, nearly five decades after his death, Wright's letters and journals have not yet been published.) Even so, in after years, when Wright had attained international fame and generally had no trouble getting published, he never moved to reissue his autobiography in the form in which he had originally written it. The second part—which he had already mined for magazine articles—appeared in book form only posthumously, in 1977, as a separate text. This publication was authorized, incidentally, by Mrs. Ellen Wright, who controls the literary estate and who has *prevented* the timely publication of Wright's letters and journals.

These textual considerations also raise a question about the form of *Native Son* as well. Editor Arnold Rampersad remarks in a note that "This text of *Native Son* is the last version of the text that Wright prepared without external intervention, and in all the other cases these texts are the last, or last-known, versions that Wright approved."[29] His reference to external intervention is a serious matter and deserves clarification. When Aswell, Wright's editor, sent a copy of the Harper proofs to the Book-of-the-Month Club, Dorothy Canfield Fisher (and perhaps other judges of the Club) objected to a passage, early in the novel, where Bigger and a friend masturbate in a movie theater while watching a newsreel clip about Mary Dalton, the rich Chicago socialite and left-wing sympathizer. Some sense of the passage is suggested by this excerpt:

> Bigger moved restlessly and his breath quickened; he looked round in the shadows to see if any attendant was near, then slouched far down in his seat. He glanced at Jack and saw that Jack was watching him out of the corners of his eyes. They both laughed.
> "You at it again?" Jack asked.
> "I'm polishing my nightstick," Bigger said.
> They giggled.
> "I'll beat you," Jack said.
> "Go to hell."
> The organ played for a long moment on a single note, then died away.
> "I'll bet you ain't even hard yet," Jack whispered.
> "I'm getting hard."
> "Mine's like a rod," Jack said with intense pride.
> "I wish I had Bessie here now," Bigger said.
> "I could make old Clara moan now."[30]

The Club was inclined to accept the novel if some three pages of this material, culminating in an orgasm, were deleted. Wright agreed to excisions deemed to be obscene. In the Library of America text, these excisions have been restored as instances of unwarranted external interference. But were they? Wright, after all, *approved* the deletions. In fact he rewrote the scene and modified later particulars (not always with perfect consistency) to harmonize with his changes. Do not these changes represent his final intention? And should that not be respected? In later years, moreover, when Wright was famous and well respected, he never complained, to my knowledge, of the editorial suggestions supplied by Aswell or the Club. And he never moved to reissue the autobiography in its original manuscript form.

In reaction to the Library's editorial decisions, James Campbell, in "The Wright Version," has raised a question about whether

Wright "would have approved the work of re-editing which has been carried out on his two most famous books." Arnold Rampersad, in his view, "appears to have overstepped his brief" by altering the texts that we have known for so long.[31] Rampersad did not, I believe, reply to this accusation. But Mark Richardson, who described himself as having assisted in the research for the Library edition, wrote a rejoinder to the effect that the Library's decisions were sound because "Wright would not have revised the two books if the Book Club hadn't asked him to. . . ."[32] On this principle, no editor's recommendation for amending substantives or accidentals (regardless of how much it improves a writer's text and regardless of the fact that the writer endorses the change) need be considered binding on a later editor. As an editorial principle this is, of course, arrant nonsense. I am sure that the in-house editors at the Library of America amended Arnold Rampersad's prose at will, just as they have done with all their collaborators. Editors are, in fact, essential figures in the publication process. Publishers need them to get printable copy, and authors need them to produce publishable work. Perhaps not all writers need close editing, but Wright was one of those who did; and it is a fact that Wright depended on Edward Aswell for help and valued his assistance.

But of course there are some people who think that no moral or social value should ever constrain the writer's imagination, which should be free to communicate whatever obscenities may pop up during the writer's always infallible creative reverie. Further, it is sometimes said that there should never be a bar to our *having* these obscenities, or having them thrust upon us, even if the writer decides, on reflection, that he will not, after all, expose us to the filthy things. In any case, when the Library's problematic texts were first brought up for discussion and criticism, Ellen and Julia Wright, the novelist's widow and daughter, announced rather grandly that

> It is important to us that Bigger Thomas, who was "castrated" because deprived of his sexual life in the edited 1940 text, is made whole again—and made human—by the reinstatement of the masturbation scene at the beginning of *Native Son* and of references to his guilt-ridden desire for rich, white Mary prior to the panic which leads him to smother her accidentally. Likewise it is important to

have reinstated *American Hunger* as an integral part of *Black Boy* because of the psychological importance of viewing Wright's account of his disillusionment with Communist Party politics as only one in a series of betrayals, the first of which takes place in *Black Boy* when young Richard is disowned by his father over the kitten episode.³³

It is not clear to me how, exactly, the acclaimed masturbation passage makes Bigger more human than (as he is sometimes called) subhuman. And the flamboyant "castration" reference, with its implication of white hoods and lynching parties, is pure race theater intended to flay whites for having lynched blacks. In my opinion, the seriousness of such crimes is trivialized by linking it with the deleted masturbation scene. Furthermore, if it has always been important to have both parts of the autobiography together, why did Mrs. Wright, the literary executor of her husband's estate, authorize the *separate* republication of *American Hunger* in 1977?

There is no question that readers will want to know about these variant versions. The question, in relation to serious bibliographical and editorial practice, is where these variants belong—restored to the text or relegated to endnotes? The fact is that Rampersad's restored passages are, in the lingo of professional text editors, *rejected substantives*. Wright himself rejected and excised them. The Library of America notes give us no evidence for thinking that Wright disapproved the decision to change the novel. The implication is that he was coerced. Was he?

Clarity on this point would be assured if only Mrs. Wright would release Wright's letters and journals and authorize the publication of them. The absence of them impedes a full critical understanding of her husband's work. While we await the facts, however, let us speculate about his possible reasons for canceling the masturbation passage.

(1) Wright may have deleted it because he wanted to please Edward Aswell and the folks at Harper's. They, after all, were in a position to publish not only *Native Son* but also *future* books of his, like the already written but unpublished *Lawd Today!* Was he being cooperative for the sake of his publishing future? Perhaps.

(2) But, on the other hand, perhaps he changed the novel because he knew that Book-of-the-Month Club sponsorship would

vastly increase the book's sales, and that meant more *money*. Money, after all, does motivate professional writers.

(3) But perhaps he didn't care about the *money*. Perhaps it was *fame* he sought. Perhaps he deleted the passage because of the vastly extended readership that Club selection implied. To become known worldwide through the Club—that might indeed validate a prudent revision.

(4) Yet isn't it possible that Richard Wright did not wish to be judged an obscene writer? After all, the line between what is and is not obscene is *very difficult* to draw, and writers often want guidance, want in fact, to be reined in, if and when they cross the line. Twain, as is well known, rarely knew when his irrepressible and irreverent Western humor had turned obscene; and he repeatedly asked people such as his wife Olivia, Mrs. Fairbanks, and William Dean Howells to identify any manuscript passages needing excision or revision. Likewise, Dreiser asked his wife and a friend, Arthur Henry, to edit the manuscript of *Sister Carrie* for style and content. They recommended a great many changes, Dreiser accepted them, and the novel was published in 1900. The impact of *Sister Carrie,* over the years, was not unlike that of *Native Son*. And Dreiser was content to let the novel stand—stand as revised with the editorial changes and excisions. Yet the recent University of Pennsylvania Press edition of *Carrie,* which restores Dreiser's original manuscript readings (especially references to Carrie's sexuality), does not respect Dreiser's final intention in accepting the changes he had asked his wife and friend to recommend. Nor did the Library of America respect the author's final intention in Wright's case. One final speculation. . . .

(5) Is it not possible that Wright might, on reconsideration, have concluded that the *aesthetic value* of his text suffered from the scene in which Bigger masturbates? We really cannot know. And, based on the evidence made public, neither the editors of the Library of America nor Mrs. Wright knows either.

What we do know is that Wright agreed to make changes; he *did* in fact make the changes; and he never afterward—to my knowledge—complained that he had been coerced by his publishers or that his books had been butchered. Moreover, since he attained international fame in the 1940s, he had every opportunity to insist that his work be republished in the form in which he had written it. In fact, as Eugene E. Miller has rightly complained, to see the cuts as "the result of a racial/political plot" to weaken Wright's novel is "fantastical," given its impact and given Wright's continuing faith in his agent Reynolds and in his editor Edward Aswell.[34] We need to have these excised passages—but they belong in the endnotes, not in the text. When later editors, on their own authority, undertake to restore canceled material, they do not honor the author's final intention and do not produce "definitive texts." While we now live in a more liberal age, where almost any obscenity can be claimed to have aesthetic merit or socially redeeming value, the imposition on a text of an editor's modern attitudes really serves to create a different book from the one the author finally intended. It produces, a book, moreover, different from the one that made an impact on the reading public of Wright's time and that shaped the reputation of the writer that we know.

Derek Walcott and the Vision of Homeric Grandeur

Derek Walcott's *Collected Poems, 1948–1984* (1986), *The Arkansas Testament* (1987), his epic song *Omeros* (1990), and the verse drama *The Odyssey: A Stage Version* (1993) suggest, by almost any standard, an impressively realized major imaginative achievement. Since nearly a lifetime of observation and poetic vision is captured in these works, they offer a timely occasion to reflect on the career of one of the most distinguished Caribbean poets writing today in English. A consideration of his principal themes and techniques, however brief, is especially warranted in view of his having been awarded the Nobel Prize for Literature in 1992. First, a few words about the man himself.

Born in St. Lucia in 1930, Walcott, like everyone else in the British Empire in the Caribbean, was taught to think of England as the center of civilization, even as the homeland of all its subjects. Black though he might be, he has observed,

> one was English. . . . *Civic Britannica sum*. I am a British subject. Until the reality of empires breaking up and the migration from the former Commonwealth and the colonies happened, every child all over the Empire—whether he was in Malaya or Fiji—belonged to the one nation. When we sang Kipling's hymn in church on Sundays, that very hymn was being sung by people of all colors all over the world.[1]

This remark suggests both the sense he had of belonging to a larger world and the radical dislocation he felt at the breakup of the empire into multi-island postcolonial confusion. In any case, accustomed in youth to think of himself as a British subject, Walcott took his degree at the University of the West Indies in Kingston, taught for a while in Jamaica, married and had children, wrote plays and directed theater productions, came north to the United States, and subsequently won many fellowships and prizes. He has taught creative writing at a number of American colleges and in recent years has alternated his residence between Boston and Trinidad.

Over the years, while teaching and traveling, he has been developing an impressive poetic virtuosity marked by an intimate feeling for the sensuous forms of nature and by a complex meditation on contemporary Caribbean, British, and North American culture. In the development of his dramatic and poetic repertoire,[2] Walcott has shown that he is capable of alternately dramatic, lyrical, elegiac, and confessional verse. The rhythms of his work are sometimes traditional, sometimes experimental; rhyme is invoked, or not, as the matter may require. The range is engaging and the voice distinctive, especially as Walcott's youthful apprentice work—with its too-frequent echoes of Auden, Thomas, Eliot, and Lowell—gives way to the idiom of the mature poet. Although he has never entirely escaped his formative influences, most of his lyrics are marked by a distinctive signature. Mark Rudman has suggested that this signature is recognizable by language garish and bold, observing that "no modernist mistrust of eloquence unseats Mr. Walcott's confidence and willingness to employ tradition."[3] That, in my view, is true insofar as Walcott is averse to the colloquial flatness of the William Carlos Williams line. But modernist verse offers a complicated kind of stimulus: Walcott, like Pound, makes it new by employing the tradition yet charging the contemporary idiom with a rhetorical verve, reminiscent of Dylan Thomas, that lifts his art above the banal.

It is, of course, impossible to do justice to Walcott's complex achievement in a mere essay. There are simply too many excellent poems and dramatic creations reflecting a mastery of form and a virtuosity in technique that are rare enough in poets today. This essay, however, is an effort to describe some of the sources of felicity produced by so rich and representative a reflection of the poet's art.

II

Scott Fitzgerald once said that a novelist has only one story to tell, which is told and retold with variations throughout the writer's whole career. This might almost be said of Walcott. To be brief about it, his imagination is fixed on the myth of a Caribbean Eden. As the myth is elaborated, he gives us the creation and emergence of an Adamic poet and his fall into knowledge; with this comes the corruption of the island Eden; and, after the transfiguration of Adam, the theme resolves itself into the worldwide odyssey of a Homeric wanderer. The volume contains much else, but this is, in my view, *the* major theme of *Collected Poems*.

Now, the idea of myth is suspect today, as is almost every so-called "totalizing gesture" that is directed toward comprehensive understanding. A studied cynicism about literary meaning of any kind, in fact, seems to prevail in the academy. But it is worth remembering that Walcott came to his majority at a time when Northrop Frye had made archetypal literature a centerpiece of criticism and when the great masters of modernism—Pound, Eliot, Yeats, and Stevens—had each founded his career upon one or another grand conception of the whole: Pound's Odyssean descent into the underworld in search of the wisdom of the masters; the Bloomian wandering about Dublin in Joyce's *Ulysses*; Eliot's far-wandering search for the Grail of spiritual rebirth throughout the ancient and modern moral waste lands; Yeats's two-thousand-year cycles of civilization, each of a divine, ornithic origin; and Stevens's supreme fiction said to produce a grand harmonium of the whole. Walcott shares in these modernists' mythographic tendencies, and he is not shy of paralleling his own experience with grand literary analogues and archetypes.

Anyone reading the *Collected Poems*, in any case, will be struck with how many of Walcott's verses circle back to the idea of the paradisal, which is recreated in the beauty of the islands of the West Indies. The Caribbean Eden is a personal myth and recurrent literary τόπος in Walcott's imagination. This *topos* attains sensuous form in his painterly evocations of the brilliant sun, the lime-green sea, the salt winds, the lush palms, the marl-white roads, and the bamboo roots "freckled with light." What about the inhabitants? "No people there, in the true sense of the word," Trollope once fatuously observed.[4] There is an immense disdain in such an attitude, as Walcott perfectly well understands. But setting aside its snobbishness, the remark has provoked Walcott to imagine—like Thomas in "Fern Hill"—a time before mankind had even appeared, when the Caribbean world had come into its first being in the breathtaking purity and perfection of its original creation.

There is properly speaking no Eden without an Adam, of course, and it is this persona who is most often invoked by the poet in the early years before *Omeros* and *The Odyssey: A Stage Version*. Adam is a figure, in Walcott's early monomyth, who begins with "no memory" and in fact does not even have a name. No Caribbean poet has a memory, of course, in the sense of a regional written poetic tradition upon which he can draw, a body of work constituting a model and point of departure for the contemporary island writer. As the child of a mute precolonial history, he hears no voices speaking from the pre-Columbian past. There are none. As the Adamic poet of the Caribbean, Walcott thus finds himself confronted with a blank: "For no one had yet written of this landscape / that it was possible."[5] Hence, one of his first tasks, as he makes plain in "Origins,"[6] is to ascertain who he is.

> The mind, among sea-wrack, sees its mythopoeic coast,
> Seeks, like the polyp, to take root in itself.
> Here, in the rattle of receding shoal,
> Among these shallows I seek my own name and a man.
> As the crab's claws move backwards through the surf,
> Blind memory grips the putrefying flesh.

Adam, for the moment, is a name that will do as well as any other. So, like Adam, Walcott takes upon himself the task of giving the Caribbean creation its names as well—that is, of transfiguring island realities into the nomenclature of song.[7] In these poems, lifted into the magical language of poetry, are St. Lucia and St. John, Adina, Antigua, Cannelles, and Andreuille, "all the *l*'s, Voyelles, of the liquid Antilles."[8]

The litany of islands

> The rosary of archipelagoes,
> Anguilla, Antigua,
> Virgin of Guadeloupe,
> And stone-white Grenada
> Of sunlight and pigeons,
> The amen of calm waters,
> The amen of calm waters,
> The amen of calm waters.

Named with love, in the *Collected Poems*, named in both the island patois and the high diction of the English poetic tradition, are the colors of the sea, the qualities of light, the vividness and beauty of the landscape of this world, and the island people who inhabit it. But this is only a part of what now seems manifestly a major element in Walcott's nearly career-long poetic project.

For the paradisal world is called into being in order to reflect on the fall, on how corruption and evil have entered this fertile and beautiful island world. Adam in Paradise implies no history, but of course the Caribbean has had a history—has had a history since Christobal Colon found it, inaugurating in that region what Walcott, in "The Great House," calls "the leprosy of empire." Before the discovery of those islands and of what Columbus's log called that "fine race of people" who possessed "No knowledge whatever of metals, not even of gold," lies a temporal blank, a history swallowed up by the sea. These ancient Caribs have all gone voiceless into the light, "and the lost Arawak hieroglyphs and signs / were razed from slates by sponges of the rain."[9] Thus the fall is a fall into history, and it has brought with it those white imperial officers in their crisp khaki uniforms and broad pith helmets. It has brought the sugar and tobacco planters and their immense baronial estates, large airy houses, and exclusive country clubs. It has brought their fine white ladies with their elegant Parisian dress and colorful parasols. And, for the natives, it has brought slavery, poverty, the corrugated-tin shacks on wooden stilts, the broken debris of civilization, disease, and death.

Walcott's disturbance at the history of imperial colonization in the Caribbean was, in his youth, sharp enough to have ignited revolutionary trouble. And, as he matured, he continued to be an anguished and bitter observer of what might be called the recurrent catastrophes in postcolonial black experience. I mean here the chaos arising after Caribbean independence; the disorders of African disengagement from European rule; the recurrent civil wars in both regions; the tribal savagery and mass dislocations producing disease and chaos (e.g., in Rwanda, Uganda, and Zaire), plague and epidemic, recurrent famines (e.g., in Biafra and Somalia), and so forth. But his anger, it seems to me, has always had an ethical ground, not an ideological one—much less a racist or a Marxist one. It is founded on his now rejected family Methodism and the morality of an island Catholicism that he has nevertheless absorbed in spite of sectarian differences. Walcott's anger in the *Collected Poems* never expressed itself in the terms of the revolutionist killer like Ché Guevara, who nevertheless figures in two works in the volume, nor has it ever resembled that of Jomo Kenyatta, whose ghastly butcheries loom on the horizon of "A Far Cry from Africa."

The revolutionary impulse appears in Walcott, as I say, but it is not subversive or self-destructive. His wounds are inflicted by the *lacrimae rerum*; and, rather like Auden, he recurs again and again to the inadequacy of words, of language, or poetry itself, to make anything happen. What could he as a poet do to help his people?

> Where is that passionate hatred that would help
> The black, the despairing, the poor, by speech alone?
> The fury shakes like wet leaves in the wind,
> The rain beats on a brain hardened to stone.

He is thus a victim of what "Return to D'Ennery; Rain" calls "the wounds that make you think." As his spokesman Shabine says in *The Star-Apple Kingdom*, "I am satisfied / if my hand gave voice to one people's grief."[10]

Shaped by a fundamental Christian humanism, Walcott was sickened to numbness by the savage excesses of the Kikuyu Mau-Maus who thought to achieve Kenyan independence from Great Britain by the random butchery of white settlers and their children in their beds. After such bloodshed, what is left of the revolutionist's humanity? This kind of anguish at violence—whether white or black—led some black activists to call Walcott insufficiently militant in his verse. Particularly during the sixties a great many black writers like him were faulted by black revolutionary activists for the heresy of a lingering humanism. Of course such an indictment was bound to produce a knee-jerk estrangement in white radicals as well. Robert Mazzocco, writing rather dismissively in 1964 in the *New York Review of Books* (the periodical that published on its cover a how-to diagram of a "Molotov cocktail" for the use of counterculture revolutionaries) complained rather wearily that "there's nothing revolutionary or proletarian as such in his work."[11] How the jaded radical intellectuals of that time, materially at ease at their writing desks on the Upper West Side, longed for poets to become bomb-throwing revolutionaries.

The Star-Apple Kingdom makes it rather plain that for a long time now European imperialism has been an obsolete ground of island social dissatisfaction and political discontent. This volume indicates why Shabine, Walcott's projected mulatto persona, can say, "I no longer believed in the revolution." The reason is simple. After the singing of "Rule, Britannia" ended, "One morning the Caribbean was cut up / by seven prime ministers who bought the sea in bolts" and then "sold it at a markup to the conglomerates."[12] They then

> retailed it in turn to the ministers
> with only one bank account, who then resold it
> in ads for the Caribbean Economic Community,
> till everyone owned a little piece of the sea,
> from which some made saris, some made bandannas;
> the rest was offered on trays to white cruise ships
> taller than the post office; then the dogfights
> began in the cabinets as to who had first sold
> the archipelago for this chain store of islands.

Walcott's island paradise, after imperial colonization has ended, is evidently no better than before and is perhaps even worse.[13] Hence the tone of Walcott's criticism is satirical and disillusioned:

> All those who promise free and just debate,
> then blow up radicals to save the state,
> who allow, in democracy's defence,
> a parliament of spiked heads on a fence,
> all you go bawl out, "Spoils, things ain't so bad."
> This ain't the Dark Age, is just Trinidad. . . .

Walcott's ambivalence about island life naturally suggests a comparison with V. S. Naipaul. Originally Walcott shared in the

Caribbean novelist's disgust at the decay of West Indian culture. He even dedicated the early poem "Laventille" to him. Walcott has remarked that "The older I get . . . the more aware I am of the banality and indifference of a place like Trinidad to any development of the arts"; and he has even expressed the fear that "nothing could ever be built among these rotting shacks, bare-footed backyards and moulting shingles." But Naipaul's growing dismay at the moral and aesthetic vacuity of island life increasingly estranged the two writers; and as Naipaul became more caustic, Walcott turned away, condemning him in "The Spoiler's Return" as "V. S. Nightfall." If the novelist's satire on Caribbean postcolonial greed, corruption, and cultural backwardness was once a valuable corrective, recently it has become "a manic fury controlled by a style that is becoming emptier with every book; the fury is dehydrating the style. . . . It's like the native going a step further than the master. You think you're bitter? I will show you, bwana, what real bitterness is. And that is just another form of servitude."[14]

Even so, some of the verses in the *Collected Poems* suggest a bitterness as intense as that of Naipaul.[15]

> This was his heaven once. It smells like hell.
> "And what is hell, my children?"
>
> *Qui côté c'est l'enfer?*
> Why, Father, on this coast.
> Father, hell is
>
> two hundred shacks on wooden stilts,
> one bushy path to the night-soil pits.
>
> Hell is this hole where the devil shits. . . .

If the islands have become a Dantean inferno, the now-liberated people there seem consumed "in the stench of their own sulphur of self-hatred."[16] Walcott cannot imagine, however, any other homeland. Deep within him is a steadying resistance to his own attraction to Rousseauistic primitivism—the attraction, for example, of the old back-to-Africa politics. "A Far Cry from Africa" defines with unparalleled clarity why Walcott is not your ordinary third-world dissident, much less a revolutionary. Like many island people, Walcott is a writer of mixed descent. Descended from black, English, and Dutch ancestry, from a white as well as black grandfather, and lacking therefore the luxury of racial oversimplifications,[17] Walcott was a divided child, and is a torn man:

> I who am poisoned with the blood of both,
> Where shall I turn, divided to the vein?
> I who have cursed
> The drunken officer of British rule, how choose
> Between this Africa and the English tongue I love?
> How can I turn from Africa and live?

A great many people of mixed descent identify and take pride in only one source of their racial heritage, but Walcott here feels poisoned by both the white and black strains. In his case, the island history of conquest and empire, independence and self-betrayal, has given him no basis on either side for self-congratulation. But, looking at that passage above, it strangely enough poses the choice as one between a place, Africa, and a language, the English tongue, not between Africa and England, or between (let us say) an East African tongue or a Creole pidgin English. As Walcott is a poet writing mainly for white middle-class readers who are literate and engaged with poetry, this seems to slant the issue considerably. Yet his appropriation of English may in fact have been finally conditioned by the racism of the black postcolonial island politicians. In "The Schooner Flight,"[18] the mulatto Shabine—in a departure from Eden that parallels that of Adam—contemplates his departure from the islands:

> After the white man, the niggers didn't want me
> when the power swing to their side.
> The first chain my hands and apologize, "History";
> the next said I wasn't black enough for their pride.

III

Some black critics have expressed contempt for English and American literature because it is written in the English language, which they regard as the instrument of slavery and oppression. Houston Baker, for one—as I note in the essay above on Richard Wright—has even expressed a sarcastic sympathy for the novelist because he had to write *Native Son* in the language of the slavemaster. Such contempt for the English language I find paradoxical in black academics. Baker, after all, is a highly paid professor of English at a major American university and a sometime president (get this!) of the Modern Language Association. This hostility to English oozes with the most arrant duplicity, especially since one sees absolutely no sign of any interest in the academics' relearning, or rather in learning for the first time, any tribal language of Africa (if the tongue of African origin could even be discovered).[19]

Walcott has commented on the speech of the original Caribs and Arawaks and discussed the several dialects and pidgins that developed and scattered worldwide throughout the black diaspora. The natives' patois he has contemplated in relation to English. Though he once called Creole "the language of slaves," the language of international commerce might be a more accurate term. In the past decade, Walcott has even bought into the notion of English as the tongue of the slavemaster. It is as if, for the soul of the Caribbean, he has decided to set himself entirely in opposition to Naipaul. In "Cul de Sac Valley,"[20] returning to the islands, he comes upon some indigenous trees remembered from his childhood, the *bois canot* and the *bois campêche*. They hiss to him:

> What you wish
> from us will never be,
> your words is English,
> is a different tree.

Does the Carib name of the tree really make it a different tree? Hardly. Nor, if the language of the old Caribs has now faded away, can history be reversed. No matter. The people of the region, descended from the Caribs, have no problem in continuing to communicate—whether in Creole, English, or French. However desirable, theoretically, it might be for a Walcott to write in the Carib tongue, Walcott's complaint is on a practical par with Yeats's not being able to write in Old Irish or Eliot's not being able to write in Anglo-Saxon. Political ideologists are always keen to hang onto the obsolete if the sense of victimization and pathos can be stoked and rekindled. But would anyone have wished Yeats or Eliot to have done so, if they could have? The mutability of language is a theme as old as poetry itself. The paradox in this poem is that if

Walcott's words are English, the names of the trees are French. Even if the French terms derive from the Carib, let us say, the point is that, in consuming languages, poetry produces something transcendent to any of them. English is particularly ravenous and swallows whole foreign-language syntax and alien vocabularies like nectar. It is poignant that "in forme of speeche is chaunge," as Chaucer put it of old, but even the pure well of English undefiled will doubtless not survive the inevitable effects of temporality.

In Walcott's case, in any event, the language of his poetry is English. About this tongue D. J. Enright has remarked, "The English language, which has so much to give if only because it has filched so much, is chameleon-like; it possesses the mysterious ability to insinuate itself into the most alien experience."[21] In recording this alien experience in the *Collected Poems*, Walcott sees the Creole as merely a different "regiment" from the Queen's English, yet both are marching along toward one destination; they frankly travel "the same road" with the speech of "soldiers from rival shires, from the brimstone trenches / of Agincourt to the gas of the Somme." If the metaphor is strangely military, Walcott may have had Eliot in mind.[22] I mean Eliot's sense of poetry as "a raid on the inarticulate / With shabby equipment always deteriorating / In the general mess of imprecision of feeling / Undisciplined squads of emotion." Walcott resolves the problem of language in this way.[23]

> Have we changed sides
> to the moustached sergeants and the horsy gentry
> because we serve English, like a two-headed sentry
> guarding its borders? No language is neutral;
> the green oak of English is a murmurous cathedral
> where some took umbrage, some peace; but every shade, all,
> helped to widen its shadow.

English has become for Walcott not only a precious acquisition but an instrument of great poetic power. He has helped to widen its shadow by extending its resources through the speech of his own region. Having "entered the house of literature as a houseboy,"[24] Walcott indisputably enriched English with Creole additions never heard before. A shabine, "the patois for any red nigger," he took his mixed descent and his classical English and Creole patois as constituting in him a new identity. He was a nation unto himself; he was a complete world, a cosmos of which he could be proud.[25]

> and I, Shabine, saw
> when these slums of empire was paradise.
> I'm just a red nigger who love the sea,
> I had a sound colonial education,
> I have Dutch, nigger, and English in me,
> and either I'm nobody, or I'm a nation.

Yet sometimes, as in "Codicil,"[26] a weariness of spirit saps this divided man, especially as he contemplates a corruption in Eden that has affected everyone around him and that corrupts even the purity of language that poetry ought to embody.

> Schizophrenic, wrenched by two styles,
> one a hack's hired prose, I earn
> my exile. I trudge this sickle, moonlit beach for miles. . . .
> ....
> Once I thought love of country was enough,
> now, even I choose, there's no room at the trough.

I am not sure that such a balance in perspective survives in *Omeros* and his *fin-de-siècle* verse.

IV

If even language is corrupted in a spoilt Eden, "To change your language you must change your life." And to change your life in Anguilla, Adina, Antigua, or Canelles usually means to fly up to the United States. But since the imperial center is, for many of these island peoples, Great Britain, even England becomes a place of exile, although some think of it as "going home." It is in his persona as an Adam in exile that Walcott hereafter becomes, ironically, "The Fortunate Traveller." This is the title of one of his volumes; it is clearly derived from Thomas Nashe's *The Unfortunate Traveller* (1593). But it reverses the title of its source because worldwide wandering is enlarging to the vision. (In fact it prepares the exiled Adam poet to become the wanderer Omeros, who projects himself thenceforward as Odysseus.) As an exile, he is the one who "had no nation now but the imagination."[27] Traveling to America, he sees the stink and litter of Greenwich Village streets, where "starved, on the prowl, / I was a frightened cat in that grey city"; he is frozen by the snowy winter of Cold Spring Harbor; and the man who loved islands is repelled by the cold New England landscape, where (Lowell's?) "God is meek but keeps a whistling sword." Moving on to England, he confronts the empire come full circle. This is a most interesting section of the poem to me, for there Walcott sees a race riot of black immigrants ("Calibans") howling down the Brixton streets "that began with Caedmon's raceless dew."[28] The notion of black race riots in white England was indeed a shocker after the collapse of empire, but Walcott is not content with a superficial sociological complaint about the displaced island poor in the realm of Elizabeth II. Walcott has a historical imagination sufficient to see that England itself was once an island colony, that it was despoiled by the imperial Roman legions,[29] and that it is actually not that much different from Andreuille, St. Lucia, or St. John:

> Ablaze with rage I thought,
> Some slave is rotting in this manorial lake,
> But still the coal of my compassion fought
> That Albion too was once
> A colony like ours, "part of the continent, piece of the main,"
> Nook-shotten, rook o'erblown, deranged
> By foaming channels and the vain expense
> Of bitter faction.
>
>   All in compassion ends
> So differently from what the heart arranged. . . .

Walcott's myth of Adam exiled from Paradise is not complete, however, until he has circled back to the idea of *Adam reborn*, the new man. He will be reborn as the Odysseus of *Omeros*. This turn is most memorably recounted in the extraordinary 150-page autobiographical poem *Another Life* (1973). There Walcott records how he "fell in love with art / and life began." In the economy of Walcott's grief, it is art that finally comes to compensate for the island possession that is lost. He accepts his new "function / as a colonial upstart at the end of an empire, / a single, circling homeless satellite."[30]

Thus far I have stressed Walcott's recurrent use of the biblical myth. But Adam is not, for this poet, the final correlative. For one thing, there is no Eve in this elaborate poetic myth of creation gone astray. The Walcott drama of Paradise Lost seems to occur before an Eve can even make her appearance on the scene. It is not that there are no women in *Collected Poems*—or in Walcott's own life, for that matter. But although the tendency to confessional self-revelation disfigures the verse of nearly all the poets of Walcott's generation, he is rather chivalrous about keeping out of the poems any intimate disclosures about women or any erotic biographical revelations that might connect with Eve or the paradisal monomyth.

What in fact occurs in these poems, at least initially, is a displacement of responsibility for the fall from Adam or Eve onto the colonial powers. It is they who at first seemed to bring evil into Paradise. But looking around at the postcolonial debris of abandoned factories, rusting machinery, empty mines, abandoned and unproductive fields and farms, it became clear to Walcott that there was too much oversimplified melodrama of white and black, of good and evil, in postcolonial militancy, too much romanticizing of the noble primitive versus the destructive white man's civilization. Walcott, I think, knew this all along, however volatile his emotions. After all, there really was not much of an improvement in the lives of ordinary Commonwealth peoples after the English ceded power and authority, and for many, a decline set in like that reflected in "A Letter from the Old Guard."[31] Here, an elderly black soldier, a veteran who had fought for king and country during World War II, remembers the pomp and majesty of Empire Day.

"I was twelve years of age

"when Edward abdicated for Mrs. Simpson,
but even today, I can recall my rage!

"I served with Lord Alexander in the Sudan,
I know his batman, I am now a night watchman.

"Then we get Independence all of a sudden,
and something went. We can't run anything,

"we black people. So far, I have not found one
I would trust. I soldiered for my King

"and island. My hands catch arthritis,
but they rendered unto Caesar what is Caesar's,

"just like the Gurkhas. What ferocious blighters!
Still, we was as good as them...."

If independence has not brought the hoped-for deliverance from the evils that infect Paradise, the problem is the intractability of fallen human nature. This innate defect calls into question the very idea of progress and stands in stark opposition to the utopian promises of the island politicians. In *The Star-Apple Kingdom*, as they sail toward Dominica,[32] Shabine and his friend Vince engage in this exchange:

"Dominica ahead!"
                    "It still have Caribs there."
"One day go be planes only, no more boat."
"Vince, God ain't make nigger to fly through the air."
"Progress, Shabine, that's what it's all about.
Progress leaving all we small islands behind."
I was at the wheel, Vince sitting next to me
gaffing. Crisp, bracing day. A high-running sea.
"Progress is something to ask Caribs about.
They kill them by millions, some in war,
some by forced labour dying in the mines
looking for silver, after that niggers; more
progress. Until I see definite signs
that mankind change, Vince, I ain't want to hear.
Progress is history's dirty joke.
Ask that sad green island getting nearer."

The adamic myth after this point becomes too difficult for the poet to sustain. Adam is not, after all, the right figure for the exiled, wandering poet, and so he turns from Adam to Odysseus as the appropriate mythic analogue. And from a place, the islands, Walcott turns to a time gone by, his childhood. The task of the lyrics then becomes something else—as *Another Life* (1973) suggests: to recreate, in St. Lucia, Antigua, and the other islands, the lost ruined Ilium of his youth and to repopulate the Antillean scene with remembered characters—Emanuel, Berthilia, Darnley, Ligier— who rise to epic dimensions in the memorial process. These are merely childhood heroes, but in the processes of poetry they are transfigured into a new constellation; they become astrological guides in a new private mythography suggesting a Caribbean *Odyssey*.

I shall return to *Another Life* (1973) in connection with a discussion of *Omeros*, for it is the seed ground of that much longer and more impressive Odyssean voyage. But for the moment let me note that *Collected Poems* concludes with a moving *ubi sunt* reflection on homelessness and memory, a meditation that gathers into itself the fate of several exiles, wanderers, and castaways—not merely Adam and Odysseus but Ovid banished from the imperial Roman court, St. John exiled on Patmos, and Defoe's stranded castaway, Robinson Crusoe. These are the literary, imaginary, or legendary figures with whom Walcott has always most identified. As to a real exile or castaway, Walcott has always had most in common with the Russian Jewish poet Joseph Brodsky, whose refusal to subordinate his art to the *diktats* of the Communist commissars led to his expulsion from the Soviet Union as a social "parasite." Brodsky came to the United States and took up English, determined in a heroic way to make poetry out of this strange new language of exile. Both he and Walcott were exiles longing for a distant homeland who found their own yearning reflected in this theme of exile.

Brodsky's *Of Grief and Reason* (1994) offers a moving discussion of this motif of exile. Walcott was possibly thinking of Brodsky's situation, and certainly of his own, when he composed "The Hotel Normandie Pool." There the exiled poet Ovid is conjured up and indeed appears whole out of the mists of imaginative memory. In an exchange reminiscent of that of Odysseus and Tiresias (perhaps in Book XII of the *Odyssey* or in Pound's *Canto I*)—or perhaps reminiscent of the "familiar compound ghost" in Eliot's *Four Quartets*, the precursor Master arises and speaks: "When I was first exiled / I missed my language as your tongue needs salt." In expressing a wisdom reserved for age, Ovid then describes his poetic dream, castigates his Roman detractors, and defines the ordeal of exile and suffering to which the poet is always fated when, in opposition to the political authority, "art obeys its own order."[33]

Art, of course, must always assert its own order against the censorship of the state. It certainly cannot obey the dictates of the politicians—even though the writer may risk the displeasure of the government. Walcott was as absorbed as Brodsky with the theme of exile. But there is another and final aspect of his personal displacement that concerns the poet and that interests the reader quite as much. It is an exile not just from a place but from his childhood past. And with the loss of his childhood comes the loss of innocence. In the fallen state Walcott expresses the crisis of belief as the paradox of a faith persisting in doubt, with poetry as an alternative mode of realizing the *Logos* in a fallen world. He concludes the volume with this reflection[34] on an abandoned place and a former time, now memorialized in the art of *Collected Poems*:

> Where's my child's hymnbook, the poems edged in gold leaf,
> the heaven I worship with no faith in heaven,
> as the Word turned toward poetry in its grief?
> Ah, bread of life, that only love can leaven!
> Ah, Joseph, though no man ever dies in his own country,
> the grateful grass will grow thick from his heart.

V

Let us turn now to *Omeros*. Both Pound and Joyce gave new prominence in high modernist poetry and fiction to Homer and the Odysseus figure. The connection between Homer's *Odyssey* and *Omeros* would be engaging to tease out. Especially absorbing would be the question of whether Walcott's work is a highly self-conscious and ironic postmodern parody of his predecessors, one that eludes and even rejects cognitive understanding; or whether it seriously embraces the Homeric tradition and recreates it with sincerity of meaning and purpose. Rei Terada in *Derek Walcott's Poetry: American Mimicry*[35] never quite resolves the matter. But in an effort to put Walcott abreast of the latest postmodernist fads, Terada virtually transforms Walcott from a poet devoted to the discovery of meaning into an ironic, self-reflexive Donald Barthelme or a meaningless John Ashbery. In other words, Terada sees Walcott's invocation of tradition as mere mimicry of poetic originals without discoverable import.

It should be conceded at once that Walcott—a college teacher, after all—is too well read in modernist and postmodernist literature and criticism not to know that it is *de rigeuer* nowadays for the artist to be *immensely* self-conscious. The narrator-poet of *Omeros*, at the death of his own character Maud Plunkett, intrudes into the poem to observe at one point: "I was both there and not there. I was attending / the funeral of a character I'd created; / the fiction of her life needed a good ending / as much as mine."[36] In the process of imagining her, the face of Maud then merges with that of the narrator's mother:

> Join, interchangeable phantoms, expected pain
> moves me towards ghosts, through this page's scrim,
> and the ghosts I will make of you with my scratching pen,
>
> like a needle piercing the ring's embroidery
> with a swift's beak, or where, like a nib from the rim
> of an inkwell, a martin flickers a wing dry.

Such reflexivity as these lines suggest *is* an element of the poem. The source of it, by the way, is John Barth's *Lost in the Funhouse* (1968). This remarkable collection of interconnected tales reinvents the Trojan War from the point of view of a marooned and enisled Homer, a protean, shape-shifting noncombatant who reappears in various historical periods and cultures in various incarnations. He missed the real action at Troy and consequently had to invent what he never really knew. Some of Barth's perceptions and techniques are introduced and reworked in *Omeros*. But the tone of the poem is markedly different from that of Barth: Walcott is serious, elevated, dignified; the poem is remote in effect from the parodic mimicry of reflexive postmodernism. Periodically the narrator refers to his boyhood reading in the great books. These references are invariably respectful. And indeed, in a dream vision of the boy's future, his father tells him that "before you return, you must enter cities / that open like *The World's Classics*, in which I dreamt / I saw my shadow on their flagstones, histories / that carried me over the bridge of self-contempt. . . ."[37] Walcott's appreciation of classic literary texts—texts that are routinely discredited by white academic Marxists such as John Guillory in *Cultural Capital: The Problem of Canon Formation* (1993)—is predicated on an understanding of the extent to which literacy and a command of the knowledge and power that literacy brings are essential to black liberation. It is in this sense that *The World's Classics* offers an escape from the self-contempt inflicted on one by the personal experience of racism.

Even so, certain it is that Walcott has strenuously denied that *Omeros* is an epic.[38] And we have every good reason to believe him. Epics are very formal long poems marked by required conventions. They invoke a muse for inspiration and attain a lofty language with complex rhetorical devices like the Homeric simile; they formally announce the argument or theme of the poem; the action is launched *in medias res* and is recounted through twelve or perhaps twenty-four books; an epic hero, a man of *virtù* incarnating the qualities of the nation-state, emerges to announce in value-defining formal speeches the issues that impel the principals toward combat; armies then engage in world-shattering battles in which the hero proves himself worthy of praise and emulation; there are conventional catalogues of ships, armories, armadas, and so forth. *Omeros*, it may be said, ignores many of these formal requirements.

Milton's Christian reconfiguration of the epic in *Paradise Lost* made it a well nigh impossible form for English and American poets coming after him. Early American epic attempts such as *The Columbiad* and *The Anarchiad* were tedious disasters that led Poe to denounce the "epic mania" of his time and to call the long poem "a flat contradiction in terms."[39] Whitman, with his studied aversion to the Eurocentric, pretended to dislike the epic, especially its inevitable motif of warfare:

> Come Muse migrate from Greece and Ionia,
> Cross out please those immensely overpaid accounts,
> That matter of Troy and Achilles' wrath, and Aeneas', Odysseus'
>   wanderings.

Yet still Whitman hankered after the fame conferred by greatness in the form and tried to recreate it as a New World innovation in *Leaves of Grass*. He kept a great many of its conventions: the epic hero—himself; the invocation of the muse—installed in the kitchen near the "gasometer"; the proclamation of the argument—"Oneself I sing"; the wrath of combat champions—soldiers in the Civil War; the long catalogues—occupations, rivers, states, trees, all tending toward ennui and stupefaction. (Whitman, as an epic poet, leaves much to be desired.)[40]

The appeal of the epic form is thus perennial. Homer set a standard that even a houseboy in the palace of literature would want to transcend. Reflecting on the epic after Dante, Ezra Pound once observed that "the best criticism of any work, to my mind the only criticism of any work of art that is of any permanent or even moderately durable value, comes from the creative writer or artist who does the next job."[41] Pound himself had done the "next job" after Whitman in *The Cantos*, especially insofar as this poem reconstituted the epic along an original Dantean line: "For forty years I have schooled myself . . . to write an epic poem which begins 'In the Dark Forest,' crosses the Purgatory of human error, and ends in the light. . . ." *Omeros*, like *The Cantos*, wants to capture that flash of light, the glow of radiant experience, "the magic moment" where the poet breaks through the quotidian into the "divine or permanent world" of the gods.[42] Elements of the Poundian plan are replicated in *Omeros*.

An inescapable instance of the artist who did the "next job" for the epic was James Joyce in *Ulysses*, who suggested a narrative possibility different from that of Homer, Dante, Pound, and Barth. And indeed, Joyce—"our age's Omeros, undimmed Master / and true tenor of the place"[43]—actually appears in Chapter 39 of the poem. This is a vision not unlike Eliot's encounter with the dead master in "Little Gidding." Joyce's *Ulysses*, we remember, parallels Bloom's wandering around Dublin on a particular day with Odysseus's wandering as Homer recounts it. Eliot said that Joyce's "mythic method" had replaced conventional linear narrative and that "in using the myth, in manipulating a continuous parallel between contemporaneity and antiquity, Mr. Joyce is pursuing a method which others must pursue after him." Walcott evidently agreed with Eliot that such a system of parallels would offer a better way of "controlling, of ordering, of giving a shape and a significance to the immense panorama of futility and anarchy which is contemporary history."[44] If the epic impulse realizes itself in the encyclopedic modern novel, Joycean *Omeros* likewise has a narrator, characters, dialogue, fictive action, a plot of sorts, and a clear tendency to storytelling.

Still, while *Omeros* reflects a number of both novelistic and epic conventions, it is *sui generis* and really unconstrained by either. *Omeros* begins to tell a story in the middle of things. But the narrative elements are not continuous on a novelistic line. Walcott found, like Pound, a form elastic enough to hold nearly everything he wanted to include, whether or not required by necessity or even logical coherence. The form is musical. With a technical debt to Dante, *Omeros* is presented in loose hexameter lines that form tercets approximating the Italian poet's *terza rima*. Unlike Pound's poem, the sixty-four units of *Omeros* are called chapters rather than cantos; they build up into seven "books" (divided into subsections), yielding, finally, 325 pages of lyric verse.[45]

What is the setting of the poem? The action of *Omeros* largely takes place on the Caribbean island of St. Lucia. This island is paradisal, and its name canonizes, as it were, the light. In imagining this paradise, Walcott draws on Pound in taking light to be "the single most significant manifestation of the Divine—*Lux enim per se in omnen partem se ipsum diffundit.*" Light is the "*bonum diffusivum sui*," the good that diffuses itself in a numinous or radiant illumination of the world.[46] "The artist seeks out the luminous detail and presents it,"[47] Pound observes. Walcott likewise wishes to make plain that the island and its people shine with a visionary radiance that makes of St. Lucia a hallowed ground, a blessed island, a sacred light, a numinous setting that illuminates the imagination itself: "*Praise Him, Morning Star, St. Lucia, Light of My Eyes.*"[48]

This island, however, is not the only scene of the action. In epic fashion *Omeros* soars over heaven and earth, and it covers a vast expanse of historical and mythic time. On our odyssey we go by various detours to black Africa (in the time of the slave kidnapings); to Lisbon (the mud-caked town Ulissibona founded by ancient Odysseus); to London—the seat of English empire in its military contests with the French over control of the Caribbean (the island changed hands fifteen times before—in 1782 in the Battle of the Saints—Admiral Rodney in *The Marlborough* defeated the Frenchman De Grasse in *Ville de Paris*); to Holland in the seventeenth century, where a Midshipman Plunkett, ancestor of one of the principals in *Omeros*, spies for Admiral Rodney; to Ireland (where Joyce, eye patch and all, makes his appearance on the Liffey); to Istanbul; to Atlanta, Georgia; and even to the American West of the nineteenth century, where Walcott recreates "The Ghost Dance" of the Sioux at Wounded Knee.

The matter of *Omeros* is the experience of some St. Lucian natives that is paralleled against that of Homer's personae and many other historical and mythic figures. When Walcott tried this kind of parallel in a preliminary way in *Another Life*, the *New York Times* reviewer Michiko Kakutani remarked in 1986 that "when Mr. Walcott attempts to invoke the classics to talk about down-to-earth subjects—comparing, say, a prostitute to Helen of Troy—the result can seem artificial and strained, the highfalutin effusions of a willfully literary sensibility, mesmerized by words."[49] I have a conviction that Walcott was stung into reworking his parallels in a way that could not thereafter be faulted. In *Omeros* some of the island characters are lightly sketched in—Chrysostom, Maljo, Placide. But fully developed as the mysterious centerpiece is of course the black Helen of the poem, the most beautiful woman in the islands whose lovely face could sink more than an epic armada. At his first vision of Helen in her madras headkerchief at an outdoor café,[50] the narrator says

> I felt like standing in homage to a beauty
>
> that left, like a ship, widening eyes in its wake.
> "Who the hell is that?" a tourist near my table
> asked a waitress. The waitress said, "She? She too proud!"
>
> As the carved lids of the unimaginable
> ebony mask unwrapped from its cotton-wool cloud,
> the waitress sneered "Helen." And all the rest followed.

Although she is no prostitute, this black Helen is married to one man but sleeps with another and is the source of the island strife that distantly parallels the Trojan War.[51] Achille (pronounced Ash-HEEL), her fisherman husband, goes out for a catch each day in his boat, a fire-hollowed log named *In God We Troust*. His rival for Helen is Hector; they fistfight ferociously, forcing their mutual friends to take sides. "What was it in men that made such beauty evil?" Maud Plunkett asks herself.[52] After taking Helen away from Achille, Hector abandons the sea for island tourism, acquires a van (named *The Comet*), and goes into business as a hack and tour guide around the island. Another native struggling to survive modernizing change is the fisherman Philoctete, the injury to whose leg has resulted in a suppurating ulcer that, like that of his namesake, will not heal and smells abominably. "He believed the swelling came from the chained ankles / of his grandfathers. Or else why was there no cure?"[53] All these figures spend time at a bar, the No Pain Café, owned by Ma Kilman, an obeah-woman possessed of magic gifts and the old ancestral lore. The creator and narrator of the poem, a poet and an exile to North America who has returned to visit his widowed mother, is not only like but is occasionally inseparable from Walcott himself. He intrudes to comment from time to time on the action and provides the poem with its occasional self-reflexive echoes. Like most of the other men in the poem he too is in love with Helen: "Sometimes the gods will hallow / all of a race's beauty in a single face."[54]

But the most important character, and indeed the fount of the poem, is Homer himself. A mercurial figure and a shape-shifting presence (like Barth's poet), Homer here goes by the name of Omeros, which, we learn from the Greek girlfriend of the narrator, is the modern form of the old name. He is invoked for inspiration by the narrator: "O open this day with the conch's moan, Omeros, / as you did in my boyhood, when I was a noun / gently exhaled from the palate of the sunrise. / . . . Only in you, across centuries / of the sea's parchment atlas, can I catch the noise / of the surf lines wandering like the shambling fleece of the lighthouse's flock./ . . . A wind turns the harbour's pages back to the voice / that hummed in the vase of a girl's throat: 'Omeros.'"[55]

The strangeness of the name offers Walcott multiple opportunities for verbal play. More important, the figure is the occasion of a serious multilayered symbolism that warrants some attention here. The name Omeros is sometimes reduced to "O." This device is a letter, a number, and a shape. It becomes, for instance, the shape of the Greek girl's mouth as she prepares to voice the name. It is also the shape of the ink-well rim and, as we have seen, the embroidery hoop that Maud will take up. "O" becomes the shape of the opening of a vase of classical form, as well as "the low-fingered O of an Aruac flute."[56] And it is the shape of the null cipher[57] to whom, according to his father, the narrator-poet might, in his recollection of the tempo of the native women coal-carriers, pray for inspiration as well:

"O Thou, my Zero is an impossible prayer,
utter extinction is still a doubtful conceit.

Though we pray to nothing, nothing cannot be there.

Kneel to your load, then balance your staggering feet
and walk up that coal ladder as they do in time,
one bare foot after the next in ancestral rhyme.

Because Rhyme remains the parentheses of palms
shielding a candle's tongue, it is the language's
desire to enclose the loved world in its arms. . . ."

It is unusual for an epic poet to pray to another poet for inspiration. Usually the artist's Muse or God is invoked. But, in fact, while the "O" here stands on a superficial level for Omeros, behind Omeros is the real origin of all poetic power, the god who inspires the poet with the divine afflatus. It is for this that poets pray; for it is divine inspiration alone that issues in transcendently powerful poetic expression. In its appeal for inspiration, these staggering feet (hexameters, actually) fuse "O" with deity. Now, the zero implies an emptiness that assuredly seems here to be associated with nihilism and nothingness. And indeed, throughout much of the poem, the narrator is imprisoned in a state of disbelief that reduces history to human carnage and religious faith to epic blindness. The zero surely expresses this atheism. The narrator even concedes as much: "I had lost faith both in religion and in myth."[58] But the number zero functions on another level and has a deeper significance that makes it the proper analogue for God as an existential reality. But before discussing the number zero as a manifestation of the real existence of God, it is necessary to explore the way the *letter* "O" functions as an analogue of the divine.

In making so much of the letter "O" throughout the poem, the narrator not only pays homage to Omeros or Homer as the original fount of his poetic inspiration, but he also merges Omeros with God, the origin of all creativity. This is expressed through the trope of the divine as the Alpha and the Omega, the first and the last, the beginning and the end, the inclusive collectanea of all language or discourse, including poetic song. In the Revelation of St. John, for instance, the letter "O" (or Ω, "Omega," the equivalent of "O" in Greek) is repeatedly identified with the deity: "I am the Alpha and the Omega, saith the Lord God" (Revelation 1:8; 21:6). Derived from this linguistic symbolism of the letter "O" is that ancient sense of God as "an infinite circle, the center of which is everywhere, the circumference nowhere": *Deus est sphaera infinita, cuius centrum est ubique, circumferentia nusquam.* Walcott probably derived this ancient notion of the circle as a trope for the divine by working backward through Pound's use of the metaphor in *The Cantos* to Dante's formulation of it in Canto XII of the *Vita Nuova*.[59]

If we read the "O" as a zero, however, the effect is still the same. Central to mathematical thinking, from the ancients onward, is the relation of number to infinity. The idea of the infinite, which has always been identified in theological and philosophical discourse with God, derives from the evident fact that no matter how high I count, I cannot exhaust numeration (there is always another, higher number). Since human reason cannot grasp the ultimate extension of number into infinity, the mind is forced to resort to metaphors and analogues to suggest the nature of the infinite or to characterize the boundless infinitude of God. Nicolaus Cusanus, as Karsten Harries points out, was only one of many philosophers of old who believed that "given the necessity of relying on symbols in our search for the divine infinite, we had best rely on mathematical symbols, which are distinguished by their 'incorruptible certainty.'" A mathematical symbol like zero was an indispensable trope for imaginatively grasping what reason could not—the *"actualissimam Dei existentiam*, the absolute reality of God's creative existence."[60] The narrator's prayer, "O Thou, my Zero," thus turns out to be not so impossible an orison after all, for instead of restricting us to the narrowness of the narrator-poet's atheism, the trope turns itself into a figure for the endless and immense sphere of God's omnipresent inspiring creativity.

Winslow Homer is also invoked in the poem. He is a painter whose name is of value not just for its echoing effect. He is a source of inspiration because of the brilliance of those seascape canvases, like *The Gulf Stream*, that may be said to pictorialize the action of *Omeros*. Homer's seascapes, according to Walcott, parallel Hemingway's superb prose descriptions of the Caribbean in *The Old Man and the Sea* and *Islands in the Stream*.[61] A marble bust of Homer, full of iconic significance, recurs in the poem, and even comes to life and speaks; this bust has a parallel in the inner image of the Master conjured up by the narrator from his reading of the

Iliad and *The Odyssey*. If this original Greek Homer, now called Omeros, is the font of Walcott's epic invention, he also appears in several historical or mythic disguises. For our purposes, the most important of these is the nameless blind island singer who, because he has been around the world, goes by the name of "Monsieur Seven Seas." Though lacking external sight, he has Tiresian insight, or prophetic knowledge, and understands the realm of those who have already passed into the light. At one point Seven Seas materializes on the steps of the Church of St. Martin's-in-the-Fields in London, clutching the manuscript of his epic poem, but is ejected by the curate for loitering. It is he who comments to the narrator on the affair of Helen and on the lives of the others, and who is even the means of the narrator's realizing a transhistorical and transtemporal vision of human affairs. On occasion his words are delphic, not clear to others, seem Greek to his listeners, "or old African babble."[62]

Let us turn now to the action of the poem. Helen is a waitress, but she has lost her job because "she was too rude, 'cause she dint take no shit / from white people and some of them tourist—the men / only out to touch local girls; every minute— / was brushing their hand from her back side so one day / she get fed up with all their nastiness. . . ."[63] If she rebuffs the lecherous tourists, she does not take any abuse from her boyfriend Achille either. Unable to cope with his jealousy, she quarrels with him, and they separate. She then is taken on as a housemaid for Maud and Major Plunkett, displaced colonials who have remained on the island after independence. This island St. Lucia, we learn, originally had another name: "A Genoan wanderer / saying the beads of the Antilles named the place / for a blinded saint. Later, others would name her / for a wild wife."[64] Before it was St. Lucia, then the island was named St. Omere, and then afterward Helen.

Maud is a gardener and seamstress whose needlework (à la Penelope) stitches the principal story of the island into a "fabulous comforter." Her husband is a retired working-class regimental sergeant major who was wounded serving with Montgomery in Africa in World War II. He is in love with black Helen and has had an affair with her. Achille, in fact, feels that Helen is selling herself, as the island is selling itself to the tourists, and nobody cares. Since the major is among other things a pig farmer, his lust has put him in a fair way of being transformed, like Circe's victims, into a swine. Maud fires Helen. In response she steals one of Maud's dresses (with an open back in the shape of a V) and wears it defiantly in public. Their transgression known to Maud, the sacked Helen leaves the house, and the major displaces his desire for Helen onto an amateur historical research project. He starts to investigate the history of Helen (or St. Lucia), culminating in the victory of Admiral Rodney over De Grasse. What makes *Omeros* tonally different from the *Collected Poems* is that a new militancy seems evident, a clear tendency to slant matters in favor of the natives of the West Indies.[65] Major Plunkett, for instance, doubtfully remarks: "We helped ourselves to these green islands like olives from a saucer, / munched on the pith, then spat their sucked stones on a plate, / like a melon's black seeds."[66] While his research project is a manifestation of his love for both the woman and the island, who are finally inseparable, the major recognizes that "all colonies inherit their empire's sin / and these, who broke free of the net, enmeshed a race."[67]

Major Plunkett (a "khaki Ulysses") had earlier taught the black narrator-poet when he was in the college cadet force. The narrator thus senses "a changing shadow of Telemachus / in me, in his absent war, and an empire's guilt / stitched in the one pattern of Maud's fabulous quilt."[68] If Plunkett, far from home, is a white father-figure to the narrator, Maud's image (as we have seen) merges with the image of his own mother. Thus the narrator, a spiritual child of this couple, is able to grasp Plunkett's pain at knowing that "History will be revised, / and we'll be its villians, fading from the map / (he said 'villians' for 'villains'), and when it's over / we'll be the bastards!"[69] Still, in reflecting on these whites, the narrator is "tired of their fucking guilt / and our fucking envy!"[70] He therefore turns away from Plunkett toward Seven Seas, away, that is, from his white heritage to his black, and from history to poetry as a mode of knowing and understanding the past.

While the major pursues his research, Helen moves in with Hector, whose business as a tour bus driver steadily declines and fails to support them as he had hoped. Then comes the realization that Helen is pregnant. While the child's paternity seems ambiguous for a time (is the father Achille? Hector? Plunkett?), the matter is eventually resolved in favor of Achille. He has continued to maintain himself as a fisherman, though the fleets of commercial trawlers, with their immense seines and onboard factory processing, have practically depleted the seas.[71] When Hector is accidentally killed in *The Comet,* the pregnant Helen returns to the lonely Achille, who has come to see how she wished

> for a peace beyond her beauty, past the tireless
> quarrel over a face that was not her own fault
> any more than the full moon's grace sailing dark trees,
>
> and for that moment Achille was angrily filled
> with a pity beyond his own pain.

Maud in the course of things passes away. Helen gets another job as a waitress. And, toward the end, Philoctete is healed by Ma Kilman, who conjures up a native herbal remedy.

I have remarked that the narrator of the poem is a kind of spiritual son to Maud and Major Plunkett. This is the kinship that makes it possible for him to understand not only the native perspective but that of the colonizing whites. Indeed, if we presume him to be a shabine, his knowledge of the Plunketts is a mode of self-understanding.[72] But the narrator goes even further in ascribing to himself a "wound in the head" identical to that of the major:

> This wound I have stitched into Plunkett's character.
> He has to be wounded, affliction is one theme
> of this work, this fiction, since every "I" is a
>
> fiction finally. Phantom narrator, resume: . . .

The theme of affliction is indeed important, but Walcott's portentous remarks about the fictive self fall below the fundamental intelligence of the work. In my view they are simply desperate ways of trying to signal to the academic reader that Walcott has read Foucault, Barthes, Adorno, and other MLA gurus who were so frequently invoked in the 1980s in the vain effort to deny the existence of a "self" or the "bourgeois subject." How quaint, and indeed risible, their observations seem today.

It is the wound of racism and colonial exploitation that both men suffer from, a wound that reopens and closes in smoke when memory resurrects the evils inseparable from the history of the island. This occurs especially in the Soufrière scenes, which approximate the horror of Dante's *Inferno* and Pound's "Hell Cantos."[73] There, as the narrator climbs up the high volcanic peak, St. Lucia's historical past and political present dissolve into the scene of perdition:

> It was a place where an ancient fear
> increased as he neared it. Holes of boiling lava
> bubbled in the Malebolge, where the mud-caked skulls
>
> climbed, multiplying in heads over and over, while the
> zircon gas from the flues climbed the bald hills.
> This was the gate of sulphur through which he must pass,
>
> singeing his memory, though he pinched his nostrils
> until the stench faded into verdurous peace,
> like registering skulls in the lime-pits of Auschwitz.

Auschwitz carries with it the full weight of the Holocaust; and the reference requires us to reflect for a moment on Walcott's intention. Does he wish us to believe that the treatment of island people by the colonizing white Europeans was no different from what the Nazis did to the Jews in the World War II era? No one would wish to justify the mistreatment of the natives by the *conquistadores* and those who followed. But candor forces the observation that Walcott's poem conveniently ignores several incontrovertible facts of Caribbean history. One is that there was no "final solution," or political agenda, according to which these colonial powers intended to exterminate the natives. Indeed, a great many authorities in imperial Spain, Portugal, England, and France ordered the local *alcaldes* or governors to preserve the native population and indeed to increase its number—if only for the sake of free slave labor. Second, there is no recognition in the poem whatsoever of the extent to which natural catastrophes like starvation and disease inadvertently decimated a great number of the natives. Europeans cannot be blamed for transmitting fatal smallpox or measles any more than natives can be blamed for transmitting to the Europeans their own illnesses such as syphilis. (A great many English, Dutch, Spaniards, and Frenchmen died of identical illnesses in the early years of exploration.)

The poem does not care to recognize a most salient fact evident to the early explorers: that the island basin was a primordial tribal battleground; that it was split between the Caribs and the Arawaks; that the Caribs were violent and bloodthirsty, even by savage standards, practicing a repellent cannibalism. Walcott simply fudges the fact that the Caribs were notorious for the butchery of their enemies; and that the Arawaks pleaded with the Spaniards and French to protect them from their inhuman native oppressors.[74] Finally, Walcott ignores the fact that the most telling arguments on behalf of the sanctity of Indian life as an ethical principle were not made by the natives but were frankly urged by Europeans. I mean Christian eyewitnesses like the Bishop Bartolomé de las Casas, whose *Historia de las Indias* indicted as a moral evil all violence directed against God's children in those islands. Such strictures as his eventually led the king and court to punish the most violent overseers of the *encomiendas* and *repartimientos*, or the agricultural estates, where Indian slaves were worked. None of this comes through in *Omeros*, which merely repeats, uncritically, some of the anti-Columbus diatribes that bizarrely erupted at the time of the quincentenary of the Genoese admiral's remarkable discovery of the New World.

These remarks serve to remind us that while a poem is not a political tract, it may reflect a polemical bias. In one section of the poem, for instance, Achille, in *In God We Troust*, goes out too far at sea, remains there overnight, and is feared lost for good. As he suffers under the boiling sun, the sea swift seems to lure him outward and eastward to Africa. He then has a dream vision (or sunstroke) in which he is taken to the birthplace of his race somewhere in the interior of Senegal or Guinea. There he finds a tribe of natives, curious at his clothes and his person, who adopt him. In this hallucinative realm of the dead, the vanished natives show Achille the African origin of various festivals, rituals, and customs that are still practiced in St. Lucia. He is taken to a chief, Afolabe, who turns out to be his father. What seems most interesting to the chief is what Achille is named in "that other kingdom" and what the name means. When he learns that Achille does not know and has even lost the knowledge of the African name his father gave him, namely, Afolabe, the father virtually disowns him. In this, it seems to me, Walcott passes a doubtful judgment on the modern black who has little interest in an uncivilized African past, the civilized black who is content to be a citizen in the modern country of his birth. This section of *Omeros* frankly romanticizes black Africa and reflects the mythological power, in the black poetic imagination, of a primitive but highly idealized native homeland. In any case, no African experience of old could be complete without the slave traders' raid on the village. There, in the village of Achille's father, in a shower of arrows and bloody axes, fifteen men are captured and taken upriver to the waiting slave boat. Achille suffers for these victims locked in the hold of the ship. And the narrator remarks: "But they crossed, they survived. That is the epical splendour."[75] The dream vision concludes with Achille's return to St. Lucia:[76]

> ... God said to Achille, "Look, I giving you permission
> to come home. Is I send the sea-swift as a pilot,
> the swift whose wings is the sign of my crucifixion.
>
> And thou shalt have no God should in case you forgot
> my commandments." And Achille felt the homesick shame
> and pain of his Africa. . . .

A similar dream vision—again having nothing really to do with the contemporary action of the poem—begins with the Trail of Tears and resurrects the Cherokees, Choctaws, and Creeks who were marched to reservations in Oklahoma. We are also shown the Crow Indians and the Sioux, stunned by the advent of the white man and his railroads. Condemned for trying to effect their deliverance through dancing the "Ghost Dance," they are massacred at Wounded Knee. It is not clear what these episodes are meant to show, other than the evil that men do in human history, especially the evil done to defeated people of color. But although *Omeros* is slanted, it cannot be missed that when Achille tries to intercept the raiders and free some of the imprisoned villagers, the raider he kills is a black like himself: blacks are betrayed by their own. Likewise, the Indian butchery of white Catherine Weldon, who devoted her whole life to the welfare of Native Americans, qualifies Walcott's sympathy for the red man, reminding us that if whites tore up the Indian treaties, there was "mutual treachery" or recurrent betrayals on both sides.[77]

The vision of human history, from Troy onward, has been a panorama of continual evil sufficient to generate a universal anathema and the condemnation of the malefactors to a burning hell. In Chapter 58 Walcott visualizes this hell by means of a nightmare of the narrator-poet. In it the sightless marble bust of Omeros becomes animate and guides him into the boiling sulphur mists of Soufrière. After a time they arrive at the Pool of Speculation. Who are the damned? There boil the "souls who had sold out their race"; "the traitors / who, in elected office, saw the land as views / for hotels and elevated into waiters / the sons of others, while their own learnt something else"; those who had "rented the sea / to offshore trawlers" with thirty-mile seines; the thieves running the casinos; and others who "kept making room for slaves to betray their brothers / till the eyes in the stone head were cursing their tears."[78]

In this hell appear Bennett and Ward, "two young Englishmen" whose business exploited the island paradise. We also encounter Hector, who had abandoned the sea to make money off the tourists. If "A man who cursed the sea had cursed his own mother. / *Mer* was both mother and sea,"[79] Hector is a traitor to his people and a proper—if rather crudely allegorized—victim of island tourism and industrial development. Then the poet-narrator is drawn down further toward the lake where the damned poets suffer, those who are "condemned in their pit to weep at their own pages."[80] The causes of poetic damnation are selfishness and the preoccupation of writers with "surfaces in nature and men," overweening pride in their craft, and egotistical self-promotion.

> I slid, and kept falling
>
> towards the shit they stewed in; all the poets laughed,
> jeering with dripping fingers; then Omeros gripped
> my hand in enclosing marble and his strength moved
>
> me away from that crowd, or else I might have slipped
> to that backbiting circle, mockers and the self-loved.

There is no reflexive parody or mimicry in such scenes. Walcott is in dead earnest. At last they descend further down to the Devil, who, as in Dante's ninth circle of the Inferno, is encased in ice. There the "ice-matted head" hisses at the narrator, ordering him to ask himself "whether a love of poverty helped you / to use other eyes, like those of that sightless stone?" He wants to know whether the poet-narrator has attained insight, like the bust of blind Homer, now come to life, that guides him through this nether world.

The devil's query is only one of many challenges to the narrator's self-consciousness about his own attitudes and prejudices in relation to his poetic material. Disgusted by the persistence of poverty, filth, and disorder in the islands, still he has nothing but sarcasm for the politicians and the disc jockeys who scream out "'WE MOVIN' MAN! WE MOVIN'!' / but towards what?"[81] In Chapter 45, angry at the signs of modernization that have polluted his paradise, the narrator wonders:

> Didn't I want the poor
> to stay in the same light so that I could transfix
> them in amber, the afterglow of an empire,
>
> preferring a shed of palm-thatch with tilted sticks
> to that blue bus stop?

He observes that "Art is History's nostalgia," the expressed preference for the way it was; it prefers "a thatched roof / to a concrete factory"; and he suspects the authenticity of his own motives: "Hadn't I made their poverty my paradise?"[82]

In an early discussion of *Omeros* that virtually coincided with its publication, John Figueroa posed as a preliminary question for criticism the extent to which "a certain sort of fatalism and quietism" may be said to characterize the ending of the poem. This way of putting it seems to me to presuppose that if one is a black writer, he is required to be an activist who will change things. That is of course nonsense, but it is a common pressure still exerted on almost all black writers by racial activists. The term "fatalism" also slants matters by suggesting that Walcott could feel a paralyzing resignation at the intractability of the problem of racial prejudice and so is inert when he might be marching on Washington. One man's notion of fate may be another's conception of Providence, however, and it may be that Walcott believes that the unfolding of human history is driven by an agency anterior and exterior to the individual poet. About this it is difficult to be sure, especially since Walcott stresses that his is a worship of a heaven in which he has lost faith.[83] Still, Walcott's verse is saturated in Christian imagery and thought. However we may interpret it, Figueroa has rightly suggested that the "*Salve Regina* aspect of the poem" might offer a clue to Walcott's fundamental intention in *Omeros*.[84] This lead deserves, I believe, fuller elaboration.

If the original blind Homer had insight, or other eyes, the poet-narrator eventually attains a deeper level of insight himself. This takes the form of a realization that a divine beatitude inheres in the gift of life, out of the sea, that "drenched every survivor with blessing."[85] It is no accident that the poem ends at the Christmas season and expresses a sense of Christian forgiveness that, in my view, serves to eclipse the violence of history—or at least render it more intelligible as a part of a not yet fully understood aspect of the divine plan. Reflecting on the hero of the poem, the narrator-poet thinks that history had simplified Achille, and "its elegies had blinded me with the temporal lament for a smoky Troy." He is hopeful about the future and comes to see Achille as strong, as "strong as self-healing coral," out of whom "a quiet culture / is branching from the white ribs of each ancestor."[86] With reverence for the luminous world of the spirit, intermittently apprehended through the experience of the actual, the narrator breaks into a lyrical exultation, a jubilate of sorts, a "deep hymn / of the Caribbean":[87]

> O Sun, the one eye of heaven, O Force, O Light,
> my heart kneels to you, my shadow has never changed
> since the salt-fresh mornings of encircling delight
>
> across whose cities the wings of the frigate ranged
> freer than any republic, gliding with ancient
> ease! I praise you not for my eyes. That other sight.

The epic poem written by Seven Seas, to which we have no direct access in *Omeros*, evidently contained "gods and demi-gods" that, the narrator complains, "aren't much use to us." And it is true that, since Nietzsche, modern readers have been told that God is dead and the sense of the divine has vanished from the world. "'Forget the gods,' Omeros growled, 'and read the rest.'"[88] Yet if God is dead, what—Seven Seas wonders to himself—was the original fault? Could original sin be merely "the incurable / wound of time" that has pierced them all? Although Pound certainly thought that time is the enemy, that explanation hardly seems sufficient, however important it may be. (When Seven Seas observes to Ma Kilman that Major Plunkett will heal in time, she replies "We shall all heal.")[89] And indeed, in visiting the conjure woman, the major does have a vision of Maud, attains with her spirit a final reconciliation, and is ethically transformed, coming to accept, finally, the blacks who work for him.

But more than an escape from the change that time brings or that death achieves is implicit in the narrator's struggle with his own skepticism. Although the tourists condescend to the islanders and even ridicule their simplicity (like the comic misspelling on Achille's boat *In God We Troust*), they do not understand what really gives meaning and purpose to the natives' lives. Almost as remote from the natives as the tourists, he also tries to grasp what sustains them. Walcott suggests that central to the existence of these islanders is a profound religious faith rooted in Christianity but containing vestiges of something even more ancient. At the beginning of the poem, the Major—clearly a product of English dissent and chapel anti-Catholicism—sees the island people as "Encouraged to screw like rabbits / by estates who liked labour and, naturally, by / a Church that damned them to hell for contraceptives." But even Plunkett cannot deny that "there were ikons in their lives— / The Virgin, the Virgin Lamp, the steps lined with flowers."[90] These ikons are precious symbols of their faith in the unseen benignity at the heart of things. On Sunday "the fishermen in black, rusty suits" meet at the church,[91] where their anthem makes itself heard even to the ears of the old pagan Seven Seas:

> "*Salve Regina*" in the pews of a stone ship,
> which the black priest steered from his pulpit like a helm,
> making the swift's sign from brow to muttering lip.

The swift, that magical bird (*l'hirondelle des Antilles*), mysteriously appears in the poem at critical moments of inspired imaginative reflection. In Achille's dream vision, as we have seen, God calls the swift the sign of his crucifixion. Here the swift is explicitly identified with the sign of the cross made by the priest—with the name of the Father, the Son, and the Holy Spirit. If we ask why Walcott moves his conclusion toward this Christian prayer, Figueroa reminds us that the *Salve Regina* is addressed to "that Star of the Ocean, Star of the Sea, Mary, the mother of Jesus: *Salve Regina,*

Mater misericordiae, vita, dulcedo et spes nostra, salve. Ad te clamamus, exules filii Hevae. Ad te suspiramus, gementes et flentes in hac lacrimarum valle. 'We cry to thee; we are exiles, children of Eve, groaning and weeping in this valley of tears.' And it ends 'after this exile show unto us the blessed fruit of thy womb, Jesus.'"[92]

Toward its conclusion, then, the poem thus invokes a Christian longing for an end to the separation from the divine that marks all historical existence. The Battle of the Saints points to not merely the victory of Rodney over De Grasse. It reminds us that the whole region of islands is named for saints: St. Thomas, St. John, St. Martin, and so on. In discussing the name St. Lucia, I have emphasized its significance in relation to the *light* as a figure for the divine. But St. Lucia, we must remember, is also one of the most well known of the virgin martyrs, a Christian whose purity and faith are memorialized in an ecclesiastical tradition dating from the fourth century.[93]

What the Battle of the Saints finally points to is the victory of these common island folk, saints, really, who troust in an eventual spiritual reunion with the divine. The poem's end is rather like Eliot's *Ash-Wednesday*, with its culminating prayer to the Queen of Heaven: "Sister, mother, / And spirit of the river, spirit of the sea, / Suffer me not to be separated / And let my cry come unto Thee."[94]

The most interesting reflection of the narrator's self-consciousness is his doubt about his own method of coercing the reality of island life into a parallel with Homer's Troy. Plunkett, in his historical project, "had tried to change History into a metaphor, / in the name of a housemaid." He himself had used an opposite tack, turning a literary metaphor into history. Both, he feels, are equally guilty of falsifying reality. Toward the end, the poet-narrator grasps the absolute adequacy of the real and longs, like Wallace Stevens, for "The poem of pure reality, untouched / By trope or deviation, straight to the word, / Straight to the transfixing object / At the exactest point at which it is itself, / Transfixing by being purely what it is."[95] Walcott asks himself, "Why not see Helen / as the sun saw her, with no Homeric shadow, / swinging her plastic sandals on that beach alone, / as fresh as the sea wind?" He longs for the time when he will not "hear the Trojan war in two fishermen cursing in Ma Kilman's shop." He speaks of "All that Greek manure" and wonders "When would it stop, / the echo in the throat, insisting, 'Omeros': / when would I enter the light beyond metaphor?"[96]

Walcott ends the poem by plunging us back again into the raw order of experience, immersing us completely in a *de profundis* of the real. In the final lyric, Achille lands with his catch in *In God We Troust*, then cuts a wedge of dolphin for Helen, and finally heads for the No Pain Café. Although all classic literature seems dismissed in this reduction of its narratives to mere ordure, no one can fail to see that all of this "Greek manure" has wonderfully served to fertilize a vivid modern poetic imagination. "When he left the beach the sea was still going on."[97]

Ralph Ellison: Indivisible Man

> *For by a trick of fate (our racial problems notwithstanding) the human imagination is integrative—and the same is true of the centrifugal force that inspirits the democratic process. And while fiction is but a form of symbolic action, a mere game of "as if," therein lies its true function and its potential for effecting change. For at its most serious, just as is true of politics at its best, it is a thrust toward a human ideal. And it approaches that ideal by a subtle process of negating the world of things as given in favor of a complex of man-made positives.*
>
> —Ralph Ellison, "Introduction," *Invisible Man*

Despite the recent death of Ralph Ellison (1914–1994), he has perhaps never been more visible to those with an eye for distinguished American fiction and criticism. And certainly his work has never been more necessary to American literary culture and racial relations than it is today. The salient sign of his visibility is of course his one and only novel, *Invisible Man* (1952), a work that won him the National Book Award.[1] It is in my view the best novel ever written by an African American, and it may well be the best novel written since World War II. Certainly millions of copies of it have been sold and read; and it has become an inevitable assignment in school and college courses in the American novel, thanks to its splendid narrative account of the apprenticeship of a young black boy struggling to be seen, struggling to define himself against the forces of poverty, educational incompetence, white racism, political manipulation by Communists and black nationalists, and even personal exploitation by sex-crazed white women.

I do not mean to suggest that *these subjects* lifted *Invisible Man* to international importance. But Ellison's mastery in the handling of scene and dialogue, his vivid characterization and plotting, and his dazzling repertory of styles and symbolic devices—all these elements of his tragicomic poetry made for stunning intellectual richness and an aesthetic delight greatly superior to anything produced by the "Harlem Renaissance" novelists (Claude McKay, Jean Toomer, Zora Neale Hurston, *et al.*) or even by the prolix Richard Wright or William Attaway during the 1930s and 1940s. Though he wrote only one novel, I think it fair to say that Ellison also towered over his near contemporaries—e.g., James Baldwin, LeRoi Jones (Imamu Amiri Baraka), William Melvin Kelley, and John A. Williams. Indeed, compared to Ellison's great achievement, the more recent contemporary adulation of Jamaica Kincaid, Alice Walker, and Toni Morrison seems grotesque. If these comparisons to other blacks segregate Ellison from white fiction and seem to diminish him as merely "a credit to his race," let me go further and say that in my view *Invisible Man* towered over anything produced by Mailer, Bellow, Malamud, Roth, and later by Updike, Cheever, Barth, Vonnegut, Pynchon, Hawkes, and Barthelme.

I shall have more to say about *Invisible Man* in due course. But another sign of Ellison's intellectual presence—and pertinence for literary culture now at the end of our century—is the recent collected edition of his nonfiction prose. *The Collected Essays of Ralph Ellison*[2] includes all of Ellison's published and unpublished expository writing. Readers familiar with his already available volumes *Shadow and Act* (1964) and *Going to the Territory* (1986) will find these books completely reprinted here. In addition, more than a score of other uncollected writings have been brought together to complete this huge volume. In all there are some sixty-one essays expressive of Ellison's thinking about a wide range of cultural subjects. Aside from autobiographical reminiscences and interviews with journalists and editors, there are a great many celebrations of American music. In his youth Ellison had a deep desire to play the trumpet and majored in music at Tuskegee; but though he never made it as a musician, his love of spirituals, the blues, jazz, and classical music shines on nearly every page. We also have here recollections of (or reflections on) memorable performers like Mahalia Jackson, Charlie Parker, Jimmy Rushing, Simon Estes, and Jessye Norman. There are likewise observations on the visual arts (especially the work of Romare Bearden); appreciations of other writers (Mark Twain, Richard Wright, Stephen Crane, Alain Locke, Bernard Malamud); several lectures and addresses at colleges and universities; the original working notes for—and a thirtieth-year introduction to—*Invisible Man*; a great many reflections on race in America; and extensive commentary on the indivisibility of American culture as a fusion (to be celebrated) of distinctive ethnic, racial, and cultural elements.

There is so much richness in the *Collected Essays* that it is impossible briefly to summarize Ellison's critical perspectives. A simple way to view the book would be to say that it is the work of a mid-century American artist and intellectual reflecting seriously on elements of both high and low culture in the public life. Nowadays the term "intellectual" stands in derision, as it is associated with power- and publicity-hungry freaks in the academy. But Ellison came to his majority as a writer just after World War II, when the term had some dignity as a vocation and it was still possible to aspire to be one. His conception of the life of the mind and art was shaped by T. S. Eliot, Henry James, André Malraux, Kenneth Burke, Yeats, Auden, Bellow, and the writers then associated with the *Partisan Review*. He did not always agree with them about politics, race, and culture, but he conducted his arguments with great seriousness, personal dignity, and an actual knowledge of racial and cultural experience in the America to the west of the Hudson River (a world largely unknown to the *Partisan Review* crowd).

Perhaps some sense of this remarkable writer's mind can be suggested by attention to several themes that run through this definitive essay collection. First, a great many pieces deal with how American culture has been and is being formed and shaped as a dynamic process that fuses into one entity a wide range of human activities. Ellison was always preoccupied in some part of his mind with the way elements of any race's cultural expression filter into the mainstream of (and thus help to form) American culture. He thought black American culture immensely rich, as indeed it is. But in the 1930s black culture had been grossly oversimplified by white American leftists and others who reduced blacks to the stereotype of the wretched of the earth. Segregated and excluded from the inner circle of American life, blacks were thought to be so desperate for a better life that they could and should be manipulated to bring about the socialist revolution. In this struggle, black artists were supposedly useful agents. Ellison saw how the Communists had seduced and abandoned black writers such as Richard Wright, and he had no intention of being coopted by the left. Later, in the sixties civil rights movement, in order to further the political cause of desegregation, political liberals (both black and white) once again reduced blacks to this stereotype of the racial victim who has been excluded from American culture.

Ellison was himself at first drawn to the radical left in the thirties and forties (he even wrote for the *New Masses*), and he was supportive of integration and black civil rights in the fifties and sixties. But he would not let this reductionist stereotype of black culture go uncriticized. Black life was too positive and various in its engaging forms. As he remarked in "That Same Pain, That Same Pleasure": "I have no desire to write propaganda. Instead I felt it important [in *Invisible Man*] to explore the full range of American Negro humanity and to affirm those qualities which are of value beyond any question of segregation, economics or previous condition of servitude. The obligation was always there and there is much to affirm."[3] As these essays make plain, whatever the legal condition of slavery and desegregation may have meant, in the domain of culture and society blacks had always been fully involved in the national life. Though long reduced to menial work as cooks, domestics, share-croppers, yardmen, and manual laborers, there had nevertheless developed over the years a great many important black ministers, teachers, lawyers, musicians, editors, businessmen, union leaders, and college presidents—all of them defining and expressing a rich and diverse and creative black culture. In their preoccupation with black victims, few liberal whites seemed to notice these blacks or to speak about their contributions to American life. Indeed, this complex black culture was so diverse that no single *black* could speak for it.

Not only was North American black culture immensely diverse, it was also so rich and influential that, in Ellison's view, many of its forms had already entered the mainstream culture of America and had been assimilated into the consciousness of whites long before many whites were even aware of it. Much of Ellison's essay writing was devoted to showing this contribution blacks had made to the national experience in its broadest terms, that is, in both high culture and the popular culture. But his point was never merely a pride in individual black achievement. What interested Ellison most was how a national culture gets formed in the first place. In these essays he shows that the forms of folk culture (white as well as black) are invariably already integrated in America. Spirituals, the blues, and jazz were originally distinctive forms of more or less anonymous black folk consciousness. But such was their moral and aesthetic power, despite the fact that no one person had "originated" them, that they permanently changed mainstream popular music. But it hardly ends there. Folk culture, which is this already intermixed and continually integrating amalgam of creative elements, was itself for Ellison the fertile seedground of superior artistic genius. Spirituals, the blues, and jazz, for instance, not merely influenced mainstream popular music but also reemerged in transfigured form in the musical expression of brilliant individual composers such as George Gershwin, Aaron Copland, and Igor Stravinsky, to name just a few.

Ellison, for many years the Schweitzer Professor of the Humanities at New York University, was a colleague and friend of mine. And when he learned that I knew John Lewis, the founder and director of the Modern Jazz Quartet, he was keen to meet him. Lewis had also been trained in the conservatory tradition of classical music. Bach, Mozart, and Stravinsky were as familiar to Lewis as Duke Ellington, Satchmo, and "Bird" Parker. And Lewis's jazz compositions—and not merely those in the "Third Stream" phase—were brilliant realizations of Ralph Ellison's tenaciously held belief that the lines of creative influence flow from black culture into white and back again, and from low culture into high and back again, all this producing a single, unified, dynamic national culture. In fact, for Ellison American culture was a rich seamless tapestry of varicolored elements in which there were so many black contributions that, after a while, it was sometimes impossible to identify them as such.

A second theme running through these essays is the role of the writer in America. Ellison certainly saw himself as a figure in the continuum of black writing. But, more broadly, he knew himself to participate in a wider current of mainstream American fiction. Beyond that, he saw himself as a citizen of the republic of letters that included the Frenchman Malraux, the Pole Joseph Conrad, the Russian Dostoevsky. Since "white literature" was continually influenced by black writing, and vice versa, he did not believe in the segregation of black literature in college courses such as "The Negro Novel," and so forth. During his Schweitzer professorship, I chaired the English Department, worked out with him an annual program of lectures, and used to talk with him at great length about the American masters who were our common pedagogical enthusiasms. As a teacher, his was truly a "rainbow curriculum" of various writers exploring the multicultural aspects of American life in a democratic polity. But his choice of books and writers was always based upon considerations of art rather than race.

During the sixties black power movement, Ellison's lectures and essays on the unity of an American culture to which blacks had made an inseparable contribution brought him under shrill and sometimes raucous censure from radical separatist blacks who thought him too subservient to racist honky culture, which they wanted to demolish. Some black radicals could never forgive him for his portrait of Ras the Exhorter, the black nationalist rioter in *Invisible Man*, who romantically solicited and indeed incurred his own destruction—and that of his people. The abuse Ellison suffered in those years of the New Left, as a so-called "Uncle Tom," was wholly undeserved, as *Invisible Man* and his nonfiction works are one long brilliant protest against the continuing forms of American racism. But the courage and dignity with which Ellison bore insult from even his own people—evident in the interview "Indivisible Man"—were signs of great personal magnanimity.

II

It is of course this novel, *Invisible Man*, on which his reputation ultimately rests, and something must be said about its essential character before discussing some of the other themes reflected in his criticism. This novel is so rich and complex a work of art that no one can do it justice in a brief essay. But several aspects of the narrative, in light of the cultural themes explored in his essays, perhaps deserve further amplification. Generically a *bildungsroman*, *Invisible Man* traces the development of a naive young Southern boy who collides head on with the fact of his blackness—or rather with his invisibility to mainstream white culture. In this respect he is like Yank in O'Neill's *The Hairy Ape,* the lower-class maritime stoker who is never seen by the Fifth Avenue swells who continually collide with him while strolling along the street. The first lesson of the Invisible Man in the brutal education that American racism imposes on blacks is that his only value to the white businessmen who fund his college scholarship is mere entertainment—which he and other black boys provide in "The Battle Royal," a staged slugfest, in blindfold, for the after-dinner amusement of the white Establishment. How blacks are induced to turn on each other by the white racists who manipulate society, after blacks have ceased to amuse, is an implicit meaning of this degrading battle, which effectively robs the boy of the mind, the intellectual faculty, his education is meant to cultivate.

With his scholarship in hand, the unnamed boy then enrolls at a Southern black college. Given the assignment of escorting important visitors around the campus, the boy misunderstands the institutional illusions created by the wily black president of the college. These illusions serve to create a public relations front intended to deceive the Northern white trustees, and the boy is summarily expelled for letting Mr. Norton, a white trustee, see what he should not have seen. No one has satirized so artfully as Ellison the deceptions practiced upon white educational benefactors by the administrators of historically black colleges, like Tuskegee, which Ellison attended in the 1930s. But the cost to the boy is his matriculation and his chance at a formal education.

Heading north to make his fortune, the unnamed protagonist then lands in Harlem, where he enters the black work force. Manufacturing Optic White Paint (by mixing into it a measured black additive), the boy with no name and no identity misunderstands the right mix of black and white and causes an accidental explosion—with hysterically funny aftereffects. Escaping the pursuing police and appalled at the racism of American culture, he is an easy mark for "The Brotherhood," a thinly disguised portrait of the Communist party.[4] The party recruits him with the promise of racial equality. Since the boy has a gift for oratory, he is assigned to the task of speaking out on the race question, thus propagandizing the Communist party line. Through his speeches he attains a local reputation and develops into a potential "race leader"—until Moscow orders a shift in party priorities, "The Black Question" is shelved, and the Invisible Man is reassigned to propagandize the party line on "The Woman Question."

The protagonist's lectures on feminism provide Ellison with rich opportunities for farce in satirizing the white tendency (especially evident in radical white women) to romanticize the black man as the embodiment of some primitive sexual energy unaffected by the effeteness of white civilization. After one of his lectures, a white woman sympathetic to the party line invites him back to her apartment in the Village in order to discuss, presumably, the party's position on women. Before long her sexual motive becomes apparent. After she has poured the wine, she proposes a toast to the party and says:

> "Oh, I'm so pleased to have you agree with me. I suppose that's why I always thrill to hear you speak; somehow you convey the great throbbing vitality of the movement. It's really amazing. You give me such a feeling of security—although," she interrupted herself with a mysterious smile, "I must confess that you also make me afraid."
>
> "Afraid? You can't mean that," I said.
>
> "Really," she repeated, as I laughed. "It's so powerful, so—so *primitive!*"
>
> I felt some of the air escape from the room, leaving it unnaturally quiet. "You don't mean primitive," I said.
>
> "Yes *primitive*; no one has told you, Brother, that at times you have tom-toms beating in your voice?"
>
> "My God," I laughed, "I thought that was the beat of profound ideas."[5]

Profound his ideas are not: they are basically the party-line pamphlets recycled for platform presentation. But neither is the Invisible Man a mindless stud whose only use is to service bored radical groupies. Implicit in this scene is the myth of the black's reversion to the jungle type, as Zora Neale Hurston has put it, according to which "No matter how high we may *seem* to climb, put us under strain and we revert to type, that is, to the bush. Under a superficial layer of western culture, the jungle drums throb in our veins."[6]

Because both the Communists and the black nationalists exploit black dissatisfaction with poverty and racism, they foment a disorder that, at the end of the novel, erupts into a race riot. While a great many mere opportunists are looting the businesses on Lenox Avenue and 125th Street, the police undertake to track down those who have supposedly started the riot—party functionaries such as the Invisible Man and revolutionaries such as the black nationalist Ras, a crazy Jamaican radical. It is a question whether Ellison's protagonist will be shot by the police as a Communist provocateur or lynched by Ras and the black separatists, who have targeted him as an accommodationist and a traitorous tool of the white power structure. In a display of self-destructive bravado, Ras mounts a dray horse and, waving a spear, is himself shot down in the streets while inciting Harlem to riot. Meanwhile, chased by the police into an apartment building, the protagonist lands in a hidden basement room, where he holes up and literally becomes the underground man.[7] Throughout these events the American identity of the unnamed hero is the absorbing correlate of his violent educational experience of race in America.

While there are many other engaging matters in *Invisible Man*, two central questions engage the reader's attention. The first of them follows directly on the boy's disastrous seduction by the Communist party. While basing its claims on universal brotherhood, the party had really had no interest in American blacks as such but merely wished to inflame racial unrest in America and so provoke the race riots that would trigger the armed revolutionary overthrow of the government. This is the lesson that Ellison had learned so directly from the experience of Richard Wright. In the novel, the Brotherhood wishes to exploit the black community's sorrow at the death of Tod Clifton, a popular boy senselessly shot down only because he is black. Tod's death arouses the outraged community, who memorialize him in a long cortege that slowly files its way down into Central Park:

And crowds approached the park from all directions. The muffled drums now beating, now steadily rolling, spread a dead silence upon the air, a prayer for the unknown soldier. And looking down I felt a lostness. Why were they here? Why had they found us? Because they knew Clifton? Or for the occasion his death gave them to express their protestations, a time and place to come together, to stand touching and sweating and breathing and looking in a common direction? Was either explanation adequate in itself? Did it signify love or politicalized hate? And could politics ever be the expression of love?[8]

The question of whether politics could ever be the expression of love derives directly from the work of the man Ralph Waldo Ellison was named for—the nineteenth-century transcendentalist Emerson. Now, the American democratic system had been designed by the Founders as an equilibrium of political operations and agencies—legislative, executive, and judicial. Thanks to the inbuilt method of political checks and balances, no one branch could dominate the others. Since divisiveness and factionalism are inevitable in the state, the Founders likewise arranged it so that no organized faction could dominate the political process. No political party (like the Whigs), no vocational group (like the farmers or unions), no religious sect (like the Methodist church), no ethnic or racial bloc (like the Irish or blacks), and no sexual lobby (like women or gays) can conceivably dominate our institutions because of the freedoms allowed to rival factions in courting the allegiance of the people and because of the political protections afforded to numerical minorities.

Emerson was inherently skeptical of the absolute value of American democracy. He regarded it as essentially just a political system (one among many). It fitted our conditions well enough for now, just as the monarchy had satisfied American political interests in the pre-Revolutionary past. For Emerson, as the essay "Politics" makes plain, the essential function of any political system is education. The aim of the state is to provide opportunities for the education and development of a man's character. When the man of character appears, the state is no longer needed and can, frankly, wither away. Since the judgment of the man of character is always in harmony with God's will, he is a Majority of One; and he need not, and indeed should not, compromise his principles for the sake of political expediency. Implicit in Emerson's thinking is the idea that the man of character can govern himself and consequently will always be the embodiment of equity and justice in his dealings with others. To compromise with others over a political issue is to defile the divine law that he, above all others, grasps and embodies. If Emerson's doctrine sounds morally authoritarian and subversive to the give and take of the American democratic process, let there be no mistake about it: it is.

The Founders, on the other hand, understood the moral imperfection of mankind. Brought up in the Christian view of fallen human nature, they took as a given that self-serving ambition, base motive, even criminal intent will at times motivate human behavior. The political system they devised took self-interest and factionalism into account and designed constraints to prevent some of their more sinister political effects. Emerson, however, was a transcendental romantic who thought of men as potentially godlike if only they lived up to the divine intuitions communicated to them by the World Soul, or the Oversoul, or the Universal Current of Being, as he sometimes called it. At the center of Emerson's optimistic moral doctrine in "Politics" is the idea that if every man listens to the voice of the divine within him, if every man embodies the ethical vision he knows by intuition to be true, political factionalism is bound to cease, brotherhood will replace civil strife, and men will live in harmony and justice. For Emerson, the basis of political arrangements in America had to be changed: "The power of love, as the basis of a State, has never been tried."[9] Emerson then comments on the political scene as it presented itself in the early 1840s:

> We live in a very low state of the world, and pay unwilling tribute to governments founded on force. There is not among the most religious and instructed men of the most religious and civil nations, a reliance on the moral sentiment, and a sufficient belief in the unity of things to persuade them that society can be maintained without artificial restraints, as well as the solar system; or that the private citizen might be reasonable, and a good neighbor, without the hint of a jail or a confiscation. What is strange too, there never was in any man sufficient faith in the power of rectitude, to inspire him with the broad design of renovating the State on the principle

of right and love. All those who have pretended to this design, have been partial reformers, and have admitted in some manner the supremacy of the bad State. I do not call to mind a single human being who has steadily denied the authority of the laws, on the simple ground of his own moral nature.[10]

In Emerson's thought, then, love is the only workable public policy. As a political philosophy, Emerson's position grandiloquently affirms human greatness, but it is wildly utopian and out of touch with the sinful nature of man and the real world of political wheeling and dealing wherein Americans are obliged to negotiate a resolution of their differences, frankly by compromising their principles, to the extent that they can, if they can, instead of resorting to violence.

Invisible Man holds in a delicate equilibrium those counterpoised views of human nature and of political action that are suggested in Emerson's "Politics." Implicit in identity politics is political contention, or what the Invisible Man calls "politicalized hate"; it is the dark underside of our factional disagreements in the political forum. Yet with exceptional sympathy for the ethical thought of his transcendental forebear, Ellison nevertheless raises the question of what would the effect be if we reorganized our politics on the basis of love. While it is easy to dismiss Emerson's thought as wildly impracticable and out of touch with human nature, as Emerson sagely reminds us in "Politics," love as the basis of political action has never really been tried.

The second question posed by *Invisible Man* is the meaning of the deathbed advice of the protagonist's grandfather, who had been a slave in antebellum days. The grandfather's remarks presuppose that racial politics is implicitly a war all right, but, like all wars, there are rules of combat, an ethic of behavior touching how blacks are to relate to the white majority that is repressing them.

> "Son, after I'm gone I want you to keep up the good fight. I never told you, but our life is a war and I have been a traitor all my born days, a spy in the enemy's country ever since I give up my gun back in the Reconstruction. Live with your head in the lion's mouth. I want you to overcome 'em with yeses, undermine 'em with grins, agree 'em to death and destruction, let 'em swoller you till they vomit or bust wide open. . . . Learn it to the young-uns."[11]

This advice, which the young protagonist struggles to fathom throughout the novel, stresses a positive strategy not just for survival but for winning the war for racial equality with whites. But what does it mean to say *yes* to whites or to allow oneself to be swallowed by them? Toward the end of the novel, after the riot has run its course, the protagonist again raises the question of the meaning of his grandfather's advice and poses a series of possible interpretations that give hermeneutic depth and richness to the oracular wisdom of the old slave. While a degree of interpretive ambiguity must always inhere in the syntactic and rhetorical formulation of the question, *Invisible Man* implicitly commends an ethic of interracial relations that makes survival possible for blacks and hope possible for whites.

> Perhaps he hid his meaning deeper than I thought, perhaps his anger threw me off—I can't decide. Could he have meant—hell, he *must* have meant the principle, that we were to affirm the principle on which the country was built and not the men, or at least not the men who did the violence. Did he mean say "yes" because he knew that the principle was greater than the men, greater than the numbers and the vicious power and all the methods used to corrupt its name? Did he mean to affirm the principle, which they themselves had dreamed into being out of the chaos and darkness of the feudal past, and which they had violated and compromised to the point of absurdity even in their own corrupt minds? Or did he mean that we had to take the responsibility for all of it, for the men as well as the principle, because we were the heirs who must use the principle because no other fitted our needs? Not for the power or for vindication, but because we, with the given circumstance of our origin, could only thus find transcendence? Was it that we of all, we, most of all, had to affirm the principle, the plan in whose name we had been brutalized and sacrificed—not because we would always be weak nor because we were afraid or opportunistic, but because we were older than they, in the sense of what it took to live in the world with others . . . ? Or was it, did he mean that we should affirm the principle because we, through no fault of our own, were linked to all the others in the loud, clamoring semi-visible world, that world seen only as a fertile field for exploitation by Jack [the Communist organizer] and his kind, and with condescension by

Norton [the Northern trustee] and his, who were tired of being the mere pawns in the futile game of "making history"? Had he seen that for these too we had to say "yes" to the principle, lest they turn upon us to destroy both it and us?[12]

Whatever the old man had meant, the several possibilities elucidated by his grandson here are all alike in stressing the necessity of blacks' affirming the principle on which the country had been founded—this despite the manifest failure of whites to honor it and indeed in spite of whites' betrayal of the principle itself in their brutalization of black people. *Invisible Man* thus rejects the call to violence voiced by revolutionary communism and the separatist ideology espoused by black nationalists from Marcus Garvey to Louis Farrakhan. It likewise sets itself against the kind of counterculture violence that would emerge in the protests of Eldridge Cleaver, Malcolm X, H. Rap Brown, Bobby Seale, and the Black Panther gangsters of the sixties. At the same time it passes the severest judgment on white racism in its historic character and as a still-extant midcentury (and indeed *fin-de-siècle*) phenomenon.

Invisible Man, it must be remembered, was written before the great civil rights legislation of the fifties and sixties. A great many of the sources of oppression felt by the black protagonist of the novel back then have now, consequently, been effectively remedied; and indeed, beyond the question of mere laws, there has come about in the past half-century a significant reduction in the level of white racism infecting the culture. Black activists regularly deny this, but the degree of change for the better has frankly been breathtaking. There will doubtless always be prejudice arising from people's racial differences. But Ellison's novel points to an avenue of escape from the pain and suffering of prejudice and the reactive impulse to lash out violently at the felt sources of racism. This way of escape is transcendence through love and transcendence through art. Toward the end, Ellison's Invisible Man remarks:

> The very act of trying to put it all down has confused me and negated some of the anger and some of the bitterness. So it is that now I denounce and defend, or feel prepared to defend. I condemn and affirm, say no and say yes, say yes and say no. I denounce because though implicated and partially responsible, I have been hurt to the point of abysmal pain, hurt to the point of invisibility. And I

> defend because in spite of all I find that I love. In order to get some of it down I *have* to love. I sell you no phony forgiveness, I'm a desperate man—but too much of your life will be lost, its meaning lost, unless you approach it as much through love as through hate. So I approach it through division. So I denounce and I defend and I hate and I love.[13]

Not all of us can attain the transcendence of the artist who resolves his troubled self-division through his personal creativity. But all of us can attain it in an indirect way through a deep appreciative immersion in those works of art that deal with the human condition in the most profound and illuminating way. Such an immersion is bound to clarify one's vision of reality and enlarge one's awareness and understanding of racial complexities. Similarly, opening up oneself to the capacity to love delivers one from the negations that drain life of its richness, its power, and beauty. Ellison's Invisible Man escapes the paralysis attendant on black rage and is thus able to speak on the lower frequencies for both blacks and whites who are seeking a way to live together in peace and harmony.

III

As a black novelist and intellectual, Ellison saw his role as the affirmation and celebration of American life as a whole. This position—evident in the novel as well as in the essays—also put him at odds with white radicals, who wanted him to sign off and merely denounce America for her history of slavery and continuing racism. I have already mentioned Ellison's critique of the Communist party in *Invisible Man*. Yet even socialists like Irving Howe and some of the others in the *Partisan Review* crowd wanted Ellison to abandon his commitment to high art and merely to reproduce Richard Wright's savage denunciations of white racism in *Native Son* (1940), *12 Million Black Voices* (1941), and *Black Boy* (1945). In "Black Boys and Native Sons" (1963), Howe excoriated "accommodationists" like Ellison:

> In response to Baldwin and Ellison, Wright would have said (I virtually quote the words he used in talking to me during the summer of 1958) that only through struggle could men with black skins, and for that matter, all the oppressed of the world, achieve their hu-

manity. It was a lesson, said Wright, with a touch of bitterness yet not without kindness, that the younger writers would have to learn in their own way and their own time. All that has happened since bears him out.[14]

But has Wright proved prophetic? I do not think so, nor did Ellison. In *Invisible Man* Ellison dealt frankly, comically, and horrifyingly with the forms of white racism. But at the same time he knew that Wright's posture of alienation and feverish militancy was not the only stance. Nor was it a necessary stance for the black writer. Hence he refused to reduce his unnamed protagonist to the subhuman condition of Wright's Bigger Thomas, and he deplored Wright's dismissal of what Wright had called "all that art for art's sake crap." For Ellison fiction was not racial propaganda. As he remarked in "The World and the Jug," "what an easy con-game for ambitious, publicity-hungry Negroes this stance of 'militancy' has become."[15] And he liked to quote (of all people!) President Lyndon B. Johnson, who had remarked quite rightly that art is not a social weapon. For Ellison, the demand—whether made by white or black critics—that the Negro writer subordinate his art to antiracist propaganda denies the writer his own vision:

> For I found the greatest difficulty for a Negro writer was the problem of revealing what he truly felt, rather than serving up what Negroes were supposed to feel, and were encouraged to feel. And linked to this was the difficulty, based upon our long habit of deception and evasion, of depicting what really happened within our areas of American life, and putting down with honesty and without bowing to ideological expediencies the attitudes and values which gave Negro American life its sense of wholeness and which render it bearable and human and, when measured by our own terms, desirable.[16]

He said that for this reason black writers often failed "to achieve a vision of life and a resourcefulness of craft commensurate with the complexity of their actual situation. Too often they fear to leave the uneasy sanctuary of race to take their chances in the world of art."[17] It was in the world of art and according to aesthetic standards that Ralph Ellison wanted *Invisible Man* to be judged. And his artistic standards were so high and exacting that he was never able to complete a second novel (especially after a fire in his New England summer house destroyed the manuscript of it). He painstakingly undertook to reconstruct it, from scratch, but he never completed the novel.

A final theme that runs through his *Collected Essays* and that is brilliantly illustrated in *Invisible Man* is Ellison's love of the American language as a vernacular medium adequate to the highest art. Few American writers, white or black, have been as sensitive as he to the evolution of the American language out of the whirling maelstrom of immigrant experience. He immensely admired Twain's ear for Southern speech, studied the Mississippi dialect in Faulkner's prose, and listened for and learned from James's vernacular locutions. Ellison was naturally sensitive to the speech of blacks as a distinctive form of our "American version of English." In his speech to Haverford students in 1969, he noted how "the American language owes something of its directness, flexibility, music, imagery, mythology, and folklore to the Negro presence."[18] In "Going to the Territory" he called the slaves and their successors ingenious in developing the linguistic skills necessary to communicate in a mixed society, and he particularly praised blacks for their "melting and blending of vernacular and standard speech and a grasp of the occasions in which each, or both, were called for." In fact, Ellison called the vernacular style "the American style":

> But by "vernacular" I mean far more than popular or indigenous language. I see the vernacular as a dynamic *process* in which the most refined styles from the past are continually merged with the play-it-by-eye-and-by-ear improvisations which we invent in our efforts to control our environment and entertain ourselves. And this not only in language and literature, but in architecture and cuisine, in music, costume, and dance, and in tools and technology. In it the styles and techniques of the past are adjusted to the needs of the present, and in its integrative action the high styles of the past are democratized. From this perspective the vernacular is, no less than the styles associated with aristocracy, a gesture toward perfection.[19]

Richard Kostelanetz once called Ellison a "brown-skinned aristocrat." This sounds like "reverse color prejudice" to me, as well as class prejudice: it implies that he was too "white" to be a black, and snooty as well. Many blacks do have white ancestry, through no responsibility of their own. Ellison even had Cherokee ancestry; and when he learned that I too was from the South and had a Cherokee grandmother, it sealed our friendship. In his own selfhood he was the living personification of the interrelation of racial and cultural elements in America that was his dominating theme. He saw me in that light as well. And from this I drew the lesson that, to the extent that we acknowledged ourselves to be united by what we have in common, to that extent we added our mite to racial harmony in America.

Was he an aristocrat? Indeed, he did carry himself as if he were A Visible Somebody, but without arrogance. He *was* an aristocrat, but only in the way that every American man and woman is—as an heir to, as entitled to, incalculable cultural wealth. Ellison's whole career, insofar as I understand it, was devoted to making clear that elements of the high style—like the elements of popular culture—are available to *everyone for everyday life*. He had started out as a poor boy in Oklahoma, looking at magazines like *Vogue* and *Harper's,* and recognizing in them a style that was higher and better and more distinguished than what he saw roundabout him. It was like the difference between his daily clothes and his Sunday-go-to-meeting clothes. The boy decided that he wanted to wear glad rags every day of the week, and so he became one of the most elegantly dressed men I have ever known. Further, as a youth he found in Conrad, Hemingway, and Eliot a literary imagination superior to that of the bestsellers and poetasters common to the popular culture, and he wanted what these artists had to give. Mozart and Rossini were his inheritance—as available to him (or to any black boy or poor white boy) as to a Marian Anderson or a Jessye Norman. High culture, the fusion of black and white influences and much else besides, was his for the taking, as it is for all of us. He was as comfortable—clad in a tuxedo, listening to chamber music in the staid, large reading room of the Century Club, to which Henry James had belonged—as he was in an all-black jazz nightclub toe-tapping to local riffs. In every aspect of life Ellison worked to bring the high style, the patrician, the best, into our common everyday possession; and to lift vital, worthwhile folk expression into general consciousness as values in themselves and as a common American legacy offering inspiration to rising genius. This was, for Ralph Ellison, what a democratic culture was all about.

Notes

Preface

1 My arguments in defense of the capacity of language sufficiently to represent reality are set forth in *Vital Signs: Essays on American Literature and Criticism* (Chicago: Ivan R. Dee, 1996) and *A Fine Silver Thread* (Chicago: Ivan R. Dee, 1998).

2 Ronald Takaki, *A Different Mirror: A History of Multicultural America* (Boston: Little, Brown, 1993).

3 See Bell's *Faces at the Bottom of the Well: The Permanence of Racism* (New York: Basic Books, 1992); Hacker's, *Two Nations: Black and White, Separate, Hostile, Unequal* (New York: Ballantine, 1995); and Coleman's, *Long Way to Go: Black and White in America* (New York: Atlantic Monthly Press, 1997).

4 See Patterson's *The Ordeal of Integration: Progress and Resistance in America's "Racial" Crisis* (Washington, D.C.: Civitas/Counterpoint, 1997).

5 See Paul M. Sniderman and Edward G. Carmines, *Reaching Beyond Race* (Cambridge: Harvard University Press, 1997); Abigail and Stephan Thernstrom, *America in Black and White: One Nation, Indivisible* (New York: Simon and Schuster, 1997); and Richard Bernstein, "Optimists Disputing Decades of Pessimism on Race Relations," *New York Times*, November 8, 1997.

6 "Race Panel Excludes Critics of Affirmative Action Plans," *New York Times*, November 20, 1997, p. A-24. See also Abigail Thernstrom's "Who's Afraid to Debate Affirmative Action?" *New York Times*, November 22, 1997, p. A-15.

7 David Stove, "Racial and Other Antagonisms," in *Cricket versus Republicanism and Other Essays*, eds. James Franklin and R. J. Stove (Sidney: Quaker's Hill Press, 1995), p. 100.

8 For an excellent discussion of the rational necessity (even the inevitability) of prejudging men and situations based on the inescapable horizon of one's own prior experience, see Martin Heidegger in *Being and Time*,

trans. John Macquarrie and Edward Robinson (New York: Harper and Row, 1962), passim; and Hans-Georg Gadamer, *Truth and Method* (New York: Crossroad, 1986), p. 235ff.

9   "The Negro Writer as Spokesman," in *The Black American Writer*, ed. C. W. E. Bigsby (2 vols. Deland, Fla.: Everett–Edwards, 1969), I, 245–259; paperback reprint by Penguin Books, Inc., 1971.

10 *Richard Wright: Early Works* (New York: Library of America, 1991) includes *Lawd Today!*, *Uncle Tom's Children*, and *Native Son*. *Richard Wright: Later Works* (New York: Library of America, 1991) includes *Black Boy (American Hunger)* and *The Outsider*.

11 I do not think, incidentally, that the committee really meant to say that the other essay was "fulsome" in its praise of Zola. "Fulsome" means so extravagantly flattering as to be obviously insincere and therefore mendacious. Fulsome praise is, in fact, an insult. This error, though slight, still indicates the low level of language competence in those recruited by government bureaucrats. See Roger Kimball, "Diversity Quotas at NEA Skewer Magazine," *Wall Street Journal*, June 24, 1993, p. A-12.

12 Sarah Boxer, "Hanna Bercovitch, 63, Who Rescued Texts," *New York Times*, October 25, 1997, p. D-16.

13 Candor compels me to disclose that I myself was once one of those consultants. I was enlisted for *The Works of Washington Irving. Volume I: History, Tales, and Sketches* (New York: Library of America, 1984). There I became familiar with Ms. Bercovitch's methods. She insisted, for instance, that I prepare the 1809—rather than the 1848—edition of Irving's *A History of New York*. As the two books were substantially different, and no significant editorial principle was at stake, I assented. But it was clear that her selection of texts would prevail. I was not aware of her role in the Wright fiasco until the publication of her obituary revealed it.

14 Anthony Appiah, "The Uncompleted Argument: Du Bois and the Illusion of Race," in *"Race," Writing, and Difference*, ed. Henry Louis Gates, Jr. (Chicago: University of Chicago Press, 1986), pp. 35–36. See also Gates, "Talkin' That Talk," in *"Race," Writing, and Difference*, p. 403.

15 Derek Walcott, *Collected Poems, 1948–1984* (New York: Farrar, Straus, and Giroux, 1986), p. 505.

16 Henry Louis Gates, Jr., *Thirteen Ways of Looking at a Black Man* (New York: Random House, 1997), p. xvii.

17 See Nathan Glazer, *We Are All Multiculturalists Now* (Cambridge: Harvard University Press, 1997); and Stanley Crouch, *Always in Pursuit: Fresh American Perspectives, 1995–1997* (New York: Pantheon Books, 1998).

18 The death-blow to black America's romance with Africa has recently been struck by black journalist Keith B. Richburg in *"Out of America": A Black Man Confronts Africa* (New York: Basic Books, 1997). Richburg's eyewitness accounts of the political, social, and moral barbarism he encountered, in country after collapsing country, makes for harrowing

reading and reflection. See also Stanley Crouch, "Don't Get Smug About Slavery," *New York Daily News*, December 3, 1997, p. 41.

19 Orlando Patterson, "Racism Is Not the Issue," *New York Times*, November 16, 1997, Section 4, p. 15. A fuller development of his assessment of the improvement of racial relations in America can be found in *The Ordeal of Integration*.

The Mind of a Black Abolitionist: Frederick Douglass

1 On the slave narrative as a genre, see Marion Wilson Starling, *The Slave Narrative* (2d ed.; Washington, D.C.: Howard University Press, 1981); Charles H. Nichols, *Many Thousand Gone: The Ex-Slaves' Account of Their Bondage and Freedom* (Leiden: E. J. Brill, 1963); Wayne L. Andrews, *To Tell a Free Story: The First Century of Afro-American Autobiography, 1760–1865* (Urbana: University of Illinois Press, 1986); and *The Art of Slave Narrative*, eds. John Sekora and Darwin T. Turner (Macomb: Western Illinois University Press, 1982).

2 Fortunately the recent Library of America edition now makes it possible to study all three autobiographies together. Hence, all quotations from the Douglass narratives are drawn from *Frederick Douglass: Autobiographies,* ed. Henry Louis Gates, Jr. (New York: Library of America, 1994).

3 *Frederick Douglass: Autobiographies*, p. 37.

4 *Frederick Douglass: Autobiographies*, p. 38.

5 *Frederick Douglass: Autobiographies*, p. 42.

6 This accusation was quite odd, as the record shows that Auld was not present at the escape attempt, did not march Douglass to Easton, and had no intention of selling the boy.

7 *Frederick Douglass: Autobiographies*, pp. 416–417.

8 *Frederick Douglass: Autobiographies*, p. 53.

9 *Frederick Douglass: Autobiographies*, pp. 53–54. And at Covey's farm, over a period of several months, Douglass was flogged so often that he finally snapped.

10 *Frederick Douglass: Autobiographies*, p. 58.

11 *Frederick Douglass: Autobiographies*, p. 72.

12 *Frederick Douglass: Autobiographies*, p. 316.

13 *Frederick Douglass: Autobiographies*, p. 319.

14 *Frederick Douglass: Autobiographies*, pp. 92–93. Douglass is no more explicit about how he escaped in the 1855 *My Bondage and My Freedom*. In fact, the intervening Fugitive Slave Act of 1850 had now turned all officers of the court into slave-catchers, and Douglass's situation was even more perilous since his fugitive status and his owner's identity were by 1855 a published fact. The 1881 *Life and Times of Frederick Douglass,* written well after Emancipation, gives a full account of the means of his escape to freedom.

15 Further, it is not clear whether Nathan Johnson or Douglass added the final *s* to the name of Sir Walter Scott's Lord Douglas, but the choice of an aristocratic cognomen was by no means unintentional.

16 *Frederick Douglass: Autobiographies*, p. 65.

17 Donald B. Gibson has observed that the black minister who married the Douglasses also conveys this meaning of freedom, as a subjective condition or state of mind, in his own autobiography. After seeing his father whipped, J. W. C. Pennington observed in *The Fugitive Blacksmith* (1849) that "Although it was some time after this event before I took the decisive step [of running away], yet in my mind and spirit, I never was a *Slave* after it." See Gibson's "Reconciling Public and Private in Frederick Douglass's *Narrative*," *American Literature*, 57 (December 1985), 556; and *Great Slave Narratives*, ed. Arna Bontemps (Boston: Beacon Press, 1969), p. 211.

18 *Frederick Douglass: Autobiographies*, p. 591.

19 Quoted in Philip S. Foner, *The Life and Writings of Frederick Douglass: Early Years, 1817–1849* (New York: International Publishers, 1950), p. 83.

20 *Frederick Douglass: Autobiographies*, p. 126.

21 William S. McFeely, *Frederick Douglass* (New York: Simon and Schuster, 1991), p. 32.

22 Julia Griffiths, it should be said, was only one white woman with whom Douglass's name was romantically linked. Another was Ottilia Assing, a German revolutionary journalist who came to him in 1856, translated the second autobiography, and remained an intimate friend until her suicide in 1884. Anna having died, that was the year that Douglass was remarried to another white radical, Helen Pitts.

23 David Brion Davis, "The White World of Frederick Douglass," *New York Review of Books*, May 16, 1991, p. 15.

24 Jean Fagan Yellin, *The Intricate Knot: Black Figures in American Literature, 1776–1863* (New York: New York University Press, 1972), p. 166.

25 *Abraham Lincoln: Speeches and Writings, 1832–1858*, ed. Don E. Fehrenbacher (New York: Library of America, 1989), pp. 556–557. This edition includes the reporter's parenthetical depiction of the crowd reaction.

26 Quoted in Gabor S. Boritt's useful *Lincoln and the Economics of the American Dream* (Memphis: Memphis State University Press, 1978), p. 174.

27 Benjamin Quarles, *Frederick Douglass* (Washington, D.C.: Associated Publishers, 1948), p. 213.

28 William S. McFeeley, *Frederick Douglass*, p. 213.

29 William S. McFeeley, *Frederick Douglass*, p. 383.

30 See Robert G. O'Meally, "Frederick Douglass's 1845 *Narrative:* The Text Was Meant to be Preached," in *Afro-American Literature: The Reconstruc-*

tion of Instruction, ed. Dexter Fisher and Robert B. Stepto (New York: Modern Language Association, 1979), pp. 192–211.

31 The one conspicuous use of black dialect writing appears only in the second and third autobiographies—in the scene representing the speech of the slave Sandy Jenkins, who almost certainly betrayed their escape attempt. On revising the scene, Douglass seemed to feel that an illiterate dialect was the most appropriate vehicle for characterizing the superstitious and morally reprehensible betrayer.

32 Henry L. Gates, Jr., "Binary Oppositions in Chapter One of *Narrative of the Life of Frederick Douglass an American Slave Written by Himself*," in *Critical Essays on Frederick Douglass*, ed. William L. Andrews (Boston: G. K. Hall, 1991), p. 93n.

33 Gates, "Frederick Douglass and the Language of the Self," *Yale Review*, 71 (1981), 592–611.

34 Baker, "Autobiographical Acts and the Voice of the Southern Slave," in *Critical Essays on Frederick Douglass*, pp. 101–103.

35 Ziolkowski, "Antitheses: The Dialectic of Violence and Literacy in Frederick Douglass's *Narrative* of 1845," in *Critical Essays on Frederick Douglass*, p. 150.

36 For a discussion of black criticism of Douglass, see the Epilogue to Waldo E. Martin, Jr., *The Mind of Frederick Douglass* (Chapel Hill: University of North Carolina Press, 1984).

37 *Frederick Douglass: Autobiographies*, pp. 876–877.

38 It was perhaps Douglass's capacity for forgiveness and reconciliation that made J. Saunders Redding declare that "*Life and Times* is his best book." See *To Make a Poet Black* (Chapel Hill: University of North Carolina Press, 1939), pp. 37–38.

39 *Frederick Douglass: Autobiographies*, p. 875.

The Mind of a White Abolitionist

1 *Selections from Ralph Waldo Emerson*, ed. Stephen E. Whicher (Boston: Houghton Mifflin, 1957), p. 308.

2 Mary Thacher Higginson, *Thomas Wentworth Higginson: The Story of His Life* (Boston: Houghton Mifflin, 1914), p. 68.

3 This view is a dangerous one in the impatient, the young, and the irrational. It leads to the excesses we have seen in certain paramilitary groups in the South and West whose antigovernment rantings tend to be incomprehensible and unrelated to contemporary political reality.

4 *Walden and Other Writings of Henry David Thoreau*, ed. Brooks Atkinson (New York: Random House, 1950), p. 645.

5 Quoted in Tilden G. Edelstein, *Strange Enthusiasm: A Life of Thomas*

Wentworth Higginson (New Haven: Yale University Press, 1968), pp. 102, 105–106.

6 Mary Thacher Higginson, *Thomas Wentworth Higginson*, p. 112.
7 Thomas Wentworth Higginson, *Cheerful Yesterdays* (Boston: Houghton Mifflin, 1898), pp. 130–131.
8 Anna Mary Wells, *Dear Preceptor: The Life and Times of Thomas Wentworth Higginson* (Boston: Houghton Mifflin, 1963), pp. 83–84.
9 Edelstein, *Strange Enthusiasm*, p. 152.
10 Mary Thacher Higginson, *Thomas Wentworth Higginson*, p. 144 .
11 Mary Thacher Higginson, *Thomas Wentworth Higginson*, p. 145.
12 Edelstein, *Strange Enthusiasm*, pp. 159, 118, 162.
13 Higginson, *Cheerful Yesterdays*, p. 166.
14 Mary Thacher Higginson, *Thomas Wentworth Higginson*, pp. 173, 178–179.
15 Mary Thacher Higginson, *Thomas Wentworth Higginson*, p. 190.
16 Edelstein, *Strange Enthusiasm*, p. 233.
17 Edelstein, *Strange Enthusiasm*, p. 199.
18 Mary Thacher Higginson, *Thomas Wentworth Higginson*, p. 210.
19 Howard N. Meyer, *Colonel of the Black Regiment: The Life of Thomas Wentworth Higginson* (New York: W. W. Norton, 1967), p. 244.
20 To Mrs. Howe, Higginson later wrote: "Our Oldport will always be dear. The new-Newport . . . seems a sort of dusty daylight place that must be hard to dream in; in which picturesque, romantic, unique figures . . . have no part." *Letters and Journals of Thomas Wentworth Higginson, 1846–1906*, ed. Mary Thacher Higginson (Boston: Houghton Mifflin, 1921), p. 232.
21 Edelstein, *Strange Enthusiasm*, p. 304.
22 Edelstein, *Strange Enthusiasm*, pp. 302, 304.
23 Edelstein, *Strange Enthusiasm*, p. 297.
24 Mary Thacher Higginson, *Thomas Wentworth Higginson*, p. 263.
25 "Introduction," *The Works of Epictetus*, trans. Thomas Wentworth Higginson (Boston: Little, Brown, 1866), p. ix.
26 Mary Thacher Higginson, *Thomas Wentworth Higginson*, p. 262.
27 Howard Mumford Jones, "Introduction," *Army Life in a Black Regiment* (East Lansing, Michigan: Michigan State University Press, 1960), p. ix.
28 Mary Thacher Higginson, *Thomas Wentworth Higginson*, p. 282.
29 Edelstein, *Strange Enthusiasm*, p. 378.
30 Edelstein, *Strange Enthusiasm*, pp. 389–390.
31 Edelstein, *Strange Enthusiasm*, p. 391.

32 Edelstein, *Strange Enthusiasm*, p. 392.
33 Samuel Eliot Morison and Henry Steele Commager, *The Growth of the American Republic* (New York: Oxford University Press, 1962), I, 756.
34 Thomas Wentworth Higginson, *Army Life in a Black Regiment* (Boston: Houghton Mifflin, 1900), pp. 4–5.
35 Higginson, *Army Life in a Black Regiment*, p. 3.
36 Higginson, *Army Life in a Black Regiment*, p. 9.
37 Higginson, *Army Life in a Black Regiment*, p. 11.
38 Higginson, *Army Life in a Black Regiment*, pp. 112–113.
39 Higginson, *Army Life in a Black Regiment*, pp. 124–125.
40 Higginson, *Army Life in a Black Regiment*, p. 128.
41 Higginson, *Army Life in a Black Regiment*, p. 163.
42 Higginson, *Army Life in a Black Regiment*, pp. 129–130.
43 Higginson, *Army Life in a Black Regiment*, p. 133.
44 Higginson, *Army Life in a Black Regiment*, pp. 176–177.
45 Higginson, *Army Life in a Black Regiment*, pp. 135–136.
46 Higginson, *Army Life in a Black Regiment*, pp. 142–143.
47 Higginson, *Army Life in a Black Regiment*, p. 206.
48 Higginson, *Army Life in a Black Regiment*, p. 359n.
49 Higginson, *Army Life in a Black Regiment*, p. 21.
50 Meyer, *Colonel of the Black Regiment*, pp. 241–242.
51 Higginson, *Army Life in a Black Regiment*, p. 173.
52 Higginson, *Army Life in a Black Regiment*, p. 229.
53 Higginson, *Army Life in a Black Regiment*, p. 156.
54 Higginson, *Army Life in a Black Regiment*, p. 227.
55 Higginson, *Army Life in a Black Regiment*, p. 246.
56 Higginson, *Army Life in a Black Regiment*, p. 247.
57 Higginson, *Army Life in a Black Regiment*, p. 251.
58 Higginson, *Army Life in a Black Regiment*, p. 252.
59 Higginson, *Army Life in a Black Regiment*, p. 13.
60 Higginson, *Army Life in a Black Regiment*, p. 14.
61 Higginson, *Army Life in a Black Regiment*, pp. 13–14, 6, 29.
62 Higginson, *Army Life in a Black Regiment*, pp. 31, 43.
63 Higginson, *Army Life in a Black Regiment*, pp. 72–73.

64 Higginson, *Army Life in a Black Regiment*, p. 269.
65 Higginson, *Army Life in a Black Regiment*, p. 271.
66 Higginson, *Army Life in a Black Regiment*, p. 271.
67 Higginson, *Army Life in a Black Regiment*, pp. 276, 299.
68 Higginson, *Army Life in a Black Regiment*, p. 300.
69 Higginson, *Army Life in a Black Regiment*, pp. 295–296.
70 Meyer, *Colonel of the Black Regiment*, p. 235.
71 Higginson, *Army Life in a Black Regiment*, p. 37.
72 Higginson, *Army Life in a Black Regiment*, p. 338.
73 Higginson, *Army Life in a Black Regiment*, p. 334.
74 Higginson, *Army Life in a Black Regiment*, p. 346.
75 Higginson, *Army Life in a Black Regiment*, pp. 352–353.
76 Higginson, *Army Life in a Black Regiment*, p. 359.
77 Higginson, *Army Life in a Black Regiment*, pp. 366–367.
78 Higginson, *Army Life in a Black Regiment*, pp. 386–387.
79 Higginson, *Army Life in a Black Regiment*, pp. 374, 387.
80 Higginson, *Army Life in a Black Regiment*, p. 376.
81 Thomas Wentworth Higginson, "Intensely Human," *Part of a Man's Life* (Boston: Houghton Mifflin, 1905), pp. 127, 136.
82 Howard Mumford Jones, "Introduction," *Army Life in a Black Regiment*, pp. xvi–xvii.
83 Meyer, *Colonel of the Black Regiment*, pp. 244–245.

An Uncertain Abolitionist: Lincoln in Fact and Fiction

1 William Safire, *Freedom* (Garden City, N.Y.: Doubleday, 1987).
2 William Safire, *Freedom*, p. 87.
3 William Safire, *Freedom*, pp. 118–119.
4 William Safire, *Freedom*, p. [xiii].
5 William Safire, *Freedom*, p. 978.
6 Hayden White, *Tropics of Discourse: Essays in Cultural Criticism* (Baltimore: Johns Hopkins University Press, 1978), p. 83.
7 At a recent roundtable on the status of history, historian Arthur Schlesinger, Jr., denied the problem of cognitive nihilism now infecting the study of the past. Yet for a detailed discussion of the virtual collapse of academic history as a profession, see Keith Windschuttle's brilliant analysis in *The Killing of History: How Literary Critics and Social Theorists Are*

Murdering Our Past (New York: Free Press, 1997). A like argument is advanced in Tuttleton, "Parkman and the Emptiness of Postmodern History," in *Vital Signs: Essays on American Literature and Criticism* (Chicago: Ivan R. Dee, 1996), pp. 3–25.

8   William Safire, *Freedom*, p. 689.

9   William Safire, *Freedom*, p. 916.

10 Grant's order to Hurlbut of November 9, 1862, contained a like command: "Refuse all permits to come south of Jackson for the present. The Israelites especially should be kept out." See *Ulysses S. Grant: Memoirs and Selected Letters*, eds. Mary Drake McFeely and William S. McFeeley (New York: Library of America, 1990), p. 1015.

11 On these matters see J. G. Randall, *Lincoln the President* (Volume I, *Springfield to Gettysburg*; Volume II, *Midstream to the Last Full Measure* (1946–1955; rpt. New York: Da Capo, 1997); Benjamin Quarles, *Lincoln and the Negro* (1962; rpt. New York: Da Capo, 1991); David Zarefsky, *Lincoln, Douglas, and Slavery* (Chicago: University of Chicago Press, 1990); and David Herbert Donald, *Lincoln* (New York: Simon and Schuster, 1995).

12 "Speech on the Kansas-Nebraska Act at Peoria, Illinois" (October 16, 1854), in *Abraham Lincoln: Speeches and Writings, 1832–1858*, ed. Don Fehrenbacher (New York: Library of America, 1989), p. 338.

13 It is easy in retrospect to blame the war upon those political figures, Northern and Southern, who flourished between the founding of the nation and the Civil War. Had the compromisers acted in 1783 as the abolitionists of 1860 wanted, the results might very well have been comparable to the effects of the Soviet Revolution of 1917 — the destructive consequences of which will still be with the former Soviet peoples for centuries to come.

14 David Herbert Donald, *Lincoln*, p. [13].

15 David Herbert Donald, *Lincoln*, p. 14.

16 See David W. Dunlap's "When Today's Agenda Is a Prism for the Past," *New York Times*, October 6, 1995, p. E-3.

17 David Herbert Donald, *Lincoln*, p. 15.

18 J. G. Randall, *Lincoln the President*, II, ii, 370.

19 Donald, *Lincoln*, p. 15.

20 J. G. Randall, *Lincoln the President*, II, ii, 371.

21 *Abraham Lincoln: Speeches and Writings, 1859–1865*, ed. Don Fehrenbacher (New York: Library of America, 1989), p. 627.

22 Donald, *Lincoln*, p. 514.

23 *Abraham Lincoln: Speeches and Writings, 1859–1865*, ed. Don Fehrenbacher (New York: Library of America, 1989), p. 687.

24 *Abraham Lincoln: Speeches and Writings, 1859–1865*, ed. Don Fehrenbacher (New York: Library of America, 1989), p. 358.

25 Donald, *Lincoln*, p. 14.

26 Safire, *Freedom*, p. 1083.

27 Safire, *Freedom*, p. 1084.

28 J. G. Randall, *Lincoln the President*, II, i, 232–233.

29 Safire, *Freedom*, p. 94.

30 *Thomas Jefferson: Writings*, ed. Merrill D. Peterson (New York: Library of America, 1984), p. 1231.

31 Donald, *Lincoln*, p. 14.

Lincoln's Generals: Grant and Sherman in Their Memoirs

1 *William Tecumseh Sherman: The Memoirs of General W. T. Sherman*, ed. Charles Royster; *Ulysses S. Grant: Memoirs and Selected Letters*, eds. Mary Drake McFeely and William S. McFeely (New York: The Library of America, 1990).

2 *William Tecumseh Sherman: The Memoirs of General W. T. Sherman*, p. 171.

3 Allan Nevins, *The War for the Union: War Becomes Revolution, 1862–1863* (New York: Scribner's, 1960), p. 301.

4 *William Tecumseh Sherman: The Memoirs of General W. T. Sherman*, p. 279.

5 It is worth remarking that many of these generals were also West Point graduates. Even Jefferson Davis, president of the Confederacy, had graduated from the academy. Before Fort Sumter he had served in the Black Hawk War, and he had also commanded Mississippi troops during the Mexican War. See Burke Davis, *The Long Surrender* (New York: Random House, 1985), p. 8.

6 *William Tecumseh Sherman: The Memoirs of General W. T. Sherman*, p. 30.

7 Emory M. Thomas, *The Confederate Nation, 1861–1865* (New York: Harper and Row, 1979), p. 270.

8 *William Tecumseh Sherman: The Memoirs of General W. T. Sherman*, p. 716.

9 *William Tecumseh Sherman: The Memoirs of General W. T. Sherman*, pp. 601, 705.

10 *Marching with Sherman: Passages from the Letters and Campaign Diaries of Henry Hitchcock*, ed. Mark A. DeWolfe Howe (New Haven: Yale University Press, 1927), pp. 82, 125, 168.

11 Charles Royster, *The Destructive War: William Tecumseh Sherman, Stonewall Jackson, and the Americans* (New York: Alfred A. Knopf, 1991), pp. 271, 356, 89.

12 James Reston, Jr., *Sherman's March and Vietnam* (New York: Macmillan, 1984), p. 8.

13 William C. Davis, "Massacre of Saltville," *Civil War Times Illustrated*, 9–10 (1971), 4–11.

14 Reston, *Sherman's March and Vietnam*, p. 6.

15 Royster, *The Destructive War: William Tecumseh Sherman, Stonewall Jackson, and the Americans*, pp. 356, 358. For a full discussion of the spurious uses to which the symbolic Sherman has been put and his supposed responsibility for twentieth-century military savagery, see pp. 352–359, 496n.

16 Winston S. Churchill, *The American Civil War* (New York: Dodd, Mead, 1961), pp. 128–129.

17 Quoted in Burke Davis, *To Appomattox: Nine April Days, 1865* (New York: Rinehart, 1959), p. 121.

18 *Ulysses S. Grant: Memoirs and Selected Letters*, p. 716.

19 *Ulysses S. Grant: Memoirs and Selected Letters*, p. 735.

20 *Ulysses S. Grant: Memoirs and Selected Letters*, p. 735.

21 "General Sherman's Opinion of General Grant," *Century Magazine*, 31 (April 1897), 821.

22 *Ulysses S. Grant: Memoirs and Selected Letters*, p. 231.

23 *Ulysses S. Grant: Memoirs and Selected Letters*, pp. 531–532.

24 William S. McFeely, *Grant: A Biography* (New York: Norton, 1981), pp. 510–511.

25 Bruce Catton, *Stillness at Appomattox* (Garden City, N.Y.: Doubleday, 1953), p. 83.

26 Shelby Foote, *The Civil War: A Narrative* (New York: Random House, 1958–1974), III, 119.

27 Quoted in *The Civil War: An Illustrated History* (New York: Alfred A. Knopf, 1990), p. 276.

28 *William Tecumseh Sherman: The Memoirs of General W. T. Sherman*, p. 266.

Twain's Huck: Fresh Tears and Race Flapdoodle

1 Quoted in Rita Rief, "How 'Huck Finn' Was Rescued," *New York Times*, March 17, 1991, p. H-38.

2 See Mark Twain, *Adventures of Huckleberry Finn: A Comprehensive Edition*. With an Introduction by Justin Kaplan, foreword and addendum by Victor Doyno. New York: Random House, 1996.

3 Twain, *Adventures of Huckleberry Finn: A Comprehensive Edition*, p. 64.

4 The discovery of the lost section of the manuscript requires a complete reexamination of the composition of the novel. That is beyond the scope of the present essay. But it may be noted here that part of the work has already been done in two early studies that made use of the then-available manuscript fragment: Walter Blair's splendid *Mark Twain and Huck Finn*

(Berkeley: University of California Press, 1960) and Victor Doyno's *Writing "Huck Finn": Mark Twain's Creative Process* (Philadelphia: University of Pennsylvania Press, 1992).

5 See Dierdre Carmody, "What Huck and Jim Really Said in That Cave," *New York Times*, May 16, 1995, p. C–13.

6 The Random House text follows a disturbing new trend that is, alas, likewise evident in the University of Pennsylvania edition of Theodore Dreiser's *Sister Carrie* and the Library of America edition of Richard Wright's *Native Son*. Both of these editions, as I argue below in the chapter on Wright, wrongly restore to an author's approved text passages that the author had canceled in manuscript or had revised on the advice of editors or trusted advisers. In each case the "modernized" text reflects a late-twentieth-century editor's hankering for more sexually explicit language — even at the expense of the author's wish to delete such material in the interests of the design and reception of his art.

7 Daniel Menaker, "The Phoenix-Like Manuscript of *Adventures of Huckleberry Finn*," *At Random*, December, 1995, p. 46.

8 For a recent discussion of the novel see R. Kent Rasmussen, *Mark Twain: A to Z* (New York: Oxford University Press, 1995), pp. 372–379.

9 All scholars have noted Twain's penchant for the morbid, the grotesque, and the funerary. Delancey Ferguson has rightly remarked of Twain's tale "The Undertaker's Love Story," which Howells and Olivia Clemens both nixed, that "one inclines to support their judgment sight unseen." See Ferguson's "The Case for Mark Twain's Wife," *University of Toronto Quarterly*, 9 (October 1939), 14.

10 *Mark Twain's Letters*, eds. Harriet Elinor Smith and Richard Bucci (Berkeley: University of California Press, 1990), II (1867–1868), 248. See also *Mark Twain to Mrs. Fairbanks*, ed. Dixon Wecter (San Marino, Calif.: Huntington Library, 1949), p. xxvii.

11 Quoted in Edward Wagenknecht, *Mark Twain: The Man and His Work* (Norman: University of Oklahoma Press, 1961), p. 165.

12 Van Wyck Brooks, *The Ordeal of Mark Twain* (New York: E. P. Dutton, 1920), pp. 122–123.

13 It is worth citing Walter Blair on Brooks's slander of Olivia Clemens: "Both Clemens and Howells had semi-invalid wives who were unusually gentle, and their private joke (not novel in husbandly humor) was to picture them as shrews. Failure of biographers to see this indicates a lack of humor, something of a handicap for students of a humorist's biography." See Blair's *Mark Twain & Huck Finn* (Berkeley: University of California Press, 1962), p. 31.

14 *Mark Twain's Letters*, eds. Smith and Bucci, II, 275.

15 Quoted in Albert Bigelow Paine, *Mark Twain: A Biography* (New York: Harper and Brothers, 1912), II, 774–775.

16 *Mark Twain's Autobiography* (New York: Harper and Brothers, 1924), II,

89–90. See also Susy's *Papa: An Intimate Biography of Mark Twain*, ed. Charles Neider (Garden City, N.Y.: Doubleday, 1985). Sydney J. Krause, who made a close study of Livy's actual handwriting in Twain's manuscripts, concludes that "The ultimate impression one gets of Livy is decidedly *not* that of a woman who wasted a fair portion of her married life dictating literal propriety to a recalcitrant husband and making his prose less salty than it might otherwise have been. No, . . . Olivia Clemens reveals herself to have been only, alas, a poor plodding, pedestrian proofreader, and a rather erratic one, at that, who let go many more serious improprieties than she caught." See Krause's "Olivia Clemens's 'Editing' Reviewed," *American Literature*, 39 (1967), 330.

17 *Mark Twain's Letters to His Publishers, 1868–1894*, ed. Hamlin Hill (Berkeley: University of California Press, 1967), pp. 19–20.

18 *Selected Mark Twain–Howells Letters, 1872–1910*, eds. Frederick Anderson, William M. Gibson, and Henry Nash Smith (New York: Atheneum, 1968), p. 227.

19 "Note on the Text," in Mark Twain, *Adventures of Huckleberry Finn*, eds. Walter Blair and Victor Fischer (Berkeley: University of California Press, 1985), p. 449.

20 Twain's natural irascibility may have been aggravated here by a dental problem.

21 *Selected Mark Twain–Howells Letters, 1872–1910*, eds. Anderson, Gibson, and Smith, pp. 232, 234.

22 Twain, *Adventures of Huckleberry Finn*, eds. Blair and Fischer, p. 450.

23 Twain, *Adventures of Huckleberry Finn*, eds. Blair and Fischer, pp. 450–451.

24 Quoted in Justin Kaplan's "Introduction," in *Adventures of Huckleberry Finn: A Comprehensive Edition* (New York: Random House, 1996), p. ix.

25 Peaches Henry, "The Struggle for Tolerance: Race and Censorship in Huckleberry Finn," in *Satire or Evasion? Black Perspectives on "Huckleberry Finn,"* eds. James S. Leonard, Thomas A. Tenney, and Thadious Davis (Durham, N.C.: Duke University Press, 1992), p. 26.

26 Quoted in Justin Kaplan, "Selling 'Huck Finn' Down the River," *New York Times Book Review*, March 10, 1996, p. 27.

27 S. I. Hayakawa, *Language in Action* (New York: Harcourt, Brace, 1939), pp. 76–79.

28 *Mark Twain's Autobiography*, I, 101.

29 *Mark Twain's Autobiography*, I, 101.

30 See Sterling Brown's "Negro Characters as Seen by White Authors," *Journal of Negro Education*, 2 (January 1933), 180–201.

31 Quoted in Philip S. Foner, *Mark Twain: Social Critic* (2nd ed. New York: International Publishers, 1966), p. 192.

32 *Selected Mark Twain–Howells Letters, 1872–1910*, eds. Anderson, Gibson, and Smith, p. 241.

33 Shelley Fisher Fishkin, *Was Huck Black? Mark Twain and African-American Voices* (New York: Oxford University Press, 1993), p. 4.

34 The term "Ebonics," evidently made up in 1966 in Oakland, is compounded, it seems, from "ebony" and "phonics." A like recent innovation is Kwanzaa, a supposed African seasonal holiday that was concocted in the United States in the 1960s by Ron Karenga, a militant activist who did not want blacks to have a white Christmas.

35 "Black English Plan Baffles Some Students in Oakland," *New York Times*, December 21, 1996, p. 8.

36 That racial victimization, black separatism, and milking the government of bilingual education money is at the heart of the Ebonics concoction is suggested by the Oakland school board's claim that students would be taught "in their primary language and in English" and that teachers who were "bilingual in Nigritian Ebonics" and English would be eligible for extra pay and other perqs. The U.S. Department of Education is, for the moment, not amused. See Jonathan Schorr's "Give Oakland's Schools a Break," *New York Times*, January 2, 1997, p. A–19.

37 *Mark Twain's Autobiography*, II, 174.

38 Ralph Ellison, "What America Would Be Without Blacks," in *Collected Essays of Ralph Ellison*, ed. John F. Callahan (New York: The Modern Library, 1995), p. 581.

39 See Gerald Graff, *Beyond the Culture Wars: How Teaching the Conflicts Can Revitalize American Education* (New York: W. W. Norton, 1993).

40 Mark Twain, *Adventures of Huckleberry Finn: A Case Study in Critical Controversy*, eds. Gerald Graff and James Phelan (Boston and New York: Bedford Books of St. Martin's Press, 1995). The Julius Lester quotation, cited above, appears on p. 432. Graff and Phelan reprint the authorized 1885 text. This is the right text to reprint, but their reason for choosing it shows how little interested they are in questions of exacting editorial procedure. As they observe on p. v, "We do not include the raftsmen's passage, which was not part of the 1885 text and is not directly relevant to any of our three controversies." While the passage surely should be rejected, Graff and Phelan's reason for not including it is a poor one. Editors of classic American novels should not include or reject substantives based on whatever may be the extraliterary controversies of the moment. Feminism, gay liberation, and racial relations may seem urgent to some people now, but they should not dictate editorial procedures any more than saving the whales, ending dependence on fossil fuels, outlawing cigarettes, restricting immigration, or any other such sociological issues. In fact, only controversies relevant to the *form* of the novel, its aesthetic character, belong in the *literature* classroom.

41 Twain, *Adventures of Huckleberry Finn: A Case Study in Critical Controversy*, eds. Graff and Phelan, p. 11.

42 Twain, *Adventures of Huckleberry Finn: A Case Study in Critical Controversy*, eds. Graff and Phelan, p. 504.

43 Lauriat Lane, Jr., "Why *Huckleberry Finn* Is a Great World Novel," *College English*, 17 (October 1955), 2.

44 *Adventures of Huckleberry Finn*, eds. Blair and Fischer, p. 271.

45 *Adventures of Huckleberry Finn*, eds. Blair and Fischer, p. 361.

46 Twain, *Adventures of Huckleberry Finn: A Case Study in Critical Controversy*, eds. Graff and Phelan, p. 516.

47 See Charles Reade's *The Cloister and the Hearth* (New York: Dodd, Mead, 1944), p. 491; and Blair, *Mark Twain & Huck Finn*, pp. 129–130, 400 n32.

48 Leslie Fiedler, "Come Back to the Raft Ag'in Huck Honey!," *Partisan Review*, 15 (June 1948), 664–671; reprinted in *An End to Innocence* (Boston: Beacon Press, 1955), pp. 142–151.

49 Leslie Fiedler, *Love and Death in the American Novel* (New York: Criterion Books, 1960).

50 Twain, *Adventures of Huckleberry Finn: A Case Study in Critical Controversy*, eds. Graff and Phelan, p. 545. The argument that Twain was queer originated in Andrew J. Hoffman's "Mark Twain and Homosexuality," *American Literature*, 67 (March 1995), 21–49. The evidence that Hoffman adduced was so preposterous, tenuous, and hermeneutically contorted that even the author was obliged to admit that, after all, he had no proof of any homosexual experience on Twain's part: As to "*proof* of my hypothesis," Hoffman conceded, "there is none" (p. 25). Anyone can imagine anything nowadays and call it literary criticism. But the question is whether such speculative drivel should ever see the light of day. (That *American Literature* published this essay marks the collapse of a once-great journal of scholarship into a shameless propaganda organ of Queer Nation and its friends.)

51 Liz McMillan, "New Theory About Mark Twain's Sexuality Brings Strong Reactions from Experts," *Chronicle of Higher Education*, September 8, 1993, pp. A8, A13.

52 Swift's diatribe in *Gay Community News* is quoted in Eugene Narrett, "Letter from Massachusetts: The Sex Quiz," *Chronicles: A Magazine of American Culture*, 20 (October 1996), 35.

53 For a fuller discussion of the meaning of slavery and freedom as a "bipolar" movement between the shore and the raft, see Henry Nash Smith, "Introduction," in *Adventures of Huckleberry Finn* (Boston: Houghton Mifflin, 1958), pp. x–xi.

Pride and Shame: The Winning of the West

1 *The West*. Directed by Stephen Ives. Senior Producer: Ken Burns. Produced by Stephen Ives, Jody Abramson, and Michael Kantor. Written by Geoffrey C. Ward and Dayton Duncan. Narrated by Peter Coyote. A Turner Home Entertainment Production. Nine cassettes.

2. *Lewis and Clark*. A film by Ken Burns. A production of Florentine Films and Wota, Washington, D.C., 1997. Two volumes. Produced by Dayton Duncan and Ken Burns. Written by Dayton Duncan. Edited by Paul Barnes and Erik Ewers. Narrated by Hal Holbrook.

3. Dayton Duncan, *Lewis and Clark: The Journey of the Corps of Discovery* (New York: Alfred A. Knopf, 1997). Duncan, it should be observed, also co-authored the script of *The West*.

4. The journals of Lewis and Clark were never completely published until 1904. They run to eight volumes in Thwaites, the standard scholarly edition produced in 1904 by the Wisconsin Historical Society. A convenient reprint of this standard text is *The Original Journals of the Lewis and Clark Expedition, 1804–1806*, ed. Reuben Gold Thwaites, 8 volumes (New York: Arno Press, 1969). Jefferson's charge to Lewis and Clark is given in an appendix to a recently reprinted one-volume abridgment of the record of this expedition: *The Journals of Lewis and Clark*, ed. Bernard DeVoto (rpt. Boston: Houghton Mifflin, 1997), p. 483.

5. *The Journals of Lewis and Clark*, ed. Bernard DeVoto, p. 92.

6. The DeVoto edition of the journals preserves the eccentric spacing and spelling practices of the authors; American usage had yet to be standardized by native lexicographers like Noah Webster. *The Journals of Lewis and Clark*, ed. Bernard DeVoto, pp. 27, 476.

7. Ken Burns, "Preface: Come Up Me," in *Lewis and Clark: The Journey of the Corps of Discovery*, p. xi.

8. Ken Burns, "Preface: Come Up Me," p. xi.

9. Ken Burns, "Preface: Come Up Me," p. xii.

10. Duncan, "Introduction," *Lewis and Clark: The Journey of the Corps of Discovery*, p. xix.

11. The "gentle Tasadays" were a prehistoric native tribe supposedly discovered a few years ago in the South Pacific. Journalists and anthropologists were delighted with their nakedness, primitivism, and peaceful disposition. (They supposedly had no word for "hate," "enemy," "weapon," etc.) The Tasadays were held out to us as proof of the reality of the "noble savage," who lived a splendid primitive existence outside the constraints and corruptions of Western society. The tribe turned out to be a hoax. It was perpetrated by some government officials to induce tourism in the region.

12. *The Journals of Lewis and Clark*, ed. Bernard DeVoto, p. 49.

13. Francis Parkman, *France and England in North America*, ed. David Levin (New York: Library of America, 1983), II, 484.

14. *The Journals of Lewis and Clark*, ed. Bernard DeVoto, pp. 438–439.

15. Ambrose is the author of *Undaunted Courage: Meriwether Lewis, Thomas Jefferson, and the Opening of the American West* (New York: Simon and

Schuster, 1996), a book immensely popular on the liberal left because of its politically correct, revisionist, historical shame-mongering.

16   "Author Says Indians Keyed Success of Lewis and Clark," Casper (Wyoming) *Star-Tribune*, July 17, 1997, p. B-4.

17   "Author Says Indians Keyed Success of Lewis and Clark," p. B-4.

18   Quoted in Duncan, *Lewis and Clark: The Journey of the Corps of Discovery*, p. 93.

19   Duncan, *Lewis and Clark: The Journey of the Corps of Discovery*, p. 60.

20   *The Journals of Lewis and Clark*, ed. Bernard DeVoto, p. 76.

21   *The Journals of Lewis and Clark*, ed. Bernard DeVoto, p. 38.

22   *The Journals of Lewis and Clark*, ed. Bernard DeVoto, p. 301.

23   *The Journals of Lewis and Clark*, ed. Bernard DeVoto, p. 19.

24   Francis Parkman, *France and England in North America*, II, 532–533.

25   Parkman's account of the ubiquity of Indian violence, catalogued at horrific length in his seven-volume history of France in the New World, is extended in *The Oregon Trail* and *The Conspiracy of Pontiac*, ed. William R. Taylor (New York: Library of America, 1991). For yet another account of the readiness of the Western Indians to go on the warpath, see Thomas E. Mails, *The Mystic Warriors of the Plains* (1972; rpt. New York: Marlowe, 1995), pp. 15ff.

Ethnic Blues and All That Multicultural Jazz

1   Ronald Takaki, *A Different Mirror: A History of Multicultural America* (Boston: Little, Brown, 1993).

2   Takaki, *A Different Mirror: A History of Multicultural America*, p. 17.

3   Roger Kimball, "Legislating History," *New Criterion*, 15 (November 1996), 1–2.

4   Takaki, *A Different Mirror: A History of Multicultural America*, p. 208.

5   Takaki, *A Different Mirror: A History of Multicultural America*, pp. 155, 270, 314, 286.

6   Quoted in Takaki, *A Different Mirror: A History of Multicultural America*, p. 331.

7   Quoted in Takaki, *A Different Mirror: A History of Multicultural America*, p. 176.

8   Takaki, *A Different Mirror: A History of Multicultural America*, p. 15.

9   For a detailed discussion of immigration issues and patterns, see Bernard Bailyn's *The Peopling of British North America: An Introduction* (New York: Knopf, 1986); *Clamor at the Gates: The New American Immigration*, ed. Nathan Glazer (San Francisco: ICS Press, 1985); and John Bodnar's *The*

Transplanted: A History of Immigrants in Urban America (Bloomington: Indiana University Press, 1985).

10 Quoted in Takaki, *A Different Mirror: A History of Multicultural America*, p. 17.

11 Edith Wharton, *A Backward Glance* (New York: Scribner's, 1934), p. 7.

12 For a consideration of the changing origin of immigrant peoples, see *Still the Golden Door: The Third World Comes to America*, ed. David Reimers (2nd edition; New York: Columbia University Press, 1985).

Loathing Western Civilization

1 William Shakespeare, *Othello*, Act I, Scene 3, Lines 145-147, in *The Complete Works of Shakespeare*, ed. David Bevington (3rd ed., Glenview, Ill.: Scott, Foresman), p. 1131.

2 Perhaps the most egregious distortion of the savage is a modern phenomenon after all. I refer to the contemporary treatment of Caliban in Shakespeare criticism of *The Tempest*. In developing the dramatic parable of Prospero's exile, abandonment, and return, Shakespeare allegorically split the human body and soul into Caliban and Ariel, figuring the grosser appetites in the carnal figure of the darker Caliban, reserving for the pale and ethereal Ariel the more intangible spiritual qualities of mankind. Third World ideologues have seized upon this allegory and its color symbolism as really a form of theatrical realism that baldly exhibits the immorality of Shakespeare's racism, the British colonial enslavement of native peoples, Caribbean island exploitation, devastation by European invaders, and so on. This is the Alice-in-Wonderland approach to criticism: anything is so if you say it is.

3 The quotations from Royal and Vitoria appear in Robert Royal, "Who Put the West in Western Civilization?" *Intercollegiate Review*, 33 (Spring 1998), 11-13.

4 I am aware that the high priests of psychoanalysis claim that Freud has been misinterpreted by those who abjure repression, exalt the id, and revere instinct. Still, Freud's doctrine is known, among other ways, by the fruit it bears. Whether the phenomenon I have sketched out is a popular misreading of Freud or not, the social effects of the doctrine known as "Freudianism" have been disastrous.

5 Richard Waswo, *The Founding Legend of Western Civilization* (Hanover, N.H.: Wesleyan University Press, 1997).

6 Forrest G. Wood, *The Arrogance of Faith: Christianity and Race in America from the Colonial Era to the Twentieth Century* (New York: Alfred A. Knopf, 1990).

7 A sad commentary on this contemporary assault on Christianity is suggested by the title of David Martin's recent book *Does Christianity Cause War?* (Oxford: Clarendon Press, 1998). The title is of course meant to be provocative, but even to entertain the question momentarily

suggests the kind of calumnies against which Christians must now continually do battle.

8 St. Augustine, *The City of God*, Book XIX, Section 16.

9 St. Augustine, *The City of God*, Book X, Section 20.

10 Eugene Genovese, review of *The Arrogance of Faith: Christianity and Race in America from the Colonial Era to the Twentieth Century*, in *The New Republic*, 203 (August 13, 1990), 35.

11 Wood's bizarre thesis that whites were slaveholders *because* they were Christians cannot explain why non-Christian American Indians regularly enslaved their captives after village raids. Nor can it account for why, throughout their long history, Muslims and Jews also engaged in the slave trade. The eradication of slavery, to the extent that it has been achieved (African slavery is still practiced today—notably in the Sudan, a fundamentally Islamic nation), represents the triumph of Western contemporary Judeo-Christian values.

12 For a partial introduction to this vital manifestation of modern Christianity, see Sylvia R. Frey, *Come Shouting to Zion: African American Protestantism in the American South and British Caribbean to 1830* (Chapel Hill: University of North Carolina Press, 1990); Jeff G. Johnson, *Black Christians—The Untold Lutheran Story* (St. Louis: Concordia, 1991); Donald G. Mathews, *Religion in the Old South* (Chicago: University of Chicago Press, 1977); and Cyprian Davis, *A History of Black Catholics in the United States* (New York: Crossroads, 1990).

Countee Cullen at "The Heights"

1 See Margaret Perry, *A Bio-Bibliography of Countee P. Cullen, 1903–1946* (Westport, Conn.: Greenwood Press, 1971), p. 29.

2 Perry, *A Bio-Bibliography of Countee P. Cullen, 1903–1946*, pp. 28–30.

3 Countee Cullen, *Caroling Dusk* (New York: Harper and Brothers, 1927), p. 179.

4 "The Literary Spotlight," Doran, 1924, p. 77.

5 *Editor's note:* This description of the writer was first published in "Edna St. Vincent Millay," *Bookman*, 56 (January 1922), 272–278, and was reprinted in *The Literary Spotlight*, ed. John C. Farrar (New York: George H. Doran, 1924). Some dispute as to its authorship has arisen. Norman A. Brittin, in *Edna St. Vincent Millay* (New York: Twain, 1967), identifies the author as Floyd Dell. But another critic, John J. Patton, in "A Comprehensive Bibliography of Edna St. Vincent Millay," published in *The Serif*, argues that Farrar is the author.

6 "American Poetry Since 1900," Louis Untermeyer, Henry Holt, 1923.

7 "The New Era in American Poetry," Louis Untermeyer, Henry Holt, 1919.

8 *Editor's Note:* Although Cullen quotes and provides a superscript number in the text here, he neglected to provide a footnote identifying his source.

9   *Editor's Note:* Cullen silently deletes here these intervening sentences in the text being quoted: "Its title gives an indication of its cynical optimism. Previous to this volume she had been known as the author of 'Renascence,' and had gained the devout admiration of a few poetry lovers, but no popular audience."

10 *Editor's Note:* Professor Rollins, to whom Cullen submitted this thesis for grading, underlined the word "immortal" and posed a question mark in the right margin.

11 *Editor's Note:* No footnote is provided, nor is Carl Van Doren listed in the "References" at the end of the essay. Cullen's source was either Van Doren's "Youth and Wings," *Century*, 106 (June 1923), 310–316, or his book *Many Minds* (New York: Alfred A. Knopf, 1924), which reprints the article.

12 Letter of Hyder E. Rollins to Dean A. L. Bouton, February 11, 1920. NYU Archives.

13 For a discussion of Rollins's career at Harvard, see Herschel Baker's *Hyder Edward Rollins: A Bibliography* (Cambridge: Harvard University Press, 1960).

14 Keats's influence on Countee Cullen is often mentioned but rarely treated in depth. Yet see Perry, pp. 28–30.

15 Hyder E. Rollins to A. L. Bouton, February 28, 1921. NYU Archives.

16 Chancellor Elmer Ellsworth Brown to Henry Allen Moe, Guggenheim Foundation, October 21, 1925. NYU Archives.

17 Hyder E. Rollins to E. E. Brown, January 15, 1924. NYU Archives.

18 Shucard rightly remarks that "it is to Cullen's credit that, whatever the version or versions of the frequently reprinted old ballad he was familiar with, his treatment is more dramatic than those presented, for example, in two standard collections, *The Oxford Book of Ballads* and *The Ballad Book*." *Countee Cullen* (Boston: Twayne, 1984), p. 110.

19 *The English and Scottish Popular Ballads,* ed. Francis James Child (New York: Dover, 1965), II, pp. 179–199.

20 Shucard, *Countee Cullen*, p. 110.

21 Houston A. Baker, Jr., *A Many-Colored Coat of Dreams: The Poetry of Countee Cullen* (Detroit: Broadside Press, 1974), p. 45.

22 Blanche E. Ferguson, *Countee Cullen and the Negro Renaissance* (New York: Dodd, Mead, 1966), p. 39.

23 Shucard, *Countee Cullen*, p. 125, n18.

24 Ferguson, *Countee Cullen and the Negro Renaissance*, p. 39.

25 George Lyman Kittredge to Countee Cullen, December 8, 1923. Amistad Collection, Tulane University. See *Guide to the Microfilm Edition of the Countee Cullen Papers, 1921–1969,* compiled by Florence E. Borders (New Orleans: Amistad Research Center, 1975).

26 H. E. Rollins to Countee Cullen, January 9, 1926. Amistad Collection.
27 Chancellor E. E. Brown to Countee Cullen, October 20, 1925. Amistad Collection.
28 E. E. Brown to Countee Cullen, March 17, 1926. Amistad Collection.
29 A. L. Bouton to Countee Cullen, October 28, 1929. Amistad Collection.
30 Charles Norman, *Poets and People* (Indianapolis: Bobbs-Merrill, 1972), p. x.
31 Martin Russak, "Countee Cullen," *The Critical Review* (NYU literary publication), March 1928, p. 7.
32 For representative opinions on Cullen's verse in relation to the black tradition and to poetic modernism, see Shucard, pp. 111–114; Mercer Cook and Stephen E. Henderson, *The Militant Black Writer in Africa and the United States* (Madison: University of Wisconsin Press, 1969), p. 116; and David Littlejohn, *Black on White: A Critical Survey of Writing by American Negroes* (New York: Grossman Publishers, 1966), pp. 55–56.
33 James B. Munn, "Introduction," *Some Recent New York University Verse,* ed. David L. Blum (New York: New York University Press, 1926), pp. vii–viii.
34 Eda Lou Walton, "The Undergraduate Poet," *The Critical Review,* March 1928, p. 7.
35 H. E. Rollins to Countee Cullen, May 15, 1926. Amistad Collection.
36 H. E. Rollins to Countee Cullen, October 28, 1929. Amistad Collection.

The Negro Writer as Spokesman (1969)

1 Robert Penn Warren, *Who Speaks for the Negro?* (New York: Random House, 1965), Foreword, n.p.
2 W. E. B. Du Bois, *The Souls of Black Folk,* in *W. E. B. Du Bois: Writings* (New York: Library of America, 1986), pp. 364–365.
3 James Baldwin, "Many Thousands Gone," *Notes of a Native Son* (New York: Bantam, 1968), p. 33.
4 Baldwin, "Many Thousands Gone," p. 27.
5 James Baldwin, "Alas, Poor Richard," *Nobody Knows My Name: More Notes of a Native Son* (New York: Dell, 1961), p. 157.
6 See Maurice Charney's "James Baldwin's Quarrel with Richard Wright," *American Quarterly,* 15 (1963), 67–75.
7 Irving Howe, "Black Boys and Native Sons," *A World More Attractive: A View of Modern Literature and Politics* (New York: Horizon Press, 1963), p. 112.
8 Robert Bone, "Ralph Ellison and the Uses of the Imagination," *Anger, and Beyond: The Negro Writer in the United States,* ed. Herbert Hill (New York: Harper & Row, 1966), p. 102.
9 Hoyt W. Fuller, "Towards a Black Aesthetic," *Black Expression: Essays by and*

About Black Americans in the Creative Arts, ed. Addison Gayle, Jr. (New York: Weybright and Talley, 1969), p. 268.

10 Quoted in Abraham Chapman, Introduction, *Black Voices: An Anthology of Afro-American Literature,* ed. Abraham Chapman (New York: New American Library, 1968), p. 48.

11 LeRoi Jones, "State/Meant," *Home: Social Essays* (New York: William Morrow, 1966), p. 251.

12 Neal, "Statements on Poetics," *The New Black Poetry,* ed. Clarence Major (New York: International Publishers, 1969), p. 141.

13 *The New Black Poetry,* p. [5].

14 *The New Black Poetry,* p. 15.

15 *The New Black Poetry,* pp. 48–49.

16 *The New Black Poetry,* p. 140.

17 Fuller, "Towards a Black Aesthetic," p. 264.

18 Hoyt W. Fuller, review of Dan McCall's *The Example of Richard Wright, New York Times Book Review,* May 18, 1969, p. 8.

19 Larry Neal, "Statements on Poetics," *The New Black Poetry,* p. 141.

20 "Statements on Poetics," *The New Black Poetry,* pp. 141–142.

21 Quoted in Chapman, pp. 48–49.

22 Ralph Ellison, "The World and the Jug," *Shadow and Act* (New York: New American Library, 1966), p. 130.

23 Gayle, "Introduction," *Black Expression,* pp. xi–xii.

24 *Black Fire,* eds. LeRoi Jones and Larry Neal (New York: William Morrow, 1968). Of such poems Jack Richardson has observed, in "The Black Arts" (*New York Review of Books,* December 19, 1968), that an insidious madness is now infecting "Negro literature and . . . the criticism surrounding it. Dragged out into America's social chaos, the new literature, instead of analyzing the lunacy behind the slogans of racial struggle, has begun to embody it. The Black Fire view of art may be extreme, but the madness filters into much better writers than those in this anthology, and it is a madness far from divine: deadening, awkward, simplistic, strident—in every way inimical to the antic, the unique, the odd and personal. It is the madness in monuments and behind lapidary epigrams, and it settles like a stylish uniform on those who let themselves be drafted into its service" (p. 11).

25 *The New Black Poetry,* p. 54.

26 "Seminar on Black Culture Begins at Columbia," *New York Times,* March 2, 1969, p. 49.

27 Ellison, *Shadow and Act,* p. xviii.

28 Gayle, Introduction, *Black Expression,* p. xv.

29 "Robert Penn Warren and Ralph Ellison: A Dialogue," *The Reporter*, 32 (March 25, 1965), 48.

The Problematic Texts of Richard Wright

1 The set is in two volumes. *Richard Wright: Early Works* (New York: Library of America, 1991) includes *Lawd Today!*, *Uncle Tom's Children*, and *Native Son*. *Richard Wright: Later Works* (New York: Library of America, 1991) includes *Black Boy (American Hunger)* and *The Outsider*. Arnold Rampersad, author of the acclaimed biography *The Life of Langston Hughes*, wrote the notes for both volumes.

2 Ralph Ellison, "Remembering Richard Wright," *Going to the Territory* (New York: Random House, 1986), p. 210; Irving Howe, "Black Boys and Native Sons," in *Critical Essays on Richard Wright*, ed. Yoshinobu Hakutani (Boston: G. K. Hall, 1982), p. 41.

3 For a discussion of the "Wright School" of black naturalists, see Robert A. Bone's *The Negro Novel in America* (New Haven: Yale University Press, 1965), pp. 157–160.

4 Michel Fabre, *Richard Wright: Books and Writers* (Jackson: University Press of Mississippi), p. 40.

5 See Fabre, *Richard Wright: Books and Writers*, p. 72.

6 Ralph Ellison, *Going to the Territory*, p. 212.

7 Baldwin meant that "Richard cared more about his safety and comfort than he cared about the black condition." See *Nobody Knows My Name: More Notes of a Native Son* (New York: Dell, 1961), p. 168; Cecil Brown, "Richard Wright's Complexes and Black Writing Today: The Lesson and the Legacy," *Negro Digest*, 18 (December, 1968), 45–50, 78–82. See also Nick Aaron Ford, "A Long Way from Home," *Phylon*, 19 (Winter, 1958), 435–436.

8 Baldwin said that he "distrusted" Wright's "association with the French intellectuals, Sartre, de Beauvoir, and company" because "there was very little they could give him which he could use." Baldwin found that, to these existentialists, "ideas were somewhat more real to them than people" and that they "were no more capable of seeing this jewel [Wright] than were the people of his native land. . . ." See Baldwin's "Alas, Poor Richard," *Nobody Knows My Name*, p. 148. *The Outsider* suggests that Wright's gift for creating people was thinning out as he turned toward philosophical abstractions. But for a more sympathetic treatment of Wright's relation to French thought, see Michel Fabre's "Richard Wright, French Existentialism, and *The Outsider*," in *Critical Essays on Richard Wright*, pp. 182–198.

9 J. Saunders Redding, "The Alien Land of Richard Wright," in *Soon One Morning*, ed. Herbert Hill (New York: Knopf, 1963), pp. 50–59.

10 See Russell Carl Brignano, *Richard Wright: An Introduction to the Man and His Works* (Urbana: University of Illinois Press, 1970), p. 53.

11 *Richard Wright: Early Works*, p. 235.

12 In an inscribed gift of *Black Boy* to Sylvia Beach, Wright said that Lenin's words had "influenced me more than any other words in my life." See Fabre, *Richard Wright: Books and Writers*, p. 94.

13 *Richard Wright: Early Works*, p. 874.

14 Robert Bone sees Dreiser (in *An American Tragedy*) as the source of Wright's "guilt-of-the-nation thesis" and of his "environmentalist view of crime." See *The Negro Novel in America*, p. 143.

15 *Richard Wright: Early Works*, p. 818.

16 Nathan A. Scott, Jr., "The Haunted Tower of Richard Wright," *Black Expression: Essays by and About Black Americans in the Creative Arts*, ed. Addison Gayle, Jr. (New York: Weybright and Talley, 1969), p. 299.

17 James Baldwin, *Notes of a Native Son* (New York: Bantam, 1964), pp. 27–28.

18 Ralph Ellison, "The Seer and the Seen," *Shadow and Act* (New York: New American Library, 1966), p. 36.

19 Scott, "The Haunted Tower of Richard Wright," p. 300.

20 Hakutani, *Critical Essays on Richard Wright*, p. 2. For an ampler discussion of this point, see the valuable essay "Beyond Naturalism," in Michel Fabre's *The World of Richard Wright* (Jackson: University Press of Mississippi, 1985), pp. 56–76.

21 Scott, "The Haunted Tower of Richard Wright," p. 309.

22 Houston A. Baker, Jr., "Racial Wisdom and Richard Wright's *Native Son*," in *Long Black Song: Essays in Black American Literature and Culture* (Charlottesville: University Press of Virginia, 1972), pp. 128, 133. A comparable effort at critical deflection away from Wright's sociological interests is Eugene E. Miller's *Voice of a Native Son: The Poetics of Richard Wright* (Jackson: University Press of Mississippi, 1990), which likewise tries to make Wright out to be "intuitive, emotional, even visionary and semi-mystical" (pp. xiv–xv). This makes Wright sound like William Blake rather than the dedicated Marxist he was.

23 Baldwin reports that Wright, like Du Bois, insisted that "*All* literature is protest. You can't name a single novel that isn't protest." Baldwin's rejoinder was that "all literature might be protest but all protest was not literature." See *Nobody Knows My Name*, p. 157.

24 Keneth Kinnamon, "*Native Son*: The Personal, Social, and Political Background," *Phylon*, 30 (Spring 1969), 66–72; reprinted in *Critical Essays on Richard Wright*, p. 124.

25 Baldwin has remarked that Max's speech is "one of the most desperate performances in American fiction" (*Notes of a Native Son*, p. 22). The reason for this desperation, as David Daiches has rightly noted, is that Wright was "trying to prove a normal thesis by an abnormal case." See Daiches, "The American Scene," *Partisan Review*, 7 (May–June 1940), 245. See also Phyllis R. Klotman, "Moral Distancing as a Rhetorical Technique

in *Native Son:* A Note on 'Fate,'" CLA Journal, 18 (December 1974), 284–291.

26 *Richard Wright: Early Works,* p. 862.

27 See Introduction, *New Essays on Native Son,* ed. Keneth Kinnamon (Cambridge: Cambridge University Press, 1990), p. 6. See also Kinnamon's excellent full-length study *The Emergence of Richard Wright* (Urbana: University of Illinois Press, 1972), pp. 121–125.

28 Henry Seidel Canby, in "'Native Son' by Richard Wright," *Book-of-the-Month Club News,* February 1940, pp. 2–3, and Edward Margolis, in his *Native Sons: A Critical Study of Twentieth-Century Negro American Authors* (Carbondale: Southern Illinois University Press, 1968) are both typical of one school of Wright criticism. This group emphasizes, as Kinnamon puts it, "the psychological dimension of Wright's story as a way of evading the social message." See *New Essays on Native Son,* p. 22.

29 *Richard Wright: Early Works,* p. 909.

30 *Richard Wright: Early Works,* pp. 472–473.

31 James Campbell, "The Wright Version," *Times Literary Supplement,* December 13, 1991, p. 14.

32 "Letters," *Times Literary Supplement,* January 24, 1992, p. 15.

33 "Letters," *Times Literary Supplement,* January 31, 1992, p. 17.

34 See "Letter," AFRAM *Newsletter* (a publication of the Centre d'Etudes Afro-amèriçaines of the Sorbonne in Paris), 35 (June 1992), 30.

Derek Walcott and the Vision of Homeric Grandeur

1 Quoted in James Atlas, "Derek Walcott: Poet of Two Worlds," *New York Times Sunday Magazine,* May 23, 1982, p. 34.

2 The plays are beyond the scope of this paper. Among Walcott's published theater works—aside from *The Odyssey,* which I stress here for its relevance to my argument touching *Omeros*—are *Dream on Monkey Mountain and Other Plays* (1970), *The Joker of Seville and O Babylon!* (1978), *Remembrance and Pantomime* (1980), and *Three Plays: The Last Carnival; Beef, No Chicken; A Branch of the Blue Nile* (1986). For an account of Walcott as a man of the theater, see Bruce Alvin King's *Derek Walcott and the West Indian Drama: Not Only a Playwright but a Company, The Trinidad Theatre Workshop, 1959–1993* (New York: Oxford University Press, 1995).

3 Mark Rudman, "Voluptuaries and Maximalists," *New York Times Book Review,* December 20, 1987, p. 12.

4 Or was it Trollope who said this? I quote here from Walcott's Nobel Prize acceptance speech. This talk was separately published as *The Antilles: Fragments of Epic Memory* (New York: Farrar, Straus, and Giroux, 1994), but I quote from the version given as "The Sigh of History," in the *New York Times,* December 8, 1992, p. A-25. In the poem "Air," Walcott

attributes this remark (it is his epigraph) to Froude in *The Bow of Ulysses*: "There has been romance, but it has been the romance of pirates and outlaws. The natural graces of life do not show themselves under such conditions. There are no people there in the true sense of the word, with a character and purpose of their own." See Derek Walcott, "Air," in *Collected Poems, 1948–1984* (New York: Farrar, Straus, and Giroux, 1986), p. 113.

5   Walcott, *Collected Poems, 1948–1984*, p. 195.

6   Walcott, *Collected Poems, 1948–1984*, p. 14.

7   Walcott, *Collected Poems, 1948–1984*, p. 294.

8   Walcott, *Collected Poems, 1948–1984*, pp. 45–46.

9   Walcott, *Collected Poems, 1948–1984*, pp. 19, 11, 196.

10 Walcott, *Collected Poems, 1948–1984*, pp. 29, 360.

11 Robert Mazzocco, "Three Poets," *New York Review of Books*, December 31, 1964, p. 18.

12 Walcott, *Collected Poems, 1948–1984*, pp. 390–391.

13 Walcott, *Collected Poems, 1948–1984*, p. 434.

14 Atlas, "Derek Walcott: Poet of Two Worlds," *New York Times Sunday Magazine*, pp. 39–40.

15 Walcott, *Collected Poems, 1948–1984*, p. 179.

16 Walcott, *Collected Poems, 1948–1984*, p. 269.

17 Walcott, *Collected Poems, 1948–1984*, p. 18.

18 Walcott, *Collected Poems, 1948–1984*, p. 350.

19 For a number of African tongues, there has not been, until recently, any kind of alphabet or written language (and for some there is still none), much less a body of poetry and fiction or scholarship and criticism.

20 Derek Walcott, *The Arkansas Testament* (New York: Farrar, Straus, and Giroux, 1987), p. 9

21 D. J. Enright, "Frank Incense," *New Republic*, November 2, 1987, p. 46.

22 T. S. Eliot, *Four Quartets*, in *Collected Poems, 1909–1962* (New York: Harcourt, Brace and World, 1970), p. 189.

23 Walcott, *Collected Poems, 1948–1984*, p. 506.

24 Walcott, *Collected Poems, 1948–1984*, p. 219.

25 Walcott, *Collected Poems, 1948–1984*, p. 346.

26 Walcott, *Collected Poems, 1948–1984*, p. 97.

27 Walcott, *Collected Poems, 1948–1984*, p. 350.

28 Walcott, *Collected Poems, 1948–1984*, p. 483.

29 Walcott, *Collected Poems, 1948–1984*, pp. 20–21.

30 Walcott, *Collected Poems, 1948–1984*, p. 405.

31 Walcott, *The Arkansas Testament*, p. 42. For a more sympathetic perspective, readers may wish to consult *Postcolonial Literatures: Achebe, Ngugi, Desai, Walcott*, eds. Michael Parker and Roger Starkey (New York: St. Martin's Press, 1995).

32 Walcott, *Collected Poems, 1948–1984*, pp. 355–356.

33 Walcott, *Collected Poems, 1948–1984*, pp. 443–444.

34 Walcott, *Collected Poems, 1948–1984*, p. 510.

35 Rei Terada, *Derek Walcott's Poetry: American Mimicry* (Boston: Northeastern University Press, 1992), pp. 183–212.

36 Walcott, *Omeros* (New York: Farrar, Straus, and Giroux, 1990), p. 266.

37 Walcott, *Omeros*, p. 187.

38 See D. J. R. Bruckner, "A Poem in Homage to an Unwanted Man," *New York Times*, October 9, 1990, p. C-13.

39 Edgar Allan Poe, "The Poetic Principle," in *Selected Writings of Edgar Allan Poe*, ed. Edward H. Davidson (Boston: Houghton Mifflin, 1956), pp. 468, 464.

40 Walt Whitman, "Song of the Exposition," in *Walt Whitman: Poetry and Prose*, ed. Justin Kaplan (New York: Library of America, 1982), p. 342.

41 Ezra Pound, "Paris Letter: *Ulysses*," in *Pound/Joyce: The Letters of Ezra Pound to James Joyce, with Pound's Essays on Joyce*, ed. Forrest Read (New York: New Directions, 1967), p. 197.

42 See *The Letters of Ezra Pound, 1907–1941*, ed. D. S. Paige (New York: Harcourt, Brace, 1950), p. 210.

43 Walcott, *Omeros*, p. 200.

44 T. S. Eliot, "'Ulysses,' Order, and Myth," in *Selected Prose of T. S. Eliot*, ed. Frank Kermode (New York: Harcourt Brace Jovanovich, 1975), p. 177.

45 Some sections of *Omeros* are formally anomalous. A cinematic technique, productive of montage effects, is occasionally introduced: in Chapter 45, section 2, the terms "pan," "cut to," and "rewind" are invoked to "direct" what and how we see. Chapter 25, section 3, is written as a dramatic scene with formal speeches. Chapter 33, section 3 ("House of umbrage, house of fear"), dealing with the breakup of the narrator's marriage, abandons the hexameter in favor of tetrameter couplets with an insistent use of Whitman's characteristic epanaphora.

46 See Michael Bernstein, *The Tale of the Tribe: Ezra Pound and the Modern Verse Epic* (Princeton: Princeton University Press, 1980), p. 86.

47 Ezra Pound, "I Gather the Limbs of Osiris," *Ezra Pound: Selected Prose, 1909–1965*, ed. William Cookson (New York: New Directions, 1973), p. 23.

48 Walcott, *Omeros*, p. 11.

49 Michiko Kakutani, "Books of the Times," *New York Times*, January 15, 1986, p. C-19.

50 Walcott, *Omeros*, pp. 23–24.

51 While Walcott's personae are black, he wisely makes no effort to exploit the preposterous claims of Martin Bernal—in *Black Athena: The Afroasiatic Roots of Classical Civilization* (New Brunswick: Rutgers University Press, 1987)—that Homer and Hellenic culture generally are derivative of black African sources.

52 Walcott, *Omeros*, p. 124.

53 Walcott, *Omeros*, p. 19.

54 Walcott, *Omeros*, p. 318.

55 Walcott, *Omeros*, pp. 12–13.

56 Walcott, *Omeros*, p. 152.

57 Walcott, *Omeros*, p. 75.

58 Walcott, *Omeros*, p. 293.

59 *Ezra Pound: Selected Prose, 1909–1965*, p. 29.

60 See Karsten Harries, "The Infinite Sphere: Comments on the History of a Metaphor," *Journal of the History of Philosophy*, 13:1 (January 1975), 8–10. Especially valuable is Harries's analysis of the shift in phrasing, according to which "universe" was later (as in Pascal's formulation of it) substituted for "God."

61 Walcott himself is a painter. *Omeros* features a jacket cover by the poet that portrays, after the manner of Winslow Homer, some Caribbean fishermen out at sea.

62 Walcott, *Omeros*, p. 18.

63 Walcott, *Omeros*, p. 33.

64 Walcott, *Omeros*, p. 286.

65 I find this troubling tone evident in Walcott's book for the disastrous musical *Capeman* (1998), co-authored with the aging rock star Paul Simon. This joint production, it must be said, went beyond mere political correctness: it presented a pathological Hispanic teen-age killer as the victim of white society. (Too few whites were willing to pay the exorbitant Broadway price to be racially insulted—especially with such bad music. So the production closed after sixty-eight performances.)

66 Walcott, *Omeros*, p. 25.

67 Walcott, *Omeros*, p. 208.

68 Walcott, *Omeros*, p. 263.

69 Walcott, *Omeros*, p. 92.

70 Walcott, *Omeros*, pp. 269–270.

71 Walcott, *Omeros*, p. 115.
72 Walcott, *Omeros*, p. 28.
73 Walcott, *Omeros*, p. 59.
74 For chilling eyewitness accounts of intertribal violence—stupefying even to the sanguinary Spanish navigators Ojeda, Niceusa, Rivera, Vasco Nuñez de Balboa, and Ponce de Leon—see Don Martin Navarette's *Colección de los viages y descubrimientos, que hicieron por mar los españoles desde fines del siglo XV* (5 vols., Madrid: Royal Historical Society, 1825–1837).
75 Walcott, *Omeros*, p. 175.
76 Walcott, *Omeros*, p. 134.
77 Walcott, *Omeros*, p. 175.
78 Walcott, *Omeros*, pp. 289–290.
79 Walcott, *Omeros*, p. 231.
80 Walcott, *Omeros*, p. 293.
81 Walcott, *Omeros*, p. 112.
82 Walcott, *Omeros*, pp. 227–228.
83 Walcott, *Collected Poems*, p. 510.
84 John Figueroa, "*Omeros*," in *The Art of Derek Walcott*, ed. Stewart Brown (Dufour, Wales: Seren Books, 1991), p. 208.
85 Walcott, *Omeros*, p. 296.
86 Walcott, *Omeros*, p. 296.
87 Walcott, *Omeros*, pp. 321, 298.
88 Walcott, *Omeros*, p. 283.
89 Walcott, *Omeros*, p. 319.
90 Walcott, *Omeros*, p. 64.
91 Walcott, *Omeros*, p. 310.
92 Figueroa, "*Omeros*," p. 209.
93 St. Lucia is also memorialized in the internationally popular song "Santa Lucia." See "Lucy," in *The Oxford Dictionary of Saints,* by David Hugh Farmer (3rd ed., New York: Oxford University Press, 1992), pp. 304–305.
94 Eliot, *Ash-Wednesday*, in *Collected Poems, 1909–1962*, p. 95.
95 Wallace Stevens, "An Ordinary Evening in New Haven," in *Collected Poems of Wallace Stevens* (New York: Alfred A. Knopf, 1964), p. 471.
96 Walcott, *Omeros*, p. 271.
97 Walcott, *Omeros*, p. 325.

Ralph Ellison: Indivisible Man

1. Ralph Ellison, *Invisible Man* (New York: Modern Library, 1952).

2. *The Collected Essays of Ralph Ellison*, ed. John F. Callahan, with an Introduction by Saul Bellow (New York: Modern Library, 1995).

3. *The Collected Essays of Ralph Ellison*, p. 76.

4. I am aware that Ellison has specifically denied the identification of the Brotherhood with the Communist party, wishing instead to suggest that a number of other organizations were guilty of the same kind of political manipulation of blacks. (See *The Collected Essays of Ralph Ellison*, p. 538.) Still, the rationalizations of Jack and the maneuvers of the Brotherhood so exactly parallel the policy flip-flops on "the black question" of the CPUSA that the identification is irresistible.

5. Ellison, *Invisible Man*, pp. 311–312.

6. Zora Neale Hurston, "How It Feels to Be Colored Me," in *I Love Myself When I Am Laughing and Then Again When I Am Looking Mean and Impressive: A Zora Neale Hurston Reader*, ed. Alice Walker (Old Westbury, N.Y.: State University of New York Press, 1979), p. 172. This tendency to associate the black with an atavistic reversion to savagery is precisely the dismaying conceit of O'Neill's *Emperor Jones*, complete down to the divestment of his clothes and the expressionistic beating of the jungle tom-toms.

7. For a splendid discussion of the relation of Ellison's protagonist to Dostoevsky's *Notes from the Underground* and Richard Wright's "The Man Who Lived Underground," see Robert A. Bone's *The Negro Novel in America* (New Haven: Yale University Press, 1965), pp. 201–203.

8. Ellison, *Invisible Man*, p. 341.

9. Ralph Waldo Emerson, "Politics," in *Ralph Waldo Emerson: Essays and Lectures*, ed. Joel Porte (New York: Library of America, 1983), p. 569.

10. Emerson, "Politics," in *Ralph Waldo Emerson: Essays and Lectures*, p. 570.

11. Ellison, *Invisible Man*, pp. 12–13.

12. Ellison, *Invisible Man*, pp. 433–434.

13. Ellison, *Invisible Man*, pp. 437–438.

14. Quoted in Ellison, *Collected Essays*, p. 161.

15. *The Collected Essays of Ralph Ellison*, pp. 170–171.

16. *The Collected Essays of Ralph Ellison*, p. 58.

17. *The Collected Essays of Ralph Ellison*, p. 59.

18. *The Collected Essays of Ralph Ellison*, p. 430.

19. *The Collected Essays of Ralph Ellison*, p. 608.

Acknowledgments

Some of the material in *The Primate's Dream* has previously appeared elsewhere. But while most of it has been rewritten or revised, often extensively, I still want to thank the several editors and publishers of the entries below for granting permission to reprint sections of the following: "The Many Lives of Frederick Douglass," *The New Criterion*, 12 (February 1994), 16–26; reprinted in *Against the Grain: The New Criterion on Art and Intellect at the End of the Twentieth Century*, eds. Hilton Kramer and Roger Kimball (Chicago: Ivan R. Dee, 1995), pp. 236–250. Selections from *Thomas Wentworth Higginson* by James W. Tuttleton (Boston: Twayne Publishers, 1978). "Preserving the Union," *Commentary*, 85 (February 1988), 90–92. "Demystifying Lincoln," *The New Criterion*, 14 (November 1995), 65–68. "Lincoln's Generals: Sherman and Grant in Their Memoirs," *The New Criterion*, 9 (October 1990), 63–70. "Mark Twain: More 'Tears and Flapdoodle,'" *The New Criterion*, 15 (September 1996), 59–65. "The Winning of the West," *The New Criterion*, 15 (October 1996), 23–27. "Through a Glass Darkly," *The New Criterion*, 11 (June 1993), 65–69. "Arrogance and the Canons of Historical Scholarship," *The New Criterion*, 9 (December 1990), 66–70. "The Negro Writer as Spokesman," in *The Black American Writer*, ed. C. W. E. Bigsby (2 vols., Deland, Fla.: Everett-Edwards, 1969), I, 245–259; paperback reprint by Penguin Books, 1971. "Countee Cullen at 'The Heights,'" *The Harlem Renaissance: Revaluations*, eds. Amritjit Singh, William S. Shiver, and Stanley Brodwin (New York: Garland Press, 1989), pp. 101–137. "The Problematic Texts of Richard Wright," *Hudson Review*, 45 (Summer 1992), 261–271. "One People's Grief," *National Review*, 38 (June 20, 1986), 51–52. "The Achievement of Ralph Ellison," *The New Criterion*, 14 (December 1995), 5–10.

Index

Adams, Henry, 60
Addams, Jane, 38
Adventures of Huckleberry Finn (Twain), 91–115; banning of, 101–102, 104; dialects in, 105–106; differences between old and new versions, 93–94; feminist argument against, 109, 111–112; finding of lost half of manuscript, 91–92; homosexuality and, 112–113; morality and, 109–111; republication with Twain's cuts included, 94–95, 97; typesetting of, 99–100; women and, 109
Adventures of Tom Sawyer (Twain), 100
Aeneid (Virgil), 161
Alamo, 131
Algren, Nelson, 224
Ambrose, Stephen E., 125, 126, 127
American Articles of War, 82, 83
American Indians. See Native Americans.
American Poetry Since 1900 (Untermeyer), 189
Anderson, S. E., 214
Anthony, Aaron, 3, 4
Anthony, Susan B., 28
Appiah, Anthony, xxii
Aria da Capo (Millay), 187–188
Army Life in a Black Regiment (Higginson), 34, 36, 39–51, 52–53

Arnold, Matthew, 88
Arrogance of Faith: Christianity and Race in America from the Colonial Era to the Twentieth Century, The (Wood), 165; central theme of, 170; criticism of, 171–175; omissions in, 174–175; slavery depiction in, 171–172
Assing, Ottilia, 16
Aswell, Edward, and Richard Wright, 236, 238, 239, 240, 242
Attaway, William, 281
Attucks, Crispus, 207
Auld, Hugh, 4, 5, 9, 12, 24
Auld, Lucretia Anthony, 4, 24
Auld, Sophia, 4, 5, 24
Auld, Thomas, 4, 5, 6, 7, 9, 22–23, 24

Bacheller, Irving, 54
Backward Glance, A (Wharton), 154
Bailey, Betsey, 4
Bailey, Frederick. *See* Douglass, Frederick.
Bailey, Harriet, 3
Bailey, Henny, 7
Baker, Jr., Houston A., 21, 22, 200; hypocrisy of, 251–252; on *Native Son*, 233–234, 251–252
Baldwin, James, 210, 211, 212, 281, 294; criticism of *Native Son*, 232; on self-exile of Richard Wright, 226

Ballad of the Brown Girl, The (Cullen), 199, 200
Ballad of the Harp Weaver and Other Poems, The (Millay), 186–187, 189, 199
Baraka, Imamu Amiri, xviii, 214, 218, 281; on black writer's role in America, 213–214
Barth, John, 260, 262, 265, 281
Bates, Edward, 67, 72
Bearse, Austin, 29
Beauregard, Pierre G. T., 77
Beecher, Henry Ward, 174
Being and Time (Heidegger), xvii
Bell, Derrick, xiii
Benford, Lawrence, 219
Benjamin, Walter, 162
Bercovitch, Hanna, xxi, xxii
Beyond Good and Evil (Nietzsche), 164–165
Bigsby, C. W. E., xvii
Bingham, Caleb, 5
Black aesthetic definition, 213
Black Boy (Wright), 209, 224 225, 235–236, 294; alternate title, 236; different version of, 237, 240
Black Christ and Other Poems, The (Cullen), 201, 205
Black Culture and Black Consciousness (Levine), 144
Black Elk, Charlotte, 136
Black Expression (Gayle), 217
Black Fire, 218
Black folksongs, 47–49
Black militancy after World War II, 38–39
Black Panthers, xviii
Black Power: A Record of Reactions in a Land of Pathos (Wright), 227
Black soldiers' pay and the Civil War, 43–44
Black writer as spokesman, 207–221; Baraka (LeRoi Jones), Imamu Amiri, 213–214, 218; Baldwin, James, 210–211, 212; Benford, Lawrence, 219; black aesthetic definition, 213, 217; critics and, 216, 219, 220; Edwards, Harry, 214–215; Ellison, Ralph, 211–212, 217, 219–220, 221, 295; Fuller, Hoyt, 215–216, 217; Gayle, Jr., Addison, 217, 220; Giovanni, Nikki, 219, 220; Karenga, Ron, 214; Killens, John O., 219; Knight, Etheridge, 216–217; Neal, Larry, 212–213, 214, 216, 218, 219; Rahman, Yusuf, 218, 219; Warren, Robert Penn, 208–209; Wright, Richard, 209–211
Blacks as permanent victims, xiii
Blair, Walter, 100
Blair family, 60
Bliss, Elisha, 99
Blum, David L., 203
Bone, Robert, 212
Bontemps, Arna, 224
Boothe, John Wilkes, 65
Bouton, Archibald L., 192, 196, 197, 198, 201
Bowditch, Henry, 29
Bowie, Jim, 131
Brady, Matthew, 55, 60
Bragg, Braxton, 77, 78
Breckinridge, John Cabell, 55, 59
Bright, John, 12
Brignano, Russell Carl, 228
Brodsky, Joseph, xxv, 258, 259
Brooks, Gwendolyn, 216
Brooks, Van Wyck, 96
Brown, Dee, 144
Brown, Elmer Ellsworth, 198, 201
Brown, H. Rap, 293
Brown, John, 16, 32, 131
Brown, Sterling, 105
Brown on exile of Richard Wright, Cecil, 226
Browning, Orville, 57
Bryan, William Jennings, 37
Buell, D. C., 77
Burns, Anthony, 28–29, 30
Burns, Ken, 116, 117, 120; waxing nostalgic for land of Lewis and

Index

Clark's time, 120–122. *See also Lewis and Clark: The Corps of Discovery.*
Burnside, Ambrose E., 78
Burton, Annie L., 3
Bury My Heart at Wounded Knee: An Indian History of the American West (Brown), 144

Calley, William, 83, 84
Camarillo, Albert, 144
Campbell, Ben Nighthorse, 137
Campbell, James, 238–239
Cannady, Charles T., xiii
Capitein, Jacobus Elisa Joannes, 169–170
Carmines, Edward G., xiii
Carroll, Anna Ella, 55, 59, 72–73
Carson, Kit, 130
Catton, Bruce, 89
Césaire, Aimé, 226
Channing, W. F., 30
Charney, Maurice, 211
Chase, Kate, 55
Chase, Salmon P., 55, 57, 59, 60
Chen, Jack, 133
Chestnut, Mary, 89
Chestnutt, Charles, 223
Chicanos in a Changing Society (Camarillo), 144
Chief Joseph, xxvii, 130, 133
Child, Francis James, 199, 200
Child, Mrs., 26
Chinese treatment by Americans, 147
"Christian-bashing," 165
Christianity and race in America, xiv, 156–175; moral law and, 157, 158; Nietzsche and, 164–165; slavery and, 166–170; Waswo and, 160–164; Wood and, 165–175
Churchill, Winston, 82
City of God, The, 157, 167–168
"Civil Disobedience" (Thoreau), 26–27
Civil War: averting question of, 78; Battle of the Wilderness description by Grant, 88–89, 90; first black regiment in, see 1st South Carolina Volunteers; Jews and, 61–62; "March to the Sea" by Sherman, 79–81; memorial to, 74–75; pay for black soldiers, 43–44; Richmond, capture of, 79, 85–86
Civilization and Its Discontents (Freud), 158–159
Clarkson, Thomas, 14
Cleaver, Eldridge, xviii, 293
Clemens, Samuel L. See Twain, Mark.
Clinton, William Jefferson, xi, 56; open meetings on race convened by, xiii–xiv
Cloister and the Hearth, The (Reade), 112
Cody, Buffalo Bill, 130
Coleman, Jonathan, xiii
Collected Essays of Ralph Ellison, The, 281–282, 296
Collected Poems, 1948–1984 (Walcott), 243, 245–259; anger within, 248; comparison to *Omeros*, 269; conclusion of, 28; excerpts from, 246–257, 259; language and, 251–253; theme of, 245–246; women in, 256 *Color* (Cullen), 177, 193, 194, 199, 201, 203
Columbian Orator, The, 5
Colvin, J. B., 73
Connerly, Ward, xiii
Conrad, Joseph, 163, 224, 285, 297
Conroy, Jack, 224
Copper Sun (Cullen), 193, 194, 199, 203
Coronado, 130
Countee Cullen (Shucard), 199
Countee Cullen and the Negro Renaissance (Ferguson), 176
Covey, Edward, 7–8, 10
Cricket versus Republicanism (Stone) and definition of racism, xvi
Critics and black writers, 216
Crockett, Davy 131

Crouch, Stanley, xxviii
Cullen, Countee, xv, 176–206; education of, 190–192; examples of Rollin's influence on, 199; first publication of poems, 193–194; Kittredge letter to, 200, 201; resemblance to other poet's works, 177; similarities to Edna St. Vincent Millay, 177–178; transcripts of, 191–193
Cultural Capital: The Problem of Canon Formation (Guillory), 260
Cultural diversity, xxvii–xxviii
Cultural miscegenation, xxviii
Cusanus, Nicolaus, 267
Custer, George Armstrong, 130, 131

Dana, Richard Henry, 30
Dances with Wolves, 141
Darwin, Charles, xxiv, 159, 160
Darwinian theory of evolutionary development, xxiv
Das Kapital (Marx), 161
Davis, Ben, 225
Davis, David Brion, 15
Davis, Jefferson, 68, 69, 85
Death in the Afternoon (Hemingway), 219
de Beauvoir, Simone, 226
Democracy (Adams), 60
Derek Walcott's Poetry: American Mimicry (Terada), 259
DeVitoria, Francisco, 158
Devons, Charles, 27
DeVoto, Bernard, 97, 100
Dewey, John, 38
Dickinson, Emily, 25
Dietz, Paula, xviii
Different Mirror: A History of Multicultural America, A (Takaki), xii, 145, ', 150; rainbow curriculum and, 145; women in, 147–148
Dinkins, David, 153–154
Discrimination and American immigrants, 148–150
Dissertatio Politico-Theologica de Servitute, Liberatati Christianae, non Contraria (Capitein), 169–170
Donald, David Herbert, 62–63, 64–67, 69, 71, 73
Donne, John, 162
Douglas, Stephen, 16–17, 63
Douglass, Anna, 10, 13, 19
Douglass, Frederick, xiv, xxvii, 1–24, 26; autobiography of, 2–3; Baker on, 21; birth of, 2, 3–4; Douglas on, 16–17; education of, 5; escape to freedom by, 9–10; Gates on, 20–21; Higginson and, 37; legal freedom of, 12; McFeely on, 14–15; name change of, 10; *North Star* start by, 13; publication of his *Narrative*, 12; reconciliation with former master, 22–24; remarriage of, 19; Republican party and, 16, 19; "Sisterhood of Reforms" and, 16; Stanton on, 18; thoughts on slavery by, 5–6; Yellin on, 16
Douglass, Helen, 19, 20
Doyno, Victor, 94
Dreiser, Theodore, 224, 233, 241
Drumgoold, Kate, 3
Du Bois, W. E. B., 28, 52, 209, 223; Library of America series and, 222
Duke, David, xiii
Dunbar, Paul Laurence, 19, 203
Duncan, Dayton, 122, 125, 126, 127–128

Earp, Wyatt, 130
Ebonics, 106–107
Edgar, John Gaston, 193
Edwards, Harry, 214
Eisenhower, Dwight David, 153
Eliot, T. S., xviii, xxv, 108, 203, 204, 206, 216, 244, 245, 252, 258, 262, 278, 282, 297
Ellison, Ralph, xv–xvi, xxviii, 107, 207, 211–212, 217, 219–220, 221, 234, 280–297; black radicals' view of, 285; blues and jazz and, 284; *Invisible Man*, 280–297;

Kostelanetz on, 296; language and, 296; on *Native Son*, 222, 232; rainbow curriculum of, 285; role as viewed by, 294; themes of, 282–285; views on Negro writers, 295; works of, 281; Wright and, 226, 283, 288, 294–295
Emancipation Proclamation, xiv, 3, 33, 59, 70, 90, 174
Emerson, Ralph Waldo, 26, 33, 35, 289–291
Emersonian transcendentalism, 25
Emigrants and Exiles: Ireland and the Irish Exodus to North America (Miller), 144
Engels, Friedrich, 160
English and Scottish Popular Ballads, The (Child), 199
English and Scottish Popular Ballads, The (Kittredge), 199
Enright, D. J., 253
Epic poems, requirements for, 261–262
Ethnic alienation today, 151
Ethnic cleansing, 155
Ethnic discrimination, 153
Ethnic diversity, xxvii–xxviii
Ethnic history of twentieth century, views on, 139–140
Ethnic prejudice and immigrants, 147–150
Ethnic rage, 152

Fairbanks, Mary, and Mark Twain, 96, 97, 101, 241
Fanon, Frantz, 212
Farrakhan, Louis, xiii, xxviii, 293
Farrell, James T., 224
Ferguson, Blanche E., 176, 200, 201
Few Figs from Thistles, A (Millay), 184
Fiedler, Leslie, 112, 113
Figueroa, John, 275–276, 277–278
Finnegan, Joseph, 42
Finney, Charles Grandison, 174
First black regiment in Civil War. See 1st South Carolina Volunteers. 1st South Carolina Volunteers, 34, 39–51
Fischer, Victor, 100, 101
Fisher, Rudolph, 223
Fishkin, Shelly Fisher, 105, 106, 107
Fitzgerald, F. Scott, 245
Foote, Shelby, 69
Foster, Stephen S., 12
Foucault, Michel, 138, 161, 162, 270
Founding Legend of Western Civilization, The (Waswo), and criticism of, 160–164
Franklin, John Hope, xiii
Frederick Douglass (McFeely), 14
Frederick Douglass' Paper, 16
Freedom (Safire), 54–62, 71
Freeland, William, 8
Frémont, John C., 75
Freud, Sigmund, 139, 158–159, 160
Frye, Northrop, 245
Fugitive Slave Law, 26, 27, 31; test case of, 27
Fuller, Hoyt, 215–216, 217
Funkhouser, Erica, 128

Gadamer, Hans-Georg, xvii
Gaia Atlas of First Peoples, 163
Garrison, William Lloyd, 12, 13, 14, 15, 16, 18, 26, 28, 33
Gates, Jr., Henry Louis, xxi, xxii, xxiii, xxvi, 20–21
Gayle, Jr., Addison, 217, 220
Geertz, Clifford, 162
Genovese, Eugene, 171
Getridge, Carolyn M., 106
Gide, André, 226
Gilson, Etienne, 157
Giovanni, Nikki, 219, 220
Glazer, Nathan, xxvii
Gluck, James Fraser, 92
God That Failed, The (Wright), 228–229
Gold, Mike, 225
Gone with the Wind, and taking of Atlanta, 79

Graff, Gerald, 108, 112, 113, 114
Grangerford, Emmeline, 114
Grant, Ulysses Simpson, xiv, 19, 55, 59, 65, 78, 80; Battle of the Wilderness description, 88–89; biographical sketch of, 76–77; concern for casualties, 89–90; death of, 90; as defender of Sherman, 87; on food supplies, 79; as general-in-chief, 77, 78; Jews and, 61, 62; Lee's surrender to, 86; memoir reviews, 87–89; military commander of Union armies, 77, 78; and Richmond, taking of, 85–86; Sherman's view of, 87; surrender terms of, 86; view of Sherman by, 87–88
Grant: Memoirs and Selected Letters, Ulysses G. (Grant), 75, 87
Greeley, Horace, 28, 55, 70
Greenhow, "Wild Rose," 55, 56, 60
Griffiths, Julia, 13, 15
Grimké sisters, 26, 174
Guillory, John, 260
Gurney, Mrs. Eliza P., 68
Gwaltney, Bill, 133

Habermas, Jurgen, 162
Hacker, Andrew, xiii
Half-Century of Conflict, A (Parkman), 124, 136
Halleck, Henry W., 65, 77, 78, 80
Hamlet (Shakespeare), 70
Hardee, William J., 79, 80
Hardy, Thomas, 106
Harlem Renaissance authors, 281
Harries, Kersten, 267
Hay, John, 55, 59
Hayakawa, S. I., 103
Hayden, Robert, 217
Heart of Darkness (Conrad), 163
Heidegger, Martin, xvii
Helms, Jesse, xiii
Hemingway, Ernest, 211, 219, 267, 297
Henry, Peaches, 102

Hermeneutic circle, xvii
Herrick, Robert, 184
Higginson, Thomas Wentworth, xiv, 25–53, 174; on arming black troops, 50–51; attempted rescue of Anthony Burns, 28–30; Civil War feelings of, 33–34; and Douglass, 37; emancipation articles in the *Atlantic*, 33; and John Brown, 32; and 1st South Carolina Volunteers, 34, 39–51; and Fugitive Slave Law, 26–31; and Kansas, 31–32; on mixed marriage, 52; and Negro spirituals (folksongs), 47–49; and Reconstruction era, 35, 51; Worcester pastorate, 28; works of, 36
Himes, Chester, 223
Himmelfarb, Gertrude, 170
Hirst, Robert H., 101
Historia de las Indias (la Casas), 272
Historical revisionism, xi–xii
History of Mary Prince: A West Indian Slave, The, 3
Hitchcock, Henry, 80
Holliday, J. S., 133
Homer, xxv, 164, 259, 260, 264; epic poems and, 261–262; *Omeros* and, 265, 266, 268,   278
Homer, Winslow, 267
Hood, John B., 79
Houseman, A. E., 177, 203
"How to Change the U.S.A." (Edwards), 214–215
Howe, Irving, 144, 145, 149; on Ralph Ellison, 294–295; on *Native Son*, 294
Howe, Julia Ward, 35
Howe, Samuel Gridley, 26, 29, 32
Howells, William Dean, 38, 96, 97, 99, 101, 241
Hudson Review, xviii, xix, xx, xxi, xxii
Hughes, Langston, 203, 206, 216
Hurston, Zora Neale, xxvii, 281, 287–288
Hussein, Saddam, 84

Ichioka, Yuji, 144
If He Hollers Let Him Go (Himes), 223
Immigration Act of 1965, 152
Immigration to America, some reasons for, 148, 155
Income levels and ethnic hostility, 153
Indians. See Native Americans.
Innocents Abroad (Twain), 99
Invisible Man (Ellison), 211–212, 234, 280–297; Emerson's "Politics" and, 291; passages from, 287, 288–289; plot of, 286–288; question raised by, 291–293
Irish famine of mid-nineteenth century and New York state legislature ruling, '
Issei: The World of the First Generation Japanese Immigrants, The (Ichioka), 144
Ives, Stephen, 116–117, 130, 131, 132–133, 134, 137. See also West, The.

Jackson, Andrew, 73
Jackson, Helen Hunt, 35
Jackson, Jesse, xiii, xxviii, 103, 175
Jackson, Stonewall, 81
James, G. P. R., 112
James, Henry, xxvii, xix, 60, 222, 282, 296, 297
James, William, 222
James Baldwin's Quarrel with Richard Wright (Charney), 211
Japanese internment during World War II, 147
Jefferson, Thomas, 26, 73; Lewis and Clark expedition and, 117, 118; Louisiana Purchase and, 117
Jeffries, Leonard, xiii
Jehlen, Myra, 111
Jewish Defense League, 152
Jews and the Civil War, 61–62
Jim Crow laws, 3, 51
Jim Crow racism, 105
Johnson, Andrew, 35, 87
Johnson, Lyndon Baines, 72, 153, 295

Johnson, Nathan, 10
Johnston, Joseph E., 86, 90
Jones, Howard Mumford, 36, 52
Jones, LeRoi. See Baraka, Imamu Amiri.
Jordan, Michael, xxvii
Joseph, Chief, xxvii
Joyce, James, 262, 245, 259

Kakutani, Michiko, 264
Kaplan, Justin, 94
Kelley, William Melvin, 281
Kelly, Abby, 12
Kemp, William, 29
Kennerley, Mitchell, 181
Kerner Report of 1968, xii, xiii, xxviii
Killens, John O., 219
Kimball, Roger, xix–xx, ', 160
Kincaid, Jamaica, 281
King, Jr., Martin Luther, 207
King, Rodney, 144, 145, 153
Kinnamon on *Native Son*, Keneth, 234
Kittredge, George Lyman, 195, 196, 198–199, 200, 201, 205
Knight, Etheridge, 216–217
Knock on Any Door (Motley), 223
Kostelanetz, Richard, 296
Kwan, Andrew, 147

LaCapra, Dominick, 58
La Farge, John, 35
Lamp and the Bell, The (Millay), 187, 188–189
Lane, Lauriat, 110
Language in Action (Hayakawa), 103
Larsen, Nella, 223
Las Casas, Bartolomé de, 158, 272
Lavender, Lizzie, 15
Lawd Today! (Wright), 228, 240
Lawrence, D. H., 159
League of Struggle for Negro Rights, 224
Leaves of Grass (Whitman), 261
Lee, Robert E., 55, 65, 71, 78, 83; Battle of the Wilderness and, 89,

Lee, Robert E. *(continued)*
90; Richmond, taking of, 85–86; surrender of, 86
Lester, Julius, 104
Letters from the Earth (Twain), 98
Lévi-Strauss, Claude, 138, 226
Levine, Lawrence, 144
Lewis, John, xvi, xxvii
Lewis, Meriwether. *See* Lewis and Clark expedition.
Lewis and Clark expedition: commissioning of, 118; disappearance of what they saw, 121–122; end of, 120; hazards of, 119–120; importance of Indians to, 125–126; Native Americans and, 122–126; Omaha Indians disappearance noted by, 135; reason for, 118; route of, 119; Sacagawea and, 126–128; start of, 118–119; waterways named by, 119; weapons of, 124; women and, 126–129; years of, 118
Lewis and Clark: The Corps of Discovery (Burns), 116, 117, 120, 129–130; exaggeration of role of women in, 122, 126–127; Indian women and, 128–129; look of, 129–130; Native American life distortion in, 122; period dealt with by, 117
Liberator, The, 12, 13, 15
Liberty Party Paper, 15
Life and Times of Frederick Douglass (Douglass), 3, 11, 22
Life on the Mississippi (Twain), 93, 101
Lincoln, Abraham, xiv, 33, 54–73, 222; actions at outbreak of hostility and legality of, 58–59, 71–72; beginnings of, 64–65; homosexuality question and, 66; and McClellan firing, 60, 78; military rule and, 61; religion and, 67–69; saving the Union, 70; slavery issue and, 63–64
Lincoln, Mary Todd, 65, 66, 68
Lincoln (Donald), 63, 64–66, 71

Lincoln: A Novel (Gore), 54, 55
Lincoln and the Negro (Quarles), 62
Lincoln, Douglas, and Slavery (Zarefsky), 62
Lincoln, the President (Randall), 62, 67
Lippmann, Walter, 154
Little Big Horn, 131
Lloyd, Daniel, 4
Lloyd, Edward, 4
Longstreet, James, 78, 89
Looby, Christopher, 112, 113
Lost in the Funhouse (Barth), 260
Love Is Eternal: A Novel about Mary Todd and Abraham Lincoln (Stone), 54
Lucas, Curtis, 223

Mailer, Norman, 281
Major, Clarence, 214
Malcolm X, xviii, 207, 293
Man for the Ages, A (Bacheller), 54
Many-Colored Coat of Dreams: The Poetry of Countee Cullen, A (Baker), 200
Mark Twain's America (DeVoto), 97
Marx, Karl, 159, 160, 161
Marx, Leo, 108
Massachusetts Anti-Slavery Society and Frederick Douglass, 12, 13, 14, 16
May, Samuel, 28
Mazzocco on Derek Walcott, Robert, 249
McCarthy, Mary, 81
McClellan, George B., 55, 59, 65, 71, 78; firing of, 60, 77, 78
McFeely, William S., 14, 89
McKay, Claude, 203, 206, 216, 281
Melting pot as American ideal, 151
Memoir of Old Elizabeth: A Coloured Woman, 3
Memoirs of General W. T. Sherman (Sherman), 75, 87
Memories of Childhood's Slavery Days (Burton), 3

Menaker, Daniel, and *Adventures of Huckleberry Finn*, 94, 95, 96
Metahistory (White), 58
Meyer, Howard N., 49, 53
Midsummer (Walcott), xxiii
Millay, Edna St. Vincent, xv, 177, 203, 205; excerpts of poems, 182, 183, 184, 185, 186, 187, 188, 189; "God's World," 182; physical description of, 180–181; plays of, 187–189; poems about death, 184–186; reprint of Cullen's thesis on, 180–190; similarities between Cullen and, 177–178. *See also Poetry of Edna St. Vincent Millay: An Appreciation, The* (Cullen).
Miller, Eugene A., on *Native Son*, 242
Miller, Kerby A., 144
Modern Jazz Quartet, xvi
Momaday, N. Scott, xxvii, 134
"Morality and *Adventures of Huckleberry Finn*" (Lester), 104
Morgan, Frederick, xviii
Morrison, Toni, 281
Motley, Willard, 223
Mott, Lucretia, 28
Munn, James B., 203
Murray, Anna. *See* Anna Douglass.
My Bondage and My Freedom (Douglass), 3, 6, 14, 16

Naipaul, V. S., 249–250, 252
Narrative of the Life of Frederick Douglass, An American Slave (Douglass), 2–3, 8, 9, 10, 12, 14, 16, 21
Nasby, Petroleum V., 60
Nashe, Thomas, 254
Nason, Arthur Huntington, 203
National Endowment for the Arts, xix, xx, xxii, 74; and Ken Burns, 116
National Negro Conference, 38
Native Americans; disease and, 135; history rewritten to tone down savagery of, 147; land and, 134–135;
Lewis and Clark expedition and, 122–126; spiritual equality and, 158; as Stone Age–like people, 140–141; treatment of in *The West*, 133–136; treatment of women by, 128–129; tribal disappearance of, 131; tribal warring of, 122, 124, 125, 136, 137; women and, 126–129
Native Son (Wright), xviii, xx–xxi, 209–210, 211, 228, 230–235, 237–238, 239, 294; Baldwin on, 232; critiqué of, 222–223; Ellison on, 232; Kakutani on, 233; Kinnamon on, 234; origin of, 234–235; passage cut from original version of, xx–xxi, 238, 240–242; plot of, 230–231; publication of, 225
NEA. *See* National Endowment for the Arts.
Neal, Larry, 212–213, 214, 216, 218, 219
Negro Digest, 212
New Black Poetry, The, 214
New Criterion, The, xix
New Era in American Poetry, The (Untermeyer), 189
Newton, Huey P., xviii
Nietzsche, Friedrich Wilhelm, 160, 175, 276; attack on Christianity by, 164–165, 167
Nigger: arguments for and against usage of the word by Mark Twain, 102–103, 108; origins of the word, 102
Nineteenth-century ethnic discontent, xiv
Norman, Charles, 202
Norman, Jessye, xxvii, 282, 297
North Star, 13, 15
Noyes, John Humphrey, 128

Odetta, xxvii
Odyssey (Homer), 164, 258, 259, 268
Old English Ballads, 1555–1625 (Rollins), 196
Oldtown Folks (Stowe), 36

Omeros (Walcott), 243, 246, 254, 255, 258, 259–279; action of, 268–274; affliction theme in, 270; comparison to *Collected Poems*, 269; ending of, 276–279; excerpts from, 260, 264–266, 270–271, 273–277; Figueroa on, 275–276; Guillory on, 260–261; Holocaust comparison in, 271; Homer in, 265, 268; Homer's *Odyssey* and, 259, 260; Kakutani on, 264; letter "O" usage in, 266–267; setting of, 263–264; Terada on, 259

On Being Brought from Africa to America (Wheatley), 174–175
One in a Thousand (James), 112
Ord, O. C., 77
Organization of Black American Culture, 213
Outsider, The (Wright), 227
Owens, Mary, 65

Padmore, George, 227
Paine, Tom, 67
Pan-Africanism or Communism? (Padmore), 227
Parker, Theodore, 26, 28, 29, 32, 33
Parkman, Francis, 124, 136, 222
Parrinder, Geoffrey, 173
Part of a Man's Life (Higginson), 52
Patterson, Orlando, xiii, xxviii–xxix
Peel, Robert, '
Penn Warren, Robert, xvi
Perry, Margaret, 177
Petry, Ann, 223
Phillips, Abby Foster, 28
Phillips, Wendell, 12, 14, 18, 26, 29, 33
Pillsbury, Parker, 12, 18
Pinkerton, Allan, 55, 56
Pitts, Helen. *See* Douglass, Helen.
Plessy v. Ferguson, xiv
Pliny, 156
Poetry of Edna St. Vincent Millay: An Appreciation, The (Cullen), 176–206; physical appearance of original copy of, 179; reprint of actual thesis, 180–190

Poets and People (Norman), 202
Poitier, Sidney, xxvii
Pope, Alexander, xxv, 162
Pound, Ezra, xviii, 202, 203, 206, 216, 244, 245, 258, 259, 262, 263, 267, 271, 276
Powell, Colin, 84
Primitive, glorifying, 163
Prince and the Pauper (Twain), 99
"Problematic Texts of Richard Wright" (Tuttleton), xviii
Pudd'nhead Wilson (Twain), 96

Quarles, Benjamin, 18, 62

Racism and Christianity in America, xiv
Racism, definition, xvi, xvii
Rahman, Yusuf, 218, 219
Rainbow coalition, 154
Rainbow curriculum, 145; and Ralph Ellison, 285
Rampersad, Arnold, xviii, xx, xxii; and Wright's works, 228, 237, 239, 240
Randall, J. G., 62, 67, 68, 70
Reade, Charles, 112
"Reading Gender in *Adventures of Huckleberry Finn*" (Jehlen), 111
Reality of the past, xii
Red Cloud, 130
Redding, Saunders, 217, 227
"Reformers and Young Maidens: Women and Virtue in *Adventures of Huckleberry Finn*," 109
Reisner, Marc, 133
Renascence (Millay), 177, 181, 182, 189
Republican party formation, 16
Reston, Jr., James, 82, 84
Revisionism, xi–xii
Richard Wright: Early Works, 227–230, 236, 238
Richards, Ann, 141, 142
Richardson, Anna and Ellen, 12

Index

Richardson, Mark, 239
Ridge, Martin, 133
Robinson, Edward Arlington, 177, 187, 203, 205
Rollins, Hyder E., 179, 192–193, 195, 200–201, 203, 204–205; biographical sketch of, 195–199; and Keats, 196, 197, 198; publications of, 197
Romo, Ricardo, 133
Roosevelt, Franklin D., 72, 73
Roughing It (Twain), 95–96
Rousseau, Jean-Jacques, 156, 159, 160
Royal, Robert, 158
Royster, Charles, 81, 83
Rudman, Derek, 244
Russak, Martin, 202–203, 204
Russell, John, '
Rutledge, Ann, 65

Sacagawea, 126–128
Safire, William, 54, 55–62, 64, 71, 72, 73
St. Augustine, 157, 158, 167, 168
Saint-Gaudens, Augustus, 74
Sanborn, Frank, 32
Santa Anna, 131
Sartre, Jean-Paul, 226, 227, 233
Saxton, Rufus, 34, 39, 42
Schlesinger, Jr., Arthur, 154
Schwartzkopf, Norman, 84
Scott, James Brown, 158
Scott, Nathan, 232, 233
Scott, Walter, 47
Scott, Winfield, 76
Seale, Bobby, xviii, 293
Second April (Millay), 184–185
Senghor, Léopold Sédar, 226
Separate-but-equal legislation, xiv
Seward, William, 55, 60
Shakespeare, William, xxv, 70
Sharpton, Al, xxviii, 152, 175
Shaw, Robert Gould, 39
Sheridan, Phil, 85
Sheridan, Richard Brinsley, 5
Sherman, William Tecumseh, xiv, 62, 65, 78; anti-Sherman sentiment, 81–83; biographical sketch of, 75–76; death of, 90; destruction of property versus people and, 81–83; Grant's view of, 87–88; "March to the Sea" by, 79–81, 85; as modern war creator, 83–84; predictions of length of Civil War, 77–78; and Richmond, 79, 85–86; statue of, 74–75; taking of Atlanta and, 79; view of Grant by, 87
Shucard, Alan R., 199, 200
Signifying Monkey, The, (Gates), xxiii
"Sisterhood of Reforms," 16
Sitting Bull, 130, 131
Slave Girl's Story, A (Drumgoold), 3
Slavery, 2; Bible and, 165–166; Christianity and, 166, 167–170; Douglass on, 5–6, 11; Fugitive Slave Law, 26–31; religion and, 166, 167–170; St. Paul and, 11, 168; Wood on, 171–175
Slaves, books written by and about, 3
Smith, Gerrit, 15, 32
Smith, James McCune, 14
Sniderman, Paul M., xiii
Sontag, Susan, 111
Spanish Origin of International Law, The (Scott), 158
Speed, Joshua, 65, 66
Spenser, Edmund, 162
Stanford, Leland, 130
Stanton, Edwin, 55, 59, 60, 87
Stanton, Elizabeth Cady, 18, 28
Stearns, G. L., 32
Stein, Gertrude, 226
Stone, David, and definition of racism, xvi, xvii
Stone, Irving, 54
Stone, Lucy, 26, 28
Story of Mattie Jackson, The, 3
Stowe, Harriet Beecher, 36
Stowell, Martin, 29, 30
Strangers from a Different Shore: A History of Asian Americans (Takaki), 145

Street, The (Petry), 223
Sutter, John, 130
Swift, Michael, 113–114
Symbionese Liberation Army, xviii

Takaki, Ronald, xii, 133, 145, 147, 148, 149, 150, 153, 154; bribes for peacekeeping, 154; income levels and ethnic hostility and, 153
Tannenbaum, Marc, xiii
Tanselle, Thomas, 236
Tappan, Arthur and Lewis, 174
Taylor, Zachary, 76
Terada, Rei, 259
Thernstrom, Abigail, xiii
Thernstrom, Stephan, xiii
Third Ward Newark (Lucas), 223
Thirteen Ways of Looking at a Black Man (Gates), xxvi
Thomas, Emory M., 79
Thomas, George H., 78
Thompson, W. Scott, 66
Thoreau, Henry David, 26, 27, 35
Thornwell, James Henley, 169
Thorpe, Jim, xxvii
Todd, Mary. See Lincoln, Mary Todd.
Toomer, Jean, 281
"Towards a Black Aesthetic" (Fuller), 215–216
Trilling, Lionel, 108
Tropics of Discourse (White), 58
Truman, Harry S., 153
Truth and Method (Gadamer), xvii
Tukey, Marshal, 27
Turner, Frederick Jackson, 130
Twain, Mark, xix, 3, 19, 91–115, 130, 222, 223, 282, 296; *Adventures of Huckleberry Finn* by, 91–115; editorial advice solicited by, 96, 97–98, 241; homosexuality claims on, 113; printing instructions and his books, 98–99; publication of Grant's memoirs and, 88; racism charges against, 101–102, 103; works, 111
Twain, Olivia, 96, 97–98, 101, 241

Udall, Stewart L., 141, 142
Ulysses (Joyce), 245, 262
Uncle Tom's Children (Wright), 225, 228–230
Unfortunate Traveller, The (Nashe), 254
Uniform Code of Military Justice, 83
Untermeyer, Louis, 181, 182, 189

Vallandigham, Clement L., 71, 73
Van Doren, Carl, 186
Vidal, Gore, 54, 55
Villard, Oswald Garrison, 38
Virgil, xxv, 161, 162
Volney, C. F., 67
Voltaire, François-Marie Arouet, 67

Wade, Benjamin, 57
Walcott, Derek, xxiii–xxvi; biographical sketch of, 243–244; comparison between *Omeros* and *Collected Poems*, 269; on Darwinian theory of evolution, xxiv; excerpts from poems, 246–257, 259–260, 264–266, 270–277; exile as subject, 257–259; Figueroa on, 275–276; Kakutani on, 264; language and, 251–254; Mazzocco on, 249; mixed heritage of, 250–251; Naipaul and, 249–250, 252; Nobel Prize for Literature, 243; range of his work, 244; Rudman on, 244; Terada on, 259; and vision of Homeric grandeur, 243–279; women in his poems, 256; works, 243. *See also Collected Poems 1948–1984; Omeros.*
Walker, Alice, 281
Walker, Nancy A., 109, 110
Wall Street Journal, xix
Wallace, John, 102
Walton, Eda Lou, 204
Ward, Artemus, 19, 60
Warren, Robert Penn, 208
Was Huck Black? (Fishkin), 105
Washington, Booker T., 22, 38, 51, 52

WASPS, and prejudice against, 149–150, 152, 153
Waswo, Richard, 160–164
Watkins, T. H., 133
We Are All Multiculturalists Now (Glazer), xxvii
Webster, Charles, 99, 100
Weld, Theodore Dwight, 174
Welles, Gideon, 57
Wells, Ida B., 20
West, area defining, 117
West, The (Ives), 116–117, 118, 120, 129–130, 141; biographic sketches in, 130; contents, 130, 131, 133; Coyote as narrator, 132; daguerreotype and camera photographs in, 130–131; Indian women and, 128; look of, 129–130; minority treatment in, 133; Native Americans in, 133–136, 137; period covered, 117–118; slanted view of Native Americans in, 137; tribal disappearance in, 131; typical episode of, 132; voice-over personalities in, 132
West African Religions (Parrinder), 173
Western civilization founding, 160–164
Wharton, Edith, xxi, 154, 222
Wheatley, Phyllis, 174–175
White, F. M., 96
White, Hayden, 58
White, Richard, 133
White, Walter, 177
White Hat, Albert, 142, 143
Whitman, Walt, 55, 261, 262
Whittier, John Greenleaf, 27, 37
Who Speaks for the Negro? (Warren), 208
Whole World Temperance Convention, 28
"Why *Huckleberry Finn* Is a Great World Novel" (Lane), 110

Williams, John A., 281
Williams, Raymond, 162
Wilson, Edmund, 88
Wilson, Henry, 56
Windschuttle, Keith, 170
Wings of the Dove, The, (James), xxvii–xxviii
Women and Lewis and Clark expedition, 122, 126–128
Wood, Forrest G., 165; criticism of, 167–170, 172–175; exposé of, 171–172
Works and Papers of Mark Twain, The (Blair and Fischer), 100
World of Our Fathers: The Journey of East European Jews to America (Howe), 144, 149
World Temperance Convention, 28
Wright, Richard, xviii, xix, xx–xxi, xxii, 209–211, 222–242, 281, 282, 283, 288, 294–295; and Aswell, 236, 238, 239, 240, 242; autobiography of, 224, 224, 235–236; Baldwin's criticism of, 210–211; biographical sketch of, 223–227; communism and, 224, 225–226; critiqué of, 227, 232; first breakthrough for, 225; Library of America series and, xix, xx–xxi, 222, 227–230, 236; problematic texts of, 222–242; reediting of his works, 236–240; self-exile of, 226; works, 209, 227. *See also Native Son* (Wright).

Yates, Richard, 78
Yellin, Jean Fagan, 16
Young, Brigham, 130, 132

Zacharie, Isachair, 61–62
Zarefsky, David, 62
Zoilkowski, Thad, 22

A NOTE ON THE AUTHOR

James W. Tuttleton, who died in November 1998, was a professor of English at New York University. Born in St. Louis, he studied at Harding University and the University of North Carolina. He wrote on a wide range of American literature in such periodicals as *The American Scholar*, *The New Criterion*, *The Times Literary Supplement*, and *The Yale Review*. He was also the author of *The Novel of Manners in America*; *Thomas Wentworth Higginson*; *Vital Signs: Essays on American Literature and Criticism*; and *A Fine Silver Thread: Essays on American Writing and Criticism*. He was the editor, among other books, of *The Works of Washington Irving: History, Tales and Sketches* for the Library of America.